PRAISE FOR LA BRIGANTESSA

This is a beautiful novel, one that vividly recreates the heart-break and drama of one of the most turbulent periods in Italian history.
—NINO RICCI, award-winning author of *The Origins of Species, Testament,* and *Sleep*

In the writing and storytelling of *La Brigantessa,* Rosanna Battigelli reflects the very passion and glory, the suffering and hope of the times that her Gabriella Falcone must endure and over which she must triumph. *La Brigantessa* is written with great heart and conviction—such that, in an era when truth is at a premium, no one will question the truth of this narrative. In fact, the great achievement of this novel is that Rosanna Battigelli is able to make fiction feel truer than truth, truer than non-fiction. Bravo!
—JOSEPH KERTES, founder of The Humber School for Writers and author of *Gratitude* and *The Afterlife of Stars*

In this historically accurate novel, Rosanna Battigelli uses every detail from pigeon soup to Southern Italian traditions to bad omens, bad luck, and retaliation. As unpredictable as summer storm clouds, as enjoyable as homemade Calabrian sausages, you should read this book with a glass of strong red wine and a supply of Baci chocolates.
—MARIA COLETTA MCLEAN, author of *My Father Came From Italy* and *Summers in Supino: Becoming Italian*

Based on actual events, *La Brigantessa* is the triumphant, epic tale of a young woman's incredible courage and resilience during one of Italy's most tumultuous decades. This heart-wrenching, unforgettable novel was an addictive read that will stay with me for years.
—Mirella Sichirollo Patzer, author of *The Orphan of the Olive Tree* and *The Prophetic Queen*

La Brigantessa is a feast for the senses. The author's visceral descriptions of events, both terrifying and exhilarating, instantly transport the reader to the sun-bleached hills of Post-Unification Calabria. The novel is a meditation on class, politics, and women's roles without losing sight of intrigue and adventure.
—Michaela Di Cesare, playwright and author of *In Search of Mrs. Pirandello* and *Successions*

La Brigantessa

We gratefully acknowledge the support of the Canada Council for the Arts and the Ontario Arts Council for our publishing program. We also acknowledge the financial support of the Government of Canada through the Canada Book Fund.

La Brigantessa is a work of fiction. All the characters and situations portrayed in this book are fictitious and any resemblance to persons living or dead is purely coincidental.

Cover design: Val Fullard

Library and Archives Canada Cataloguing in Publication

Battigelli, Rosanna, 1959-, author
       La brigantessa / Rosanna Micelotta Battigelli.

(Inanna poetry & fiction series)
Issued in print and electronic formats.
ISBN 978-1-77133-553-9 (softcover).-- ISBN 978-1-77133-554-6 (epub).--
ISBN 978-1-77133-555-3 (Kindle).-- ISBN 978-1-77133-556-0 (pdf).

       I. Title. II. Series: Inanna poetry and fiction series

PS8553.A83B75 2018   C813'.54   C2018-904361-X
                                                  C2018-904362-8

Printed and bound in Canada

MIX
Paper from
responsible sources
FSC® C004071

Inanna Publications and Education Inc.
210 Founders College, York University
4700 Keele Street, Toronto, Ontario, Canada M3J 1P3
Telephone: (416) 736-5356 Fax: (416) 736-5765
Email: inanna.publications@inanna.ca   Website: www.inanna.ca

La Brigantessa

A NOVEL BY

ROSANNA MICELOTTA BATTIGELLI

Inanna poetry & fiction series

INANNA PUBLICATIONS AND EDUCATION INC.
TORONTO, CANADA

In memory of my parents,
Assunta (née Adavastro) and Nicola Micelotta.
Their courage and resilience continue to inspire.

Home is where one starts from....
In my end is my beginning.
—T. S. Eliot

The journey of a thousand miles
begins with one step.
—Lao Tzu

Nel mezzo del cammin di nostra vita
mi ritrovai per una selva oscura,
ché la diritta via era smarrita.
—Dante Alighieri

PART I: CHANGES

February-March 1862

THE HOG IS LIMP, having shuddered its last breath after a single blow to the head with a mallet. Gabriella and some of the neighbourhood women watch her father Lorenzo and his friends, huffing and perspiring, urge each other on with cries of "Pull, pull!" as they hoist the hog with a crude rope and pulley system. The thick ropes have been drawn through a gash made in the hog's hind legs to expose the hamstring, pulled over a log projecting from a hollow in the stone wall of the rectory, and nailed into a fork of the adjacent chestnut tree. When the beast is suspended, her father pulls out his sharpened knife and plunges it into the hog's jugular vein. Blood gushes into a waiting bucket.

Gabriella wrinkles her nose. In the crisp February air, the scent of sweat from the men's exertion mingles with that of the coals smouldering in the nearby fire. She watches as several of the children, fascinated with the orange flames licking wildly out from under the huge iron cauldron, throw in small twigs they have snatched from the chestnut tree, squealing and jumping back at the crackle and leap of fiery tongues.

Her seven-year-old brother Luciano, wearing a faded cap and well-worn knickers criss-crossed with dozens of sewing repairs, turns and cocks his head at his friend's dare to touch the flame with his finger. A sudden breeze whips the fire at his backside and the handkerchief dangling from the back pocket of his breeches alights. Gabriella gasps and dashes through the shrieking children to get to Luciano, throws him on the ground, and rolls him back and forth on the dusty earth as if she were kneading dough to make a huge *filone*.

When she is certain that the flames have been spent, she pulls Luciano to his feet and scowls at him. His tears are trickling down earth-streaked cheeks, exposing red mottled skin underneath.

"Enough tears," she says in her sternest voice, wiping his face with the edge of her apron. "Consider yourself lucky. If you hadn't roasted your bottom, I'd be roasting it right now with *this*." She lifts her hand menacingly. "And *then* you'd have reason to cry. Now get yourself into the house so I can check you."

One of the boys calls out, "Hey, Luciano, show us your roasted *culo*."

Gabriella reaches for Luciano's hand, but he pulls away, his face reddening. He flashes her a look of accusation before scampering toward the back entrance of the rectory.

"I won't be long," Gabriella reassures the women who are beginning to shuffle back toward the hog dressing area. She strides into the rectory. Her eyes adjust to the diminished light, and noting that her brother is not there, she grumbles under her breath and lifts her long skirts to mount the narrow stairway leading to the bedroom they share.

Luciano is lying face down on his straw pallet, his sobs stifled by his feather pillow. She feels herself softening. The sight of her only brother with his thatch of unruly hair and spindly arms and legs always brings out the protective, mothering side of her. Her eyes fly to his singed breeches and her heart jolts at the thought of her brother suffering even for a moment.

Gabriella sits on the edge of the bed and caresses the back of his head. "Come now, Lu, even the hog didn't fuss this much. Let me see if you really have something to cry about." She peeks into the back of his trousers. "There, there, you're still covered in skin, thank God. Other than being as pink as a newborn piglet, you're fine. Now wipe your face, and let's get going. You don't want to miss the cooking, do you? Don't you remember how good the *suffrittu* tastes? Well, if we don't get back to work, we won't be able to enjoy your favourite stew. Hurry, let's go."

Luciano sniffles loudly as he sits up, and Gabriella hands him a fresh handkerchief from her apron pocket. She smiles as he gives his face a quick swipe and then hands it back. With renewed vigour, he bolts down the stairs and tumbles into the waiting group of friends. Like a flock of sparrows, they swoop off to the hog dressing area.

The whole spectacle holds such fascination for them, from the cornering of the alarmed beast to the slitting of its throat and the subsequent butchering. She shivers. The sight of blood always reminds her of Luciano at birth—a bellowing, unrecognizable creature matted with clots. his quivering body washed out by an endless gush of red that spread over the sheets like the Ionian Sea battering an empty beach in winter.

Gabriella squeezes her eyes to stop the tears and memories. She reaches the area where her family's closest neighbours and friends are gathering, as they do every year at this time, to butcher the hog of the parish priest, Don Simone. He will be back from his monthly spiritual retreat tomorrow. She smiles, knowing how much he anticipates the feast awaiting him.

She has known Don Simone all her life. Her father has always worked the church lands, tending the priest's animals and crops. In return, her family has never lacked food and shelter. Peasants though they be, they have been blessed with goat's milk aplenty, and gifts coaxed from the fields, the result of her father's daily toil: olives and figs, pears and medlars, beans and squash. What her father planted and picked, her mother Elisabetta prepared and preserved, when she wasn't tending to other rectory chores. Don Simone was happy to have them stay at the rectory; he had left his family in northern Italy and having a young family around him made him feel less bereft.

The village midwife Nicolina is hobbling into the church property, one hand gripping her hand-carved cane and the other clasping a cloth bag that Gabriella knows contains the spices and other ingredients for the blood pudding she is renowned for in their hamlet of Camini.

The hog has been lowered onto a wooden pallet, and Salvatore Vitale, the village butcher and his eldest son, Tonino, are pouring scalding water on it from the nearby cauldron to loosen its bristles. Some of the women are preparing the long wooden trestle table that will be used for the sausage-making, while others are busy stoking the coals that will shortly heat the second cauldron, the one that will soon sizzle with pieces of lard and pork.

Her glances keep returning to Tonino, who has begun to scrape off the bristles in long, experienced strokes until most of the hair is off the hide. Suddenly, he looks up and winks at her. Gabriella's cheeks burn as a feeling of warmth spreads through her in ways that both shock and intrigue her. A quick scan of the group satisfies her that no one has caught the exchange. She takes over the stirring of the coals, determined not to look back at Tonino.

Young and inexperienced though she might be in the ways of men and women, for months now, she has wondered if Tonino didn't seem to be making it a point to deliver the priest's butchered meat to her at the rectory every week instead of sending his younger brother who usually handled such jobs.

At Tonino's sudden exclamation, she glances up. His job is done, and he steps back as Gabriella's father and the men rehoist the hog, head down. After another dousing of scalding water over the carcass, and the scraping of any missed spots by Tonino, her father announces that the hog is ready to gut.

"Not the kind of work one does without a little *vino*," calls out Salvatore, her father's friend since childhood. A bottle materializes from the laughing crowd, passed man-to-man until it reaches Lorenzo. He takes a healthy swig and passes it on to Tonino, waiting until the younger man lifts the bottle to his lips before giving him an approving swat on the back. Tonino chokes on the vermilion liquid and it spills onto his linen shirt.

The whole crowd bursts into laughter amidst cries of "To your health! Spilled wine is a sure sign of a wedding to come!"

Gabriella finds herself laughing with the rest of her friends and neighbours, and her eyes link with Tonino's for the second time. He holds up his hand to lick the wine off it before unbuttoning his shirt and pulling the wet cloth away from his skin. Again, she quickly looks away, trying to convince herself that she didn't purposefully look at Tonino's bare chest, thatched with curly, dark brown hair....

A tug on her skirt draws her attention to Luciano, who is imploring her, "Gabriella, please, convince *Papà* to let me help cut the hog."

Gabriella looks down at shining chestnut eyes. "Now, Lu, why would you want to get yourself all covered in blood?" Without waiting for a reply, she pushes him to their father. "Papà, do you have a job for this young man? He's ready and willing, God bless him."

She can tell by the look on her father's face that he feels proud of his "Little Man," as he often calls him. He waves to his friend. "Hey, Salvatore, bring over that wine for my helper here, before we begin." He hands the bottle to Luciano, who starts sputtering after a tentative first swallow, tipping the bottle accidentally over his shirt. This time, Luciano doesn't seem to mind the laughter around him. When he cockily attempts to take another drink, Gabriella's arm flies out to stop him, but her father succeeds first and hands the bottle back to Salvatore.

"Enough play." Her father's guffaws subside. "Luciano, take this knife, and I'll help you begin." With a firm grip on Luciano's hand, Lorenzo makes a long cut down the underside of the hog, from the crotch to the chin. Gabriella sees Luciano's eyes widen when the gut cavity opens and the membrane holding the intestines is sliced, allowing the red, coiled entrails to drop into a waiting tub.

"That's a good start," her father says. "Now you can watch the rest of it."

Luciano steps back with a ready nod, his puckered face the colour of an unripened quince. His friends slap his back and take their spots around him to watch.

With a few experienced stabs, her father cuts around the base of the hog's head, and through the throat, until he is able to twist off the head completely. He dumps it into a pail, which is duly carried off by his other friend Rocco, who will singe off any of the hairs or bristles left, cut out the eyes, and further quarter the head and leave it to soak overnight in a pot of fresh water. Rocco's wife Francesca will occupy herself with the rinsing and subsequent cooking of the head, tongue, and brains the first thing next morning, and they will all feast on it at suppertime, along with Don Simone, who should be back from his monastic retreat in Gerace by then.

Gabriella lifts her skirts slightly to avoid some of the spilled hog's blood from Rocco's pail as he strides past her.

In the meantime, Salvatore carves up the rest of the hog. While the carcass is still hanging, he removes the leaf lard that holds the intestines, and throws it into the cast iron *cardara* sitting atop the coals. He cuts the liver free and removes the gall bladder; he trims the valves, veins, and arteries off the heart; he then retrieves the stomach, kidneys, and small intestines. Once that is done, he dumps the liver, heart, stomach and intestines into a pail of clean water and hands it to Gabriella, who washes them thoroughly before throwing them into the iron cauldron with the lard, except for the small intestines, which will be thoroughly drained, and used as casings for the sausages they will make the following day. With an oversized wooden spoon, she stirs the contents of the cauldron, slightly raised from the ground, and around which two heaps of live coals begin the slow, even cooking of the *frittuli*.

Gabriella looks up from her stirring to see Salvatore make one cut down the middle of the back into the backbone. Then, when Tonino, her father and the others have taken the carcass down and put it on its back on the chopping block, Salvatore takes his axe and chops all the way down both sides of the backbone until he can lift it out. While he cuts off the shoulders and hams and the side meat, his wife Beatrice takes over the stirring.

Feeling hot from standing over the embers, Gabriella welcomes the break and walks away to pour herself a cup of water from the terracotta *gozzarella* that she has filled from the natural spring tapped thirty metres from the rectory.

"Did you leave me a drop or two?"

Gabriella splutters at the sudden voice behind her, flushes at Tonino's teasing tone.

She turns and hands him the pitcher and an unused cup. "There's plenty left, and if that's not enough for you, there's more out there." Gesturing toward the spring, Gabriella realizes how serious she sounds. She adds a smile that she hopes doesn't seem flirtatious, and then glances beyond him.

Her father and the others are stacking the large pieces of meat at the end of a long oak table. Luciano has run off to play in the fields with his friends, and the women are occupied with different tasks: Beatrice is tending the lard cauldron; Francesca, having left the hog's head to soak, is now cleaning out the small intestines and rinsing them in a mixture of water, lemon, and salt; and Nicolina, the old midwife, is heading into the kitchen, where she will mix together the hog's blood in her bucket with other ingredients for the blood pudding.

Gabriella usually helps her make the *sanguinaccio*—it is one of her favourite tasks—by preparing the mixture with milk, coffee, sugar, bitter cocoa, wine must, and a dash of cloves, cinnamon, and mandarin zest.

As Nicolina's back disappears past the door, Gabriella turns again to Tonino, whose cup is still full.

"Gabriella, I want to talk to you." His voice is husky, urgent.

She swallows. "Yes?" She stifles the desire to wipe the beads of sweat from his forehead.

Tonino shakes his head. "Not now. This is not the right time. Or place." He searches her face for a moment. "Will you meet me down at the river this afternoon, past the place where you do your washing?" He clears his throat. "By the abandoned vineyard?"

Gabriella feels her cheeks burn. She looks away. Is Tonino trying to set up a secret tryst? Does he think she will agree to a secret meeting instantly, as if she has no scruples, no thought for her reputation? What reason does he have to think that she will agree? For as sure as her middle name is Lucia, after *Santa* Lucia, she knows that her father would not approve of such a meeting, even with the son of his best friend. She turns back to him with a frown.

He coughs. "I just want to talk to you. Nothing more."

"You can talk to me now." She glances at him sideways.

"There's no time. In a minute, my father will be calling me to chop up the meat for the sausages."

"I'll be helping with the sausages."

"I don't want an audience when I talk to you."

Gabriella wants to ask, "Why not," but bites back her words at Salvatore's booming call.

"Eh, Signor Antonino, how are you supposed to perfect your father's trade if you're playing with girls? Get your apprentice's ass back here."

Amid the laughter, Tonino looks wryly at Gabriella with a "What did I tell you?" expression. He sets down his cup on the rough stand and begins to walk away. He stops and turns around after a few paces. "I'll be there at mid-afternoon," he says. "By the abandoned vineyard."

Gabriella watches as he strides away, noticing how his linen shirt clings to his back in places. She lifts her face to the crisp breeze from the Ionian Sea in the distance and inhales deeply, trying to steady the drumming in her chest.

Hoping that her face doesn't betray her, she walks briskly to the others, who are ready to begin the chopping and mixing of the sausage meat. She rinses her hands with the rest of the water from the jug and takes a spot at the long oak table. After Salvatore and Tonino chop up the larger pieces of pork shoulder, her father cuts them up further and slides them over to her. All chatter seems to die down suddenly, as if they are taking in a solemn church service. Gabriella salts, peppers, and sprinkles the ground pork with fennel, stirring to distribute the spices evenly, before placing it in a wooden vat, where it will remain until the following day. Occasionally, she steals a glance at Tonino, and to her surprise and pleasure, he happens to be gazing at her on every one of those occasions.

She flushes with the sudden conviction that she *will* be meeting Tonino later by the river, forbidden or not.

ASCENDING THE WESTERN SLOPE of Mount Gallica, Don Simone Oliveri anticipates his retreat with his friend Don Filippo, abbot of the Monastery of the Capuchins in the hamlet of Gerace. He prods his mule Vittorio around a series of ruts toward the last stretch of road leading to the monastery.

Don Simone waves at the appearance of Don Filippo. The abbot is striding toward him, his cassock billowing. Don Simone dismounts, and as he embraces his friend, another monk takes the mule away to be tethered, groomed, and fed. Don Filippo opens the thick domed door of the monastery. Their shoes slap the slate floor as they pass through a series of rooms and narrow halls that lead to an open courtyard.

Don Simone feels the fatigue of his two-hour journey begin to dissipate as he breathes in the familiar herbal scents around him. Sweet basil, thyme, rosemary, and mint thrive in the garden maintained by Brother Domenico, who enjoys a well-earned reputation both within the monastery and outside its walls for his tisanes and culinary concoctions. Even the most simple of meals becomes a celebration of abundance with Brother Domenico's touch. Nothing is wasted; much is conserved for winter use or for the weekly soup dinners made for charity. People travel from as far away as Gioiosa Ionica to line up at the monastery gates every Saturday, carrying a *tiana*, its glazed terracotta interior keeping the soup or vegetables and beans protected until later use.

A giant fig tree towers in one corner of the courtyard, and in another corner, a prickly-pear cactus drapes the outer wall, and spreads along the mountainside. A lone persimmon tree stands nearby, its fruit long picked. Don Simone has his fill of its fiery orange fruit every autumn, and the thought of its extraordinary succulence always makes his mouth water. *It is as tempting as any fruit could be in the Garden of Eden,* he muses.

Don Filippo and Don Simone turn into a vine-edged doorway and continue down the slate corridor until they reach a sitting room that houses the abbot's desk and bookcases. In one corner, a table has already been set with fresh linen and cutlery.

Brother Saverio, the newest member of the Order, enters the room and offers Don Filippo and Don Simone a tray with two cups, a steaming kettle of fennel tea, and several fresh golden-brown *panini* that are split in half and drizzled with olive oil and oregano, accompanied by several wedges of sheep's cheese that Don Simone knows is made on the premises. Don Simone thanks him and the monk retreats to the refectory to reassume his duties as bread-maker and assistant cook to Brother Domenico.

"Eat, eat," Don Filippo bids Don Simone.

The edge of his hunger appeased after finishing his *panino*, Don Simone leans back before retrieving a parchment from within his cassock. It is affixed with the formal seal of the State of Piedmont. He recalls the shock of reading its contents two days earlier. "I have some news to share with you, Filippo." His voice catches. "Not good enough, however, to warrant a celebration."

"Simone, what is it?" Don Filippo leans forward, frowning. "Has something happened to a family member?"

Don Simone takes a deep breath. "No, nothing like that, thank God." He hands the letter to Don Filippo. "I have been informed by the State that my church lands have been sold." He slumps back in his chair while Don Filippo reads the letter.

"I'm truly sorry for you, Simone. It is a disgrace, the number of religious orders that are being suppressed by the new State. Church properties auctioned off like fattened goats to the land-owning classes."

"Yet *your* monastery and the Convent of St. Anna here in Gerace will remain open, Filippo. And the Sisters of Charity in the Aspromonte have been spared also, apparently for their dedication in caring for Garibaldi's wounded."

Don Simone bites his lip. General Garibaldi's victory in ousting the Bourbons under King Francis II from the southern territories in The Kingdom of the Two Sicilies has brought changes none of them could have foreseen. How many bodies maimed and lives lost to become one nation under King Victor Emmanuel II! Months after Garibaldi's victory in Naples and Sicily, the territories were called to pledge their allegiance to the new State by way of a plebiscite. And those voting "yes" seemed to be enjoying special privileges in the aftermath of Unification.

Don Simone's jaw tenses. It is a known fact that the dozen or so monasteries that were known to have voted "no" for the plebiscite for the annexation of regions for Italian unity, were shut down by the new State, including the House of the Holy Redemptor and the Monastery of the Capuchins in Stilo. He clears his throat. "So, tell me, good brother, how did you...?"

"Manage not to get shut down?" Don Filippo rubs his chin. "I think, perhaps, we were not as openly hostile to the annexation proposal as some of our brothers. Out of the twelve of us, only eight of us—including myself—quietly voted 'no' without stirring up the villagers, as some of our more outspoken and subversive brothers have been doing."

Don Simone sets down his tea. "I am neither overly outspoken nor subversive and yet...." He hears his voice crack. Unable to go on, he wipes the corner of his eyes with his handkerchief.

"Oh dear," Don Filippo places a hand on his arm. "What a shock this has been for you." He glances again at the letter. "You'll still conduct masses," he offers consolingly.

"Apparently so," Don Simone says drily. "But on whom am I to depend with no land, no food, no animals? The collection provides barely enough to pay for a basket of figs. And I don't intend to seek charity from the poor villagers, either. They're barely subsisting as it is." He thinks of his labourer, Lorenzo Falcone, who farms and tends the animals for a portion of the crops as well as eggs, goat milk, and the occasional meat after the yearly hog slaughter. How will Lorenzo's family subsist if the new owner dismisses them? "Poor Lorenzo," he murmurs. "I shudder to think what this news will do to him."

"Must they leave?"

Don Simone purses his lips. "They may have no choice. You read the letter. It specifically states that once Alfonso Fantin, the new proprietor from northern Italy, takes ownership in July, he may require all vassals and livestock to be dispersed of as quickly as possible."

"Why does he want the lands if not to work them?"

"Like so many northern men of status, Fantin has no interest in anything other than ownership. An absentee landlord, that's what he'll be. I should have paid more heed to what's been going on in the *latifundia* all over Calabria." Don Simone feels anger coiling in his stomach. "If the Piedmont government can seize half the Papal States after Unification, why *wouldn't* it extend its greedy reach to every corner of Italy?"

Don Simone takes a loud sip of his tea and sets it down, his eyes starting to prickle again. *Damn the liberals.* How else to pay for the cost of war and independence, and to pay the expenses needed to make the new nation a viable entity in the competitive, industrial world? How else but to sell expropriated church property and inundate the new nation with taxes?

"These are troubled times for the brotherhood, Filippo." He shakes his head. "And to think that most people thought their 'yes' vote in the plebiscite would result in a greater freedom for all. Those poor, deluded souls. If anything, Unification has only brought about more poverty." His mouth twists.

The clanging of the bells announcing vespers startles him. His elbow hits his cup and it falls, cracking against the slate floor. He apologizes profusely to Don Filippo, who rings for assistance.

As he stoops to pick up the bigger pieces, he thinks how his life and Lorenzo's family's life will shortly become as jagged and shattered as the cup....

TONINO SPRINTS THROUGH THE WEED-LADEN PATH of the abandoned vineyard. The late afternoon breeze whips his face. He can smell the imminent downpour in the air. He has grown up in this valley, shadowed on one side by the dusky, jagged foothills of the Aspromonte mountain range, and bordered on the other by the endless Ionian. The salt-laced wind is blowing in from the sea. He welcomes it; his body is suffused with the same kind of heat he felt in early December during the mass commemorating the death of *San* Nicola in the Church of Santa Maria Assunta.

Tonino's glance was not transfixed on the altar, where a life-sized statue of the saint gazed at the congregation with luminous eyes that some swore blinked miraculously from time to time. Tonino's eyes were fastened onto the back of Gabriella's head, draped in a black kerchief with fringed ends.

While Don Simone chanted the Psalms, Tonino chanted silently: *Turn your head, Gabriella, so I can catch a glimpse of your saintly face.* She truly *was* a saint. Anyone who did what Gabriella was doing—devoting herself to her family, housekeeping and cooking for Don Simone—deserved such a title.

Tonino was rewarded moments later when a latecomer entering the church with cumbersome steps drew the attention of many and caused heads to turn and faces to scowl. Gabriella turned, bestowing Tonino with a flash of her profile, and a glimpse of her plum-red lips and bright eyes that matched San Nicola's in lustre. Her hair, thick and wavy, looked eager to burst from its kerchief restraint. Her eyes didn't meet his, but he was almost relieved, for his knees would surely have buckled.

The procession started after the mass. Tonino thrust himself into every opening in the thick cord of followers, hoping to get closer to Gabriella, but something or somebody always thwarted his progress: old Nicolina, the village midwife, who sought support for her arthritic knees; Signora Danone, who at seven months pregnant lumbered along, praying aloud to San Nicola to bless her unborn child; or a boisterous group of youngsters who were hardly willing to give up their spot with their companions.

Every once in a while, Tonino would lose sight of Gabriella, and the hope he felt would plummet, until a wave in the ocean of limbs leaving the church restored her to his view and then he felt like a saved man. *God forgive me,* he murmured to himself, *for thinking of Gabriella instead of venerating* San Nicola. But surely God would see that his heart and actions were pure when it came to Gabriella. His heart ached whenever he thought of her, and whenever he saw her. Tonino felt a tremor course through him that had nothing to do with a threatening roll of thunder that momentarily caused the processional cries, laments, and devotions to cease. Moments later, the first drops of rain began to fall.

As the procession shuffled through the main road of the village and out into the open countryside, the rain intensified. The six robust men carrying the statue on a platform with extended wooden arms ploughed ahead, their heads bent. Mothers held their children near, fathers sheltered the older folk, and the younger ones fended for themselves.

Tonino felt a jolt of envy as he saw a villager, Dino Poletti, offer his cloak to Gabriella. His heart twisted as he glimpsed the grateful smile she offered the recently widowed neighbour. As the procession reached its destination to the cemetery on the outskirts of the hamlet, Tonino's heart felt increasingly heavier. It seemed that everything and everyone was contriving to keep him from getting close to Gabriella.

As the rains turned into a deluge, the men set down the statue, and everyone headed frantically back toward the hamlet, shrieking as lightning forked the sky. Tonino lost sight of Gabriella in the scattering crowd, and by the time he reached his house, he was shaking uncontrollably. He dried himself by the hearth, but the chills continued. He spent the night in torment, seeing Gabriella's eyes over and over again, her smiling face directed at Poletti.

He discovered later that his mother and *nonna* had stood by his bedside incessantly during his feverish thrashing and outcries, taking turns applying cool cloths and giving him elixirs to bring out the fever. Another day and they were ready to call the village exorcist, so great was their fear that some envious villager had laid a deadly curse on him.

After two days, the fever broke and he came out of it feeling like the cloths the washerwomen would wring out and slap against the limestone outcroppings by the river. He was weak, weaker than he had ever felt in his life, but his conviction about Gabriella was stronger than ever. Slowly, with his daily intake of the pigeon broth his *nonna* prepared, making sure to add the yolks of freshly laid eggs, his physical strength returned. And being the son of a butcher, he didn't lack for liver or sweetbreads to build up his constitution.

In the weeks of recuperation and for weeks afterward, Tonino thought of ways of approaching Gabriella. He played them all out in his head, knowing full well that there were expected

procedures to follow if he was contemplating a serious court-
ship, and that some of his imaginings would not likely ever
take place. He would never compromise her in any way; no, he
had every intention of doing the right thing by her. He would
approach her father first, or maybe he could take his father
into his confidence and have him talk to Lorenzo.

There was also the matter of Dino Poletti to consider, who
might very well be looking for a new wife to tend to his three
children. He made some discreet inquiries about the widower
and was ecstatic to hear that Poletti was making plans to go
live with his mother up in the hills of Serra San Bruno, and that
his second cousin, a spinster, was promised to him in marriage.

Tonino returned to work with renewed vigour and health.
He made sure that *he* and not his brother delivered meat to
Don Simone, and he would leave the rectory after hand-deliv-
ering the package to Gabriella with a sense of breathlessness
and excitement that almost drove him mad with the effort of
keeping his feelings a secret. He couldn't help but drink in
as much of Gabriella as he could with thirsty eyes in the few
moments it took for the exchange, and any accidental contact
of her fingers against his ignited his senses like a torch. To his
mortification, Gabriella once made mention of this after her
usual inquiries as to his parents' health.

"And how are *you*, Antonino?"

"I...I'm well, thank you." He wondered why she was peering
at him with furrowed brows.

"Your face is quite flushed. Are you sure you're well? Perhaps
you have a fever."

Tonino inwardly cursed his traitorous skin. "No, no, I'm not
ill; I just ran to get here, as I have to head into town very soon."

"Well, don't overexert yourself." Gabriella gave him a shy
smile. "Or you might get sick again, and then Don Simone
will have us all reciting the rosary after Sunday mass to pray
for your recovery."

Tonino's cheeks burned. Was she joking with him? He gave

a laugh that sounded like a croak and thanked her for the payment. "*Arrivederci.*" He tipped his cap and turned away.

"*Ciao,* Tonino."

Tonino froze. She had used the short form of his name. It had been uttered with a soft familiarity that warmed him like his grandmother's pigeon soup. He turned around. Gabriella was still in the doorway of the rectory, her face and eyes bright with genuine innocence and purity. His heart sank. There was nothing there but neighbourly concern and camaraderie. He tipped his cap again and then sprinted away, vowing to find a way to make her want him the same way he wanted her. He hoped one day her eyes would let him know....

On the day of the hog slaughter, Tonino finally got up enough courage to ask her to meet him at the river. And now he has made his way there, his heart in his throat the entire way. Tonino catches sight of a shawl-draped figure sitting on a large stone near the riverbank. His heart pounds. *She came!*

ALFONSO KNOWS THAT HE AND HIS BROTHER Claudio are about as different from each other as any two brothers can be. If one didn't know they were related by blood, one would be hard-pressed to find any characteristic that might even vaguely hint at a familial connection.

Claudio, the eldest by seven years, is as mature as his outward appearance implies. His impeccable clothes and grooming habits befit his superior position as head physician at Torino's biggest hospital. He is always clean-shaven, save for a neatly clipped moustache with immaculately tapered tips, and his ear and nose hairs are perennially trimmed—he has his wife tend to them religiously every Sunday. His dark brown hair glistens and his nails are clipped to perfection—a crescent of white at both ends.

Claudio's face is not ruggedly masculine; it is handsome in a refined sort of way, with its blue eyes inherited from his Visigoth ancestry and a chiselled jawline that carries no pockets of fat around the jowls, like so many of his less-disciplined colleagues. His frame is lean but firm. Keeping physically in form is a priority; he has repeatedly said that he abhors the thought of aiding in the body's deterioration by eating excessively, drinking excessively, or doing *anything* excessively.

Alfonso realizes that Claudio is not-so-subtly trying to suggest that *his* lifestyle is excessive, and that a few more years of unbridled excess will most surely result in a state of deterioration. Alfonso laughs every time Claudio mentions it. He isn't at all worried. At twenty-five years of age, his features are solid but not flabby. His hair is flaxen, which his last lover likened to an undulating wheat field in the August sun. His eyes are dark brown with hazel specks. His body suits him the way it is: broad shoulders, a barrel of a chest, sturdy legs. A man of substance.

Claudio is concerned chiefly with Alfonso's excessive pastimes, which include women and gambling in Venice. Alfonso smiles. "*La Serenissima,*" as his favourite city is known, draws him with a bevy of delights that hold him willingly captive with its countless gambling havens and wealthy patronesses who are more than willing to test his skills in their salons and in their boudoirs.

Occasionally, when Claudio sees that he is indulging heavily in any one area, he does what he has always done since Alfonso was old enough to follow him around and since the death of their father shortly after Alfonso's birth. He assumes a paternal role, advising if need be, and inevitably scolding.

Claudio is never mean-spirited even when he scolds. And although Alfonso usually nods in an attempt to seem remorseful, he and Claudio both know that disciplining Alfonso is pretty much nothing more than a ritual Alfonso tolerates.

"I don't like that glint in your eye, little brother. It's going to get you into trouble one day," Claudio has often told him.

Alfonso scowls as he ponders how Claudio's prophetic words became reality this past autumn, shortly after hiring a new chambermaid, the young niece of Antonietta, his cook....

Alfonso took a liking to the girl, whose plain skirts and cotton blouses seemed to emphasize, rather than conceal, her budding voluptuousness. She had a pretty face and eyes with thick lashes that fluttered like the wings of a butterfly in a mating dance, taunting him with veiled messages, inflaming him with the occasional glide of her tongue over swollen lips.

"Clara offered me the apple first," Alfonso blurted when Claudio confronted him with the news of the girl's shameful condition, revealed to him by the sobbing Antonietta.

"You didn't have to take it," Claudio snapped. "The Fantin name has always been a respected one. Now it is besmirched as a result of your...your...*excessive stupidity.*" Spittle flew from the corners of his mouth. "A plan has to be concocted before this unfortunate incident becomes public knowledge and destroys the reputation our parents worked so hard to build." His eyes bore into Alfonso. "This is going to cost you dearly, brother. You can't keep indulging in the desires of the flesh and never expect your seed to take fruit."

Alfonso bit his lip. "It doesn't have to take fruit. There are ways...."

"That is not her wish."

"How do you know?"

"Your cook came to me, remember? This is just as shameful for her family as it is for ours, especially if word gets out."

"Who knows?"

"Just Antonietta; Clara couldn't bear to come to you."

"Maybe she'll listen to me." Alfonso's voice hardened. "She can't keep it. I never intended—"

"To marry her?"

"Of course not." Alfonso snorted. "She's a servant, for God's sake."

"So, you don't love her?"

"Love?" Alfonso scoffed. "I never bedded her because I loved her. And I found out quickly enough that Clara's appetite for bedding had been whetted before me. I wasn't the first." He began to pace the room. "Perhaps this was a scheme from the start. Entice your master, have him impregnate you, and then arrange for blackmail money so the news doesn't leak out to the wrong people." Alfonso turned sharply to Claudio. "Has there been mention of money exchanging hands?"

"Cook hinted as much. She mentioned a friend in Lombardy who would take the girl in for a sum that wouldn't result in hardship for her family, and that Clara would be willing to spare everyone the shame."

"*Puttana!*" Alfonso spat, clenching his teeth. He could feel the vein in his temple throbbing, his face flushing in an unstoppable wave.

"You have to recognize your part in this," Claudio said quietly. "This was bound to happen with the lifestyle you insist upon. Did you not think of sheathing yourself?"

Alfonso snorted. "This was not a planned overture, or yes, I would have, brother dear." He had always heeded Claudio's clinical lessons, arranging with the family butcher to supply him pig intestines, and except for the first time with Clara, he always made sure he was well equipped for his amorous adventures. "It must have happened on that first occasion, goddammit!"

He began pacing again, recalling the events of the night he had stumbled into the *palazzo*, after a night of successful gambling and celebratory drinking. His missteps in the hall past the servants' quarters had awoken Clara, who had appeared sleepily at her door in a flimsy night shift. Her hair, usually in a bun by day, cascaded over her shoulders in a thick mass of curls. In his kneeling position, Alfonso had seen the firm outlines of her body beneath the shift, and the solid peaks and dark valleys had aroused the manly desires within him that the effects of his drinking had not been powerful enough to stifle. He had risen clumsily toward her, grinning as Clara pushed her door open invitingly....

The primitive desire Alfonso had felt for Clara in that first month after his initial entry into her room had waned instantly when he found out that she was pregnant. He had felt angry, betrayed, and regretful that the lustful unions they had shared would no longer continue. Clara, unlike his other partners in the past, had had no modest inhibitions. She had not just lain like a virtuous debutante of the social class he shared, feigning a delicate attempt to protect her maidenhead. No, Clara had been as lustful, if not more, that he. She had strutted around him with no fig leaf to hide her modesty. She had ridden him like a wild bandit, her hair streaming over her ripe breasts and gyrating abdomen, grinding into him until he felt himself explode. Unlike the inexperienced young women who had lain passively in bed after he had feasted on their virginity, still quaking at their first experience but not yet aroused themselves, Clara had been insatiable. There was *nothing* that Clara had demurred about when it came to bedding.

And now she had gone and spoiled everything. She had extinguished his ardour as surely as the candle she snuffed out upon his nightly arrival in her chamber, preferring the light of the moon during their tempestuous relations.

Alfonso stopped seeking her out immediately and grudgingly gave orders to his personal secretary and advisor for the financial transaction to be made discreetly, and with haste, so that she could be out of his sight before she swelled out. On the one occasion that they crossed paths, Alfonso gave her an icy half-nod of acknowledgement, and her face darkened and twisted.

"*Vigliacco!*" she spat, her eyes narrowing. She lifted her hand without hesitation and struck him in the face, leaving him speechless as she flounced away.

I should have followed her and given her what she deserved for lifting her hand to me, he had thought regretfully on many occasions later, but he ended up consoling himself that the whore and her bastard were out of his life for good. To heal his wounded spirit, he deliberately stayed away from women and filled his time with gambling, the only other activity that aroused his passion. A particularly profitable night at the tables brought him satisfaction a week after Clara's departure to Lombardy. His good humour restored, he set about making investments and purchasing as much property as he could, as he had done before he had allowed Clara to infringe upon his life.

His connections with officials in the Piedmontese government—he was good friends with the Minister of Finance—let him in on some succulent deals before they became public knowledge. He was particularly interested in the church properties that were to be expropriated throughout Italy, due to the ruling liberal party's ongoing anticlerical reforms. Alfonso fancied owning property all over the newly formed nation; it excited him to think of his bourgeoning wealth and prestige.

Alfonso never attended the auctions himself—he employed others to carry out that task. What he enjoyed the most was the ritual of travelling to survey his recently acquired land. The labourers lined up for inspection by their new landlord. He felt like a youthful monarch as he strode past them, and as they curtsied and bowed, he intuitively looked for signs of diffidence. If it served his interests, he kept them on, working the *latifundia* and providing at the same time for their families; if he sensed a disgruntled worker—and he delighted in sniffing them out like a hunting bitch—he smiled at them with the merest hint of condescension, sometimes even picking up their small children like a benevolent godfather ("snotty-nosed little beggars," he'd refer to them afterwards) and then, upon his return to Piedmont, he would give orders to have them dismissed with only a mere pittance, completely indifferent to their plight.

"I can't be responsible for feeding everyone," he reasoned curtly to Claudio when he was reporting the details of a shared investment. "But my employees tell me that the tenants have found work elsewhere."

This was a downright fabrication more often than not, but Alfonso didn't allow himself to feel guilty at all for lying to his brother as he knew it would help ease Claudio's strong moral conscience.

My brother's only character flaw, Alfonso thinks with a fond smile.

GABRIELLA GLANCES AT HER HANDS. Rough, calloused, the colour almost the same as the burnished terracotta floor in Don Simone's rectory. Always moving, these hands, from dawn to dusk, and often after that. She sighs. Is it any wonder she has old hands or at least older-looking than her nineteen-year-old face?

She stares at the bucket of dirty laundry she has brought with her. A young girl, no matter what age, would not be wandering toward the river for no reason, so she has thrown together items that needed washing anyway: her father's clothes, grimy and stained from working in the fields and with the animals, a pair of Luciano's torn breeches that look like they might not stand up to another hand scrubbing with the wash-stone, and her own shifts and skirts, their hems encrusted with mud from the last downpour.

"I'm glad I kept walking. You weren't at your usual washing place."

Gabriella turns slowly and nods a greeting but says nothing. She glances first at Tonino's scuffed shoes and slowly draws her gaze upward, past the trousers, slowly counting the buttons on his linen shirt before meeting his eyes. It strikes her how handsome Tonino is.

They have virtually grown up together in the hamlet of Camini, where it seems that just about everybody has a hand in the raising of a child. Rarely does a mother or father panic at the disappearance of a child—there are far too many watchful eyes in the village. If the child isn't at old Nicolina's house indulging in an *uovo sbattuto*—a thoroughly beaten egg yolk with a dash of *marsala* in it and plenty of sugar—then surely he or she might be in neighbour Betta's *cattoio,* scattering the feed to the motley group of chickens and pigeons, or in Francesco Carlini's garden, a favourite spot for the young to feed on golden plums in the summer, orange persimmons in the fall, plump pears and oranges in the winter, and medlars in the spring.

The old man always feigns fury at spotting children in his garden, frowning menacingly while attempting a cane-assisted chase through the neat rows of tomatoes, and the children shriek and scurry off like alarmed ants to hide behind the gangly bean stalks, finding this beloved ritual even more fun than the actual picking of the fruit. Secure in the knowledge of Signor Francesco's benevolence, and the fruitful outcome, they are regular interlopers of the Carlini garden.

Gabriella can still remember the time when she and Tonino had run off in the usual delirious panic, Tonino successfully finding a spot behind the giant fig tree, and she, skidding on a rotten fig on the ground and landing unceremoniously in a nearby prickly pear cactus. Signor Francesco had to pluck the tenacious thorns from her hands and legs, enduring her shrill howls with patience developed from experience. He had twelve grandchildren of his own, eight of them girls with high-pitched voices that became even more higher pitched in moments such as these. And after comforting her with a beaten egg yolk—fixed with an extra shot of marsala that he thought would benefit her under the circumstances—he sent her home with Tonino as her guardian to make sure she didn't land in any more thorny bushes.

"What are you thinking of?" Tonino returns her smile.

She feels herself reddening, realizing she has been staring. "Signor Francesco.... Do you remember?"

"How could I ever forget?" Tonino lets out a deep laugh. "I got a venomous scolding from your mother for allowing such a thing to happen, and a strict order to stay out of Signor

Francesco's prickly pears."

"Which both of us ignored, naturally."

"Naturally, being only eight and ten. It didn't make sense to stop having fun."

Gabriella smiles wistfully, watching the water gushing a short distance from her feet. She and Tonino had a lot of fun as children. And now, here they are, childhood and adolescence over, with a new *feeling* between them. An awkward feeling. Gabriella can't deny that there has been something different in the air between them for months.

Is *he* aware of it too? Is that why he wanted to talk to her? Gabriella's stomach tightens in anticipation as Tonino sits down on a flat rock next to her.

"Gabriella, I want you...."

She lifts her head.

Tonino's dark chestnut eyes are intense. "...For my wife."

Gabriella feels her heart jolting uncontrollably. Perhaps deep down she *has* been expecting a declaration of some sort, a modest expression or show of affection, but *this?* Realizing that her mouth has opened slightly, Gabriella clamps it shut and bites her lip, not knowing how she should reply.

She doesn't pull away when Tonino takes her hand in his. She likes the way his big hands cover hers. They are hard but warm and gentle at the same time, and Gabriella doesn't know if the pulse she feels originates from him or herself. She allows herself to linger in their warmth, feeling as safe as she has ever felt in all their youthful escapades together.

"*Mi vuoi*, Gabriella?" he says softly, his thumb beginning a circular caress on her palm. For a moment, as the river whispers and gushes, she wonders if he has really spoken, but when he repeats the words, she knows it wasn't her imagination.

Do I want him? she muses, dazed. She has never dared to think this far. *He wants me as his wife....*

"Yes," she finally whispers, her cheeks aflame.

When she meets Tonino's gaze again, she is overcome by the

sight of his eyes misting. She takes his hands in hers and squeezes them with all the affection that she has ever felt for him. Her lips quiver at his first tentative kiss, their locked hands held between them as they sit side by side. When Tonino's lips part from hers, she can see the intensity in his eyes. For countless moments, they sit looking at each other, with only the river and the sparrows breaking the silence. At one point, Tonino walks over to a nearby oleander bush and snips off a few blossoms. He arranges the blossoms in her hair. "For my *calabrisella*," he murmurs against her ear. "My Calabrian girl."

Long after he has departed, and she is back at the rectory with her laundry washed, scrubbed and wrung out, Gabriella wonders how she shall tell her father and Don Simone when they come home....

DON SIMONE GIVES HIS MULE AN AFFECTIONATE PAT as he approaches Camini. "Come on, Vittorio," he coaxes the animal, whose gait is considerably slower than when they headed out earlier. "*Forza!* Don't quit on me now. A reward awaits you at home." The animal neighs in response and kicks up his heels, making Don Simone chuckle at its seeming comprehension.

Humming a chorus of the *Te Deum,* Don Simone straightens in the saddle and surveys the triangle-shaped hamlet on the mountainside. Camini.... Home for the last ten years. He smiles wistfully, remembering his bittersweet departure from his home in Friuli in the north at the age of twenty-nine.

His position as head priest of the wealthy parish of San Bartolomeo was guaranteed; it was just a matter of time before his Superior, Monsignor Brunello, would succumb to the congestive lung ailment that was weakening him from day to day. But Don Simone had been having nagging feelings of doubt. *Everything is too easy for you here,* an inner voice kept telling him. *You need to serve where there is poverty, suffering, devastation. You need to bring light and faith to areas of darkness and despair.*

The feelings began assailing him at night. He had one partic-ular recurring dream of being tenderly embraced by a woman with limpid chestnut eyes and a blue veil. She had a timeless beauty. A soft, peachy glow highlighted her delicately sculpted cheeks. Her lips were the colour of wild poppies, and her hair framed her face like a silky curtain. She exuded an air of purity and grace, and as she embraced him, she would whisper, *Serve those below you.*

Upon hearing the news a few days later that the southern tip of the country had been rocked by an earthquake, the woman's words came back to him. *Below you.* Surely, the dream was a sign; *those below* must be the survivors of the earthquake that devastated seven villages in Calabria. Hundreds killed, injured and left homeless.

And then Don Simone heard the words of his inner voice: *Serve where there is poverty, suffering, devastation, and de-spair.* Unable to control his emotion at the realization that was growing at the core of his being, Don Simone collapsed into tears, knowing that he had received his calling. When he had recovered, he sought Monsignor, who was propped up against an arc of pillows on his bed, and humbly asked for his blessing to leave the parish of San Bartolomeo in order to aid one of the parishes in the devastated zone. Monsignor Brunello, to his surprise, tried to dissuade him, citing the Calabrians as a barbaric, uncivilized people, living in a state of abject poverty and illness.

"Their coastal villages are infested with malaria," he rasped after a fit of catarrhal coughing. "And if you don't die of that, you most surely will perish at the hands of brigands." He crossed himself and his shrunken eyes widened. "It is a wild, lawless region, Don Simone, why would you want to leave all *this*?" He stretched out his arms feebly, indicating his ornately decorated bedchamber and the doorway that led to the hall that would eventually connect to the gilded confines of the sanctuary. "One day soon, when God receives me into His

Kingdom—may His will be done—you will be head priest."
Monsignor gasped for air and sank back against the pillows.
"You're too cultured to subject yourself to a life among peasants and outlaws. Come now, son," he entreated, slipping into their Friulan dialect, "stay with your people." He succumbed to another spasm of coughing before grasping the brass bell by his night table.

Don Simone kissed Monsignor Brunello's blue-veined hand and retreated to his room as soon as the attendant arrived. As he sank into the comfort of his own bed, he pondered the words of his Superior, words that made him see the Monsignor in a new light. He felt his respect for the old priest diminishing, while his desire to leave for Calabria grew even stronger.

Don Simone gives his mule a pat on the back. "Come on, Vittorio. You can make it. We're almost home." *Home*. The place where he intended to stay for the rest of his life. *Camini*. For a moment, his smile freezes at the thought of the impending loss of his church lands, and then he forces the thought out of his mind, anticipating the pork feast he will soon be sharing with his friends and neighbours.

He doesn't *have* to tell them the bad news today.

WHEN GABRIELLA REALIZES THAT THE HEN—a faithful provider since her father purchased it at the fall fair in Locri—is singing stridently, as if to mock the old rooster who has just ceased his matinal crowing, she drops the basket of eggs with which she has been heading to the rectory and stands watching it in horror.

"*A crowing hen bodes nothing but ill luck,*" Gabriella recalls her mother saying years ago, when she was twelve, helping her mother scatter feed to the scrawny group of hens in the enclosure. "*It must be killed at once.*" And without hesitation, Gabriella's mother sequestered the offending bird and promptly twisted its neck, murmuring, "*Death to you, and health to those who eat you.*"

Gabriella remembers how she burst into tears and scampered off into the fields beyond the rectory, where her father was hoeing the fields. She flung herself into his arms, and when the storm of her trauma was spent and the flood of her tears had subsided, she stayed with him until the clanging of the outdoor bell announced suppertime. Both brushed the earth off their clothes, washed their hands at the outside spring, and sat down to a steaming bowl of broth, which she fortunately didn't connect to the recently killed fowl.

And then her mother started her labour. A gush of fluid suddenly appeared on the terracotta floor beneath her mother's skirt, and her father jumped up to hastily wipe it with a rag and shout at Gabriella to run to the neighbouring cottage to get Nicolina, who had brought more than half the children of the village into the world.

The sky was smeared in shades of plum and amber, and as the sun began its descent into the dark strip beyond the hills into the Ionian Sea, Gabriella tried not to think of spiders, mice, snakes, and other horrid creatures skittering across the fields. It didn't bother her during the day when the cats and the dog were present, but now that they were all in their enclosure, what would stop those stealthy, slithering field creatures from brushing against her, biting her with those sharp, vermin teeth, wrapping their scaly, serpentine bodies around her slender legs, crawling up her bare skin with their multiple legs?

Gabriella felt her stomach tightening at the thought of the snakes that could be poised to strike: the *serpa colubrida,* with its fiery markings, and even worse, the *vipera aspis,* whose venom even Nicolina cannot weaken with her most potent herb concoctions. The chant Gabriella learned as a child reverberated in her mind:

If you're bitten by a serpa colubrida, church bells will be rung,
If struck by a vipera aspis, light a candle; your life is done.

She had no choice but to obey Papà. Her mamma's time had come. She bolted down the narrow, weedy path through the fields, muttering the Ave Maria eight or nine times before an unknown creature scurried past her and made her squeal in terror. With a burst of speed she never thought possible, she made it to the neighbouring cottage.

The trek back took longer, for Nicolina was not young anymore—she had actually delivered Gabriella's mother—and she needed a cane to help support her swollen knees. But Gabriella found her fear diminishing with Nicolina's presence and the sight of her cane, until the low grumbling of thunder that had seemed so far off suddenly reverberated threateningly around them. The amber hue of the sky had been replaced with what seemed like hundreds of purple swollen bellies like her mother's, ready to burst. Her moon-shaped face uplifted, Nicolina started reciting the Pater Noster, the Ave Maria and the Gloria in a loud, somewhat defiant voice, as if daring the heavens to split open over the words of God.

When they finally reached her mother's bedside, the downpour began, and Nicolina shot a triumphant glance at Gabriella, as if to emphasize the power of her prayers over the turbulent storm. Confident that the midwife would work her same magic with her mother, Gabriella retreated to the kitchen to wait. Moments later, the baby's first cry and her mother's last one shattered the air....

By the time she was fourteen, Gabriella could wring a chicken's neck with the same diffidence she bestowed upon any household chore. She had done it countless times since her mother's death, initially under the experienced tutelage of Nicolina, who had patiently weathered her protestations, furious sobs, and foot-stomping. The midwife recognized that Gabriella's rage and remorse was not so much the girl's reaction to the killing of a fowl, but a necessary mourning for the passing of her mother, and the passing of childhood for Gabriella. The girl now had had no choice but to assume the position of cook and caretaker in the home. Her father Lorenzo had enough work to do in the fields, which earned him a roof over his head and a small plot of land for his own use, but not enough to employ a woman to take care of his children and do the cooking and cleaning for the parish priest, as Gabriella's mother had done.

At twelve, Gabriella had assumed all of her mother's previous chores. She rose at dawn, awakened by the strident crowing of the old rooster, and pulling her woollen coat over her shift, she stumbled downstairs to light the fire in the kitchen. After warming her shivering body for a few moments, she would go out into the courtyard and scatter feed to the chickens and hen, collect the eggs, milk the goat, and go back inside to prepare breakfast for her father and Don Simone, who by this time would be sitting by the roaring fire, chatting.

Of the two, Lorenzo was the heartier eater, devouring the *frittata* Gabriella would make along with a hunk of cheese and thick bread he would dip in olive oil. He needed his strength for the demanding work in the fields, he'd declare. Whereby Don Simone would reply, after a meagre wedge of bread dipped into a cup of tea slaked with goat's milk, "'The joy of the Lord is your strength.'" And Lorenzo, who had little patience with the Lord since He had seen fit to take his beloved wife Elisabetta from him, would merely snort and help himself to another *frittata*, which Gabriella had learned to make so well with eggs, milk, parsley, and whatever tidbits she had available in the larder.

And then Don Simone would sadly shake his head, whisper a prayer for the healing of Lorenzo's spirit, thank Gabriella for her toil, and tucking his breviary under his arm, he would saunter off to the church, to begin the daily seven o'clock service. Lorenzo would leave shortly afterwards, with a haversack holding bread, olives, cheese, and a small flask of wine. Gabriella wouldn't see him again until late in the evening.

Alone, she would clean up and hope to get a few essential tasks done before Luciano woke up, whimpering for his first feed of milk of the day. In the first six months after Luciano's birth,

Lorenzo had no choice but to enlist the services of a wet nurse. After offering three hens and a baby goat that Don Simone had graciously donated for this purpose, Lorenzo readily handed Luciano into the capable and experienced hands of Genoveffa Marcucci, a buxom young villager of twenty-two who was nursing her fifth infant. Genoveffa's breasts were overflowing with milk, her husband Umberto would declare proudly among the men in the town square. They would congratulate him for his virility and his wife's fecundity as they exchanged knowing winks to which the strutting Umberto would be oblivious, along with the knowledge that a great number of them, even those who were married, secretly fantasized about the fertile Genoveffa, slyly eyeing her perennially engorged bosom and swollen abdomen with stifled arousal.

Genoveffa welcomed Luciano at her breast. Umberto was working like a beast to provide for the lot of them, she told Lorenzo, and some extra hens and a goat were a godsend. To Lorenzo's relief, Luciano latched on immediately when Lorenzo brought the infant to her. Embarrassed by Luciano's loud, suckling noises and Genoveffa's lack of embarrassment, Lorenzo murmured his thanks and retreated hastily back home. It was agreed that Luciano would be returned to his care after six months. At that time, Gabriella could administer goat's milk to the infant and tend to his needs. She would be thirteen, a *signorina,* more than ready for the responsibility of taking care of her brother. At sixteen, many of the village girls were already betrothed or married....

Having promptly wrung the neck of the crowing hen before placing it in the cellar, Gabriella now stirs the *suffrittu.* She inhales the scent of pork stew from the oversized cauldron brought out for special occasions when there would be more for supper than just her family and Don Simone. It is a tradition that Gabriella loves, the feast held the day after the slaughtering. A meal of gratitude for the abundance of food in their life and for the abundance of friends. Don Simone taught her about gratitude early in life, before she could barely pronounce the word. He would bow his head solemnly at the solid oak table in the rectory kitchen. After a few moments of silence, he would murmur: "'Give thanks unto the Lord; for He is good: for His mercy endureth forever.'"

Gabriella takes a wooden spoon and dips it into the cauldron to select a chunk of pork fat to taste. She blows on it for a moment and then plops it into her mouth, savouring the pan juices covering it before compressing it satisfyingly between her tongue and hard palate.

A feeling of warmth coils within her that she knows can't be attributed solely to the pork she has just tasted. It is the prospect of seeing Tonino, being near him with this new *awareness* between the two of them.

The shuffle of feet outside sends her heart racing, and taking a deep breath, she throws open the heavy door, an expectant smile on her face. Her spirit plummets when she sees that it isn't Tonino, but she continues smiling—after all, he will be arriving soon.

"Greetings neighbours, Francesca, Rocco. Come in; you're the first to arrive. *Ciao, ragazzi.*" She greets their six children, who are between seven and fourteen years of age, and they enter noisily, the youngest scampering up the stairs to find his best friend, Luciano.

"Salvatore and Beatrice are on their way," Francesca informs her. "They wanted to get their chores done before dark. Their son Ricardo won't be coming; his stomach is unsettled, and he thought it wise to stay home and nurse a cup of chamomile tea."

What about Tonino? Gabriella wants to ask but remains silent, not wishing to draw anyone's attention. "Papà has gone to get Nicolina," she tells them, waving for them to sit down in the kitchen. "He won't be long."

"Poor Nicolina," Francesca says, shaking her head. "The years are catching up to her. All those long walks to the cemetery, summer and winter. Those poor legs of hers have done their share of walking back and forth to the grotto at Monte Stella for the yearly pilgrimage. And bad weather has never stopped her from making the journey either. Fifty or so years, through bone-chilling rains and blistering heat—no wonder her legs are stiff with rheumatism—and now she can barely walk from her place to yours."

Rocco nods his head. "She has spent her life in service to others," he says in a tone of eulogy. "It's a good thing she never married. A woman belongs in the home."

"She has been too busy bringing other people's babies into the world, including your half-dozen, to settle down and have her own," Francesca retorts.

Gabriella smiles. Nicolina has played a part in everybody's life in Camini. And as a small reward to herself after a gruelling day of delivering robust or sickly babies, or dealing with distasteful but necessary procedures on disease-ridden bodies, Nicolina indulges in smoking a pipe. Her sole vice, she laughingly declares in her recognizable smoker's rasp. She has no husband or children and nobody to please but herself. Gabriella has watched her on many a night before heading back to the rectory herself, tapping out and then refilling the pipe with her own dried hemp, tamping it down with one finger before lighting it up. She'd be enveloped by a haze that would make Gabriella wrinkle her nose, prompting her to bid Nicolina a hasty goodbye. She'd unblock her nose only when she knew she was safely out of reach of the fumes.

"Dear Nicolina," Gabriella says affectionately. "Her legs may have betrayed her, but her mind is still as sharp as my butchering knife."

A heavy knock interrupts them. Gabriella strides to the door. Tonino's parents greet her warmly. Gabriella looks expectantly beyond them, and Beatrice, catching her glance, says, "Ricardo isn't feeling well and Tonino hasn't come back home yet. He had to deliver some meat to the mayor and others in Riace."

Gabriella masks her disappointment and invites Beatrice and Salvatore to join Francesca and Rocco in the kitchen. Tonino will miss the meal. Gabriella stirs the stew and checks the loaves of bread in the brick oven. She lifts a trap door on the far side of the kitchen floor that reveals steps to an underground cellar.

The sight of the hen she has killed earlier, placed in an earthenware bowl and left in one corner of the cellar, makes her shiver. *Something terrible is going to happen. The hen crowed this morning. Dear God in heaven, don't let anything happen to Tonino.* She grabs the bottle of wine she was seeking and returns to the kitchen.

She turns to see Luciano boisterously tramping down the stairs with his friends to greet the neighbours. His antics evoke guffaws from Salvatore, his godfather, and Gabriella welcomes the distraction to slip outside. She watches her father and Nicolina approach slowly, the old midwife seated at the back of the mule cart, propped up comfortably with old blankets, and her father riding on the mule's broad back, prodding him on with the clicking of his tongue and the occasional slap on the hindquarters.

When they enter the kitchen, they are greeted with the sight of Don Simone already seated at the head of the table, smiling amidst the greetings and warm handshakes.

"Ah, how blessed I truly am, to come back to such a family as I have here. I must say, I always look forward to my retreat at the monastery, but I anticipate my return here with as much, if not more, pleasure." He waves to the children chasing each other about the rooms and chuckles. "A few days in the sanctity of silence, meditation and prayer always restores one's spirit; however, one can't deny that this…this exuberance of life is spiritual fodder as well." He winks at Gabriella. "I could smell the stew from outside the village. I pushed old Vittorio to the limit to get here before it was all gone."

"As if we would eat it all," Gabriella laughs. "We would have left you at least a corner of the pig's ear." She removes the loaves from the oven and proceeds to pass around steaming earthenware bowls. She slices the bread deftly and then turns to Don Simone.

He nods, rises, and bows his head. Everyone falls silent. "Let us thank the Lord for the blessings He has bestowed upon us." He crosses himself, blows his nose, and sits down.

"And for delivering Don Simone from the hands of brigands and gypsies," Francesca offers, crossing herself before dunking a chunk of bread into her stew.

"Brigands? God help us!" Francesca's ten-year-old daughter crosses herself. "Don't even mention them. I'll have nightmares."

"Papà, what is worse, gypsies or brigands?" Luciano tugs at his father's sleeve, his voice trembling.

"Let's change the subject," Lorenzo insists. "I want you to be able to sleep in your own bed tonight. Now eat."

Gabriella glances out the window. She shivers at the thought of Tonino journeying by himself through dusky hills and narrow roads. With a heavy heart, she sits down and begins to eat, her previous enjoyment of the meal fading with every bite. She recalls the bad omen of the crowing hen, and suddenly, her stomach twists at the thought of the many dangers that Tonino might encounter on the way home. She drops her fork with a clatter.

She meets Don Simone's eyes, and there is something in his expression that alarms her. Something unfamiliar. A look of... of *guilt*, almost. She turns away. Everyone around her is intent on enjoying the pork feast. She picks up her fork and berates herself for being so superstitious. When she looks back at Don Simone, he is dipping a piece of coarse bread in his pork stew. His shoulders are slumped, and he does not look up nor contribute to the conversation.

Gabriella finishes her stew half-heartedly. Now she is certain something is amiss.

DON SIMONE, USUALLY SO PATIENT and unflappable, seems

almost short with her the next morning. While he talks about church affairs with her father, Gabriella finds her thoughts drifting between the memory of Tonino's lips on hers and thoughts of their future together. When Don Simone's voice takes on a harsh note, Gabriella is jolted back to what he is saying. He is eyeing her with a frown, and she is about to apologize for not paying attention when he suddenly rises from the table. "I have some…some important matters to go over with both of you," he says, wringing his hands. "But I think…." He looks at her father, then back at her, then down at his hands. "I think it best that I wait until after Mass. Lorenzo, why don't you check the planks on the steps leading to the loft in the barn? Luciano noticed a loose one, You can head off to the fields after I return. Oh, and Gabriella, the good farmer Alberico came by and dropped off a couple of pigeons this morning. His wife Angelina has singed and cleaned them. How about starting a nice pot of soup?"

When Don Simone returns from saying Mass, the pigeon soup is simmering in a big pot. Gabriella throws in a few bay leaves and joins her father at the sturdy oak table. Don Simone sits down with a sigh, a letter in one hand. His brows furrow, and he begins tapping the table with his other hand. Gabriella notices the slight tremble of his hand. "I have received some disturbing news." Don Simone wipes his brow. His gaze flies to her father and back to her. "I wish I didn't have to tell you this."

At these words, her father sets down his cup of goat's milk with a clatter and frowns. "What is it? Is Farmer Basilio complaining about our animals encroaching on his pastures again?" His mouth tightens in a narrow line. "I told him I'd fix the fence and I did, but I wouldn't put it past him to loosen the post on purpose so he could collect another fine, the sneaky—"

"No, no, Lorenzo," Don Simone raises his hand in protest. "It's nothing like that."

Gabriella wipes her hands on her apron and moves closer to her father. There is something in Don Simone's voice that is causing the flesh in her arms to rise.

"A landowner from the north is investing in properties all over Italy. He...he has purchased our church property and will be arriving in the summer to view the land and to...and to establish whether he wants to keep...."

Gabriella blinks. *Purchased? Arriving?*

"*Keep what*?" Her father has leaned forward, his jaw rigid. A vein is pulsing in his temple.

Don Simone bites his lip. "Keep things the way they are. Keep the lands cultivated."

"And if he doesn't?"

Don Simone waves the letter helplessly. "I don't know what his intentions are."

Gabriella blurts, "Why else would he want the lands if not for the crops they yield? The olives, the grapes, and everything else. And how can someone buy lands that belong to the Church?" Gabriella stiffens with a new thought. "Don Simone, will you still have the church?"

"Oh, my dear, for now it seems that I will be able to stay on as the parish priest, but if this new landowner decides not to cultivate the lands, then...then...." The fingers of his free hand begin drumming on the table.

"Then we will have to find other means of employment," Gabriella's father says, each word dropping like a heavy stone.

Gabriella sinks into the chair next to him. He doesn't have to say anything else. She knows what they will have to do if they are let go. There is no work for them in Camini. There are families who have no choice but to be contented with a daily meal of whatever they can forage in the countryside. Most of them have no lands of their own to cultivate.

Many of the men in the hamlet work as day labourers on properties in neighbouring hamlets. They rise hours before dawn to travel by foot, and several by mule, to put their sweat into the land. The landlords who employ them allow them a portion of the crops, and often, the portion they get is of the poorest quality. Some landlords are even suspected of using weighted containers to measure out the quantities owed to the workers. When the men return home at dusk, the meagre contents of their haversacks are cooked and devoured, the grain set aside for the wife to bring to the miller the next day. And after barely closing their eyes for a rest, the men set off again.

Her family has been truly fortunate, working for Don Simone all these years. And a few other families have been blessed with the means to help others occasionally, like Tonino's father Salvatore, who inherited land from his father, who had ventured into North Africa and made a substantial living from working the mines.

Tonino!

Suddenly, Gabriella realizes that both men are looking at her. *Did I just utter Tonino's name aloud?* she wonders. She feels her cheeks burning.

Her father's eyes narrow. "Gabriella, did you hear what Don Simone has been saying? That church lands are being auctioned off by this new government to wealthy landowners? How many of them just want to own more and more land? If this Signor Fantin decides not to continue working the lands, we will have no choice but to leave Camini. I—"

"Can't we convince him to keep things as they are?" Gabriella hears the panic in her voice. "*I don't want to leave Camini.*" Dear God, how can she tell them about Tonino now?

"I don't want you and Luciano and your father to leave either," Don Simone says, his voice cracking. "You're my family."

Gabriella's father looks away. His jaw is clenched, and now his fingers are drumming the table.

"Come," Don Simone says, "let us leave it in the hands of God. Perhaps we are worrying for nothing, and this Signor Fantin will keep things as they are."

The way his words tremble at the end makes Gabriella

wonder later if he really believes that nothing will change. With a heavy feeling in her chest, she climbs the stairs to her room. Luciano is snoring gently, his mouth partially open. She bends down to kiss him on the forehead, knowing he is unlikely to awaken.

Lying in her own cot, she stares at the shadows cast on the wall by the moon. The leaves of the *giuggiola* tree are fluttering in the night breeze. As she listens to the whispering sounds they make, she feels the muscles in her abdomen tightening. She *has* to find a way to get this Signor Fantin to leave well enough alone.

She reaches for the rosary Don Simone gave her from a pilgrimage to Monte Stella, the Sanctuary of the Madonna of the Stars in nearby Pazzano. She keeps it under her pillow and takes it out to recite it every night, but usually, she falls asleep before the third decade. Her fingers fumble for the crucifix. She crosses herself.

She cannot leave Tonino now. *Or ever.* She has four months before Signor Fantin arrives. She *will* find a way. *Padre nostro....* She can't imagine a life without Tonino, a life they have yet to begin together. *Ave Maria, piena di grazia....*

THE *PIAZZA* IS SIMMERING WITH ACTIVITY: men arranging the sticks and logs for the fire, a bevy of women tending to boisterous children, wizened elders chatting while smoking their pipes, and adolescent boys scanning the throng for the sight of the first *signorine* who would be accompanied by unwilling chaperones—mostly brothers.

Tonino spots Luciano first, sporting his ennui like most younger siblings who are assigned chaperone duties, his head whipping to the right and then to the left, in search of friends his age with whom he can scamper off. Gabriella gives him an indulgent smile and draws nearer to the burgeoning fire, giving Luciano the subtle opportunity to make his escape. Gabriella does not look worried about his safety; if he wanders away or ventures to forbidden places, any number of their *paesani* will pass the news to her.

Gabriella is welcomed by Lola Salinaro, the bread-maker's wife, and her relatives, visitors from the neighbouring hamlet of Riace. Tonino is watching the play of smiles across their faces as they exchange greetings and conversation when he is startled by the impact of a firm slap on his back. He turns to meet Don Simone's knowing eyes. He sought the priest's counsel shortly after meeting Gabriella by the river. Confiding in Don Simone about his honourable intentions toward her softened the edge of guilt he had felt at arranging the secret meeting in the first place.

"Good evening, young man, and may God bless you. Why don't you go and offer Signorina Gabriella some chestnuts? The first batch is ready." He narrows his eyes conspiratorially. "Have you approached her father yet?"

Tonino clears his throat. "To tell you the truth, Don Simone, I have not yet summoned up the courage."

"*Be'*, well, don't leave it too long. You know the proverb: '*Chi dorme, non piglia pesci.*' You sleep, you don't catch the fish." He chuckles and when Tonino doesn't join him, he gives a knowing nod. "Eh, don't worry, lad. Gabriella's father may give the impression he is stern and unyielding, but I can't imagine that he would be upset when you tell him you want Gabriella as your wife. I am certain he will give you his blessing."

Tonino nods. "Thank you, Don Simone. But I am more preoccupied with how Gabriella will feel when I tell her the news." As the priest's brows furrow, Tonino realizes he is not aware of the latest happenings, which Tonino himself only discovered earlier this morning. "My father is sending me away to run my uncle's farm in Cosenza. *Zio* Faustino's rheumatism has gotten so bad he can no longer do the simplest chores. He collapsed several days ago, and the doctor has told *Zia* Elsa that he will never walk again. My aunt is desperate. She sent a messenger to bring the news to my father, who thought it best that I go. Family must help family, he says. And since they have no sons, I have no choice."

Tonino bites his lip. He will be gone for months, maybe longer, until suitable arrangements can be made. *Zia* Elsa may even have to sell the farm. At best, he won't be reunited with Gabriella before the summer. He feels a clenching in his stomach. It has been unsettled since his father broke the news to him this morning, and the chamomile tea he has taken has done little to remedy it.

He stares at a pigeon strutting nearby, its feathers ruffling in preparation to escape the rowdy youngsters approaching it. Their laughter as they chase it makes him cringe.

Don Simone squeezes his arm. "I understand that you're discontented at having to go away, Tonino, especially since you've made your feelings known to Gabriella. But a few months will fly, you'll see, and when you come back, there will be nothing to keep you and Gabriella from planning your wedding and life together. Perhaps you can wait until then to speak to Gabriella's father."

A cry rises up from the crowd in the *piazza*. Don Simone motions toward the fire that is now crackling in full force. "Now go on, Tonino. You must tell Gabriella." He pats him on the shoulder. "*Forza!*"

Tonino turns to nod, but the priest has already shifted away to a crowd of older men. Tonino's nose crinkles at the smoke spiralling around him from the men's pipes. He winces as his stomach contracts again. Straightening, he glances at the spot where Gabriella has been lingering. She has disappeared. The crowd has thickened, and the voices thrum around him like a discordant choir. Finally, he spots her near the edge of the church stairs. He watches as her long skirts sweep over the grey stone steps. She has tied a dark green kerchief over her head and is holding a candle. An offering for her mother, God rest her soul. He watches her disappear past the heavy oak door while others trickle out.

Tonino sighs. He will have to wait until she is back in the *piazza*, unless he wants tongues to start wagging. He mills about the square, glancing casually at the church door every few moments. When Gabriella reappears, his heart begins to drum. It is the only sound he hears as she descends the wide stone steps. He waits until she is absorbed by the crowd and then strides over to her.

There is no easy way of doing this. The news must come from *him*.

PART II
CAMINI
July-August 1862

ALFONSO RAISES HIS WINEGLASS in invitation to his brother. They sit outside an inn in Sorrento facing the Bay of Naples, after a fourteen-hour journey by rail from Piedmont. "Here's to the end of a most unpleasant journey so far."

Claudio peers doubtfully into the glass, turning it one way and then the other.

Alfonso takes a liberal sip and grimaces. "All right, this doesn't even approach one of the fine wines from your ample cellar. But remember where we are, dear brother. The coarse wine is just a reflection of the coarse territory we are entering."

As if to lend credence to his comment, a squalid group of peasants followed by an assorted and mangy bunch of goats and dogs, trundle past the inn, their voices mingling in a cacophony. The men, grizzled and sinewy thin, are discussing the paucity of wheat; the women, slick black hair drawn back severely into tight buns, are complaining about the grain tax, their voices see-sawing back and forth in alternating pitches. The children, reed-thin and happily raucous, seem oblivious to their state of abject misery, and the motley herd of underfed animals adds to the noise with their occasional bleating and barking.

The meat packed onto their ribs would barely feed a child, Alfonso thinks and looks away disdainfully. "It's obvious that these commoners lack the intelligence to elevate themselves from their squalid way of life," he says.

Claudio gazes at the retreating peasants. "Come now, Alfonso. How can you not even feel a twinge of compassion, knowing that they can never obtain the kind of medical services I provide in the north? Just imagine their mortality rate. Poor devils." He shakes his head. "The product of centuries of poverty and strife. Poverty begetting poverty. Ah, the injustices of this world!"

"Are you going to drink your wine or not?"

Claudio shakes his head. "I'd much prefer to eat something first, thank you."

Alfonso motions to the innkeeper. "We've had a long journey, and we'll be heading out to Calabria early tomorrow morning. What have you in the way of supper and a room?"

The innkeeper displays no physical signs of food deprivation, like the peasants; on the contrary, he is rather robust. He beams immediately and assures them that his wife Alma, who does all the cooking herself, will bring them an ample meal shortly. He generously refills Alfonso's wineglass and retreats to the kitchen.

The "ample" meal turns out to be a tureen of minestrone and a beefsteak. Globules of oil float on the soup's surface and cling to the oversized chunks of potatoes, string beans, and unidentifiable greens wading in the tureen. The oregano-seasoned steak plopped on each plate has an oily sheen as well and is flanked with numerous chunks of garlic.

After their hostess has ladled generous servings in earthenware bowls, she bids them, "*Buon appetito*" with a lopsided grin that reveals swollen gums and rotting teeth, and leaves them to see to guests who have just arrived. Despite the unappetizing appearance of both food and server, the brothers give in to their hunger pangs and begin to eat.

They both agree that the minestrone, despite the pockets of oil, tastes better than it looks, although the steak is a disappointment, with veins of gristle that make Alfonso wish his dog Ruggero had accompanied him, since he has the proper incisors with which to chew.

Claudio pushes the steak away after the first taste. He cannot subject his body to a piece of unyielding leather, he murmurs. Alfonso, having taken several eager bites, is now chewing in consternation.

When he has swallowed the offending lump of meat, Alfonso, face flaming, calls the innkeeper over to their table. He declares loudly that he has no complaints as to the quantity of the food, only the quality, especially that of the cut of meat. "We are unaccustomed to grappling with food of poor quality," he states coldly. The innkeeper wrings his hands and glances around nervously—the other guests have stopped talking and are listening with interest. He leans over and reassures Alfonso that he will not be charged for the meal nor the wine, and that he will be put up in one of the best rooms in the inn.

Mollified, Alfonso nods to the relieved innkeeper, who motions dramatically for the guests to resume their conversation before leading the brothers brusquely from the table.

The room has two hemp pallets covered with faintly stained but otherwise clean linen, two straw-woven wooden chairs, a whitewashed commode with two threadbare hand towels, a porcelain bowl of clean water, and a chamber pot in a bottom cupboard that is empty but discoloured. The walls are a pale whitewash, with no decorative touches, save a stark crucifix, holding an overly emaciated Jesus with dolorous eyes.

Alfonso turns to glare at the owner. Claudio puts a restraining hand on his shoulder and nods his thanks to the nervous innkeeper, who flees.

"Why didn't you let me speak?" Alfonso growls. "Look at this...this *stable*, for the love of Christ! This is the *best*?"

Claudio replies quietly, "If the poor man says this is the best, then it must be his best. Remember, *his* best will never measure up to *your* best."

Alfonso snorts before plopping himself down on one of the pallets. "Let's make sure the next inn we stay at is more to our standards, *va bene*?" He calculates how much time it would take them to reach their destination. It is unfortunate that they cannot continue their journey by night, but he and Claudio have both agreed that they should heed the advice of fellow travellers and take the safety precautions suggested. Calabria is a wild land—this is the warning they have been given by an employee of the pharmaceutical company Claudio deals with back home in Torino.

Ottavio Venturi, the youngest employee on staff, and therefore obliged to do the jobs the senior employees shun, takes a yearly trip to Calabria to dispense pharmaceutical supplies. He detests the trip, but he has no choice if he wants to remain in the employ of *La Drogheria Manarin*. And with a wife heavy with their fourth child, he has no other means of providing for their subsistence. Every trip he takes inevitably leads to one illness or another, and he curses what he calls the land of pestilence, along with God and his employer for sending him there.

"Do whatever business you have there expediently and return north without delay. If you don't suffocate from the pestilential air, you'll most likely come into contact with a worse fate...such as meeting up with the brigands roaming the countryside. I've heard stories about them that would make even the toughest man's *coglioni* shrink. Travel with an escort, if possible, and don't forget to carry your own arms. Calabria is one place I never visit without my pistol and dagger."

Alfonso and Claudio decide to heed his advice and travel with all the necessary precautions and equipment. Both are skilled hunters and are quite comfortable using firearms. And they certainly have no intention of lingering in Calabria once they have inspected Alfonso's newly acquired lands and have made the necessary adjustments and hiring of labourers to tend to the property in their absence.

Claudio turns to Alfonso, who is splashing his face with some of the water in the basin. "If we leave early tomorrow morning after breakfast, weather permitting, and barring any attack by brigands," he winks, "we should arrive in Reggio by nightfall. We'll find lodgings for the night, and after breakfast the next morning, we can dismiss our driver and journey the rest of the way ourselves to Camini."

Alfonso wipes his face, which is now devoid of his earlier scowl and holds a grin of anticipation. He thumps Claudio's back with one large hand, before opening a shuttered window to empty the washing bowl. "I must admit, brother, that I am quite looking forward to stepping foot on my new property." Closing the window, he glances slyly at Claudio. "Do you think that the fact that these expropriated church lands are now mine will extend my future stay in purgatory?"

Claudio looks up sharply after refilling the bowl. "What? A twinge of guilt for pouncing on this deal when it will obviously uproot some poor priest and his even poorer parishioners?" He shakes his head. "Oh, Alfonso, Alfonso. Perhaps you still have a conscience after all."

"Nonsense," Alfonso snorts. "I don't feel guilty in the least. I was just trying to be comical. It's obvious who has the conscience in this family, or you would have agreed to joint ownership of these lands with me."

Claudio dips a towel into the bowl, wrings it out, and wipes his face. "I prefer to inspect the lands I wish to purchase *before* I make a deal. '*Caveat emptor,*' as they say." He strides to the window and opens the shutters wide to dispose of the water. "Ah, a fresh breeze from the bay. The sea air will do us good as we sleep."

Claudio sets down the bowl and gives Alfonso a pat on the back. "Get yourself to bed, little brother. I'll pray for your redemption." He smiles as he settles onto his pallet.

Alfonso plops onto the pallet opposite him and shifts several times to get as comfortable as he can on the meagre amount of hemp placed between two scratchy linen sheets. "*Caveat emptor* indeed!" he grumbles between curses.

AS MUCH AS HE HAD WANTED TO SEE GABRIELLA as soon as he returned to Camini two days ago, Tonino knew that he would have to think up an excuse to seek out Don Simone. The rules of propriety wouldn't have changed in his absence. Tonino had planned to stop by earlier in the evening with a religious statue as a gift for the priest, but then a neighbouring farmer came by with a message that he couldn't ignore—a quickly whispered message about a meeting, like the ones Tonino attended while in Cosenza. His stomach tightened with disappointment that a possible reunion with Gabriella would have to be delayed another day, but he nodded his thanks to the farmer and went back inside his room, thinking up an excuse to tell his parents for having to step out later that night.

At dusk, Tonino makes his way through some back alleys toward the outskirts of Camini. The muted sounds of stray cats and dogs mingle with the plaintive cries of babies and children, followed inevitably by either a mother's lullaby or scolding. There is no breeze tonight, and as he strides past fields both wild and cultivated, the heat of the earth seems to be rising upward, carrying the scents of plants rooted beneath. The sweet aroma of jasmine and oleander are particularly heady. By the time he reaches his destination, the back of his collar is already damp.

Tonino steps hesitantly through a dusky grove of olive trees and onto a barely visible footpath. It comes to an abrupt stop at a horizontally-placed half-door that he lifts to proceed cautiously down a steep stairway cut into the earth. The root cellar is large but crammed, and stuffy with the mingled smells of sweat and cured sausages hanging from the rafters along with recently skinned hares.

Tonino feels the hum of energy around him. The men stand back-to-back, elbow-to-elbow, and face-to-face. Some are listening, many are talking. Spit is flying from the mouths of the most animated. Tonino sees that most of the men are from

Camini, but there is a smattering from the neighbouring hamlets as well. The owner of the place, Pietro Aji, has managed to entice a fair number of men like Tonino himself, young and hungry to change the way things are done. Some of their fathers are present, unlike his own, who has always had a complacency and a passive acceptance about life, with no desire, let alone fire in him, to become an instrument of change.

Tonino catches sight of Davide Moschetta, who is waving a greeting across the room. He waves back with a grin.

Davide's tired, shadow-rimmed eyes have a spark to them. His body, usually bent and strained after working in the fields, is straight and his shoulders erect under a threadbare shirt.

Davide is three years older than Tonino. He has been the head of his family since his father's death two years earlier, with six younger siblings to support and a mother, Evelina, who is losing herself with grief over her dead husband and succumbing to a mysterious ailment that is causing her hands, legs, and feet to swell.

The entire hamlet is aware of Evelina's deterioration, and try as the neighbours might to revive her spirit, to get her out of her bed to feed her children and herself, they have retreated in frustration and resignation to God's will for Evelina's fate.

While Davide labours in the neighbouring farms from dawn to nightfall, the youngsters roam about Camini. They have learned to quench their thirst at the two natural springs, and to appease their hunger with handfuls of wild blackberries or a feed of prickly pear—which they can peel expertly with a sharp stone—and the occasional handout from neighbours. Davide graciously accepts the goodwill of the villagers: the plucked pigeons wrapped in burlap at his doorstep; the rounds of bread that have hardened but will fill empty stomachs nicely after soaking in pigeon soup or a broth of cabbage and onion; the bits of meat and bone and sweetbreads that Tonino's father saves for the neediest families.

Tonino knows *he* fares a lot better than many around him;

he has his father's trade and the chance of a decent life. Hard nonetheless, he knows, but with a loving wife beside him, everything will be worth it.

Gabriella. The memory of her eyes and the feel of her lips by the river makes his heart thrum. A sudden commotion at the cellar door draws everyone's attention. Enzo Salinaro, Camini's bread-maker, swearing as the cellar's sturdy oak doors close behind him.

"What manner of meeting place is this?" he huffs, his meaty face red and glistening. He tells them how he has almost gotten stuck between the damp earth walls, like a cork in a bottle. Tonino laughs with the rest of the crowd.

"We would have eased you through with a good lathering of my oil," Pietro laughs, gesturing at the giant ceramic urns holding the year's supply of olive oil.

"*That* I would love to witness," chuckles a man a few feet behind Tonino, drawing another round of spirited laughs. "Enzo Salinaro, all greased up like a hog on a spit."

Enzo turns to the man and responds with a crude gesture and a toothy grin.

Tonino laughs along with the crowd and feels some of the tension in the room dissipate. Before Enzo's arrival, the groups huddled around him were much more serious, with heads bent in discussion and voices murmuring in barely suppressed anticipation. Anticipation for the arrival of a special visitor....

"Hey, Tonino," Pietro is suddenly next to him, patting him on the shoulder. "May God bless you for caring about the future of our homeland. Without men like you, and everyone else here tonight, our people will be crushed like the olives we harvested in January. And the consequences will be bitter, like oil turned rancid."

Tonino nods, not sure what to say. Pietro, unlike most of the crowd gathered in his cellar, is living well. He owns a substantial property with an olive grove and a farm, and he is not dependent on any landowner for seasonal work, unlike most of his neighbours, who travel miles every day to secure work. And when they're hired, they work eighteen hours each day, often for a pittance. Their bodies become as gnarled and bent as the olive trees, their faces gaunt and tinged yellow with malaria. Their gangly children fare no better.

Pietro is generous with his neighbours, but he alone cannot sustain an entire village. It is for the children, the families, that he has arranged this secret meeting tonight, he murmurs to Tonino. He has entreated those he can trust, those who have a high stake in this venture to change the way their lives are run.

Pietro elevates his voice to command everyone's attention. "The previous government has always controlled you. But the Bourbons are gone now. Change is coming, but it won't happen without the will of our countrymen. Your country needs you *now*, while you still have some strength left in you. *Now*, while your tired veins are still pumping some good red blood. The Bourbons have made a shambles of the Kingdom of the Two Sicilies. *Now* is the time to stitch it back together. That is why we are here tonight, my friends and neighbours.

"We must unite, as our beloved country is uniting, and lend what strength we still have to the one that has sacrificed and continues to sacrifice himself, his life, for the unity of all. We must fling ourselves with abandon to the cause of united Italy so that our children and their children will enjoy what we are still struggling for: property rights, food, security. And we will be completely united, my friends, when Rome and Venice are freed from foreign rule and can join us.

"Our great leader cannot do it alone; he needs *you*. The people answered his call in Sicily two years ago, rallying behind him to defeat the Bourbon troops in the war of independence. His Redshirts triumphed! The Kingdom of the Two Sicilies were freed to join the rest of Italy! The union sealed with the plebiscite!

"Now he needs the help of his countrymen once again for his

next mission: ousting the French from Rome." Pietro pounds his chest. "Rome belongs to *us*, to *Italy*, not to Napoleon the Third." He pauses and swivels slowly to the right and left, his eyes challenging anyone to disagree.

"I tell you, my dear neighbours, I have met the great leader himself, the man who would lead you out of these chains of poverty and struggle, of servitude and shame. Servitude to those who dangle you like marionettes over their vast estates, their invisible arms twisting you this way and that. They keep you from grasping hold of the land's abundance, deprive you of your fair share, allow vast lands to stay uncultivated, when *you* could be tending to them, the lifeblood of your family and of generations to come." Pietro wipes the corners of his mouth.

"But there will be no future generations, my dear *paesani*, if we don't take a stand *now* to change the miserable circumstances of our lives, to be strong together, to join—"

"He's here!" someone near the door cries out, and a hush settles over the group. Eyes and bodies shift to the figure now in the doorway.

Tonino's eyes freeze on the man whose gaze is sweeping over the group with the intensity of an eagle searching for food. His dark close-set eyes, however, have the benevolence and warmth that a bird of prey lacks. Tonino is but three paces away, and when their eyes meet, Tonino feels the hair on his arms rise. And then the man's gaze shifts and breaks into a warm smile under his black conical hat.

Tonino glances at Pietro, who is nodding and smiling back at the man. Pietro leaves Tonino's side to join the man, who, although unimposing in size or stature, projects a controlled power and confidence. Wearing a red shirt under a multicoloured poncho, and grey trousers, he stands with the air of a commander. He clasps Pietro's hand and shakes it vigorously, thanking him for assembling an impressive following, at least for the meeting, if nothing else. Again, the twinkle in his eyes.

Pietro announces, puffing out his chest, "Allow me, my esteemed friends and neighbours, to introduce to you...the one with whom our destinies are intertwined...our most honoured General, Giuseppe Garibaldi!"

Tonino realizes he is holding his breath. A few seconds of silence elapse, and he hears himself join the thunderous burst of cries and applause. "*Viva,* Garibaldi!"

"*Viva l'Italia unita!*" The General's eyes sweep over the men. Tonino is transfixed when they lock with his. The challenge is clear: *Follow me. Join me in my cause, in our cause for united Italy. You are the future of our country.*

Tonino notices that Garibaldi is making it a point to let his gaze settle on everyone around him. He talks steadily, convincingly, his dark eyes boring into each man watching him in wonder and admiration. He tells them to go home and to think long and hard. To think of the part they can play in history. His eyes never waiver as he tells him that he will return for his supporters the following night and lead them to chart a new course for Italy.

"Take care of your affairs tomorrow, and tomorrow night, God willing, I will see some of your patriotic faces standing here before me. I count on your discretion while making your preparations. You may tell your nearest and dearest that you plan to join me in my mission, but I beseech you to refrain from telling them that you will be leaving tomorrow night. We must leave unhindered by an anxious procession of teary mothers and ambivalent fathers. We must steal away like thieves in the night if we want our mission to proceed as it should."

The men shout, clap, and pass around bottles of wine, as they offer a toast to the General. Tonino feels a thundering echo in his chest that spreads along every nerve in his body. He is mesmerized, recalling the appeal in the General's eyes. When the fever pitch in the cellar begins to subside, Tonino feels the beating of his heart subside as well, allowing him to hear the inner voice that has been only a whisper until this moment. *Join*, it shouts, reverberating within his chest. *Join Garibaldi and his Redshirts!*

SINCE TONINO'S RETURN FROM COSENZA four days earlier, Gabriella has struggled to keep her mind on her regular tasks. These past few months have been interminable, beginning and ending each day with a prayer to the Madonna to give her patience and strength to carry on with the mundane tasks expected of her. She has tried to concentrate on baking bread and biscuits, cleaning and washing, tending the chickens and goats without thinking about Tonino, but he has always crept into her thoughts. When she is kneading the *filone,* she imagines him sitting at the table watching her, or afterwards, enjoying the hot, crusty bread drizzled with olive oil and *pecorino* cheese. When she is scrubbing Luciano's breeches and rinsing them, she remembers the day she and Tonino met by the river, sitting on the stones and looking into each other's eyes. His fingers caressing hers. His declaration of love.

At times, she has felt guilty for harbouring these thoughts while in the presence of her father or Don Simone. She has caught them looking at her in puzzlement after catching her daydreaming, and flustered, she has had to think up different excuses for her inattention. Not one day has gone by without her praying for Tonino's swift return, so he can approach her father for his blessing. And then, she and Tonino can begin to plan their life together....

On Tonino's third night back, she was preparing a late supper when he stopped by with the excuse that he had a present for Don Simone—a statue of Saint Francis that his aunt and uncle had given him for managing the farm and eventually finding a buyer. Her father and Luciano had gone to visit old Nicolina for an herbal remedy to ease Lorenzo's aching joints. While Don Simone attempted to find the right spot to display the statue and momentarily left the kitchen, Tonino reached for Gabriella's hand and brought it to his lips. Gabriella was sure her cheeks were as fiery as persimmons when Don Simone came back and her hand was still clasped in Tonino's. At Don Simone's gentle throat-clearing, Tonino released her hand, and with his back to the priest, winked at her.

Gabriella felt her knees weaken and stood there wordlessly while Don Simone poured Tonino some walnut liqueur. "Welcome back, Tonino. You were missed by your family and.... friends." He smiled at Gabriella. "Go fetch some of your lemon *biscotti*, Gabriella. And bring up some of the sausage links as well. The ones with the fennel and pepper. Tonino, come and sit at the table for a while. We won't be having supper just yet, but I'm sure Signorina Gabriella won't mind if we have a snack."

As Gabriella lifted the floor hatch and padded down the narrow steps to the cellar, she could hear Tonino talking about his time in Cosenza. She walked to the far corner where the dried sausages were hung. Tonino's voice was a murmur. She snipped off a few links and wrapped them in a cloth before depositing them in the wide front pocket of her apron. She crossed to a rough-hewn cupboard and withdrew a tin of *biscotti*. She could still feel the warmth of them from her late afternoon baking. She smiled, thinking again how wonderful it would be to bake one day for her husband and children. *Her husband Tonino.* As she ascended the steps and set down the hatch door, she realized that Tonino and Don Simone were silent. She could only see Don Simone's face, and his expression was solemn. When he saw Gabriella, he smiled weakly. He reached for the tin and set the biscuits onto a dish while Gabriella sliced up the sausage links. Don Simone brought over an edge of crusty bread to the table and offered it to Tonino, who broke off a piece with his fingers before reaching for some of the sausage. Don Simone chattered on about recent happenings and moments later, Tonino thanked them both and with the excuse that his mother was preparing a special meal to celebrate his return, he bade them farewell.

Don Simone nodded and as he turned away to tuck his bottle of *nocino* in its usual place in the corner cupboard, Tonino whispered to Gabriella, "I must speak to you alone." Something in his voice gave her a chill, and she watched him step back, his mouth pursed. "Don Simone ordered some beef liver. I'll deliver it tomorrow."

AFTER A PASSABLE BREAKFAST OF THICK, oven-baked biscuits and goat's milk, Alfonso inquires as to the means of procuring a driver and a vehicle for the journey south to Calabria. The innkeeper, who seems eager to leave them with a good impression, reassures them that their request will be granted within a half-hour. Twenty minutes later, a stalwart lad of seventeen or eighteen drives up in front of the inn and reins in his two mules. He jumps down and introduces himself as Pino. After negotiating a price that seems reasonable to Claudio and Alfonso—they know better than to accept the first offer dealt to them—they settle themselves and their bags into the carriage, and with a rush of good-natured farewells and an indecipherable dialect exchange between Pino and the innkeeper, Pino cracks his whip and begins the journey with a wave to the locals, some of whom run up and quickly hand him some figs and other foodstuff from baskets filled at the outdoor market around the corner from the inn.

Alfonso notes Pino's bronzed, muscled arms as he ascends an absurdly narrow stretch of road while munching on a pear. On either side of him, villagers and their children scurry away from the mules' path. A sudden jolt has Alfonso wondering if one of those children have been run over, and he looks back anxiously, expecting the carriage to stop. But Pino continues on, and Alfonso realizes the hump on the road is a dead hen that has fallen out of somebody's basket. He wipes the perspiration off his brow and sits back in his seat.

"Your face looks as ashen as the sky," Claudio says.

"Thank you, Doctor. I'm sure it has something to do with

my nerves, riding in this contraption."

"Close your eyes if you're feeling anxious; if it doesn't go away, I'm sure I can find something in my bag to make you feel better."

Alfonso cringes at the sight of a steep ravine. "And you have enough instruments and medicine in that bag to put my bones together after we fall over this precipice, correct?"

"This lad has probably taken this trip hundreds of times; we won't fall over, trust me."

"There's always a first time."

"Now, don't go filling your thoughts with delusions, because if you do, and your brain goes over the edge, I won't be able to help you. You'll need a psychiatrist for that." Claudio peers out at the snaking path flanked on one side by majestic oaks and poplars, and chiselled downward on the other side into an abyss of imperceptible depths. Soon, the sound of clanking hooves on the dirt path is muffled by the thunderous noise of a waterfall plunging into the ravine below. Alfonso closes his eyes.

After a less perilous stretch through chestnut and olive groves, Pino stops at a spring along the shoulder of the mountain path. He jumps down, splashes his dusty face with the water, and then fills his canteen. After drinking generously at the spring, he waits for Alfonso and Claudio to do the same, and then, whistling all the while, leads his mules to drink.

He is not a talkative sort; he has said barely a word from the time they started the journey. When he curses suddenly a few miles later, Alfonso follows his gaze. High on the mountain, on a fir tree that has been recently stripped of all its branches, hangs a human head on a spike, accompanied by a lone vulture that is perched on what remains of a bloodied patch of hair. As the carriage approaches, it becomes obvious that the bird has feasted to its satisfaction: the eye sockets are empty, and even from a distance look cavernous; most of the flesh has been ripped off, a few shreds dangling like a ragged piece of gypsy cloth; what little meat remains will shortly be devoured by the merciless scavenger.

There is no way to avoid the gruesome sight; the mule track winds around in such a way that any approaching traveller or carriage would be exposed to it fully before being able to continue his journey.

Pino stops the carriage and leaps down, immediately retching in the bracken alongside the road. Alfonso holds his hand over his mouth. Claudio hastily pulls out his medical bag and extracts a vial of smelling salts. He makes Pino and Alfonso breathe in the salts before taking a breath himself.

"A brigand," Alfonso shivers, unable to take his eyes from the head. "*A brigand!*"

GABRIELLA LIFTS THE LID OF THE TERRACOTTA *tiana* with a thick linen cloth. The broad beans are done, simmering in a broth with onions and garlic. She sets the lid back down and shifts the deep earthenware dish from its position above the coals to a corner of the hearth where it will stay warm until suppertime. She unties her apron and hurries to the vestibule of the rectory to check her appearance in the walnut-framed mirror. Her cheeks are flushed, and her eyes seem brighter than usual.

She meets the gaze of the statue of *San* Nicola in the reflection and imagines for a moment that his eyes are mocking her for her vanity. Feeling sheepish, she returns to the rectory kitchen. Sitting in the broom-woven chair by the hearth, she reaches for the note in her skirt pocket. Tonino's brother Ricardo handed it to her earlier this morning while making deliveries in the area. He hadn't said anything, but his shy smile made her realize it was a message from Tonino.

I will deliver Don Simone's order of beef liver by mid-afternoon. Good day, Tonino.

Now, reading the words again, Gabriella feels her pulse quicken. Tonino's words are hardly amorous, yet the fact that he had his brother deliver the message tells her that he wants to make sure she is there when he arrives. He is well aware that her father will be out in the fields, and that Don Simone is, as always on a Tuesday, in the neighbouring hamlet of Riace. Of course, Tonino can't predict whether or not Luciano will be around, but there is always the chance *she* will be alone.

Gabriella hears the sound of approaching footsteps outside the open window. She wipes her brow with her handkerchief. After the knocker sounds twice, she opens the door. With a tentative smile, she lets Tonino in and closes the door. Tonino hands her the package of beef liver. She takes it with a shy nod. "I'll just put it in the cellar."

When she returns, she hands him some coins from her apron pocket. As their fingers brush, Tonino's other hand comes up to cover hers while he slips the money in his trouser pocket. "*Grazie.*" He clears his throat. "Gabriella, there's something I wanted to tell you before I left for Cosenza, but everything happened so fast. We barely had two moments to ourselves in the *piazza* that day, and telling you the news that I had to leave was hard enough."

Gabriella tenses. There is something in his eyes that she doesn't recognize. Is it regret? Has something caused him to change his mind? His feelings? Her hand suddenly feels clammy, and she withdraws it from Tonino's clasp. She feels her face redden.

"I should have told you something else by the river, Gabriella, but I didn't want to spoil everything. It just wasn't the right time."

Gabriella draws in a breath. *Dear God in heaven, could it be that he told his parents and they didn't approve?*

"This isn't the best time either, or place, but I didn't want you to have to contrive some story to meet me by the river again. I don't want people to get the wrong impression of us. Of *you.*"

He is looking at her tenderly now and Gabriella takes a deep breath. "What I didn't tell you, Gabriella, is that for some months now, I have been attending secret meetings. Some of them have been here in Camini, others in the neighbouring hamlets. And some in Cosenza. An especially important meeting was called last night."

Gabriella frowns. *Dear Lord, could Tonino be embroiled in something illegal?* Her stomach clenches. Perhaps he has changed; perhaps he has been influenced or threatened by some outsiders...."

"Please hear me out, Gabriella," he says, even though she hasn't uttered a word. "You've heard the rumblings that have been going on since Unification: how being under Bourbon rule was better than the conditions existing under the new King; how the laws of the State are meant for the northern Italians and have only caused greater hardship for southern Italians, for *us* here in Calabria."

He takes both of her hands and looks at her solemnly. "There is a movement that has been growing since General Garibaldi liberated the South from the Bourbons. Garibaldi's work is not done. His mission to unite all of Italy is not completed. Rome and Venice have yet to be liberated. He wants change for all Italians, and change will come about when Rome is taken back from the French and becomes the rightful capital of our country."

Gabriella blinks. Tonino squeezes her hands comfortingly. "Gabriella, there has been a lot of discussion in secret, and until this last meeting, I wasn't completely sure that I wanted to get involved—"

"With me?" she says, hating the way her voice is quivering.

"No, silly," he smiles, cupping her chin so she is looking directly at him. "With the mission. With General Garibaldi."

Tonino's hand reaches for hers. "I want to make a difference in the building of this nation," he says, his voice growing more fervent. "General Garibaldi needs men to join his cause, to help bring about the changes we need in order to make a better life for ourselves." He squeezes her hand. "For *our* children."

Gabriella feels her heart begin to pound. *Dear God in heaven, does this mean—?*

"*He was there, Gabriella*! Giuseppe Garibaldi! That's why I couldn't miss it."

Gabriella inhales sharply at Tonino's look of rapture. It is as if he has seen the Lord Himself.

"He looked me straight in the eye, Gabriella. I couldn't live with myself if I didn't respond to his appeal, to the call of my country."

What about me, us? Gabriella bites her lip. Her eyes begin to prickle. *He is going to leave.* Risk his life in a march on Rome. She could lose him before...before their life together has even begun. She wants to scream, pound his chest, demand why he had to declare his love for her, leave her, and then come back only to tell her *this*. If he fights for Garibaldi's cause, and loses his life, then it will have been for someone else's children, not theirs.

"Wh...when will you—" She startles as the door behind Tonino opens and Luciano enters. She steps awkwardly away from Tonino, blinking rapidly.

"*Ciao*, Tonino," Luciano grins. "Did you bring us something good to eat?"

Tonino ruffles Luciano's hair. "Liver. And tripe. Don Simone told me how much you like it."

"*Acchhh!*" Luciano pretends to hold his nose before running off into the kitchen.

"Gabriella, there is something I still need to tell you—"

"Not now," she hears herself say stiffly, glancing away. There is so much she needs to say to *him*. But right now, she can't think, she can't plan.

"I meant everything I said by the river," Tonino says softly. He reaches into the pocket of his jacket and hands her a cluster of pink oleander flowers. Their sweet fragrance tinges the air between them. "I should have given them to you right away," he murmurs.

Gabriella feels numb, but she takes the slightly pressed flowers. Tonino leans forward to kiss her, but she turns away sharply. When she hears the door click open and shut, she waits for his footsteps to recede before crushing the oleander blossoms in her hand.

ALFONSO AND CLAUDIO ARISE EARLY, awakened by a discordant band of roosters and pigeons, dogs and goats, along with the cheery salutations and pleasantries exchanged by the villagers heading out to begin their work in the fields. "You'd think they were going to a *festa*," Alfonso grumbles.

"Now brother, don't deprive these poor folk of their happy spirit. God knows they don't have much to call their own except their spirit."

"They're probably too ignorant to even realize how much they don't have." Alfonso rises from the hemp pallet, stretching and arching his back. The bed barely looked like it could support him, but it has turned out to be surprisingly adequate, and Alfonso feels little of the stiffness he anticipated upon initially surveying the scrawny pallet on the iron frame.

Back home, he has always enjoyed the pleasures of a soft, ample bed. His bed chamber brings him satisfaction after a long day of tending his interests, financial or otherwise. Whether he returns alone, or with a companion, he knows he will always find his room softly lit with wall sconces, a pan of hot coals warming an oversized cauldron of water for his bath, and his bed linen freshly changed. A platter of ripe, fresh fruit flanked by a smaller dish of cheese and cured pork sausages or ham will be set out for him, accompanied by a bottle of his favourite wine.

Alfonso's servants know how much he abhors sleeping in sheets left more than two days unwashed; in fact, it is such a source of contention for him that an unaccommodating servant, acting out of carelessness, forgetfulness or some other reason, would be asked to leave his employ instantly.

He dresses quickly, anticipating the last stretch of their journey to Camini. He and Claudio proceed to the dining area, bags in hand. They each accept an oversized cup of strong black coffee, and Alfonso enhances his with a shot of brandy from a small flask inside his jacket. The host, who beams at the news that they slept well, brings them a large plate of freshly baked *biscotti,* flecked with anise and citron peel.

They finish their breakfast and bid farewell to the host, who utters a cry of surprise at the generous pile of coins left on the table by Claudio. He calls out a benediction as they step up into the cart he has procured for them and sends a street boy running after the cart with a complimentary bottle of wine. Claudio accepts it with a gracious nod and wave, murmuring to Alfonso that he will leave it with their driver upon their arrival in Camini.

"You're too damned generous," Alfonso scoffs, watching Claudio tuck the bottle in one of his bags. "Wasting your money like that." The driver of their cart manoeuvres a sharp turn that obliterates the last view of the inn. "Good riddance to that hovel and everyone in it," Alfonso mutters, settling more comfortably in his seat.

The driver cajoles the horses past the maze of narrow cobbled streets. Before long, they are on the outskirts of Reggio and onto a wider country road flanked by an orchard on one hillside and a vineyard on the other. The orchard has endless rows of fragrant orange and lemon trees, and an abundance of olive and flowering almond trees. "What a charming countryside," Claudio exclaims. "A veritable palette to feast upon with hungry eyes. So colourful."

Alfonso stares at him. "Aren't you forgetting the head on the pike we saw yesterday? *That* was more colourful if you ask *me.*" He gazes with interest at the burgeoning grapes in the vineyard that come autumn will be transformed into a robust *Greco,* according to his research. And although this area lacks the wild aspect of the hills they travelled through yesterday,

Alfonso has no conviction that the idyllic countryside around him, with its bountiful fields and beautiful views of the blue waters of the Strait of Messina, does not conceal a sinister underbelly.

He feels his stomach twinge again with the recollection of the gruesome remains in the thick of the Aspromonte mountains, and for some time he observes the woodlands they pass with some trepidation. To Alfonso's relief, there are no signs that indicate the presence of brigands, dead or alive, and with a deep breath, he leans back in the carriage and closes his eyes.

Alfonso starts as the driver announces that they are approaching the hamlet of Camini. He yawns and opens his eyes when Claudio nudges him. "Be on your best behaviour, little brother," Claudio advises with a note of sternness. "Although the parish priest has offered us accommodation in his rectory until the affairs are settled, I detected a certain tone in his letter. An indication of his feelings about the expropriation of the Church lands he manages. Not malice, certainly, but understandable discontent over the notice sent to him by our solicitor."

"Why would he put us up in his rectory if he is discontented?" Alfonso murmurs, distracted by the sight of a group of buxom peasant women balancing wicker baskets filled with freshly washed laundry. As their driver slows down the mules to pass them, the group pauses on the road to glance at them. *A trio of biblical statues,* Alfonso thinks. His eyes are drawn to the youngest woman, her long skirt brightly patterned in yellow and red against a black background. She is exceptionally pretty, a startling contrast to the two older women next to her, their heavier bodies sagging under black skirts that don't allow the sun to penetrate. *Nor probably their husbands,* he smirks, *unless the good men are half-stupid with drink and feeling nostalgic.*

The driver of their carriage nods politely as they pass, tilting his cap. Alfonso turns to his brother, trying to remember what their conversation is about.

"To answer your question, Alfonso, I think Don Simone may very well be considering staying on as parish priest of Camini, as per the solicitor's suggestion. Perhaps he feels that some negotiation might occur regarding our intentions for the rental of the Church and the administration of the accompanying lands."

Alfonso taps one foot impatiently as Claudio comments that Don Simone is not only exhibiting a fine Christian spirit, but he is perhaps hoping to sway Alfonso in some manner regarding the workings of the lands and the employ of his current farmhands, namely, the members of the Falcone family.

"Perhaps he is upset, and rightly so, that the revenues of the land will no longer be for his exclusive use, and the use of his workers," Alfonso retorts. "After all, who would be overjoyed at being uprooted?"

"He doesn't have to be completely uprooted," Claudio says. "It's his choice. You may be the new owner, but you have, most charitably I must say, given Don Simone the option of remaining as parish priest, accepting a small stipend, and continuing to administer to the spiritual needs of the villagers."

"If he chooses to remain under my conditions," Alfonso mutters. "Isn't a priest supposed to denounce worldly goods anyway? I am certainly not in opposition to his rental of the rectory," Alfonso shrugs. "And if I find his farmhands acceptable, I see no reason why they can't continue to manage the lands. But again, as my solicitor stipulated in the letter, I will make a final decision upon personal investigation of the lands and employees. Who knows? Perhaps the lands are not even worth keeping and are better off resold."

He straightens in his seat and points to a distant steeple high up in the nearby hills. The hamlet is clearly visible, spread out on the hill like a triangular shaped quilt. "*Camini!*" he nudges Claudio. "Goddammit, we made it!"

GABRIELLA GATHERS THE EARTHENWARE BOWLS in which to prepare the morning *frittata*. Signor Alfonso will no doubt expect a hearty breakfast. He had two large bowls of pigeon soup and a sizeable chunk of cheese and bread last night. Signor Claudio showed more restraint, content with one bowl of soup and a small wedge of bread.

The brothers arrived late last evening amidst an unexpected downpour. Gabriella was roused from her sleep by her father, who rushed out to shelter the horses for the visitors, and to show the driver the barn loft where he could stay for the night. She was to light the fire and heat up the cauldron of soup she had made earlier in the day. In the meantime, Don Simone would be taking the brothers to the guest room, where they would remove their drenched clothing, which Gabriella would also be expected to tend to once they had eaten and reclined for the evening.

Gabriella's stomach was churning the whole time she served the food, wondering if the visitors would make mention of their plans with Don Simone, but the meal was eaten quickly, with small talk, and little enough of that. Although she was curious about the brothers, she deliberately kept her eyes averted except for a few quick glances when their heads were bent over their soup.

Her father had gone to bed after tending to the horses and bringing the young driver some food and blankets. When Don Simone gave her the nod to leave, she curtsied and hurried up to her room. Luciano was sprawled on his back, one leg sticking out from under the covers. She felt a pang. He looked so vulnerable. The uncertainty about their fate had grown these past months and try as she might to think of a way to convince the new landlord to keep her and her father in his employ, she suspected the plea of a peasant would not be enough to sway someone of his status.

There was something about Signor Alfonso that she could not have known without seeing it with her own eyes. There was a hardness to him, despite his ample frame. A hardness around his eyes. She had caught a look that he directed at her father's back when he had come to the kitchen to get some food for the driver. It had lasted only a moment before Signor Alfonso turned around to finish his soup, but Gabriella felt a stab of dismay when she saw it—a look of disdain, disgust even. She glanced at her father then, saw him in his well-worn trousers, sodden and stained, saw his gaunt features, his hair plastered to his forehead, saw his calloused hands gripping a small tureen and a hunk of bread. A labourer. A peasant so obviously below Signor Alfonso. The slight, unnoticed by her father, stung her, and she felt herself burning, as humiliated as if the glance had been directed at her.

After burrowing under her covers later that night, she stared at the ceiling for a long time, unable to fall asleep. She felt her forehead every once in a while, wondering if she had a fever. When she eventually awoke at the rooster's first crowing, she felt as though she hadn't slept at all.

Gabriella set the bowls down and descends to the cellar to procure the flask of goat's milk, cheese, and eggs. Back in the kitchen, she mixes up the batter in the bowls and adds a palm-full of chopped parsley and lets them sit. She deftly proceeds with the cooking of the *frittata* when Don Simone comes downstairs.

Gabriella says a silent prayer as she bustles about the kitchen, setting the table with the special, gold-rimmed porcelain dishes she uses only for company, She marvels at their design whenever she takes them out: the coral rose with each intricate, overlapping petal, the slightly jagged leaves painted a dusky green and dappled with light, the unopened conical buds ready to burst, and the slender stems with their thorny peaks, all sparkling with dew spray. The set is part of the chattels bequeathed to Don Simone at his mother's passing.

A scuffling of feet behind her causes her to start, and she fumbles with a dish before setting it down shakily on the table, her heart drumming from the realization that she might have dropped and broken it.

"I beg your pardon, Signorina Gabriella. I didn't mean to startle you."

Gabriella turns to face Signor Alfonso, who is standing at the table's edge. His voice, with the gravelly cadence his brother lacks, identified him even before she turned around.

"*Buongiorno*, Signor Fantin." Gabriella nods and gives a brief curtsey, showing the deference that is expected by using his surname. "Don Simone should be here shortly." She moves over to the sideboard, where she has left her bowls and ingredients for the *frittata*. She senses Signor Alfonso's eyes still upon her as she proceeds to stir the mixture again. She stifles the inclination to glance back at him though all the while wondering at the uneasy feeling that has settled over her. She is not used to sharing the kitchen with anyone save her father and Don Simone, nor is she used to being watched while she works.

She prays for the appearance of Don Simone to take the visitor's attention off her. As she hears the familiar shuffle of steps approaching, she gives silent thanks and retrieves a pan from the sideboard cupboard. As she sets the pan upon the iron tripod over the fire, she steals a glance sideways, and to her consternation, she notices Signor Alfonso's eyes shifting to her face only after following the curves of her hips and bosom.

She knows it is not the heat from the fire that consumes her as she rustles the twigs around with an iron rod. She feels exposed, as if Signor Alfonso's murky brown eyes can somehow penetrate the coarse cloth of her garments to envision her body. She releases her pent-up breath when she hears Don Simone's "*Buongiorno*."

Gabriella prepares the large pan-sized *frittata* and sets the biscuits she made the morning before within the brick oven built adjacent to the fireplace.

The clatter of additional footsteps announces the arrival of Signor Claudio, who nods in her direction before joining his brother and Don Simone at the table. Gabriella slides the *frittata* onto a large earthenware platter and carries it to the table before retrieving the warmed biscuits. As Don Simone bids his guests help themselves, Gabriella pours coffee into three porcelain cups that have the same etching as the dinnerware. Don Simone makes a gesture for her to go to the cupboard where he keeps the walnut liqueur he offers guests, though he himself abstains from any spirits before delivering a church service.

Gabriella sets the bottle on the table, and with the excuse that she must check on Luciano, she leaves swiftly, her cheeks still burning.

GABRIELLA LETS OUT A LONG BREATH as the brothers' wagon descends the narrow lane toward the main street leading out of Camini. The young driver, Valerio Bosco, a villager often employed by Don Simone for various tasks, is only too happy to take the northerners for a tour of the church lands, some of which are located in the nearby village of Ellera.

Moments ago, after the brothers settled onto the bench in the cart, he sprinted to the rectory gate behind which Gabriella was gathering snippets from a rosemary bush.

"*Buongiorno, Calabrisella mia,*" he winked, boldly calling her "his Calabrese girl." He did not wait for her to answer; instead, he grabbed a snippet of rosemary from her hand, and held it to his heart. With a grin that flashed his dimple, he raced off to take his position in front of the cart, and with a click of his tongue, he commanded a trot from the mules, a final mischievous wink directed at Gabriella.

He is two years younger than Gabriella, and with the impetuosity of youth, has felt no hesitation in revealing his attraction to her on a number of occasions, despite the indifference she generally bestows upon him. She teases him good-naturedly when he hovers around, pretending to be on his way to or from an errand issued by Don Simone.

A few days ago, he brought over some wild fennel for Don Simone. A gift from his mother, he told Gabriella, to thank the priest for promising to recite a novena for her sick aunt.

He rambled on for several minutes until Gabriella felt her patience diminishing.

"Isn't your mother waiting for you, Valerio?"

"Come on!" Valerio jutted out his chin in a gesture of feigned offence, pursing his lips in frustration. He puffed up his chest, as if to prove he wasn't the child Gabriella thought him to be, and Gabriella almost burst out laughing, thinking that his blue linen vest and stance made him look like an outraged pigeon.

"Fine, I'll leave you alone now," Valerio shrugged, flashing a dimpled smile. "But one day, you'll wake up and realize that I'm not as young as you think, Signorina Gabriella. And my heart will take longer to heal if you choose to break it then."

Valerio generally ends his visits with outrageous comments. Gabriella looks at the rosemary in her hand now, and thoughts of Valerio dissipate. She pictures Tonino's eyes, down by the river. And his words of love. No matter what happens, she is *his* "Calabrisella" and will never belong to anyone else.

ALFONSO IS SATISFIED WITH THE MORNING'S EVENTS thus far. The boy Valerio has proven himself to be a good guide, skilled at handling horses and quite knowledgeable about Camini and its environs. Unlike some drivers, who choose to stay quiet and have to be prompted for information, Valerio demonstrates his readiness in talking about the land, the weather, the crops, the livelihood of the villagers, the politicians; in short, Valerio will discuss anything about which Alfonso asks.

His voice wears on Alfonso occasionally, though, with its perennial cheerfulness and coming-of-age inflections. Alfonso can't help wondering how Valerio can be so *allegro*, given that from the look of his tattered trousers and his threadbare shirt, his circumstances are limited.

His father died of the fever, Valerio tells them, one of many afflicted by the malarial outbreaks along the coast. Valerio bows his head in a moment of reverent silence, then crosses himself and resumes his chatter, while waving to the occasional villager along the road.

By the time they return to the rectory, Alfonso's head is throbbing from Valerio's incessant tales. He flips several coins to the boy, the amount of which suffices to silence Valerio momentarily. He then proceeds to enter the rectory, more than happy to leave it to Claudio to set up arrangements for the next day, as they have yet to inspect the church lands on the southern slopes of the mountain.

At Claudio's entry, he says, "No one seems to be present. I think I will lie down for a few hours. That boy's chatter has left me with a nasty headache."

Claudio nods with a grin. "Too bad, Alfonso. We both know that the only voice that you never tire of is your own." He ducks as Alfonso pretends to strike him. "Valerio has offered to take me tomorrow to the nearest pharmacy outside of Camini, in the town of Stilo. To tell you the truth, I'm quite curious about the medical services in this area, or lack thereof. I noticed many of the villagers Valerio greeted had a yellow tinge to them. I would be quite interested to know what treatments for malaria are available in these parts."

Alfonso stares at his brother, wondering why he would even bother, since he is not in Camini in a working capacity. He shrugs and turns away. "Do as you please. Just don't get too close to anyone and become infected yourself." His glance shifts to a statue of *San* Nicola, the town's patron saint, standing on a marble pedestal in a corner of the vestibule, squarely facing any visitor upon his entry. The luminous eyes are set in a face that is flushed with colour above a full grey beard. The saint's right hand is raised and the other holds a book and a white staff. The saint's shoulders are draped in a golden cape with scarlet lining, and on his head, a jewelled bishop's mitre points to heaven.

"You're not here to heal the sick, Claudio," he snorts, glancing back at his brother. "You're on vacation, remember? Leave the healing to *San* Nicola."

A LOW RUMBLE IN THE DISTANCE causes Gabriella to pause from her task in the hen yard. She ignores the haughty protests of the bolder hens who squawk around her skirts, attempting the occasional peck. "Luciano," she murmurs, "where are you?" She hopes he hasn't ventured to the river with his usual pack of friends; the current is swift and volatile, and Gabriella, in the tradition of Camini's womenfolk, has warned her brother of its perils.

"Remember poor Vincenzino," she has told Luciano countless times. "God bless his soul." Vincenzino had not been much older than Luciano when he ventured off with some friends. While skipping along some flat stones by the river, one of Vincenzino's shoes had fallen off, and as he tried to recover it, he slipped into the water. On a summer day, he might have had a chance to retrieve his shoe *and* swim out of the water, but November is a month for the dead after all, and everyone knows that it is not the month in which to tempt fate.

Gabriella shivers at the memory of Don Simone's solemn words—"For fate lurks under the surface of the frigid river like a funerary cloak, ready to welcome its victims with its icy embrace"—and his frequent glances at the children to make sure he had made an impression.

The washerwomen who had witnessed the boy's disappearance spoke of nothing else for weeks. "Fate took hold of Vincenzino by his ankles," they sobbed, "and pulled him into the river." Eva, the boy's mother, who had been washing clothes with her back to the group, turned at the shouts of the boys and was able to just glimpse the sight of a red-clad figure slipping into the water. With a shriek, she bolted to the river, knowing that only her son was wearing red. She thrashed her way to the flash of red, eyes fixated on it until, the women recounted, "one of fate's hands blinded Eva with a vengeful spray and she tottered backwards." When she rose, sputtering and shaking, the flash of red had disappeared.

"Vincenzino, Vincenzino," she had screamed, hands to her head, the wind whipping her hair against her face. In the distance, a rumble of thunder intensified and she stood petrified, assaulted by the spray of the water churning around her, her eyes reflecting the blackness of the water, her mouth contorted in horror.

The washerwomen swore they could hear the devil's mocking laugh reverberating in the waves around Eva, his lithe form reddening the water like the poison spray of a sea monster. Vincenzino's mother continued to scream as her eyes probed the depths. She was convinced that she could see the devil's scarlet face twisted in a triumphant grin, his pointed ears and evil talons extended, his sleek, muscled body swirling with ease as his flickering tail sliced the water like a crimson scythe.

"*U diavulu vitta*," she repeated hysterically when some labourers, having returned from the fields, pulled her out of the water a few moments later. "I saw the devil. He took Vincenzino." She started pulling at her hair in despair. "*Why? Why? What did poor Vincenzino do to him? Si finìu a vita mia; My life is over.*" Her eyes fluttered and she collapsed.

The labourers brought Eva home in the back of a hay cart. The women peeled her skirts and chemises off one by one, dried her and wrapped her in linens, and placed her on a hemp-woven chair by the fireplace. They twisted her wet clothes and hung them to dry over the canna stalks suspended horizontally between nooks in the beams.

Her husband Armando returned from the fields and didn't leave her side that night. Consumed by fever, she thrashed about, alternating between moans and shrieks. The neighbours and Armando crossed themselves with every utterance, certain that the devil had entered her soul, so shattered was it from the shock of losing Vincenzino. Armando, who couldn't bear losing his wife along with his only son, had Don Simone summoned in desperation along with Nicolina the midwife.

Nicolina had a gift that no one refuted; even outsiders travelled miles to seek her counsel and purchase her herbs and decoctions. The villagers trusted her implicitly. She had calmed neighbour Pepe's nervous tremor, eased neighbour Maria's violent headaches, cured a visiting priest, Don Alberto, of a painfully swollen abdomen, and she had successfully healed the gangrenous wound of young Domenico, who had punctured his foot with a rusty wagon nail. The villagers were certain Nicolina could concoct something to calm down Vincenzino's mother, while Don Simone performed the service to rid her body of the same devil that had taken her son.

Gabriella shivers every time she recalls the story. As she scatters feed to the hens, an ominous rumble makes her look up to the sky. *Surely, Luciano will be home soon. He hates storms....*

FROM HIS OPEN WINDOW, Alfonso hears a girl's voice. He stirs from his afternoon nap, disoriented at first, and then realizes where he is. The guest room that the priest has provided is adequate enough, with two comfortable cots and linen bed coverings, a sturdy walnut dresser and mirror, and an imposing armoire that dominates a wall on the opposite side of the room. There are few embellishments, save for the gleaming crucifix above the doorway, and the embroidered doily on the dresser, upon which a terracotta jug and two cups are placed.

Alfonso gets up, still wearing his day clothes, and ambles to the window, which looks down to the rectory courtyard. The servant girl is leaning over a rabbit enclosure, murmuring something to the creatures. She is the same pretty girl he had spotted on the way into Camini. Alfonso notices how her brown dress clings to her slender waist, which he is quite sure would fit within his hands. Her hair is arranged in a thick black braid reaching almost to her tailbone, the light catching it making it resemble the blue-black of a raven's wings. Her profile is easily distinguishable: the clear, rosy skin of her cheekbone, her straight nose, and the maroon lips that instantly invoke a painting he has of the mythical Dionysus, holding a cluster of plump grapes to his mouth.

As Gabriella's body straightens, he becomes aware of his own body stiffening. He has not indulged his desire for a woman since the fiasco with Clara months ago. Gambling has been his preferred mistress, and the monetary gains made lately at his favourite Venetian haunts have been more than sufficient to keep him positioned at the gaming table instead of over a lover.

Oh, he has thought about the pleasures of the body many times throughout his journey south, but with his brother Claudio as his constant companion, and the limited stops made along the way, the opportunity to indulge in carnal passions has never presented itself.

On one occasion at an inn near Rome, the *trattoria* owner's daughter winked at him when her father was busy settling the account with Claudio, and Alfonso was instantly inflamed by her swarthy attractiveness and revealing bodice. But there was no excuse he could think of to extend their stay. The little trollop passed by him deliberately, feigning clumsiness with a bread basket as she stumbled, brushing her bosom against him. With a giggle, she sauntered off into the kitchen. The journey from Rome to Naples had been unbearable and Alfonso had to lie when Claudio queried as to his seeming discomfort.

Alfonso straightens his clothes and slips on his burgundy jacket. As he descends the stone steps, the clock chimes mid-afternoon. He recalls that Don Simone left earlier to administer the last rites to a farmer in the neighbouring hamlet of Riace. Claudio has gone to the town of Stilo to consult with the pharmacist. The farmhand Lorenzo is out in the fields and won't be back until sunset, and his son Luciano has scampered off to spend the day with his friends.

Alfonso heads to the far door in the hallway that leads to the courtyard. The fresh air fans his face. Gabriella whirls around with a welcoming smile that fades when she sees him. "Oh, Signor Alfonso. I'm sorry. I thought you were my brother."

"I'm sorry to disappoint you, Signorina Gabriella." He gazes at the animal enclosures and the narrow path that leads to the barn and the acreage from which Don Simone and the Falcone family derive their subsistence.

The property stretches interminably. The silver-green foliage of the hundreds of olive trees is visible against the pale sky, undulating in the salt-tinged breeze. Alfonso breathes deeply and returns his gaze to Gabriella. "I didn't realize anyone was here." He gestures at the barn and beyond. "I wanted to take a closer look at this part of the property. I had no idea it was so extensive."

He notices that Gabriella is clenching her fingers. He senses she is flustered, no doubt unaccustomed to visitors in her work area. "Now that I am here, would you mind showing me about?" He makes an effort to keep his voice polite, but with an inflection of authority that will make Gabriella understand that it is not so much a request but a subtle demand to which he expects compliance.

She nods, picks up her skirts, and steps gingerly through the path strewn with hen and pigeon droppings. Alfonso follows at a leisurely pace. He half-listens as she points out the fig and plum trees, the persimmons and the medlars, and the various pots and urns filled with aromatic herbs. They arrive at the barn and its outside enclosures, where several goats are nibbling on the grassy stubble. A few cows stand flank to flank, their ears and tails twitching at the flies, their large eyes dark and vacuous.

"I'd like to see the condition of the stables." Alfonso motions for Gabriella to lead the way. He is repulsed by the overpowering smell of manure but feels a stirring at its rawness. Gabriella hesitates. She nods and picks up a knitted shawl lying on a dilapidated wicker chair and drapes it over her shoulders.

Her eyes are bewitching. Shimmering river stones, dark brown with slivers of light. And her face, smooth and peach-toned, like a fine terracotta vase, devoid of the imperfections of the typical peasant-made pottery. Her face reminds Alfonso of a soft, unmarred beach, glistening in the sun. She doesn't have the thick, dark features of many of the peasant girls and women he has seen walking along the road, their faces weathered and lined.

As they enter the stables, a mule shuffles in its enclosure, nostrils flaring. Gabriella retrieves a small apple from her apron pocket. The mule neighs and nudges her hand roughly. Gabriella frowns, and Alfonso clears his throat impatiently. She draws her shawl tightly around her and moves on.

The smell of animal dung is more intense inside the stables. It doesn't seem to bother Gabriella in the least, but Alfonso finds it smothering, and he stifles his urge to gag. He is not really interested in the sheep, the goats, the mule, or the new piglet that Gabriella tells him was procured at the fall fair in Locri, which they will feed and fatten for next year's slaughter.

He is more than happy to leave the stench of the pigsty, with its remnants of squash rinds and vegetable peelings, bruised pears, quinces, and apples. They come to the far side of the barn, its floor scattered with hay. One wall is lined with orderly bales of hay, and on the adjacent side, roughly hewn planks lead up to a hayloft. Alfonso follows Gabriella's gaze. A rectangular opening in the loft wall lets in a shaft of light. There is a cot close to the window.

"This is one of Luciano's favourite spots," she tells him. "He loves the animals and spends hours with them. Occasionally, he sleeps here at night, and more often than not, he ends up napping here in the afternoon." She smiles. "So that's where his new vest has gotten to. I'll go and fetch it. I won't be but a minute." She lifts her skirts slightly as she proceeds up the stairs. Alfonso doesn't hesitate. He follows, taking the steps two at a time.

Gabriella, grey woollen vest in hand, turns, her eyebrows furrowing. Alfonso catches her eyeing the space between him and the stairwell. She takes a step forward. He shifts his position so that the space is blocked.

"Signorina Gabriella," he murmurs, extending his hands to her arms. "I have some news to share with you. Don Simone has made mention of the preoccupation you and your father have felt over the exchange of the church lands. Please, don't be worried. As the new proprietor, I have already decided that you and your family may remain in my employ. You and your father seem to be quite capable in maintaining the crops and animals. And Don Simone will remain in Camini in his present capacity as priest." He flashes a smile that he hopes she will find reassuring. "We are to finalize the papers this evening, upon Don Simone's return."

Alfonso feels Gabriella stiffening and he realizes he has been pressing her arms. Could it be that she has been untouched by a man? He releases his hold on her. Gabriella is batting her eyes, but unlike that trollop Clara, hers are completely innocent.

"Everything will remain as before, I assure you, Signorina Gabriella," he murmurs, leaning closer. "I realize how hard it would be for your father to find employment if dismissed at a moment's notice, especially at this time of year. He would be hard-pressed to provide for you and your little brother." He steps toward her and she inches back, her pretty eyebrows furrowing.

"Don Simone tells me that his only recourse would probably be to separate your family; perhaps a convent for you and an orphanage for your little brother, the nearest of which, I understand, is situated in Gerace." Alfonso feathers Gabriella's cheek with his palm. Her face has lost its peachy tone, and she is trembling. "You wouldn't want to be the cause of your family's separation, *would you?*"

He sees a flicker in her dark eyes; the vein at the base of her neck is throbbing. Her mouth has opened at his mildly spoken words. She makes an impulsive dash to one side, but again he thwarts her. With one fluid movement, he has her flat on the cot and he is sitting beside her, holding her arms back above her head. When she opens her mouth to scream, Alfonso leans over to stifle her with his own mouth.

She tries to squirm beneath him, then goes limp. He wants to taste more of her mouth, but he releases her momentarily, and as she struggles to regain her breath, he rasps, "Don't be afraid, Signorina Gabriella. This arrangement will be to everyone's best interests."

He lets go of one hand and runs it impatiently under the folds of her skirt, until he has made contact with her stockinged leg. She cries out then, but he knows as well as she that there are no ears about to hear her, save those of the animals. Her father is not expected until sundown, and Don Simone will be detained until at least the supper hour.

Her grunts and her jerks excite him. He finds the edge of her stockings and tears them off, using his body to press against hers, and his other hand to clamp both her hands back on the cot above her head. He presses his lips to hers again, thrusting his tongue inside. She gags, and he releases her, looking down hungrily at her wild-eyed expression.

He clenches his jaw and begins to run his hands along her calves, up around her thighs and buttocks. He hears himself groan. With one hand, he yanks at her bodice. He buries his face in her heaving bosom, and without her mouth clamped, she begins to scream. Without hesitation, he releases his hold on her wrists and slaps her. He hears her suck in her breath. His own breath quickens.

"Now, Gabriella, *that* could have been avoided. Has no one taught you your place?" He has deliberately omitted the "Signorina." She is a peasant, after all. There is no longer any need to pretend at polite conventions of speech. He gazes at the side of her flaming face. His nail must have caught a corner of her mouth, there is blood oozing from her swollen lower lip. He shifts his position to unbuckle his belt. From her petrified expression, Alfonso is convinced she is untouched.

The thought of being her first lover makes him gasp. He slips his trembling hand under her skirts again and begins to pull at her undergarments, anxious to begin his exploration. Her breath is ragged now, and as she begins to sob, he continues to press down upon her.

After his self-imposed abstinence, Alfonso feels dizzy with the prospect of initiating a maiden to the carnal realities of life. The dank earthy smells of the animals around him are intensifying his urges, and he yanks off his belt, muttering a curse at the awkwardness of trying to manipulate it with one hand, while keeping Gabriella pinned down.

"What in devil's name is going on here?" a voice thunders below.

"Papà," Gabriella screams, *"Help me!"*

Alfonso jumps up, his fists clenching. Gabriella's father is leaping up the stairs, his face contorted in fury.

"You goddamned piece of shit," Lorenzo cries, hurling himself at Alfonso. "The church's lands are not enough for you? You have to take the virtue of an innocent girl as well? *Bastardo!"*

He rams his fist into Alfonso's stomach. Alfonso grunts and stumbles back but recovers in time to block Lorenzo's next punch. Lorenzo is intent on killing him, he realizes, catching sight of the old man's eyes. They are bloodshot, and his mouth is twisted in a rabid grimace. His leg shoots up to catch Alfonso in the groin, but Alfonso breaks away from Lorenzo's hypnotic gaze fast enough to deflect the hit to his thigh.

Grimacing, Alfonso steps back; this gives him the few seconds he needs to recover. He is not entirely inexperienced when it comes to settling a score in a physical manner; he has, on occasion, reserved this method for gambling partners who reason with their *coglioni* instead of their brains.

Bracing himself, he takes as much air as his lungs will hold and then rams into Lorenzo. Lorenzo gasps and then collapses, his head hitting the edge of the stairwell with a loud crack.

Alfonso watches as the forces of gravity propel the twisted body down the stairs, the blood from the gash on Lorenzo's head streaking each step, until the body slumps like a potato sack on the ground. Lorenzo looks like a crumpled doll that has been flung by an invisible hand.

Alfonso blocks Gabriella from leaping down the stairs. He feels her fists beating onto his back, but he doesn't move or flinch. He watches as Lorenzo's body twitches and then stills.

"Papà! Papà!" Gabriella's hysterical streams are close to his ear. He turns and with a back hand silences her. He picks her up and deposits her on the cot.

"*Stupid peasant,*" he mutters. "If you had kept your mouth shut in the first place, none of *that* would have happened."

Gabriella doesn't move. Her face is drained of all colour. She has fainted, he realizes, smiling. He bunches her skirts up around her thighs. The paleness of her skin makes him catch his breath as he closes his fingers around her anklebones, before caressing the swell of her calves, her delicate knee bones, and the firmness of her ivory thighs.

Sweating, he stops and rises to remove his trousers. He swears when the opening of his trousers catches. He wrenches it until it opens, tearing it in the process, and the tension he feels as he is extricating himself from the material is unbearable. He kicks his trousers away from his feet and turns to tower over Gabriella's still form.

He positions himself over her, enjoying the slow torture he is putting himself through as he rubs himself along the length of her leg. The droplets on his face have turned to rivulets, and he opens his mouth to catch them as they slip down his face. He brushes back the hair that keeps falling in front of his eyes.

The smell of the straw and the whiff of animal scents from the enclosures excite him. He drops down flat over her and begins to kiss the soft hollows of her neck. Her sudden gasps inflame him. He shifts, grunting, until he feels the rise of her bosom. He nudges her bodice down completely and his tongue begins circling over the pale mounds. Her body jerks for an instant, then stills.

His lips close over one nipple. He feels himself quivering. *Has he ever known such delirious pleasure?* He wants to bite her, suckle her, take his time, but he knows he can wait no longer. He lifts himself slightly, using one hand to quickly spread her legs. He shudders, aware that he is already drooling. He wants to drive into her, pulse against her until he explodes. As the tip of his member brushes against her softness, he groans and pulls back, preparing his thrust.

A sudden scream shatters the silence, and he realizes it is his own. Pain is searing through all the channels of his brain. It is radiating like burning embers around his neck, fragmenting his vision like the jagged shards of a smashed wineglass.

Instinctively, he clasps the area that is on fire. The hand he retracts is slick with blood. He looks down. A dagger's shaft is glistening in Gabriella's hand. Rolling from the cot, Alfonso feels his body spasm as it empties its passion on the prickly, straw-packed floor.

TONINO SHIFTS ON THE STRAW-COVERED FLOOR of the barn loft. In the scant illumination provided by a crescent moon, he can barely make out the faces of his comrades. Most of them have already succumbed to a deep sleep on the crude planks that serve as their beds. Their uneven snoring is magnified in the stillness of the night, distracting him from the putrid smells in the barn. Earlier, the General had allowed them a brief rest on the more arduous embrace of the forest floor. Despite the woollen coverlet he brought with him, Tonino felt the dampness seep into his muscles, and while he lay in discomfort, trying to accustom himself to the feel of a clump of hardened earth as his pillow and the unyielding ground beneath him, the impassioned words of the General came back to him the second night they had gathered in Pietro's cellar.

"I offer you neither rank nor honour, but toil, peril, battle, and then the sky for a tent, the earth for a bed, and God above as witness."

Tonino feels goosebumps trail a path along his arms at the memory of Garibaldi's steely delivery of that declaration, and the immediate hush that followed before a cry of solidarity burst forth from his followers, old and new. Including Tonino.

He acknowledges that he has been gripped with the scarlet fever of being a Redshirt, and although his body pulses with a patriotic fervour that he knows he must tend to, another part of him trembles with the unfulfilled promise of love that he has knowingly cast aside. He thinks of the letter Gabriella should have received by now.

Oh Gabriella, how I wish I could have told you everything before I left, especially that I had to leave so soon. But I knew that if I did, one look into the depths of your eyes would have made me crumble at your feet like a devoted slave. And perhaps I would have eventually hated myself for not allowing myself to become the man that I wanted to be; the man to fight for the cause of United Italy; the man to help bring change to this godforsaken territory we are struggling in. And even worse than hating myself, I would have died watching your love turn to hate. For how long would you be able to love a man who cowardly chose to think only of himself instead of the good that could come to many by joining the brave General Garibaldi in his cause to unify the whole of Italy? To free Rome from the French?

My dearest Gabriella, trust me when I say that leaving you was the hardest thing I have ever had to do. But I swear on the grave of all our loved ones, that I will return to you after this mission is over, and we will never be separated again. We will have the life we were meant to have together, and land, and children, and happiness.

I feel sickened, my angel, for the pain I know you will feel when you receive my letter, and for the disappointment that

I could not bid you farewell in person. Please try to understand, please forgive me, and know that there will never be anyone but you. I will hold you in my heart every day and night that I am away from you, and with God's blessing, I will be back in Camini soon, with the rest of my life to devote to you. I will console myself in the meantime with the thought that you will recite an Ave Maria *or two for me, and that the promise I first saw in those beautiful eyes of yours will remain bright and strong, awaiting my return. Tuo amore per sempre, Tonino.*

Tonino vows to pray every day until he and Gabriella are reunited. He knows that there are no promises in the life of a soldier, but he does not have the heart to inform Gabriella of the harsh realities of the mission that he has embarked upon. He recalls the look on his brother's face when he handed him the sealed letter, making him promise on Tonino's life and on his own that he would deliver it to Gabriella the day after he left. Ricardo was full of questions about Gabriella and also about Tonino's imminent departure, but Tonino told him as little as possible and swore him to secrecy. "You're a good little man," he ruffled Ricardo's hair before embracing him tightly. "One day, you'll understand too."

Tonino forced himself not to look back as he sprinted away from Ricardo, away from the house that he had lived in since he was born. He didn't want Ricardo's pleading eyes to draw him back, to make him change his mind.

Tonino shifts uncomfortably. *Did* he make the right decision? He clasps his hands behind his head. Although he cannot rid himself of the feeling of guilt for leaving Gabriella, he knows that staying behind would have eventually caused him to despise himself for letting others fight for a better Italy. And if *he* couldn't face up to himself as a man, how could Gabriella?

Between the grunts of the animals and snoring of the men, Tonino hears the wind whistling through the cracks in the barn walls. He sighs, closes his eyes, and begins to pray.

GABRIELLA STARES AT THE KNIFE IN HER HANDS. Its blade is smeared with Alfonso's blood. *Did I pull it out of him?* she wonders, dazed. Yes, of course she did. She had thrust it into the back of his neck.

Gabriella jolts into an upright position so quickly that her eyes blur. She squeezes them shut to try to regain her equilibrium; when she opens them again, the knife is still in her hands, the blood on her fingers. She gasps and lets the knife clatter to the plank floor, where it lands near Alfonso's crumpled body. She thrusts her hand in a nearby bale of straw, plunging it frantically back and forth to get the blood off, impervious to the pinching, scratching sensation. She cannot breathe. There is no light, no air. The musky, blood-tinged smell of Alfonso is making her nauseated. She picks up her skirts and steps around him to get to the stairs.

Papà. His face is turned away from her. Her heart beating a deafening rhythm, she rushes down the stairs to kneel by his side. She recoils at the sight of his head cradled in a pool of blood. "Papà," she whispers, laying a hand on his chest. His eyes are closed, and for an instant Gabriella feels a surge of hope and then a stab of recognition. She has handled enough animals to know the stiffness of death.

Her head drops to her father's chest, and she feels the hot rush of her tears soaking his work shirt. Around her, gusts of air have pushed their way through the gaps in the barn walls, making eerie moaning sounds. Tormented sounds, like a wounded animal.

She gasps, realizing they are coming from her own mouth.

PART III:
THE COLONEL AND THE BRIGAND
February-March 1862

THE MULE TRACK IS NARROW, pitted, and alarmingly slippery. A foray into hell, Colonel Michele Russo is convinced, feeling his stomach lurch again as the carriage descends the mountainside. It is the only road available for miles. The one he is accustomed to has been washed out by a mountain gorge and will stay that way until the winter rains subside.

The rains are far from over; winter has just barely begun. Russo is sick of the endless rainfall. The ashen sky hangs over the dreary countryside like a death pall. Sometimes, a soft, mournful spray douses the sullen landscape, and other times a sharp, vengeful pelting prevails, intent on punishing man and nature alike. A vendetta of nature, really. After all, there has been enough deforestation in these Aspromonte mountains in past centuries to incite the wrath of the Creator. Tonight's rain falls in the vengeful category. Russo swears under his breath as it strikes the carriage, partnered by vicious winds that seem powerful enough to topple the carriage at any time.

Earlier, he had the choice of either turning back in the direction of Gerace or continuing the journey by the alternate road suggested by his driver Dattilio, who knows this rugged, backwood country like a confident mountain goat. Russo wishes he hadn't followed Dattilio's suggestion; the inconsequential drizzle at the start of their diverted journey has now turned into a deluge.

Cursed driver! Russo grits his teeth. *Does Dattilio have to be told to slow down and find shelter somewhere, anywhere? Ignorant peasant!*

Russo realizes the carriage is slowing down. His arm around the young woman sitting next to him relaxes slightly. She looks at him with no evidence of fear. He would wager she is finding the whole experience rather exciting from the glint in her dark brown eyes. But has she sensed that he is jittery? Is she silently mocking him for his unmanly fears?

He must stop poisoning his thoughts with unfounded suspicions. Signora Liliana has shown nothing less than respect up to now. He wills his facial muscles to relax and return her smile. *Ah, the elasticity of youth,* he muses, his fingers caressing Liliana's flawless cheek, hesitating briefly at the corner of her lip before tracing its outlines.

When Liliana opens her mouth to offer the briefest flick of her tongue against his hand, Russo can't help stiffening. Her smile widens. She knows what she is doing to him…and for all his years of experience, his maturity, she always has the power to render him a pubescent *giovanotto* ready for his trembling initiation into manhood.

The carriage jolting to a stop makes Russo catapult off the seat and land hard on his knees at Liliana's feet. He feels like an awkward schoolboy. "Blasted servant! I ought to send him packing. He's put me through hell on this journey."

A rumble of thunder reverberates around them, and the rain pelting down doubles in intensity, muffling the rest of his curses. He gets up awkwardly and reaches for his overcoat and sable-trimmed hat, reassuring Liliana that he will order Dattilio to seek shelter immediately.

His servant has dismounted and is holding the reins tightly against him, trying to calm the horses, whose eyes and teeth are a white blur. They snort and stamp the ground, their heated breath fogging the crisp February air. Dattilio is a mess. His hat is long gone and rivulets are pushing his scraggly grey hair over his eyes and ears. His moustache and beard are dripping, and the rain is pouring off his drooped shoulders. His sodden, long, black coat shrouds him like the glistening wings of a raven.

The lightning that splinters the sky stills them all for a moment. Dattilio waits with his ever sullen expression, his hand stroking the horses alternately to calm them.

"Can't you find us some kind of refuge? A farmhouse, or even a cave? *This is madness.* Only a jackass would continue driving under these conditions!"

Dattilio looks away slowly, and Russo silently curses his servant's asinine nature. He wonders if Dattilio is purposefully slow, out of spite. There is something in Dattilio's yellow-tinged eyes that makes him shudder. Everything about him reminds Russo of decay: his rotted teeth, his foul breath, and his sagging, ashen skin. Dattilio's unusually prominent cheekbones, spindly limbs, and uneven gait resemble those of emaciated war prisoners. Even Liliana has mentioned pointedly that she finds that "ghastly creature" disconcerting, his yellow eyes and skin reminding her of a scaly lizard.

Dattilio turns to face him again and says gruffly, "There's a deserted farmhouse nearby. Fifteen minutes. We could wait out the storm there."

Russo nods and bids Dattilio remount, now that the horses have calmed down. Without a further word, Russo jumps back into the carriage, apologizing to Liliana for the accompanying spray of rain.

Liliana eyes his drenched hat and overcoat. As the carriage lurches forward, Russo tells her of their imminent destination. She leans into him, takes off his hat and smiles coyly. "Fifteen minutes? I think we should try to dry your clothes before then, Michele...." She pulls on his lapel meaningfully and he chuckles.

What a bewitching creature Liliana is. Not buxom, like his wife Gina, whose ample body he ravished in the early years with the insatiable appetite of youth and inexperience. Liliana is as taut and refined as a Stradivarius, with no excess at all—just a pure, rich patina and silky, mysterious hollows and curves that he can't seem to get enough of.

"I don't think I classify as a prude, generally, Lili, but I don't think...."

"Don't think at all," Liliana murmurs, tugging at his lapel. In a second, his overcoat is off. He is slipping hers off her shoulders when a deafening thunderclap wedges them apart and the carriage sways. Russo clenches his teeth. *Goddammit,* they must stop, shelter or no shelter, before they all topple over the precipice. If the weather wasn't so merciless, he would have bolted outside again to give the old bastard the verbal thrashing he deserved. Again, he vows to replace Dattilio.

He needs a younger, more stalwart driver now that he is travelling throughout the Aspromonte region in his new position overseeing the operations of the National Guard in the repression of brigandage. And he could use another armed horseman in his company. One is presently trailing the carriage, and ordinarily, one would suffice for the road Russo is accustomed to taking, as it has regular carabineer postings along the way. But travelling on this mule track, with its serpentine twists and ruts and sheer drops into fathomless ravines, he feels his stomach knotting.

Russo remembers the pistol he keeps beneath his jacket, and he feels some of his anxiety dissipate. Besides, infested though this country is with brigands, nobody with any sense at all would be wandering about in this storm. No, they would all be clustered in their mountain caves or hovels like cockroaches—*the black bastards*—until the storm abated and they could go about their nefarious schemes unhindered by nature.

Claps of thunder echo around them. "What the devil?" *Gunshots.* He wrenches himself from Liliana to reach for his pistol.

The carriage door flies open and before Russo can make a move, a masked figure in a black cloak flattens him against the seat and holds a pistol to his head. "Disarm," the intruder barks, his face obscured behind an ebony kerchief.

Russo's jaws clench. Liliana's face blanches. *God help us.* As he reaches into his holster, the brigand's pistol presses into his temple.

"Throw it outside the carriage," the brigand commands.

Russo complies. The carriage is likely surrounded by more just like him, ready to riddle him with bullets or daggers.

"Put your hands behind your back."

Russo grimaces as the brigand deftly twists a thick cord around his wrists in a blood-draining vice. He gags uncontrollably at the ill-smelling strip of cloth wedged across his open mouth and tied securely behind his head, leaving his face stretched grotesquely, his jawbone feeling about to crack.

The brigand pulls off Russo's boots and flings them outside the carriage. "It seems I have interrupted a tryst," he chuckles, glancing from Russo to Liliana. "Unless I'm wrong and this juicy young morsel *is* your wife. Ah, a wedding ring. How lovely."

He seizes her hand and his fingers close around the thick gold band. He examines the intricate filigree, and then yanks the ring off. He drops it into a pocket inside his cloak, and when his hand reappears, it is holding another rope.

Russo feels his blood flare. Liliana's eyes are wide; her back is ramrod straight in her seat. The brigand binds her hands behind her back. He cuts off the excess rope with a knife retrieved from within his cloak, allowing Russo a quick view of daggers and pistols gleaming like studded soldiers. The brigand drops down to bind Liliana's feet, and then puts the rope back within the folds of his cloak. "A lady's feet and legs are better left unbound," he laughs, running one hand slowly up Liliana's stockinged leg. "Except for occasions such as this. Let's see what gifts you have for me."

Liliana twists and recoils as the brigand's hands probe higher beneath her skirts. Russo feels rage pound through the blood vessels in his brain, and his chest constricts. The brigand laughs with a grunt of triumph. Russo knows he has found the pouch strapped around Liliana's thigh. *He* was the one who told her to conceal her valuables this way when travelling. His stomach contracts violently as the brigand, trying to remove the pouch, growls and swipes at the interfering layers of skirts. In one swift motion, he retrieves a stiletto from his cloak and slashes away at her dress and frilly underclothes. Liliana's mouth opens in a silent scream, her eyes blinking rapidly, her body jerking with every tear of satin and lace.

The brigand stops, breathing hard, and runs his gaze along Liliana's black lace stockings, held in place by garters. He reaches for the cream silk pouch attached to one garter and deftly removes it, and although the second pouch on the other thigh is just as visible, he begins to skim her leg.

The rain has stopped. The pelting against Russo's eardrums is the drumming of his heart. He feels spittle dribbling down the corners of his mouth. His loins tighten as the brigand's fingers slide upward to feel the swell of Liliana's calves and the delicate bones in her knees before splaying over each shapely thigh. The brigand squeezes, then his fingers stretch upwards to the clasps on the garters. With two tugs, the stockings are released. He retrieves the second pouch and drops it into the recesses of his cloak.

Liliana makes a strangled sound like a young goat being slaughtered. The brigand, unperturbed, watches as she writhes and strains to loosen herself, her abdomen heaving. Russo's eyes blur, and he blinks rapidly. The brigand's hands are roaming over Liliana's bare legs now, and he glances over at Russo while one of his hands disappears behind the remaining shreds of her skirts. Something about his eyes sends a chill through Russo.

Liliana's gasps and ragged breathing are unbearable. Russo's jaw is on fire, his brain an engorged mass ready to burst.

The brigand's free hand moves to Liliana's breasts. He squeezes each one and unclasps the buttons of her bodice with exaggerated delicacy before exposing her. Russo stiffens as

Liliana begins to sob, her tears spilling onto her bared breasts.

The brigand glances sideways at Russo. "Perhaps you can imagine how helpless peasants feel when they are taken advantage of, and then made to suffer even more when the law has no interest in defending them. Perhaps you should re-examine the law books, Colonel Russo. And change them before—"

Two gunshots fire off. The brigand plunges his hand within his cloak and retrieves a pistol. He kicks the door open. As he looks back at Russo and Liliana, his eyes are now clearly visible. Russo blinks, and the brigand is gone with a swirl of his cape.

His stomach clenches at the sound of approaching footsteps. *Could it be my armed horseman?* he wonders. *Or another brigand sent to finish me off?*

A figure appears at the door. Dattilio!

His servant unbinds him, explaining that another brigand restrained him while the *chief* entered the carriage, but then, at the sound of gunshots, shoved him into some lentisk bushes before fleeing. He saw no sign of Russo's armed horseman.

Russo attempts to thank Dattilio but manages only a scratchy croak. He motions to Dattilio to retrieve his boots and to procure a flask of water. Dattilio hands him the knife, lowers his gaze discreetly and descends the carriage. Russo releases Liliana from her strappings. Her face is still pale, but her eyes are blinking now. He helps her readjust what is left of her clothing and eases her trembling body into her overcoat.

At the sound of Dattilio's footsteps, Russo lunges at the door and accepts the boots and the flask. He urges Liliana to drink first. It hurts when he swallows the water. His voice cracked and hoarse, he orders Dattilio to proceed homeward.

The sooner he can get to the station, the sooner he can devise a plan to pursue his assailant. To find the bastard who did this to him and Liliana. As Dattilio urges the horses forward, Russo's jaw clenches as he recalls the brigand's tell-tale features when he kicked open the carriage door. *One brown eye, one green.*

Liliana presses her head against his chest. Russo strokes her hair gently, murmuring reassurances. He will see that justice is done. The bastard will pay, along with the informer who tipped him off as to Russo's presence and identity.

As the carriage rumbles along, Russo ponders the brigand chief's earlier words. He is harbouring a grudge and bent on revenge, obviously. Russo's stomach tightens. He will not rest until he has this devil bound and gagged, his pride in tatters like Liliana's skirts, his diabolical eyes begging for mercy. It will give Russo the greatest of pleasure to give *him* a taste of hell.

Despite his cracked lips and throbbing jaw, he smiles as he contemplates some of the methods of torture he can look forward to. Cutting off the brigand's ear with a slice of his dagger. Smashing every bone in his hands with a hunk of granite. Poking him in the testicles with a sizzling fire iron. *Something to make him pay for laying his filthy hands on Liliana*. Russo's hand trembles as he brushes Liliana's cheek softly with his fingertips.

Oh yes. The brigand chief will pay.

THE SKY IS KNUCKLED WITH BRUISES in the fading twilight. Stefano Galante scans the lifelike forms of vermilion and indigo intertwining like desperate lovers within the inky recesses of sky and feels the hair on his arms rise in reverent acknowledgement of the Creator's presence. The successful pillage of a carriage transporting Colonel Michele Russo to his villa has lifted his spirits, and he fingers the pillaged items in the pocket of his cape with a renewed sense of satisfaction.

The clouds hovering above him seem to shift with the erratic dance of the night breeze. Within a cleft of wooded hills, a mournful howl breaks off into an echo followed by the more guttural rumblings of thunder.

He feels at ease astride his mule, affected neither by the storm that is gathering once again, nor by the presence of wolves or other night creatures. This is his territory, he acknowledges in silent contentment. He has crossed every hillock, ravine, torrent, and bluff by foot or horseback. He has sheltered in numerous caves and dugouts, trenches and fields. He has taken all this wild earth has had to give, both from animate and inanimate means. He has derived his sustenance from pigeons and blackbirds, ducks and partridges, wild hares and hedgehogs, and from foxes and wild boar. He has gathered chicory and chamomile, jasmine and rosemary. The blood-red juice of the abundant cactus pear has sustained him during times of lack; the crystalline waters of gushing springs have coursed through his parched throat and body during the unforgiving heat of summer.

Stefano dismounts at the crest of a hill that has become his vantage point. The treacherous paths and ravines that have preceded him here would discourage even the most expert of horsemen. This particular hill, which he has named "Monte Galante," has become his haven, its granite shoulders offering him a barrier to the forces that would want his capture, dead or alive; its densely wooded body providing all his life's needs, like a breastfeeding mother.

He pulls out a flask from within the folds of his cloak and takes a swig. The red wine warms his throat and radiates throughout his body. He reaches for a linen sack and retrieves a hunk of hardened goat's cheese and bread. He hasn't eaten since dawn, and although he is accustomed to long stretches between meals, especially when on the run or involved in a *faccenda* with the members of his band, he savours the richness of a simple meal such as this. It is not enough to satiate him of course, but it will allow him the necessary fortitude to complete his mission.

His mule nuzzles against him, and Stefano chuckles. "No, I didn't forget you, Mastro." He pulls out a small apple from his sack. "You need your strength too."

From his position on the hill, Stefano can see the faint glow of Calvino, the hamlet nestled high on the mountainside beyond the dense valley that separates them. It is late, but not too late to accomplish the last task he deems necessary before retreating to his hideout. The others are far behind him still; by the time he returns from Calvino, they will have settled down in the camp, rewarding themselves with food and drink, and ruminating on the success of their latest pillage. He will share a celebratory drink with them, as usual, while strategizing tomorrow's events.

He pats the mule affectionately before mounting and sets off toward the muted light. Exhausted though he may be, he cannot compromise the vow he made on his life to the Blessed Virgin. He tenderly touches the scapular of the Madonna that hangs around his neck, then kisses his fingertips. Murmuring a prayer of thanks for the success of today's pillage, he yanks Mastro's reins and bolts down the hillside to the Church of the Madonna of the Poppies.

RUSSO SCOWLS AT THE MEMORY OF THE BRIGAND with the unnatural eyes. He clenches his teeth, consumed by a heat that is raging under his skin like a wildfire. With impatient fingers, he claws at his cheeks and neck to relieve himself of the itch that invariably accompanies these episodes of inner fury and then slams his palm over the bell to summon his manservant.

"Fetch me a clean cloth," he brusquely orders as Dattilio enters the study. "And a bowl of cool water with sprigs of rosemary." Liliana has mentioned more than once that he ought to try such an antiseptic remedy for his skin irritations.

Dattilio nods and retreats. Russo grimaces. He has drawn blood from scratching so hard. He stifles a curse and sits up straight in his chair. The matter of the brigand chief need not reduce him to a thousand pieces; he is made of heartier stuff than that. *Oh, the irony.* There he was, travelling through the territory of Greater Calabria South as the leader of the forces of repression against brigandage, and what was his fate? To be outsmarted by a mere brigand, a filthy outlaw who handled him and Liliana as if *they* were below *him*.

Well, the insidious bastard will be dust under his feet when he is finished with him. The brigand has won the first battle, perhaps; that much Russo will concede, but the real war hasn't even begun yet. The devil will live to regret the day he was born.

Dattilio returns, carrying an earthenware bowl and a fresh linen towel.

Russo grunts his approval as Dattilio sets them upon the desk, and at Russo's nod, retreats once more. At the sound of the door clicking behind him, Russo takes a deep breath, dips his inflamed face into the rosemary water and holds it there, forcing himself to feel its full impact.

Sighing at the temporary relief, Russo straightens in his chair as he dips his quill into the Murano inkwell. The ink splatters on the surface of his desk, but he is not particularly concerned, as the ingrained walnut and oak expanse is protected by a sheet of glass. He wipes it up with an ink cloth and proceeds to put words to paper in his latest communiqué to his superior officer:

Esteemed General Zanetti,

I pray that this latest report finds you in the most optimum health. With the aim of keeping you apprised of the state of operations in and around the districts of Gerace and Stilo, I wish to inform you of the ever-growing hostility of the peasants towards our soldiers and carabineers. They do not hesitate in attempting to provoke our men with cries of "Death to you and your leader! Shame to the cruel King Victor Emmanuel! Long live the brave and valiant volunteers of the hero King Francis, forever the head of the Kingdom of the Two Sicilies, forced to flee to Gaeta by the cursed forces of Unification!"

Illustrious General, if anything is cursed, it is the land and people of this territory in which I find myself. Not one day goes by that the signs of physical and moral deterioration do not make themselves manifest in this dejected area, with peasants that utter a savage dialect and immerse themselves in savage and barbarous customs that truly illuminate the distinction of these peoples from their northern and civil compatriots. They are lacking everything that civilized peoples enjoy: schools, decent roads and adequate homes. They live with their animals in the most unsanitary of conditions, making our animal enclosures seem like palaces in comparison.

Alas, I cannot refer to them as compatriots, as they themselves refuse to align themselves with the philosophy of Unification, and therefore, can be seen as proponents of civil dissent, perhaps even of civil war. In fact, their cries of *"All'armi, all'armi!"* would indicate that the possibility of civil revolution is steadily building. There are many who are plotting to re-establish a temporary government in the name of the ousted King Francis II, despite the presence of the National Guard. They were living in abject conditions before the Unification of the Two Sicilies, but somehow, they have determined that the new government under King Victor Emmanuel II is the cause of their perennial poverty. They have nurtured a common hate towards the wealthy, often absent landowners who have turned their face away from the pathetic living conditions of their employees to pursue more comfortable lifestyles in the North, and therefore, they resent anybody and anything that represents the distant and diffident attitude of the self-serving Northerners.

The promises of Garibaldi and the government—to elevate the state of the peasants by selling off and subdividing church and other state properties to enable them to become small landowners—have backfired and only served to balloon the already vast properties of the wealthy. It is understandable, and regrettable, that the peasants, in their ignorance, did not have the knowledge or means to bid on available properties. As a consequence, the only thing left to the peasants was their hate and frustration against the rich for keeping them shackled to their poverty and desperation. And so, it is this hate that has manifested into the festering criminality that is brigandage.

I myself have been the recent victim of a brigand attack. The villain escaped, but rest assured, General, that he and the hundreds of other outlaws in this territory will be pursued, captured, and punished to the greatest extent of the law.

Esteemed General, as your servant in the role which you have bestowed me, I will continue to hold everyone in my district accountable in maintaining order and lawfulness, and, failing to do so, will be subjected to my most stringent and dire consequences. In our military division, with our two thousand plus members of the Cavalry, along with our three hundred members of the rifle regiment, we are beginning to feel the rewards of our efforts. In the permanent garrisons of Catanzaro, Crotone, Cosenza, Rossano, Reggio, Gerace, Caulonia and Stilo, the detachments are established and are making progress. As per your request, any brigands, whether known or unknown, are to be subjected to summary execution upon capture, and any of their supporters or those who have harboured them, will also be executed by one or more members of the rifle regiment. Homes harbouring brigands will be knocked down, torched if necessary, in order to draw out the villains.

It is with extreme measures that we must combat this scourge upon the territory of Calabria. I am deeply honoured by your trust in me to lead the operations of repression, with my headquarters at the Caulonia garrison, and to know that I have your unfailing support.

Yours in the continuing battle to bring civilization to this dark part of our nation, on this, the 18th day of February in the year 1862,

I remain, your loyal subject,

Lieutenant Colonel Michele Russo

AFTER WHAT SEEMS LIKE A LONGER DESCENT than usual, Stefano dismounts and leads Mastro to a familiar grove where he knows the mule will be safe while he continues on alone. He offers the creature another apple, and drawing his cape tightly around him, disappears into the labyrinthine passageway through the grove to the cluster of houses marking the northwest limits of the village.

This is the most abject part of the area. The huts crouch together in communal squalor, some with rickety enclosures for the emaciated fowl and other creatures that keep the families from the brink of starvation.

A scuttling nearby alerts Stefano to the presence of a robust guinea pig that, sensing danger, has frozen in the shadows near him. He hesitates for an instant, raising his foot in deliberation, then shrugs and moves on. He has more important things to do besides procuring food for himself or his band. Reassuring himself with the feel of his dagger beneath his cloak, he continues along the periphery of the village, skirting from tree to bush with the fluidity of a hare, until he nears the hut he is seeking.

In the charcoal shadows between the bushy undergrowth, Stefano stops and searches for signs of human movement. His ears, accustomed to the bevy of sounds in the stillness of the night, picks up a faint wail. As he attempts to identify it, a faint light flickers within the shack he is watching.

It is Peppina Monaco's baby, the twin who survived its tumultuous birth during the earthquake on All Soul's Day. Stefano had heard that Peppina had gone into the throes of labour when suddenly the earth around her house had started to grumble, and as the midwife was trying to extricate the baby, the walls began to vibrate and crumble. Clay pots and pitchers shattered around them and Peppina, in a spasm of pain and fear, fainted.

Seconds later, the tremor had subsided and the midwife was staring at a blue-faced baby streaked with blood. No sooner had she laid the dead infant within the folds of a blanket, Peppina awoke from her faint with a series of spasms, followed by more screams before pushing out the second baby. However, her joy at the safe delivery of a baby girl dissipated when she discovered that she had already given birth to a stillborn child, a boy.

Stefano recalls watching the grim funeral procession two days later from a hiding spot up in the hills, barely making out the tiny coffin in the hands of Dante, the child's father. He cannot forget the mournful cries of Peppina and her relatives reverberating throughout the valley.

He felt genuine sorrow for Dante, a hard-working man liked by all his neighbours for his good works. Dante was especially kind to the children of the area, as he was to his own daughters, though he longed to be a father to sons. Sons to help him get out of the squalor that they were all in, working until their hands bled as day labourers on the lands of the barons and the gentry. Sons that—God bless them—would find a way out of the miserable life of a *bracciante,* a thankless existence that barely provided enough to keep themselves fed, let alone their wives and children.

And now Dante has lost the son he had so wanted. Dante's newborn daughter, Rosa, is too small and fragile to bring him solace just yet. And his other four daughters, two of whom already wear the yellow pallor of malaria, are destined to a hard, bitter life like their parents and their grandparents.

Stefano knows that Dante and Peppina's family will surely feel the lack of Providence in these bitter times, and for this reason, he is determined to help them. The children will benefit from a handout, from the looks of their scrawny limbs and sunken eyes. A surge of anger suffuses his innards as he thinks of all the other peasants suffering in the same way, unable to shake the yoke that is the burden of taxes imposed by the new government in power. *Unification!* He curses under his breath. If it has united anyone, it must be the wealthy, certainly not his countrymen, who have been breaking their backs and practically starving themselves to keep their families fed.

He realizes that the baby is no longer crying. He slips a hand inside his cloak and pulls out a small purple sack with the initial "G" embroidered in the centre with yellow thread. He holds it tightly, impeding the coins from jingling. Satisfied that there is no sign of human presence, he crouches along the side of the hut and a final leap brings him around to the front door, in front of which he places the bag before retracing his steps and crouching behind a prickly pear cactus.

Stefano feels the ground for a stone or a hardened clump of earth. When he finds it, he flings it at the door and waits. He is rewarded moments later by the sight of Dante opening the door cautiously, hastily dressed and clasping a shovel. As he moves forward, his foot bumps into the lump on the doorstep.

Stefano watches in silent satisfaction as Dante picks up the sack and loosens the drawstring. He is close enough to see the play of emotions on Dante's gaunt face under the moonlight, to hear the gasp of wonder. He watches as Dante peers out into the darkness, makes the sign of the cross, and re-enters the shack without the frown that marked his features when he first came out.

Stefano stares at the house for a moment, swallows hard and slips away. He is happy that he carried out his good deed, but he won't be fully content until he fulfills the promise he made to his protector, the blessed Madonna. Clasping the scapular, Stefano leaps into the darkness of the thicket and proceeds through a deserted path that will bring him to the rear courtyard of the church. He steps gingerly through the damp bracken, breathing in the visceral scent of fallen and decaying oak leaves.

His eyes narrow as he reaches the courtyard, at one side of which is ensconced a stone shrine dedicated to the Madonna. The statue within is reputedly hundreds of years old, found in a bed of scarlet poppies by shepherds who had been diverted from their usual path by a lost sheep. The peasants, awestruck by the sight of the shiny alabaster statue lying amidst the blood-red blooms, took it as a sign that a church should be erected at that very site in veneration of the Holy Mother, and after word reached the bishop about the miraculous discovery, the villagers combined their skills and resources to construct a small chapel with an adjacent shrine.

After three hundred years, the statue had lost its lustre, and the original chapel had been destroyed by an earthquake, and then rebuilt, only to be levelled once again by an even stronger quake in 1783. For some strange reason, however, the statue had never fallen or crumbled in the wake of either earthquake, and the poppies around it had always flourished, leaving the villagers to marvel at the power and intention of God, which was obviously to show the people of Calvino that they needed to pay attention to the Madonna, that they needed to rebuild the church beside her, and that they needed to rebuild their faith, which, Don Damiano addressed in sermon after sermon, was crumbling as far as he could ascertain.

Stefano looks into the face of the Madonna now, illuminated by an oil lamp sitting on a slab of granite at the statue's feet. Parts of her face and shoulders are speckled from the droppings of pigeons, a source of perpetual grief for Don Damiano, whom Stefano has seen scrubbing fervently at the statue from time to time.

Stefano smiles at the memory of the bowl of soup he shared with the priest after one of his nocturnal visits to the shrine. While Don Damiano was bemoaning the tendency of the pigeons to perch upon the Madonna's head and shoulders, he was smacking his lips as he ladled the steaming pigeon broth into glazed clay bowls.

Stefano's mouth waters at the thought of the flavourful soup accompanied with generous chunks of pigeon meat. He looks up at the window of the rectory for signs of Don Damiano and sees that the candle has been snuffed out for the night.

This will be a quick visit then. Stefano withdraws a pouch from the folds of his cape, identical to the one he deposited at Dante and Peppina's door, and places it behind the statue in a hollow dug out in the ground. He scatters leaves and ferns over the spot and then turns around to face the Madonna. Kneeling on the ground with his head bowed, he recites an

Ave Maria. Rising, he murmurs his gratitude for a successful mission and vows to continue to carry out further assignments under her protection.

He makes the sign of the cross, leans forward to snip off a poppy, and then plunges back into the darkness to where Mastro awaits.

STEFANO FILLS HIS LUNGS WITH THE CRISP NIGHT AIR. He relaxes his hold on the reins as he enters a serpentine path that will weave through a long stretch of dense woodland while ascending the mountainside where his band awaits him. He feels the change of air almost immediately as the sturdy pines and ilex, beeches and chestnut trees swallow up the track behind him. The pines are especially pungent, and again, he breathes in deeply, feeling comforted from the environment that keeps him buffered from his enemies.

The tension in his shoulders abates and he lets his head slump forward and to each side, tentatively stretching the corded muscles in his back and neck. He could easily succumb to sleep, knowing that he can rely on his good mule to bring him to his secret haven, but he does not allow himself the indulgence. A few good hours will restore him once he reunites with his band.

He thanks God for the presence of a half-moon tonight. It occasionally illuminates the forest with shards that penetrate through the intertwined branches. As his mule steadfastly presses on, Stefano plays the events of the evening in his head, scrupulously going over every detail: the tip his informer gave him about the carriage and the identity of its two passengers, Colonel Michele Russo, appointed to his position to bring men like Stefano to justice—and a certain Signora Liliana.

Stefano feels his abdomen tighten in desire as he recalls the journey of his fingers under the Signora's skirts and the soft curves of her legs. No woman even above the position of a peasant would be clad in such finery. Her brocaded dress, satin petticoat, exquisite boots, and her fine stockings alluded to a much higher status, perhaps as the wife of a baron.

Russo's angular face invades his memory and he finds himself thinking with satisfaction that perhaps the Colonel, once he is rescued tonight, won't have the fortitude to have his way with the Signora once they reach their destination. Fear, after all, has a way of suppressing physical desire.

And the look that flashed in the Colonel's eyes when Stefano held the pistol against his temple, *was* one of pure, unadulterated fear. Even if it lasted only for a second.

Stefano urges Mastro through a thicket that conceals the path to his hiding place. Even the most discerning eye would fail to distinguish this spot as a potential *nascondiglio* for a brigand chief and his band, so densely intertwined are the trees. The mule always balks as Stefano leads him to a solid wall of green, and then concedes as his master noses him through a narrow gap that just barely accommodates his entry. At this point, Stefano nimbly dismounts and ensures that no mule tracks or other signs of human presence are visible. Satisfied that he has taken all necessary precautions, Stefano remounts and slaps Mastro's rump before proceeding with the final stretch of the journey, his stomach coiling in pleasure at the thought of rejoining his band for some celebratory feasting.

Moments later, he is at the clearing, loosening Mastro's reins and tethering him to a tree where he will spend the night. He digs into a pocket of his cape for an apple and some carrots to reward the mule for another faithful enterprise, and then he strides over to the gleaming embers, around which his band members are each sitting on a large stump, warming themselves. At his approach, all but one member of the band arise, nodding or voicing a quiet greeting. Stefano nods silently, his eyes narrowing, and bids them sit down again with a wave of his hand. One of the men, the youngest, moves back to allow Stefano room near the firepit, and they all shuffle to rearrange themselves to include him.

The young one, Tomaso Salino, is one month short of eighteen.

Despite the fresh innocence in his countenance, Stefano has witnessed his fiery determination to be taken seriously by the rest of the band. Although he is reluctant to show favouritism to any particular member of the band, Stefano secretly considers Tomaso as a younger version of himself, and acknowledges that out of all his band members, Tomaso is the one he would most trust with his life. There are no shadows of deceit in the boy's eyes, no glint of malevolence or cruelty; he accomplishes each mission efficiently and resolutely.

The two brothers, Roberto and Raffaele Pellegrini, are much more seasoned in the affairs of brigandage, both lean and dark as polished rifles, their angular faces set with black, impenetrable pools for eyes, and each centred with a cliff of a nose. The brothers, although only twenty-one and twenty-three respectively, both have a price on their head for the murder of their sister's lover.

Upon hearing about the dishonour that a certain Ettore Nerina brought upon their fifteen-year-old sister Aurelia, the brothers stealthily followed him one night and cornered him in a dark alley, advising him to do the honourable act of marrying Aurelia or accept the gift of a serrated knife in the throat. Ettore was gallant enough to admit to having had "an adventure" with Aurelia, but nevertheless, he declared, why should *he* be the one to have to bring her to the altar when it was obvious that he was not the first to have *known* her?

Roberto, infuriated by Ettore's dirty insinuations, pulled out a dagger and lunged at Ettore. When Ettore pulled out a weapon of his own, a pistol, Raffaele intervened and stuck a knife into him from behind, while Roberto's dagger found its target in front. As blood gushed out of Ettore's body, the brothers dropped him and fled, but not before extracting their knives. As Raffaele turned his head back to the crumpled body, a flash in the alley confirmed his fears. Their act of revenge had been witnessed.

Knowing that a death sentence, or at the very best, life imprisonment awaited them, they wasted no time in taking to the hills. It was a matter of family honour, expected and just, Roberto explained, when intercepted by Stefano and his small band in a cleft of the Aspromonte mountains. Stefano had nodded curtly and allowed them to take shelter for the night in his encampment. While the brothers slept, uninhibited by guilt or remorse, Stefano had lain awake for hours, thinking about his own sister.... When he finally awoke after a troubled sleep, his first vision was of the sun crawling out from behind the distant hills, its rays streaking the sky blood-red.

A bottle of wine now passes from Roberto to Raffaele, who then offers it to Stefano. Stefano nods his thanks and takes a long swig, savouring the heat of the alcohol at the back of his throat. He sets the bottle down and proceeds to extract a piece of roasted hare from the dented pan sitting in the smouldering ashes. For a few moments, there is little conversation exchanged; the rest of the band members resume eating as well, for the feast of wild rabbits was deemed ready only minutes before Stefano's arrival. As Stefano bites into a meaty hindquarter, he nods approval at Gaetano Silvestri, whom he knows is responsible for the catch.

Gaetano is a seasoned hunter, adept at trapping and catching the most elusive of woodland creatures, with the knowledge passed down to him by his father and *nonno* Arturo, who was kept in the Baron Santoro's employ for his skills in keeping the larders full as well as the stomachs of the Baron's guests, who rarely missed the opportunity to be present at one of the Santoro galas. Gaetano is the oldest in the band; at thirty-six years of age, his hair is slivered with grey and his gaunt face is marked with lines and hollows like a dried-up riverbed. He is happy to have been assigned by Stefano as the game-catcher; his task keeps him from the more unpleasant situations the others are faced with. The blood of animals doesn't disturb him; he utilizes methods that are effective but not cruel. And in the manner of his beloved *nonno* Arturo, who was the most religious person Gaetano had ever known, he murmurs a prayer of gratitude to the beast or bird that he has killed for the sustenance of his family or of those who would partake of his forest bounty, and to the Creator for supplying humankind with the means of survival.

Stefano acknowledges Gaetano's humble nod with a wink; of all his band members, Gaetano has his greatest respect. The man is like a bird or beast himself, fleeing through the forest like a nimble deer, delving in places that would unnerve even the young Tomaso, scampering up jagged rock faces to reach the egg-filled nest of an eagle, crouching motionless in a patch of bracken until the right moment presents itself for him to lunge at a wild boar and pierce its neck with his dagger before the beast can jab its horns into his chest. Yes, Gaetano lacks the youthful passion of Tomaso and the sang-froid of the brothers, but he has skills vital to any band, the skills of procuring food to keep them alive.

Stefano's gaze rests briefly on the final member of his band, who is busy gnawing on the neck bones of one of the roasted hares. Dorotea Spinelli. Her husband Paolo was shot dead in their last mission, and she has stayed on, adamant against returning to her coastal village. Sometimes, Stefano suspects that out of all the band members, she is the most dangerous of them all. He watches her for a few seconds more as she sucks out the meat from between the bones, and then turns to the men, raising the bottle. "Here's to another successful mission," he smiles. He passes the bottle to Gaetano and then withdraws a purple bag from inside his cloak. "I've done my duty for tonight in Calvino; now it's time to share some of the gifts with *you*."

RUSSO CAN FEEL HIS SKIN CRAWLING with an unbearable itch. He nods curtly to his officer and when he is finally alone, he rakes his hand across the back of his neck, not caring if he leaves scratches. He cringes when one of his sharp nails breaks the skin, but he continues to scratch until the itching subsides.

He picks up the report that his officer has left him. Another victory for the brigands. The brigand chief Agostino Pizzelli and his dozen goons entered the village of San Luca shortly after dawn, and with the cry of "Viva Francis II! Viva Maria Sophie!" proceeded to storm into the *piazza,* steps away from the Church of *Sant'*Antonio, where a small gathering of parishioners were partaking in the morning service. The faithful spilled out of the church, wondering at the commotion, and catching sight of Agostino, one of their own, began singing along to the *Te Deum* with Agostino's brigands. By this time, other peasants began appearing, awoken by the unusual din. Emboldened by the spirited cries of support for the fallen Bourbon regime, the outlaws stormed into City Hall, tearing the national flag to shreds, smashing the portrait of King Victor Emmanuel, setting fire to the archives, and trampling to death the one townsperson who attempted to stop them.

The victim, Mario Romano, was left on the tiled floor of City Hall with a stream of blood trickling from his mouth, while the majority of the villagers followed Agostino and his band out of the *piazza* and down the main road out of the village to the holding cell. There, the latest agitators or brigands waited to be transferred to the prison in Locri where they faced either the death penalty or life imprisonment.

Arriving at the holding cell, the brigands used their assortment of weapons to break down the thick wooden doors. They promptly shot the guard and proceeded to free the inmates, while others, stirred up by the chaos, delighted in snatching any flag or sign of the Piedmontese monarch and set about pointing a stream of urine at it. Their final act before fleeing was to set the building aflame.

Russo feels a familiar rage spreading within him. It is precisely these brainless creatures he is after. Brigands who roam the countryside with the delusional idea of restoring the Bourbon order. And if the rumours are true, the deposed Francis and his

staunchest supporter, His Holiness Pope Pius IX, are supporting and organizing bands of brigands to spread and infect the
peasant masses with their preposterous ideas, inflaming them
with treasonous intentions. Intentions that are being carried
out with alarming frequency throughout the south.

Russo continues to read, his breathing growing more shallow.
When he has read the last word, he sets the page down on one
side of his desk, and with a trembling hand, takes out a fresh
piece of vellum. He dips his quill into the inkwell, and, watching
each drop spill as he taps the quill against the bottle's edge, he
vows he will capture every black heart beating in Agostino's
band and in the villagers who joined in the uprising, and he
will make them pay for their treasonous ways.

He begins writing furiously. Tomorrow, he will set out with
his rifle regiment to the village of San Luca. There, he will post
a notice to the public and conduct a thorough investigation in
the village. No villager will be excluded. By daylight's end, he
should have some of those black hearts in the palm of his hand.

Russo smiles in satisfaction as his carefully chosen words fly
across the page. When he sets down his quill, his breathing has
steadied, along with his hand, and he feels the usual fluttering of anticipation stirring in his abdomen. *It will be a good
fight*, he tells himself, glancing out the window at the setting
sun. He watches its amber halo stretching across the forested
mountains, illuminating the dark tips. It almost looks like a
path of fire that has spread across the ridge. Anxious now to
leave the station, he quickly rereads the page before him.

PUBLIC NOTICE

Having been placed in charge of the repression of brigandage in
the territory of Greater Calabria South, the undersigned attests
that anyone found to have proffered assistance, sustenance, or
shelter to any known brigand, will be immediately shot. Anyone
labouring on outlying farms will take measures to abandon their

post until further notice. Any farmhouse or shelter that is not being used by the forces of law must be abandoned within three days and boarded up so as not to be used to harbour a wanted outlaw. All the bales of straw must be burned. Every proprietor is expected to withdraw all his workers, shepherds, goatherds, existing cattle, sheep, goats, etcetera, from the woodlands around Stilo, Pazzano, Bivongi, Caulonia, Monasterace, Riace, Camini, Gioiosa Ionica, Calvino, Locri, Gerace and Roccella Ionica.

Anyone found wandering the outskirts of his village with food or supplies will be treated as an accomplice in brigand activities, and therefore shot. Hunting will be against the law for the time being; shooting is prohibited, unless it is a warning of the presence or escape of brigands. Those providing refuge, or knowing of the whereabouts of brigands, and not advising the civil, military, or legal authorities, will be shot. Those in contravention of any of the above specified orders will be treated, without exception, as brigands, and immediately shot. As head of the forces of repression in this territory, the undersigned is authorized to commission a bounty for the death or capture of any brigand chief and his band.

At present, the undersigned offers five thousand lire for the death or capture of the brigand chief Agostino Pizzelli and two thousand lire for the death or capture of any of the members in his band. Under the command of the undersigned, there are but two parties: brigands and those against brigands. A reward will be proffered for any brigand not above mentioned, whether rendered dead or alive. The same reward will be given to the brigand who kills a member in his band, with the further recompense of having his life spared. Of special interest to the undersigned is the brigand responsible for the attack upon my carriage in the previous month, and for whose capture the sum of eight thousand lire will be granted, as well as two thousand lire for each and every member of his band. The undersigned advises that this ordinance will take effect immediately, on this, the 11th day of March in the year 1862.

Lieutenant Colonel Michele Russo

Russo nods, satisfied. He can't wait to relay this latest development to Liliana. He feels a corner of his mouth lifting. She will want him to describe his every move in advance. That's what he loves about her; she *always* knows what will excite him.

STEFANO IS AWARE THAT THE LAST MEMBER to join his band is staring at him intensely, but he does not reciprocate her gaze. He extracts a side of roast hare, savouring the partially charred meat with satisfaction. After taking another generous swallow of the musky wine, one he recognizes as the local Greco, he sets down the bottle and meets the woman's gaze.

Dorotea. In the dim glow of firelight, her eyes appear inky black like the smouldering coals, but Stefano knows that in the light of day, they are a pale, silver-green, like the foliage of olive trees. Below them, permanent shadows hang like scythes. Although she is but twenty-seven, thin strands of grey have started to appear through her hair, which she usually binds in a single braid. She tends to wear a bandana, and the colourful strip of cloth, tied in a knot at the side, gives her the aspect of a gypsy, revealing her angular features: prominent cheekbones, a curved, jutting nose, and thin, pale lips. Her heritage is *grecanico,* her Greek ancestors having settled in the Ionian coastal village of Bova around the time of the millennium. The language of her people is a guttural exhalation that has been proudly preserved from generation to generation. Hers is the only southern dialect of which Stefano has no grasp.

Besides the burst of colour of her bandana, Dorotea's clothes are otherwise drab. A grey woollen vest under a loose waistcoat drapes over a boyish figure, and the trousers she dons are ill fitting as well, all previously belonging to her late husband, Paolo.

Stefano has occasionally wondered what drew Paolo to this woman. At first sight, she is unattractive and sullen. Her uncanny ability to disappear or appear out of nowhere reminds Stefano of a skittering salamander. Although young in age, her outlook and demeanour appear jaded and old. Stefano has come to realize that allowing Dorotea to join his band with her husband has turned out to be more of a detriment than an advantage....

After taking another swallow of the wine, Stefano turns and nods at Dorotea. In the firelight, her olive skin looks flushed; perhaps she has imbibed more than usual. A gleam at the top of her boots reveals a dagger with an alabaster handle. Paolo's.

Paolo was proud of his collection of daggers and pistols. His mother had sewn special pockets within his vest to enable him to carry them with him at all times. Paolo had recounted laughingly to the band how his mother had sent one of his brothers up the slopes of the Aspromonte mountains one Sunday, dressed as a shepherd, pretending to look for a lost sheep. She had instructed the boy, Carlo, to wear the vest she had made for Paolo under his garments until he met up with an old friend of Paolo's—a withered old man who tended the horses and stables for one of the *signori*.

The man could be found in his hut about a quarter of a mile up the slope, near the Black Gorge, so named for its intimidating depths. The hut would be easily recognizable, not for the structure itself, which looked like any other shepherd's hut, but for the huge, enclosed garden flanking it. The old man tended to it every moment that he could, and it provided him with an abundance of bounty, some of which he shared with the peasants of the area, or on some occasions, with any brigands who might be passing through and in need of a little sustenance. He had an understanding with them, providing for their needs in exchange for some coins, or occasionally, a gold trinket. Once in a while, the old man would venture further up the slopes, knowing that it would be dangerous for the brigands to approach his hut, as the *carabinieri* would be combing the area after a tip or a roadside robbery.

With a loaded basket in hand, filled with cabbages, potatoes, onions, chick peas or lentils, and the occasional flask of oil or wine, he would enter seemingly impenetrable sections of the wooded slopes, and after some time, return with an empty basket. The old man's coins or gold would be concealed within his own ragged clothes.

Paolo had sent word to his mother that this man was to be trusted implicitly. She sent Carlo with the concealed vest, a sack of potatoes, a round of coarse bread, and a warning—he was to say that he was searching for wild mushrooms if he came upon the forces of law or anyone who looked suspicious.

Carlo had found the old man, Paolo recounted, and the exchange of vest and food was made, after which the old man's goat proceeded to butt Carlo and nudge him away from the property. Startled, Carlo had stumbled and the goat was upon him, until the old man, guffawing, had sent the goat scuttling off with a brisk tap of his staff. The old man helped Carlo up and seeing the fright in the boy's eyes, calmed him with a cup of wine and sent him back home with a bag of wild fennel, chicory, and lentils.

When Paolo met the old man the next day on the wooded slope, they shared a convivial drink, and Paolo set off to return to the brigand camp with the provisions Carlo had brought, but not before examining the vest and discovering its array of pockets, one of which held a dagger that he recognized as a gift given to his father by a grateful employer.

And now it is strapped to the leg of Dorotea, who has made good use of it since Paolo's death. Stefano's eyes narrow at one memory of Dorotea clasping the polished handle with blood dripping from the shaft, her silver-green eyes glowing with triumph after extracting the heart of a hare captured and killed by Gaetano. And blood, purple-red like the pulpy core of prickly pears, beginning to coagulate on her face and hands after eating the raw organ. It was a family tradition, she explained once to a horrified Tomaso, who had come upon her in the middle of her ritual. Tomaso had shared his discovery with Stefano, and since then, the memory always seems to return whenever Dorotea is nearby.

Stefano catches Tomaso's eye and flicks his hand at the smouldering embers. Tomaso nods and reaches for a crude metal pitcher. He pours the last of the water into the coals. At the subsequent hiss and rising plume of smoke, the rest of the band members rise and retreat to their respective resting places. Stefano is aware that Dorotea is lingering purposefully, with the pretence of picking up traces of their meal from the forest floor. When she casts a sidelong glance at his tent and then back at him, Stefano raises his eyebrows.

She has pulled the bandana off her head, and her coarse hair has tumbled around her face, softening its angular appearance. She opens her mouth, then clamps it shut into a forbidding twist before turning and proceeding stiffly into a cleft of trees.

Stefano waits until she has disappeared and listens as she settles down onto her bed of dry bracken. He clambers up and around the mountainside to his hut. It backs onto the outcrop and is held up by a series of intertwined branches and sturdy tree limbs. A blanket is suspended in the narrow doorway. He cocks his head, attentive for several moments, assessing each snap and crackle in the distance, each thud on the forest floor. He is no stranger to the tread of a badger, the nimble tap of a leaping deer. He can distinguish the piping call of a goshawk from a kestrel, a short-toed eagle from a sparrow hawk.

Satisfied that the noises he hears originate from the creatures of the forest and not from human pursuit, he enters his hut and stretches out on a bed of soft bracken over which he has spread a well-worn blanket his mother had made. He fingers it absent-mindedly now, his mind too preoccupied to succumb to sleep. The blanket is comforting, and he runs his hand over the weave repeatedly, aware now that the only sound around him is the thudding of his heart.

Dorotea would be happy if he returned to her and invited her back to his hut on some invented pretence. She had wept profusely for days after her husband's hasty burial in an obscure mountain grave, but Stefano has noticed that her eyes have long dried, and there is a piercing luminosity in those grey-green depths that up to now he has tried to deny.

The thought that she is his for the taking causes him to suck in his breath. He is aware that he has gone without the touch of a woman for far too long. He feels his fists clenching and unclenching. Scenes flash in succession under his closed lids: Dorotea stroking a dead rabbit caught by Gaetano before plunging her own dagger into its still warm flesh, smiling at the subsequent gush of blood; Dorotea sticking her hand into its chest cavity and tugging and snapping muscle and sinew to extract the creature's heart; Dorotea crossing herself before plopping the dripping organ into her mouth; Dorotea closing the gaping cavity and looking furtively about before slinking back into the woods, thinking nobody has witnessed her.

Stefano's jaw tightens. He has never encouraged Dorotea. *And never will.*

PART IV:
PREPARATIONS
August 1862

DON SIMONE PLUCKS AN APPLE from the first in a line of fruit trees that border the church property and hang over into the abandoned property of a villager who has left the country. He hands over the treat to Vittorio and with a chuckle, leads the mule over to the stables.

He gives thanks to God for his equine companion and for another successful mission.

Not that he was able to cure old Farmer Rocco of his heart failure in the neighbouring hamlet of Riace; no, not even the doctor could do that. But at least he had arrived in time to administer the last rights to the poor man and to anoint him with the holy oil since the regular priest was away on a spiritual retreat. Every soul deserved a final spiritual cleansing before leaving the earthly world, and nothing pleased him more than to see the gratitude and relief mirrored in a dying man's eyes as he performed the ritual.

He always looked for it, that momentary gleam that brightens like a burning ember before it is snuffed out. Don Simone is aware that many people have difficulty staring into the eyes of someone who is dying, but it is such moments that give him satisfaction in his chosen vocation.

He likes to think of himself as attending to the matters of the spirit. By elevating the spirit of others, whether on the verge of death, or in more mundane situations, he in turn feels his spirit elevated. And though he knows that he should not seek any rewards for himself in carrying out his priestly duties, he cannot help but feel rewarded.

He feels especially tired. After arriving at the poor farmer's bedside, it took two hours to administer the sacrament of the sick because of the family's intermittent sobs and lamentations, another hour to console them after the farmer took his last breath, and yet another hour to return to Camini in the sweltering mid-afternoon heat. He would have arrived earlier had he ridden Vittorio, but he had chosen to walk alongside the animal, taking pauses at natural springs along the way.

He does this on every journey, wanting to ease the burden for the poor beast, and in doing so, prolong his faithful companion's life. He does it also to fulfill a lifelong vow to the Blessed Virgin since he left the parish of San Bartolomeo, for it was *she* who had appeared in his dreams, entreating him to embrace a life of service in areas of darkness. And he, in return, had mustered the courage to leave a position of comfort and security to embark upon a journey and destination wrought with danger and disease. He had prayed for her protection with the promise that if he arrived safely, and could carry out his spiritual duties, he would venerate her by demonstrating personal sacrifices weekly, if not daily.

So, one day, he would go without a meal; another day, he would double his prayers; yet another, he would walk barefoot to the sanctuary of the Blessed Virgin at the cemetery. Don Simone is proud of the fact that in the ten years that he has been in Camini, he has honoured his vows. He is certain that in doing so, the Holy Mother is interceding with God on his behalf to keep him healthy and strong, in order to continue his spiritual mission in Camini.

He may not undertake the heavy, physical tasks of the farmers and land labourers, but he makes sure that he reinforces his body as he does his soul, walking countless hours between the neighbouring villages, often choosing to traverse the rougher terrain of mountain paths and mule tracks instead of the well-trodden roads. He likes to think that this activity keeps his physical muscles stretched, while he undertakes the mission of stretching his spiritual muscles in daily prayer and meditation.

He is feeling the effects of his walk today and is relishing a quiet evening after a rejuvenating meal that Gabriella is sure to have prepared. In all likelihood, the Fantin brothers will be dining in Stilo tonight, as Signor Claudio planned, after consulting with the pharmacist.

He smiles contently as he leads Vittorio into the barn. Despite the satisfaction of conducting his priestly duties in the sprawling countryside, Don Simone feels no greater happiness than returning to his own parish and family. Gabriella, Luciano, and Lorenzo are truly his family, and he gives thanks daily that he, unlike so many in the brotherhood, is not inclined to live in solitude.

Amidst the usual bleating and snorting among the animals in their enclosures, an unfamiliar noise captures his attention. Don Simone stands rooted to the spot, trying to determine its origin, and realizes that the muffled groans and gasps are coming from the far end of the barn, and that they sound chillingly *human*.

He drops Vittorio's reins and rushes through the shadowy pathway to the sounds, which have become long, despairing sobs. Cries of lament. *What has happened? Is it Luciano? Gabriella? Mother of Jesus, help us. Ave Maria, piena di grazia, il Signore è con te....*

Gabriella is barely recognizable. She is gathered in a quivering heap on the ground, her straw-matted hair strewn over her face and shoulders, her garments are torn and blood-splattered, her body is shaking....

"*O Dio mio!*" Don Simone lunges forward when he realizes that the dark hump on the ground by Gabriella is Lorenzo. His eyes fly to the crimson halo around Lorenzo's head and his stomach recoils as if a deliberately clenched fist has made a heart-stopping impact. He falls to his knees and grabs Gabriella by the shoulders. Her sobs catch in her throat, and she gasps for breath. Don Simone looks straight at her, but her eyes are glazed, the whites laced with erupted blood vessels. His hands slide down to grip hers, and when they make contact, he feels their sticky dampness.

"Gabriella," he cries, unable to hide his anguish. "What... *how* did this happen?"

His words are like a slap. She recoils and blinks at him wordlessly, before staring at her father's rigid body. A moment later, she looks up and Don Simone follows her gaze to the loft, his heart lurching at the figure sprawled on the floor. He rises and lifting the hem of his cassock, trudges up to the loft. He feels his knees quiver as his eyes run over the still body of Alfonso Fantin, partially illuminated by the light streaming in through the window. For a moment, Don Simone's eyes follow the dust motes floating about in the air, hovering over the dead body like disembodied souls. His eyes return to Alfonso's neck wound, the streaks of concealing blood on his shirt, the stark whiteness of his trunk and loins. The bloodied shaft of the knife on the straw-scattered floor.

The bile in his throat rises as he takes in Gabriella's torn frock, her heaving bosom. He wilfully shuts those thoughts down; he needs to remove Gabriella from the barn. There is nobody else who can see to her well-being now.

He descends the steps two at a time. Kneeling down by Lorenzo, he makes the sign of the cross. "O God, the Creator and Redeemer of all the faithful, give to the soul of Lorenzo Falcone, Thy servant departed, the remission of his sins: that, through the help of our pious supplications, he may obtain the pardon he has always desired. May he rest in eternal peace and divine light, united with all your Saints. *Per Cristo nostro Signore.* Amen."

"*Papà!*" Gabriella flings herself over the inert body, erupting again into sobs, her eyes flashing with a wildness Don Simone has never seen her display, not even at the death of her mother.

My poor orphan. He gently extricates her from her father. *Of what earthly offences could you possibly be guilty to deserve such a cruel destiny?*

Supporting her quaking body, he leads her out of the dank recesses of the barn. The sun, which flickered briefly while they were in the barn, has begun to recede, and the clouds seem to be propping themselves against its luminous face in dark triumph. Don Simone feels their darkening shadows replicate themselves on his spirit. He needs to keep his mind clear, so he can figure out how he is to deal with the ramifications of the death of Lorenzo and Alfonso, but he cannot help but feel overwhelmed.

"Come." He adjusts her fallen shawl over her shivering body. "You must come with me. I will tend to your dear father afterwards." *And may our heavenly Father tend to us all in the hell to come.*

He staggers forward, biting his lip so hard that he tastes blood.

"OH, IF ONLY YOU HAD BEEN WITH US IN SICILY...." Tonino's gaze shifts from the path they are walking to the man beside him, Massimo. "You remind me of my youngest brother," Massimo continues wistfully. "I left, and now he's the man of the family. Papà died in the Battle of Volturno."

Tonino bows his head respectfully. So, Massimo's father had been a Redshirt as well, his blood shed for the cause of Unification. And now Massimo is fighting for the cause, undeterred by the possibility of sacrificing his life.

"*Sei coraggioso,*" Tonino murmurs respectfully,

"If we don't have courage, how will anything change?" Massimo looks up at the sky that is brightening with the sunrise. "We can't expect our women to fight our battles."

"Do you have a woman?" Massimo can't be but five or six years older than himself; surely he has a girl back home, or perhaps even a wife, even though there is no band on his left hand.

Massimo shakes his head. "I have been too busy being a father to my six younger brothers and sisters; I get up three hours before dawn to get to the fields. The Baron was good enough to offer me work when he heard the news about my father, who had served him faithfully for years. By the time I get back to my village, it is dusk, and there are countless jobs to do. I have no time to court anyone. And besides, what could I offer her right now? A bed to share with six others?" He laughs, but Tonino hears the edge of bitterness. "And *you*, Tonino?"

Tonino feels himself flushing. His pace slows, and he looks straight at the rising sun, a haze of pink and orange. "Her name is Gabriella," he hears himself saying and bites his lip. He has this sudden urge to weep, not only for himself for having left Gabriella, but for all the men who felt compelled to leave their loved one for the cause. For Garibaldi.

"Gabriella," Massimo repeats, and Tonino is almost jealous of the way it sounds on Massimo's lips. He's not sure if he wants to share her with anyone. "What were you saying about Sicily?" he changes the subject, his voice less vulnerable.

"Ah, yes," Massimo's eyes look up at the sky again. "Sicily. When the General and his followers arrived in Marsala, my hometown, he was greeted as if he were the resurrected Jesus. The screaming; the women weeping and holding their babies up to him; the men leaping up to touch him; the flowers flung reverently at his feet. And the music! Bands playing as if there would be no tomorrow! I can still see the men blowing with all their might on their bagpipes, their cheeks inflating and deflating, as red as our shirts! Everyone watching the General's every move. Then he disappeared and a moment later he stepped out onto a balcony overlooking the square. Everyone hushed. It seemed that even the birds and the animals knew to be still. It was like the night when Jesus was born, and the creatures and Wise Men were gazing upon the newborn with awe and wonder. I tell you, Tonino, it gave everyone goosebumps.

"And when the General cried out, 'Either Rome or death!' the silence lasted for another second, and then it was like the stars came crashing down on earth, so great was the resounding cry from the people, and yes, even the birds and the animals. If ever I doubted the mission before, well, *that* night, my doubts disappeared."

Massimo has stopped walking. He resembles a great orator, his eyes glazed in fervour, his arms outstretched, fingers splayed. The others have passed them; they are the last in line. Tonino stops and sits on a nearby stump.

"Like the fishermen who dropped their nets to follow Jesus, my Sicilian brothers made haste to join the great Giuseppe Garibaldi in his mission to liberate Rome. And when we arrived in Catania, another crowd of joyful well-wishers! The General ordered two packet ships seized in the harbour—the *Abbattucci* and the *Dispaccio*. I'll never forget the look on his face as he stood watching us cram into the ships that would shortly take us across the Strait of Messina."

Massimo shakes his head in wonder. "He was our father, his cheeks glistening with pride, his eyes burning like a lion watching his cubs. We had no doubt that he would defend us to the last. And knowing that he would lay down his life for us, for Italy, how could we not do the same for *him*?" With a tremulous sigh, Massimo raises his arm to the sky, which is now streaked with ribbons of red. "*Viva* Giuseppe Garibaldi!" he cries. "And long live United Italy!"

GABRIELLA HAS A SLIGHT BUILD, but her inert body feels like an unyielding mass of granite as Don Simone all but carries her into the rectory. Her animal-like sobs have subsided and her face, although streaked with tears, has acquired the look of an emotionless alabaster mask, like the ones sold at country fairs. He glances at the narrow steps leading upstairs to Gabriella and Luciano's room, and with a prayer on his lips, begins the ascent.

After depositing Gabriella onto her bed, he hurries out of the room, all too aware that she is lapsing into shock. He returns immediately with a flask of *grappa* that one of his parishioners regularly brings him after unloading his conscience at Confession.

"Those who do the Lord's work need extra strength," Farmer Picone assures Don Simone every time he drops by. "Besides, I swore on my blessed wife's grave that I would serve the Church for the rest of my life, if only to guarantee her soul's arrival in Paradise."

Don Simone begins to pray for the ascent of Lorenzo Falcone's soul into heaven and for a sign from Gabriella that her spirit has not died with her father. He has no delusions about the abject state her soul must be in at the present time and he will do everything he can in his capacity as priest and closest family friend to save Gabriella from the hellfire that has begun to consume her. As for Alfonso Fantin, perhaps the landowner's soul has already begun its descent into hell for what he has done. He shudders, feeling his stomach twist at the thought of Fantin's inert body lying on the floor of the loft with bits of straw stuck to his loins.

Don Simone lifts Gabriella's head slightly off the pillow and presses the flask to her lips. Her eyes are fluttering, and as she utters a low groan, he takes advantage of her partially open mouth to tip the flask. She sputters and chokes. Her body spasms as the fiery liquid sears a path through her innards. He feels like the devil himself, putting her through this, but he knows that the outcome will be worth it.

"Please forgive me, *cara mia,*" he murmurs as her shuddering subsides and she falls back on the pillow, "but this will help you, I promise." He reaches for the extra blanket folded neatly at the foot of her pallet and drapes it over her. Satisfied that her cheeks have been restored of some colour, and that she will settle into a state of rest, Don Simone descends the stairs and returns to his own room, his mind a jumble of thoughts.

Consumed with sudden anxiety, he takes a good swallow of the *grappa* and sets the flask down on his dresser before dropping to his knees. He must, first of all, pray for a clear mind, he decides, shutting his eyes. For he alone must think of how to save Gabriella from the hands of the law for the murder of Signor Alfonso Fantin, despite the fact it was obviously committed in self-defence. A wealthy landowner from the North, knifed by a peasant from the South. Don Simone has no delusions about Gabriella's fate. If she has any fortune at all, if the Holy Family and all the saints and the heavenly angels are uniting in her favour, the best she might hope for is life imprisonment.

In which case, a sentence to hang might be the most merciful judgment given to her.

DON SIMONE SNAPS HIS SATCHEL SHUT, satisfied with the provisions that he has selected: a flask of wine, a hunk of cheese, several links of cured sausage, and a half-dozen apricots. And in a separate pocket, his breviary.

He procures three wool blankets from the chest in his bedroom, then scans the room to see if he has forgotten anything. His gaze brushes the wardrobe opposite his bed, and he crosses the room in three paces to retrieve a hunting knife. He deposits it in a pocket within his cassock, murmurs a prayer to the oversized walnut crucifix hanging above his bed, and scurries out of the room and through the back door of the rectory to ready the cart in preparation for their journey.

Vittorio gives him a welcoming snort, and Don Simone pats him affectionately.

"No rest for us tonight, my friend," he murmurs. "We have important work to do."

Don Simone arranges the blankets over a thick pallet of straw lining the cart, wedges the satchel in one corner, hitches up Vittorio—whose ready compliance gives him cause to utter a grateful "Glory Be"—and heads to the rectory to carry out his final task, getting Gabriella and Luciano out of the house and away from Camini before the authorities become aware of the situation and attempt to apprehend Gabriella.

Darkness has never frightened or worried him before; his faith has always bolstered him during his nighttime trips. On this particular night, however, he cannot but feel a disturbing apprehension of forces that are out of his control. He feels the hair on his arms rising as the night breeze passes over him; he likens it to the breath of a malevolent spirit. The dampness of the earth fills his nostrils with a woody, visceral scent that reminds him of freshly dug graves. Even the moon seems menacing with its luminous grin curving mockingly from under the black blanket of sky. Shivering, he hastens to enter the rectory.

Earlier, shortly after he left Gabriella in a dejected heap on her pallet, Luciano burst into the rectory with flushed cheeks and wisps of straw enmeshed in his hair. Don Simone suspected he had been playing near the reeds by the river with his friends, and was about to scold him, but then stopped short. The boy's guilty look turned to one of confusion when Don Simone smiled, holding out his arms. Luciano walked tentatively over to him.

"Come here, young man," Don Simone urged softly, drawing Luciano closer. "I have something I must tell you. You must be strong.... There has been an accident. Your father fell down and hit his head." Don Simone's arms tightened around Luciano and he tried to hold back his tears. "Your Papà died instantly. He is with God in heaven now."

A sharp sob in the doorway announced Gabriella's presence. Luciano ran crying to her, and she dropped down to her knees and clasped him. Don Simone met her alarmed gaze. He jnstinctively understood that she didn't want him to mention Signor Fantin. He walked over and embraced them. Swallowing hard, he advised Gabriella to pack a few items of clothing for her and Luciano; they would be journeying to a place where they would be taken care of for an indefinite time.

Don Simone watches Gabriella reappear with her arm around Luciano's quivering shoulders. She pauses at the window at the top of the stairs, staring frozenly at the barn. He swallows hard. "Come, my dear children," he calls out, trying to keep his voice strong. "Vittorio is hitched up and waiting for us."

WITH EVERY JOLT OF THE CART OVER THE RUTS In the mule path, Gabriella feels something plummet within her. As they continue to descend the mountainside, she peers behind her and in the charcoal mist sees the dim twinkle of candles still burning in Camini, their configuration eerily resembling a cross. Convinced it is a bad omen, Gabriella shivers and makes the sign of the cross herself. How she wishes she could run to Tonino, collapse in his arms, let him comfort her and protect her. But how can *he* possibly protect her and Luciano? Where could he bring them to avoid the authorities? No, much as it is tearing apart her very soul to be skulking away like this with Don Simone, she knows it is the only way to avoid a life in prison, a life without Luciano. And a life with Tonino was already uncertain, given his decision to join Garibaldi's army.

How quickly a life can shatter. She feels hot tears streaming over her cheeks and doesn't bother to wipe them. *Life is so cruel, promising something with one breath and snatching it away with the next.*

She repositions herself on the mound of straw on top of which she and Luciano are huddled and draws one of the blankets around herself and her brother, who has finally succumbed to sleep. Her arm tightens around his slight body. She stares numbly at the mule's back side as it ploughs its way forward. A breeze passes over them from the nearby Ionian Sea, and Gabriella opens her mouth to gulp at the air; her lungs feel as shrivelled as the figs hanging in the cellar. The clapping of Vittorio's hooves on the ground reverberates around them, and she squints around her fearfully, expecting the police to jump out from behind the cypresses or prickly pear bushes lining the path.

A sob catches in her throat at the sight of Don Simone, his black cassock draped around his slightly bent body, walking alongside Vittorio. Don Simone, who has put everything aside to bring her and Luciano to a safe haven, and who has always been more than just an employer to Papà, and to Gabriella—he has been a trusted friend—now has the burden of taking care of them.

Orfani. That is what she and Luciano have become. Orphans lost in a storm.

The dampness of the earth rises to pervade her senses. Gabriella can tell they are near the river. Although she can't see it beyond the thick canopy of chestnut trees over the narrow path, the scent of the river tickles her nostrils like a dampened feather. Gabriella hears it slurp and gush now, and immediately thinks of Vincenzino and the tales of how the devil pulled him into the river and caused him to drown. A flash of red explodes in front of her eyes and she squeezes them shut, trying to prevent the image of the devil from attaching itself to her memory. But her eyes betray her, and she sees the alternating face of a scarlet demon and the red jowls of Alfonso Fantin.

A scurrying through the bushes makes her straighten in alarm. Since her childhood, she has heard stories of wolves, wild boars, gypsies, and brigands. Again, her eyes seek the figure of Don Simone, and his steady gait reassures her that the noises are nothing to be concerned about—perhaps a hare or quail.

Her heartbeats subside, and despite her resolution to never forgive God for allowing her Papà to be taken from her, she starts to recite the *Ave Maria* silently. Closing her eyes, she feels the presence of a quieting, calming hand, and without a doubt in her mind, she senses that her own mother, Elisabetta, is with her. Gabriella fishes for her mother's handkerchief in her pocket and wipes her tears. Letting out a long, drawn-out breath, she allows herself to drift to sleep.

VITTORIO'S HOOVES ARE DRAGGING, Don Simone realizes. The poor beast has more than doubled his usual working distance and if he is not given a rest, he will be useless. It is nearing midnight, and they have managed, with the Good Lord's help, to reach the mid-point of their destination.

The Monastery of the Capuchins of Gerace is roughly fourteen kilometres away, but much as he would like to proceed, Don Simone knows that it is imperative to give Vittorio a reprieve. He scans the moonlit sky, murmuring a prayer in reverent gratitude for its illumination. The journey thus far has been miraculously uneventful. Vittorio has plodded along tenaciously, manoeuvring the light-dappled mule path with a fortitude that brings a lump to Don Simone's throat.

He shudders at the thought of the perils and tragedies that have plagued other travellers such as stumbling over a fallen tree, the collapse of mule and cart in an indiscernible rut, a path washed out by torrential rains, a life-threatening encounter with a wild boar, or a sudden attack by brigands. No, thank God, they have met with none of those evils, and as far as Don Simone has been able to discern, there is nobody following them. *Yet.*

He glances back at Gabriella and Luciano as the cart comes to a stop. They are huddled together, but even several layers of blankets cannot stop the damp forest air from creeping through, and they are shifting uncomfortably.

Don Simone dismounts and leads Vittorio over to a black entrance, the first of a series of caves in the Gallica Valley. He knows this area quite well; it has served as a stopping point along his journey to and from his monthly retreat at the Monastery of the Capuchins. The Gallica caves have been chiselled out of granite outcrops at the base of the Gallica foothills, which are surrounded by woodlands and herald the start of the Aspromonte range.

Don Simone usually indulges in a brief rest here at mid-journey, enjoying a solitary picnic with Vittorio before meandering off for a contemplative walk among the ancient oaks, beeches, chestnuts, and pines. He particularly loves the autumn when he saunters off with a burlap sack to collect the abundant chestnuts that he knows will be enjoyed by the entire Falcone family upon his return, usually around the time of the feast of the *castagnata*.

He is pleased that they have reached this point. He explains to Gabriella, whose face is drawn and pale under wisps of hair that are now threaded with straw, that he will build a fire, and they will rest for several hours before moving on. He instructs her to bring down all the blankets and to set them in a corner of the cave. Gabriella is still in a state of shock, but he deliberately speaks to her as if nothing has changed in their lives, as if they are still at the rectory. He will not, *cannot,* show any sign that he is in shock himself, that his spirit has been shattered, that he wants to scream out the agony of his tormented soul into the silence of the night. No, that is a matter between him and God.

There will be time for mourning, as right now, he has other tasks of importance. He feels his gut clenching at the sight of Luciano, scrawny and sleepy-eyed, his breeches torn and muddied. He pushes away any further thoughts and busies himself assembling a fire at the mouth of the cave with a bag of kindling he keeps in the cart. As the flames catch the twigs and start to burn, the growing heat is absorbed into the cave. Satisfied with his effort, Don Simone pats Vittorio, who has settled down on a leaf-strewn patch of ground, before returning to huddle next to Gabriella and Luciano.

To their advantage, a granite outcrop juts over the top of the cave, providing a shield from the rain that decides at that moment to come down in a fine drizzle that reminds Don Simone of the sizzling of the *frittuli* in the cauldron after the hog slaughter. Although the drops splatter into the fire, causing it to sizzle and smoke, it remains intact, and Don Simone finds himself uttering a "Glory Be" that the weather has co-operated up to now. Even Vittorio is protected by a thick canopy of chestnut trees, unruffled by the momentary rainfall.

Don Simone glances edgewise at Luciano. The boy's eyes are luminous, long lashes blinking into the mesmerizing flames, body pressed into the protective curve of Gabriella's arm and shoulder. Gabriella's face is stony, and her eyes glassy and dark as coal. She, too, is looking trance-like into the fire, with her free arm stroking Luciano's head and temple softly, incessantly, as if she needs him to feel her touch, to know that he has not lost everyone, that he is not alone in this cold, dark world.

Don Simone senses that it is futile to say anything to Gabriella at this moment. And what would he say, anyway? That losing her father was God's will? That God deemed it necessary to deprive her of her mother *and* her father for reasons that mere humans could not possibly understand? That she needed to be strong, to keep her faith in God? Don Simone grimaces. His mind shuffles through countless sermons he has given the congregation of Camini in the aftermath of a personal or communal tragedy and the dozens of Bible quotes that he has triumphantly recited from memory, standing on the pulpit with a sea of faces reflecting alternating waves of sorrow and despair.

"'And the Lord, He is the one who goes before you. He will be with you. He will not leave you nor forsake you, do not fear nor be dismayed.'"

"'Blessed be the Father of our Lord Jesus Christ, the God of all comfort, who comforts us in all our tribulation, that we may be able to comfort those who are in any trouble.'"

And his favourite: "'The Lord is my shepherd; I shall not want. He maketh me lie down in green pastures; he leadeth me beside still waters. He restoreth my soul. He leadeth me in paths of righteousness for His name's sake. Even though I walk through the valley of the shadow of death, I will fear no evil; for thou art with me; thy rod and thy staff, they comfort me.'"

Back in Camini, Don Simone knew that some of his parishioners were on the verge of severing their belief in a just God;

he could practically see it disintegrating before his eyes, flickering desperately in the storms of their own eyes. But what a miracle it was to see some of those dying embers brightening with hope after his fervent recital from the Bible. Even if his words only bolstered one member of his congregation, Don Simone felt that his life's mission as a servant of God had been accomplished.

But they aren't in Church now. He's not at the pulpit. Reciting passages from the Bible at this time, no matter how well-intentioned, would not be the right thing to do. He frowns, pondering what *would* be the right thing to do. He glances up at the sky, which has ceased its sprinkling, and he proceeds to spread the blankets out in the cave. He rolls one into a makeshift pillow and leaves another to serve as a covering. "Please try to get some sleep for a few hours," he murmurs. "We will be safe. I will keep the fire going and wake you before dawn. *Please.*"

Gabriella turns wordlessly at his supplication. She glances at Luciano, whose eyes are drooping and she nods, shifting so that she can transfer his body down onto the blankets. Without another word, she lies next to him and pulls the extra blanket over them. Don Simone nods and makes the sign of the cross gratefully. The fire has taken the dampness out of the cave, and although it is not the most ideal sleeping arrangement, it will serve them well for several hours.

With a torrent of conflicting thoughts spiralling through his mind, he does the only thing he can think of to stop it; he extracts his rosary beads from the pocket of his cassock and starts reciting silently.

TONINO FEELS HIMSELF EXPELLING a long, drawn-out breath. "And when you landed on the mainland...?" He rises from the stump to continue walking with Massimo.

Massimo's face loses its look of rapture as he explains that upon first landing in the town of Melito di Porto Salvo on the twenty-fifth of August, they were hard-pressed to find any supporters. The locals made themselves scarce, showing their reluctance to bring provisions or invitations of hospitality, unlike the crowds that had swarmed them at Marsala and Catania. The volunteers became aware of rumours that the government in Turin was intent on stopping Garibaldi from securing the liberation of Rome.

King Victor Emmanuel II had issued a proclamation stating that *he*, and he alone would be the one to make a decision on liberating Rome, and that he would oppose anyone who proceeded to assemble a private army for such a cause without his authorization. Any such individual would be guilty of high treason as he would be foolishly waging civil war, and the Royal troops would be sent immediately to intercept them. The locals, who had started to hear accusations against Garibaldi as being a traitor, were reluctant to show any support, lest they be arrested by officials of the Royal Army in pursuit of Garibaldi.

"We could feel their uncertainty," Massimo shakes his head. "And in here, too," he pats his belly. "They gave us no baskets of bread or figs. No offers of shelter. No cheers or cries of '*Viva Garibaldi!*'" He spat to one side, as if trying to rid himself of the bitter taste in his mouth at the Calabrians' lack of welcome.

"We kept marching until we got to the outskirts of the town," he answers Tonino's unspoken question. "We kept telling ourselves that King Victor Emmanuel didn't mean what he said, and that he was secretly backing Garibaldi, as he had done in 1860, which had allowed Garibaldi to liberate the Kingdom of the Two Sicilies from Bourbon rule. And when we stopped, Garibaldi leapt on a boulder and looked down upon us, each one of us, I swear—it was as if he wanted to pierce the depths of our very souls with his eyes—and he might as well have been the great Moses himself, announcing the Ten Commandments. 'If our noble King Victor was truly against us, my dear compatriots,' he boomed, 'he would have stopped us by now. The military authorities could have broken up the camp we set up in the Ficuzza forest after we landed in Sicily. Or in Marsala. Or in the port of Catania. But the authorities *didn't* put up a fight, and I have no intention of fighting against the military authorities. They are our brothers in this United Italy, not our enemies. My sole purpose is to liberate Rome from the French troops, not to wage war with my countrymen. *Ever.*'"

Massimo shakes his head in wonder. "Complete silence for five seconds, then a burst of whistles and cheers. And when we finally stopped, the General slammed his right fist in the air high above him and shouted, 'Long live Victor Emmanuel, King of our United Italy!"

A flurry of fresh goosebumps rise at the back of Tonino's neck and rush down the length of his arms. Massimo describes how they felt invigorated after the General's impassioned rhetoric and continued to march northward, but after thirty-six hours without food, some began losing their patriotic fervour. "Fortunately, we came across a potato field and feasted on raw potatoes."

Massimo winks at Tonino. "One of our volunteers from Catania was an ex-soldier from the Royal Army who had chosen not to obey General Cugia's orders to prevent Garibaldi and us from entering Catania. Sebastiano deserted and joined us on one of the packet ships. As he's stuffing himself with potatoes, he says, 'Oh, what I would give for my wife's juicy roasted hen.'

"Another guy—Alberto—says, '*I'd* give anything for his wife's juices, too.' We're killing ourselves laughing and Sebastiano's still chewing away. Then he looks up and wants to know what's so funny. Alberto tells him, 'I said there were too many cocks around here and not enough hens.'"

Tonino watches Massimo explode into laughter again, and he waits, with some embarrassment, until Massimo wipes the tears from his eyes. "The next thing we know," Massimo continues more seriously, "we get the news that the General's envoy has come across a landowner with a substantial farm and crops, who is very receptive to providing hospitality to General Garibaldi and his men."

Tonino hears how the volunteers sprinted eagerly to this farmhouse, where they were greeted with respect and geniality, given the opportunity to refresh themselves before feasting on heaping bowls of macaroni and roasted goat and lamb, slaughtered especially for their benefit. Pitchers of the local Greco wine flowed generously all evening, and when they were sated, some set about arranging their blankets in the soft wheat fields, some in the barn loft, while the General and several others were offered accommodation inside.

"But our respected leader—unbeknownst to us then—had no intention of sleeping," Massimo grins. "The landowner, Signor Nicola Gentile, had dispatched a labourer shortly after our arrival to find a certain Pietro Aji in the nearby hamlet of Camini. This Pietro was to round up some of the local men for a secret meeting with the General in his cellar."

"To recruit more volunteers." Tonino nods slowly. "Like me." His memory flashes to that feverish meeting, the hum, the smell of curing pork sausages mingling with the sweat of young men like him, bursting with the desire to be united in the cause, instinctively knowing that their strength lay in unity. And those chestnut eyes locking with his, drawing him in, ready to sacrifice all for his country. For Italy.

"We practically flew from that cellar," Tonino continues, "stealing back to our homes like robbers in the night, filling a packsack and grabbing whatever weapon we could find—a rifle, a pitchfork, a dagger, anything—and the handful of us who could write left a note for our family. And those who couldn't, didn't have to worry, because the few who didn't catch the fever that night would let the villagers know what had happened to their missing boys or men." Tonino returns Massimo's grin. "And those of us burning with fever returned to the cellar the following night and then followed the General and the farmer out of Camini and through the back country like a pack of eager hounds. After a while, we must have looked like a sad lot, dragging ourselves up and down the hillsides, the more robust novices tumbling or collapsing from the exertion. The General mercifully allowed us to rest briefly before trekking the last few kilometres back to the farm."

"And that's where you happened to set down your things next to mine, in the hayloft," Massimo chuckles. "What a surprise, waking up in the middle of the night to find your ugly face in the space next to me." He ducks away from Tonino's good-natured swipe. "Okay, you're not so ugly. I could have had the misfortune of having Sebastiano near me. Not only is he ugly, he snores as loud as the mighty Etna." They burst out laughing.

"And then," Massimo continues, "we slept a few more hours, then woke up to a magnificent breakfast prepared by the good landowners. Fresh eggs, zucchini fritters, asparagus, *frittate*." He brings his fingers up to his lips and smacks them appreciatively as he draws back his hand.

Tonino chuckles and feels his mouth water at the memory.

After feasting, he and the others watched as the landowner bowed respectfully to General Garibaldi, followed by his more expressive wife, who pitched herself at the commander's feet and planted a fervent kiss on his gloved hand. The General graciously thanked them for having granted him and his soldiers a place of refuge and repose, and for their generosity in sharing their crops and livestock. Signora Gentile jumped up and informed him that she had set aside a store of food in an adjacent barn to which he and his soldiers could help themselves for their arduous journey onward.

Flushed with pleasure at their effusive thanks after stuffing their packsacks with potatoes, pears, coarse bread, dried sausages, and hard cheeses, she watched them take their leave, crying out blessings and the occasional, "Viva Garibaldi!" In reply, General Garibaldi boomed, as he had done in Marsala, "*O*

Roma o morte!" followed by the immediate chorus of "Either Rome or death!" by his fellow soldiers and volunteers. Tonino noticed Signor Nicola, who had placed a hand on his wife's arm to curb her unrestrained patriotic fervour, dabbing at his own eyes when she loudly prayed for the successful mission and safe return of the *"beati figli della Patria."*

Being called a "blessed son of the Fatherland" brought a twinge of unexpected tears to Tonino's eyes. Squeezing them shut for a moment, reluctant to show any vulnerability in the face of his fellow soldiers, who seemed more stalwart than ever, he fell back, reluctant to talk.

His thoughts turned almost immediately to Gabriella, and he gulped at the magnitude of his decision to leave her. This was the biggest risk of his life. A tiny voice nudged a corner of his mind. *You may never return to Camini. To Gabriella.* "No!" he found himself responding, and clamping his mouth grimly, he picked up his pace to return to the line.

He didn't want to be alone with his thoughts. Dark thoughts that would break his resolve to carry out this mission. His attention shifted to the path before him. Everything around him seemed to assume a malevolence he hadn't noticed before. The forest floor, displaced by the boots of the men before him, released a dank, rotting smell that reminded Tonino of a dead body awaiting burial after the customary two-day wake. The wild bracken tangled around his ankles as he made his way through the narrow path. The trees swayed and intertwined to block out the sun, creating eerie shadows that resembled death masks. And the sudden rustle near his feet brought to mind the venomous *vipera aspis....*

And then he caught up to Massimo, who, despite his questioning look, didn't press him for an explanation. Instead, he began recounting the story of how he came to be in Garibaldi's army....

Now here they are, both having left loved ones back home, both prepared to risk their lives along with the other men who have declared their allegiance to Giuseppe Garibaldi and to the cause of United Italy.

Taking a deep breath, Tonino gives Massimo a friendly slap on the back and picks up his pace.

He prays they'll be in this together until the end....

DON SIMONE ARRANGES THE BRUSHWOOD to maintain a slow burn while avoiding the excess spiralling of smoke into the sky. He listens for any noises that might indicate that their hiding place has been discovered. But the only sounds he hears are those he has become familiar with during his travels back and forth to the Monastery of the Capuchins in Gerace. There is the scurrying of a dormouse through the foliage of the forest floor amidst the weightier shuffle of the pine and beech martens and the tentative leap of the deer. He utters a prayer of gratitude that the sound he fears—the call of the Apennine wolf, abundant in these Aspromonte mountains—has not materialized. The haunting call of an eagle-owl startles him, sending shivers down his spine.

He stands up to stretch his legs. Gabriella and Luciano have not even shifted in their positions; they seem petrified. He doesn't have the heart to move them, though. After an interminable four hours, Don Simone kneels by Gabriella and with a gentle hand on her shoulder, murmurs her name and tells her it is time for them to move on.

Gabriella wakes up with a tortured groan. Her eyes open, lashes batting frantically like a butterfly in its first flight out of its cocoon. It reminds Don Simone of a time when, walking alongside his mule on the outskirts of the village, he noticed three of his young parishioners near a grove of milkwood. They were watching a butterfly emerge from its silky chrysalis, its spindly arms and legs working furiously. The boys took turns pulling each filament off the body, along with the brightly splotched wings.

Don Simone, usually slow to anger, felt the rage swirl up

inside him. He leapt in front of the boys, his arms extended to prevent their escape.

"You should be ashamed of yourselves, you evil children. You come to Mass with your parents every Sunday, you listen to me preach about the ways of the Lord, and you...you...do *this*? Taking the life of an innocent creature, *destroying it as it is beginning its life?* God have mercy on your darkened souls, *ragazzi*, because this poor servant of Christ," he said, pounding his chest with a clenched fist, "cannot find any mercy to forgive you at this moment for your wretched disregard for life. Every creature of God, no matter how small, deserves to live, not to be tortured and killed by your hands. Thou...shalt...not... kill," he thundered, his eyes boring into each one of them.

"*You*, Leonardo." He pointed, his finger inches away from the boy. "Shame on you, *the eldest,* for setting such a poor example. And you two, Enrico and Pepe, your actions are disgraceful. I expect the three of you to ponder your sinful acts and be prepared to make amends to God, not the least of which will be your appearance at Confession." He wiped the spittle from the edge of his mouth. "Now get home, the lot of you. I'm sure you have some chores to do for your mother. And if you don't, you will after I talk to her."

The boys fled, and Don Simone's eyes returned to the butterfly wings scattered on the road, brilliant against the dark ground. *Glorious stained-glass windows.* He sighed, bending on one knee to pick them up gently, not caring if his cassock got dirty. Eyes welling, he returned to his mule, exhausted, as usual, after battling the works of the devil.

Looking at Gabriella now, drawing her shawl tighter, he cannot help but think that she, too, is as vulnerable as a butterfly. He can only pray for the strength and the Lord's help to protect her.

Wordlessly, she nods at his instructions to gather up the blankets so they can continue on to the monastery while it is still dark. Luciano is still in a deep sleep, and when Don

Simone notices Gabriella's frantic look, he kneels beside the boy and picks him up gently, waiting until Gabriella has arranged the blankets in the wagon before setting him into the soft nest. After Gabriella has covered his body with another blanket and has settled in beside him, Don Simone hitches up Vittorio and rewards him with a pear from a bag in one corner of the wagon.

To Gabriella, he offers a wedge of cheese and coarse bread, but she shakes her head, paling visibly as she puts her hand up over her mouth. Don Simone does not insist; they are close enough to the monastery, and his brothers in the Lord will provide her and Luciano with a broth to sustain them.

He urges his mule on, anxious to complete the last stretch of the journey. It is no accident that this path is barely discernible; the monastery's location has always been intended as a haven of respite and meditation, its dense walls and unforgiving location a deterrent for any but the most devoted followers. For centuries it has been a centre for Franciscan teachings, its Capuchin brotherhood a cohesive union of local youth sent there by their families in the hope of ultimately bettering their family prospects by sacrificing one of their sons to undertake the Lord's work.

Despite its elusive location, the monastery has always kept its doors open to the stray wanderer and the poor with its tradition of providing a hearty meal of soup or beans. And now, the need seems even greater, Don Filippo has mentioned, in the aftermath of Unification. The line of peasants waiting at the monastery doors has doubled.

At the first light of dawn, the sky is wreathed in sashes of pink and violet. Don Simone feels a rush of awe mingled with relief. He commands Vittorio to stop while he takes in the golden countryside from the expansive outcrop that overlooks the winding track they have navigated since leaving the cave.

Don Simone wants to shout victoriously when the dense thicket on either side of the mule path opens up suddenly and the Monastery of the Capuchins appears, nestled within the craggy folds of the mountain as if the hand of God Himself had carved out a space expressly for a glorious shrine in His honour. The mountainsides are granite curtains, hanging motionlessly like an ancient tapestry, catching the dawn's illumination in a masterpiece of *chiaroscuro*.

Don Simone prompts Vittorio into a trot and breathes in the fresh mountain air with joy and relief. The rose window of the portal above the heavy chestnut doors suddenly catches the burgeoning rays of the sun, and Don Simone bows in silent reverence, acknowledging the Chapel of the Madonna of the Rosary that claims that space above the main floor of the monastery. It is his favourite place of prayer within the monastery walls. Murmuring an *Ave Maria* in gratitude for their safe arrival, he brings Vittorio to a halt.

He has done the right thing, he tells himself as the heavy door opens and the familiar face of Don Filippo appears. Gabriella and Luciano will be safe here. *For now.*

THE BIRDS ARE PECKING OUT HIS BRAINS, their sharp beaks foraging into the grey mash that is left inside the cracked walls of his skull. Alfonso tries to scream, but his throat feels like someone has inserted a pulpy leaf from the prickly pear bush in it, its stubby thorns catching into the tender muscles and tissues of his esophagus, tearing it further with his every effort to call out. His eyes attempt to open, but a weight on each eyelid keeps them sealed. *This is hell.* He feels terror flattening him like an olive press, crushing his bones and reducing him to an oily pulp. *God in heaven, deliver me from this inferno. I beg you, I will change. Save me! Save me!*

Suddenly, the pecking subsides, and for a few seconds, Alfonso hears nothing but the erratic drone of his heartbeat, pulsing at the side of his neck. And then, when he dares to formulate the thought that God has indeed miraculously saved him from the bloodthirsty feasting of the birds, a white-hot iron rams into what's left of his brain and he feels himself crumpling into blackness.

"HOW DREADFUL," DON FILIPPO MURMURS after Don Simone has recounted the events leading up to his return. "That poor girl...." He slides the amber bottle at Simone. "Have another drink, my friend. This has been most unsettling for you as well."

Don Simone nods, well aware of the restorative properties of the walnut liqueur before him. He fills his earthenware cup more generously than usual, hoping the *nocino* will steady his erratic heart and quell the demonic pulsing in his stomach. He savours the alcohol as it sears a path through his tightened windpipe, and he expels a long sigh, allowing his head and shoulders to slump in relaxation. He lifts drooping eyes apologetically to the abbot, who is the closest he has to a best friend in the brotherhood, and to his relief, he sees a gleam of understanding and compassion in Don Filippo's eyes. "I must protect Gabriella from the injustice that awaits her in Camini. And Luciano as well. But I cannot seem to clear this muddled head of mine and think of a way to...." His hand bats at the air in frustration.

"Simone," the abbot brings his hand back to the table and pats it gently. "You have done enough thinking for now. You must get some rest yourself, or your head will remain as thick as Brother Domenico's bread and garlic soup. Cast your worries aside for the moment. In a few hours, the answers will come to you much quicker once you have given your brain and body some rest."

Don Simone nods in silent concession. *Gabriella and Luciano are safe,* he tells himself again. Don Filippo has given strict orders to keep the monastery secured and closed to all wanderers. Should the authorities arrive with inquiries about Don Simone and his wards, there will be ample time to usher the three of them in one of the monastery's hidden rooms or cellars, while Don Filippo convinces the officers to pursue an alternate trajectory through the countryside.

Don Simone starts as the bells chime the signal for morning prayers, and he rises, anxious to retire to his usual cell before the advancing shuffle of heavy-lidded monks. He has no desire or spirit to meet his confrères and endure their curious glances and queries. He murmurs words of gratitude to his friend for his hospitality and support, and after a warm embrace, he gulps down the last of the *nocino,* grabs his packsack, and proceeds through an arched passageway to his cell.

THE WEIGHTS OVER HIS EYELIDS ARE GONE. The periphery of his eyes are crusty and gummy, but after several attempts, Alfonso manages to open them a slit. He has no sense of whether he is dreaming or awake. He stares groggily through the cracks and sees filaments of light and darkness. The sound of footsteps intensifies and from somewhere around him, a door opens. He does not have the strength to turn his head, and his eyelids close again, but the figure that has stopped to stand by him carries a scent that is familiar to him. He winces as he tries to will the fog away from his brain. "You're going to live, little brother," the voice murmurs, wavering, before placing his hand over Alfonso's. "*Grazie a Dio.* Thanks be to God."

Alfonso's eyes flutter. He groans, startling himself with the sound—a grating rattle that reminds him of a dying goat.

"Don't try to speak, Alfonso," Claudio says, now at his side. "Squeeze my hand if you understand me."

Alfonso can smell Claudio's cologne. Fresh, like pine forests. He breathes in deeply before squeezing the hand Claudio has placed under his. A stream of cool air brushes his face. He is near a window or perhaps the balcony. Is he in his own bed, in Don Simone's rectory? He tilts his face toward the breeze. He feels his brother's hand on his forehead.

"You still have a fever, Alfonso. Lie still, and I will cool you down with some wet cloths."

Alfonso welcomes the feel of the cloths on his flaming face. His hand moves to his neck, but Claudio stops it and brings it back to his side. "You must not touch your wound," he says firmly. "I imagine it hurts like the devil and probably itches, but I don't want you to re-open the sutures. Understand?" Alfonso squeezes his hand harder than before.

"Well, some of your strength is back," Claudio murmurs. "Alfonso, we need to have a serious talk when you are better. I just want you to be aware of a few things, now that you are conscious." He pauses, and Alfonso hears him let out a long, drawn-out sigh. "Where do I begin? First of all, you might be wondering how I discovered you.... When I returned to the rectory after my visit to Stilo, the house was empty. I thought it quite strange; usually Signorina Gabriella rushes to the door when I knock. I let myself in, and by the statue of *San* Nicola, I saw a note addressed to me. It was from Don Simone."

Alfonso's stomach twists. He feels the urge to turn his face away or to cover it with his bed sheet, to avoid the look that certainly must be on Claudio's face at this moment.

"Don Simone came home and heard screams from the stables," Claudio continues more softly. "He rushed in and saw Signor Lorenzo dead on the ground with Gabriella next to him, and you were lying on the floor of the loft, blood covering your neck. He surmised what had happened: that you had attempted to dishonour Gabriella, and that her father arrived inconveniently earlier than usual and tried to stop you. Don Simone couldn't say for certain how Signor Lorenzo had died, but he guessed that Gabriella had tried to defend herself and in so doing, unwillingly caused your death."

Alfonso's feels his face burn. The throbbing in his neck feels like a vice, squeezing and releasing. He gulps for air.

"Don Simone knew he had to take Gabriella away. He knew I would be returning to the rectory." Claudio's voice is trembling. "He wanted to do the honourable thing and tell me what had happened." He clears his throat. "He said he would be gone indefinitely with Gabriella and Luciano, and that he would make arrangements with another priest to take care of the funeral arrangements for both you and Signor Lorenzo. He was deeply sorry for the events that had transpired, and he would pray for both your souls, and, for your families."

Alfonso feels Claudio grip his hand suddenly. "I can't possibly know what you're feeling right now, Alfonso, and perhaps you don't want me to know. But there is one thing you must realize. If Don Simone hadn't left me this letter, I would not have rushed into the stables and found you lying there with barely a thread of a heartbeat. I may have sewn you up, and for that, you may be grateful, but the one you owe your life to is not me. It's Don Simone."

Alfonso winces, though it is not at his brother's words, but at the scene that has just returned to his memory—the flash of Gabriella's porcelain skin before that excruciating pain in his neck. Trembling with a rage that he is fighting to suppress, he squeezes Claudio's hand hard, and forgetting his earlier promise to God to change, he silently vows to find Gabriella—if it takes his last breath—and make her pay for what she has done.

TONINO AND MASSIMO MAKE UP THE REAR of the re-energized line of fifteen hundred volunteers. All are travelling by foot save the General, his commander-in-line, and a few others, including his son Menotti and his old surgeon, Dr. Ripari. They trudge along, the line of Redshirts flowing along like fresh blood through the artery that is the forest path. The blood of soldiers ready to sacrifice their lives for the cause of unity.

A widening in the forest and the accompanying light in the clearing reveal a grove where it is decided they will rest until the midday heat has abated. They quench their thirst at a nearby stream. It gurgles over a bed of gleaming volcanic stones smoothed by the gentle but constant pressure of the water flowing over them.

Unlike many of the lower-lying areas of the region, where

gushing streams of past centuries have become little more than useless trickles, or worse still, dried-up beds showing their faces of deep lines and sun-bleached whiskers, this stream flows with a pulsating fertility, spraying the men's faces as they bend down to taste its freshness. Laughing in delight as they feel their vigour renewed, the men set about feasting on the good farmers' bounty, before spreading themselves on the soft flanks of the foothills and succumbing to a welcome slumber.

Upon awakening, they await to hear what General Garibaldi has decided is the trajectory that would best take them northward through the Aspromonte, avoiding areas that will surely be heavily guarded with troops eager to suppress them. They will reassume their stealthy march at nightfall.

For the next few hours, some chat, some play card games of *briscola* or *scopa,* some pace anxiously, some pray, some go back to sleep, some write. Massimo has wandered off, a cigarette dangling from his lips. Tonino watches him for a moment before stretching out, laying his head on a soft clump of moss. He closes his eyes, eager to delve into each and every memory he has of Gabriella. He smiles, recalling the soft blush of her cheeks and her sweet scent. The perfume of oleander blossoms by the river. Intoxicating....

GABRIELLA BLINKS IN THE SUN-DAPPLED ROOM. The burst of light from a tiny arched window is so bright that it hurts her eyes. She shuts them immediately and instinctively knows that she is not in her own room but cannot seem to clear the fog from her head to distinguish her whereabouts. She prods her memory until a vision of a flask emerges, its contents poured into a cup by Don Simone, who is urging her to drink from it for its soothing and medicinal properties. She recalls that it had a slightly bitter taste, with tones of chestnut and fennel, and that after she swallowed the last drop, mere minutes passed, and she was sent to rest in a novice's cell that had been readied for her and her brother.

Luciano. Papà. Alfonso Fantin. The journey by cart. The series of events that have brought her to this place march through her mind like the death knell rung in Camini, and as her eyes wedge open, she feels the pain of her loss pushing into her chest and stomach like a clenched fist. She gasps before bursting into quiet sobs. *Luciano.* She jerks upright on her pallet, her blurred eyes seeking her brother's figure, and when she makes out nothing but a crumpled blanket on his cot, she wipes her eyes frantically, puts on her shoes, and dashes across the room to open the cell door.

She immediately slams into a body, and mortified, she looks up into the surprised but kind eyes of the abbot, Don Filippo, who had greeted them at the door of the monastery upon their arrival. Don Simone is just a few paces behind him. Luciano is absent.

"*Scusatemi,*" she apologizes, and glancing back and forth at them, wringing her hands, says hoarsely, "Where is Luciano?"

Don Simone places a hand over hers. "Do not worry, Gabriella. Luciano woke up some time ago and is now in the chapel with the good brothers. He is safe. We are all safe here."

"Yes, but…" Don Filippo clears his throat and exchanges a glance with Don Simone, "but you must have something to eat. You will need your strength." He gestures at an archway. "Brother Domenico has prepared a fine meal for all of you; he delights in displaying his culinary skills to visitors—"

"I…I'm not hungry," Gabriella murmurs. "My stomach—"

"Do not worry, Signorina. Brother Domenico's bread and garlic soup will replenish you in both body and spirit. Come."

Gabriella follows the abbot and Don Simone, anxious to reunite with Luciano. She has no interest in eating. And as far as she is concerned, her spirit is dead.

THE OFFICER ON DUTY BURSTS UNCEREMONIOUSLY into Russo's office, beads of sweat clinging to his flushed face. Russo sets down the latest letter from General Zanetti, and thin-lipped,

hears the officer's stuttering explanation for this most unchar-
acteristic of interruptions. The officer explains that there is
a man—aggressive and insistent—who is here to see Russo
about a personal matter. Not a little curious as to the identity
of the man who would reduce a usually unflappable officer
to such a state, Russo curtly orders his officer to allow the
man entry. "Get another carabineer immediately and prepare
to stand by, in case I need to have this lout thrown out of
my office." The officer nods and as quickly as he arrived, he
is gone.

Russo remains seated as the man strides into his office and
stops at one of the chairs opposite his desk. Russo taps his
fingers impatiently against his thigh, unobserved by his visitor.

"You wished to see me?" he says brusquely. He fixes an unblinking gaze on the man, who, clearing his throat, removes his
fedora and accords him the expected nod of deference. Russo
inclines his head in acceptance. "Please sit down."

"Thank you, Colonel Russo."

Russo's glance lingers on the linen cloth wrapped around
the man's neck. It is not a scarf, as he thought when the man
entered; it is some sort of bandage, and a darkened area beneath it indicates a recent flow of blood. The man is not from
these parts; his skin and hair are too fair. His ruddy countenance and build hint at a prosperous lifestyle, reinforced by
his tailored jacket and trousers, the cut and colour of which
allude to the styles favoured by the Milanese couturiers. His
hands are large yet strangely delicate; Russo doubts that
this man has had to use them for any strenuous labour. The
heavy gold ring on the third finger of his right hand boasts
the biggest emerald that Russo has ever seen. Here is a man
with money, perhaps power, and if Russo's hunch is correct
and the man's hawkish eyes are any indication, a good measure of ruthlessness.

"Thank you," the man continues, with a flourish of his ring
hand, "for allowing me the opportunity to present my case

to you." The man twitches suddenly, and his hand flies to his neck. "Please forgive me. I am recovering from a knife wound that was perpetrated upon me by an assailant who has fled the village. Please allow me to introduce myself. I am Alfonso Fantin, the new proprietor of the Church of Santa Maria Assunta in Camini and its associated properties. My brother Claudio and I have journeyed from Turin to take possession of the establishment and to evaluate the current staff and their viability in the future."

"Camini." Russo nods. Since his appointment as Colonel in charge of the forces of repression in Greater Calabria South, he has tried to acquaint himself with the myriad tiny villages and hamlets scattered about the countryside. He has heard the name "Camini" in connection with the feast of *San* Nicola, but he has had no occasion to visit as yet. "Is it the crime to your person that you wish to report?"

"Indeed. I—"

"May I ask when this attack occurred?"

"Three days ago." At Russo's arched eyebrows, he adds quickly, "I was not in any condition to move, let alone contact the authorities. My brother found me lying unconscious and proceeded to tend to my wounds. He is a physician." He twitches again. "He tells me I am healing, but I continue to be tormented by stabs of pain, both in my neck and head. He also tells me it is a miracle that I am alive."

"Where are you staying? Were there no others about that could have alerted the *carabinieri* immediately?"

Fantin grimaces. "We have been staying at the rectory of Don Simone in Camini. Unfortunately, I was stabbed in the barn, and my brother, upon finding me, feared for my life and therefore, did not attempt to move me into the house. Having his medical bag with him, he staunched the flow of blood and monitored me through the night, leaving only once to procure blankets, water, and spirits from the rectory. The following day, I was overcome with fever and occasional seizures, and

Claudio was again afraid to leave me. He thought my chances for survival were better if I was kept still."

"Where was Don Simone? Was there no one in the household to assist your brother in getting help? A farmhand? A servant?"

"There was nobody else in the rectory." Fantin winces and presses his fingers to his right temple. He draws in a deep breath. "Don Simone had left to tend to a dying man in the nearby hamlet of Riace and was expected to return by late afternoon. The priest's servant girl, Gabriella Falcone, was the only person present at the time that I was inspecting the property and livestock. She offered to show me around the premises. Inside the barn, she implored me to keep her hired. She had no other prospects, she said, and if I dismissed her and her father, the priest's farmhand, they would surely be separated.

"I don't want to sound crass, Colonel Russo, but the girl, obviously desperate, began to divest herself of her bodice, and threw herself upon me. It was at this unfortunate moment that her father, returning from the fields, came upon us, and enraged, sprang at me with a pickaxe. I managed to side-step him and kicked the pickaxe out of his hands. He came charging at me again, and this time I defended myself with my fists. Regretfully, he stumbled and fell, hitting his head hard on the ground." Fantin shudders. "He died instantly."

His eyes, which have been focused unblinkingly on the stark, whitewashed wall behind Russo's desk, now shift to meet Russo's gaze. "The girl started screaming and collapsed on the ground by her father. I turned away, intent on seeking help, but I had taken no more than a few steps when I felt a searing jab in my neck. I collapsed and the girl fled, leaving me to die, no doubt happy to have exacted revenge upon me."

Russo has watched Fantin closely as the story has unfolded. The latter's cheeks have erupted in an angry flush; his eyes are blinking rapidly and a vein in his temple is swollen, the bluish filament pulsing under the skin.

"And die I would have," Fantin grounds out with teeth clenched, "had my brother not found me."

"Did Don Simone not return?" Russo's eyes narrow and he straightens in his chair, his hands now entwined on the desk.

"Oh yes, the good Father returned, took me for dead, and must have decided that his servant needed protection. He left a note for my brother, stating that I had been killed and that he would be gone indefinitely, taking the girl and her young brother with him." He gives a bitter laugh. "I suppose I ought to thank him for the letter. At least my brother knew where to find me."

Russo's eyebrows lift. Fantin's presence seems amplified in the modest space of his office, and from his movements, his bandage has shifted, allowing Russo to catch the scent of blood and disinfectant. Russo stifles the urge to rise and open the shuttered windows. "You wish to procure my aid in finding this young woman?" He takes his fountain pen and makes a notation in the book before him.

"My wish exactly. Her father's death was an unfortunate accident. I was merely protecting myself, but the crime she committed in revenge must surely warrant the involvement of the greatest forces of law and justice." Fantin reaches within the folds of his overcoat and withdraws a bulky package. He sets it down on the desk and places his ring hand on it, fingers outstretched. "I expect you are extremely busy, Colonel Russo, in your efforts to maintain the law in this lawless territory. As a supporter of the strictest tenets of law and order, I am happy to make a donation to support you in your formidable but worthy mission here in Greater Calabria South." He takes a deep breath and his eyes shut briefly as his head twitches. "Please understand that should my offering not be sufficient, I will be more than pleased to demonstrate continued support. It would be an honour to provide you and your forces sufficient resources to aid you in your many enterprises."

Including the one you have brought to my attention today. Russo cups his chin with one hand, his eyes never wavering from Fantin. He does not have to thumb through the billfold to know that it will exceed any expectation of worth on his part. He inclines his head slightly and at the gesture, Fantin rises, reaches for his hat and bows respectfully. "*Viva* Victor Emmanuel II, King of Italy."

Russo nods. "Long live the King." He watches the large figure as it retreats. When the door has clicked shut, he slowly slides the billfold closer to him and smiles. A sharp knock makes his head snap up.

"Colonel Russo?" his first officer calls.

Russo's smile fades. He slides the package under some files in his top drawer and closes it deftly. "Come in."

GABRIELLA KNOWS, BEFORE DON SIMONE SAYS anything, that something is wrong. His erratic tap at her cell door a moment ago, his unusually strident voice calling her name, his knitted brow when she opened the door, and his clasped fingers working furiously like the movements of an ant have ignited a drumming in her chest.

"Don Simone, what is it?" She looks past him down the long corridor, her stomach clenching.

"We have to leave the monastery." Don Simone's words are calm, but his eyes are blinking rapidly. "Don Filippo has just gotten word that the carabineers, under orders from their superior officer Colonel Russo, are questioning the villagers and farmers in the area as to our possible whereabouts, and any associations and relatives we may have in the outlying area. It is only a matter of time before they discover my affiliation with Don Filippo if they don't already know. We must seek asylum elsewhere."

Gabriella feels her stomach twist again. "How does Colonel Russo know…?"

Don Simone reaches for her hands. "Signor Alfonso went to

find him." He frowns. "His brother found him in the stable—barely alive—and tended to the wound" He shakes his head. "I left him for dead…and now he is recovering…."

Gabriella's knees buckle. She sags against Don Simone as a wave of nausea hits her. *He is alive.* Clasping Don Simone's sleeve, she gasps, "What are we going to do? What will they do to me? What will happen to Luciano? We must leave." She straightens, knowing there is no time to be weak. "But where can we go?"

Don Simone winces and Gabriella realizes that her fingers are digging into his arm. She lets her hands fall to her sides.

"Don Filippo and I will discuss this while you prepare your brother. Luciano will remain here, Gabriella."

"*Here*?" Gabriella hears the near shriek in her voice. "I can't leave him. *I won't.*"

Don Simone clasps her by the shoulders. "Look, Gabriella. Don Filippo has an excellent idea. Luciano will be sheltered with the good Sisters of the Convent of Saint Anna here in Gerace. The orphanage is their life's work. Don Filippo will send Brother Martino to deliver him safely into the Sisters' very capable hands." He squeezes her shoulders. "Gabriella, Brother Martino is expected already with the usual delivery of oil, fruit, and root vegetables. Luciano will travel safely in the cart with the supplies."

Gabriella starts at the approaching footsteps. It is only Don Filippo. Heart pounding, she listens as the abbott adds, "I will apprise the abbess of your situation, and I can assure you that Luciano will be as safe as if protected by our Holy Mother herself. You have my word."

Gabriella searches his eyes for any sign of insincerity and finds none. He smiles at her kindly. "If God be with you, who could be against you?"

She feels the mass of knotted muscle in her stomach dissolving as his warm brown eyes envelop her. She nods and flees to get her brother.

Gabriella shudders as a salt-tinged breeze from the Ionian Sea slaps her cheeks. Even from this elevation, they can hear the churning and slapping of the waves against the rocky shoreline. In the distance, the muffled cry of a goshawk sounds like an injured child. Gabriella's sob catches in her throat as the cart carrying her brother is engulfed by the swaying poplars on either side of the path. She feels Don Simone's reassuring squeeze on her shoulder.

"Luciano will be safe," he murmurs. "The abbess at the Convent of Saint Anna will provide everything he needs. She is well-known for her special devotion to orphans."

I am an orphan too. Gabriella's stomach contracts, though not from lack of sustenance. Brother Domenico has made it his personal mission these last two days to ensure her compliance at mealtimes. She might as well have been eating hemp, though; each bite has been an ordeal. The hearty bean soup served earlier, thick with garlic, onions, and potatoes, and consumed with gusto by Don Simone, almost brought her to the point of retching with its overpowering smell. She took a few sips to appease Brother Domenico, and then fortunately he and Don Simone were summoned urgently by Don Filippo, and her discarded bowl went unnoticed.

She is aware of Don Simone's concern. She can read the subtle messages on his face by the familiar telltale signs: eyes that blink more rapidly than usual under furrowed brows, a perplexed twitch of the lips, and his right hand stroking his chin. His every gesture is as familiar to her as those of everyone in her family. He *is* her family. He and Luciano are the only family she has left. And now Luciano is gone. Something inside her wants to believe Don Simone that he will be safe, but a louder voice is insisting that she should have kept him with her.

Oh Luciano. She looks up to the sky, praying for a sign that God has not forsaken them. Then she remembers that she is angry with God; she wants nothing more to do with Him. He has failed her and her family. He has led her to believe she had a future with Tonino, and now her beloved has other plans for the future. Whether she likes it or not, she has to accept the fact that Tonino may never come back to her alive. She can't bear to even imagine what Tonino is thinking or doing now, for surely he knows that she has fled Camini.... *Oh God, what torment!*

God! He is as dead to her as her father. Yet despite herself, she cannot help but recall one of the many psalms that Don Simone has preached about: "'He shall set me high upon a rock. And now my head shall be lifted up above my enemies.'"

She grunts, refusing to gain any comfort or assurance from the words. The only one who can protect her from her enemies now is Don Simone. She takes his outstretched hand, and they hurry into the monastery to pack a few supplies before fleeing.

ALFONSO HAS MIXED FEELINGS ABOUT CLAUDIO leaving. Although he trusts his brother implicitly—Claudio has assured him that his neck wound is healing and that he need only change the dressing regularly and apply the medicated balm to restore the damaged tissue—there is something that is troubling him. It is the matter of the pulsating jabs on the left side of his head. He has never suffered from head ailments in the past, save perhaps, for the throbbing after an occasional night of revelry to celebrate an outstanding success at his favourite gambling house in Venice. And even then, the pain was more of a constant thrum as opposed to these intermittent jabs that feel like lightning striking.

Claudio suspects nerve damage. He has supplied Alfonso with a vial of nerve pills and cannot say for certain how long the pains will last. "What do I do when the pills are finished?" Alfonso sounds like a helpless child even to himself.

"Go to the pharmacy in the town of Stilo." Claudio writes an indecipherable message on a piece of vellum and hands it to Alfonso. "I met the pharmacist last week when I took the journey with the boy Valerio. He's learned and well-respected.

He will take care of your every need." He checks his pocket watch and looks pointedly at Alfonso. "Must you pursue this?"

Alfonso knows Claudio is not referring to the pills. "I suppose you disapprove," he rasps, propping himself up in his bed with a grimace. The shifting precipitates a jab to his head. He has been resting all afternoon; the trip to the military station in Caulonia to consult with Colonel Russo thoroughly drained him.

"Alfonso, how could I not? I don't know what you were doing when we were taught our catechism at school, but pursuing this matter...pursuing *her* goes against anything we—"

"Don't spew morality at me, brother. We're long past those guilt-provoking lessons of our youth. Or at least *I* am."

"Forget your pride and return with me," Claudio insists. "She was only trying to defend herself." Claudio opens his mouth as if to continue and then clamps it shut. He returns to his own room. Alfonso hears him fiddling with the straps of his suitcase and then he is back, setting the bag down before approaching the bed. Alfonso returns Claudio's stiff embrace and shifts his eyes to the window, reluctant to see any further disapproval in his brother's eyes.

He sighs, wishing Claudio could prolong his stay. He does not relish the thought of being alone in this barbarous region. Now that Don Simone has gone, he has no one but the ignorant peasants in the village with whom to associate. Even the mayor, whom he and Claudio met shortly after their arrival in Camini, appeared to be barely more respectable than the villagers. Alfonso had taken in the almost threadbare elbows on his jacket, his stained teeth, his unclipped fingernails, his coarse pastoral dialect. He had offered his hand when introduced by Don Simone, and it took everything Alfonso had not to extract it precipitously out of his clammy grasp.

Alfonso almost regrets having purchased the church property in Camini. It is the first expropriated property south of Naples to be added to his land holdings. He recalls the warnings and scoffing of some of his associates in Turin upon hearing that he was considering making the purchase and planning to travel the length of the country to inspect his investment personally.

"You're descending into hell itself," Ottavio Venturi from the pharmaceutical company proclaimed.

"I hear the peasants are barely more civilized than their African neighbours to the south." his banker said with a sneer.

"The most cultured women are coarser than our northern whores. Or does the thought of sticking it into a near-savage excite you?" one of his gambling friends in Venice guffawed, adding an obscene gesture.

Alfonso's jaw clenches. Gabriella Falcone, despite her lowly status, had no outwardly "savage" attributes. Her eyes, devoid of the dullness of the barefooted women returning from the fields, were shiny and alert, her movements nimble and purposeful as she carried out her kitchen tasks. Her hair, thick and immaculate—no greasy sheen or sun-dried thatch crowning her soft face. *That face.* Perhaps that is why he wanted her. The softness of that skin, a hint of coral on those cheekbones, lips that looked like they were meant to....

Alfonso gasps as a pain shoots down the side of his head. The left side. Always the left side. "*Dio bestia,*" he swears. Were it not for that girl, he *would* be returning to Turin with his brother. To hell with the church lands. He'd unload them without a second thought.

But he cannot leave before he has found Gabriella. Surely, she cannot outsmart him even with the aid of the priest. He has the money, and now, the forces of law on his side to help him track her down and punish her for her crime. Secretly, he hopes to locate her before Russo's men. He *must.* Despite his neck wound and the infernal jabs to the head, he has been sustained by thoughts of how he will enact his own brand of justice on the girl.

Moments later, he hears the *clip-clop* of hooves and the accompanying clang of the cart's wheels. Valerio will lead the mule out of Camini to Locri, where Claudio will await the train heading north.

His brother knows him far too well. Claudio knows that he will not be content until his pride has been assuaged. The only way to do that is to find the girl and....

Alfonso smiles, thinking of what he will do to Signorina Gabriella before turning her over to Russo. *If he is lucky enough to find her first.*

GABRIELLA CRINGES WITH EVERY STEP she takes through the forested mountain path. They have been walking for at least three quarters of an hour. Her shoes offer little protection from the grizzled roots that occasionally break through the sun-scorched earth. Every coarse pebble strewn across the forest floor feels like a spike. Despite their elevation, the midday August heat is still unbearable. Gabriella's soles are burning. *This is what St. Joan of Arc must have felt like as the flames began to lick the bottoms of her feet.* She cries out as a sharp stone penetrates the thin flap of sole on her right foot. She lifts her foot, sways, and falls in a heap near a clump of wild sage.

Don Simone gasps. "Did you twist your ankle?"

Gabriella shakes her head. "My foot's bleeding, though."

Don Simone mumbles something under his breath that sounds suspiciously like a curse of some kind, and Gabriella looks at him in wonder. She has never heard him utter a bad word in her life.

"*Dio, perdonami,*" he adds immediately, and despite her pain, Gabriella almost feels like laughing. Don Simone, the most holy man she knows, swearing, and then asking God's forgiveness. "We must take care of this right away," he tells her, removing her shoe, "before it becomes infected." He reaches into his cassock and pulls out a flask. Gabriella looks away and braces herself. She flinches as the alcohol makes contact with her open wound. Her foot feels as if it is engulfed by flames. Shuddering, she attempts to pull her foot away, but

Don Simone holds it firmly. She can see that he is trembling, though, and his face looks as pained as she feels. He reaches again into his cassock and produces a handkerchief, which he folds before tying it around her foot.

"How can I walk like this?" She winces as Don Simone helps her wedge her foot back into the torn shoe.

Don Simone takes a deep breath, his finger tapping one side of his face. "We will rest for a while. But we cannot stay in this spot." He straightens, looks around, and then nods in satisfaction. "See that grove of poplar trees? Beyond it is a shepherd's hut; we can stop there. Besides, you need to eat. Come."

Gabriella cannot put her full weight on her foot. Leaning against Don Simone's arm, she limps the thirty or so paces to the grove, and squeezes through a narrow opening into a field of mixed grasses intertwining in wild profusion. Gabriella can easily identify them: myrtle and rosemary, thyme and fennel, lavender and sage, and the abundant soapwort. The field is so overgrown that at first, the hut is easily missed. Don Simone points to it excitedly. "There. I knew it would be here."

The door creaks as they enter. He helps Gabriella into a dilapidated woven chair before sitting down on a rough bench. "I come this way occasionally on my travels," he says, taking a couple of apricots and a hunk of cheese from his packsack. "The shepherd whose hut this belongs to lives on the outskirts of town with his daughter, who works as a housekeeper at a villa in the area. His wife is dead. The fellow always invites me to have a little tipple with him—ahem, of tea, mostly—when I pass through. He told me to stop in even if he wasn't here, if I needed a rest or goat's milk." Don Simone chuckles. "I imagine he's out to pasture with his goat, or we could have enjoyed some fresh milk."

Gabriella accepts Don Simone's offering of fruit. For the first time since they left Camini, she feels hunger gnawing at her stomach. She bites into the apricot, savouring its sweetness. She watches as Don Simone pulls out a jackknife and cuts the *pecorino* cheese into wedges. He hands her a couple of generous wedges, takes one for himself, and puts the rest in the packsack. Her foot is still throbbing, but for a moment she allows herself to be content for the food and the rest.

Don Simone begins to say "Grace," but she plops the second apricot into her mouth, ignoring his frown at her obvious disrespect. Whatever respect and devotion she had for God died with her father and her dreams of a life with Tonino.

AFTER BIDDING CLAUDIO GOODBYE in the *piazza*, Alfonso sends a shoeless ragamuffin in search of Valerio Bosco, who had previously taken him and Claudio for a tour of the church lands. Before leaving the rectory that day, Alfonso had watched Valerio conversing with Gabriella. He couldn't hear what they were saying, but the look of adulation on Valerio's face was obvious.

It was clear to Alfonso that Gabriella did not feel the same. Her face, though flushed, did not mirror the boy's infatuation, and her drawn eyebrows and pursed lips inferred a touch of irritation. She had smiled, though, after he left, and Alfonso had observed her secret amusement with a flurry of mixed feelings. It was the first time he had seen her smile since his arrival.

"I know the area, Signor Alfonso," Valerio is saying confidently. "I can help you find Signorina Gabriella." His face clouds over. "I was very sad to hear about her father's death. Signor Falcone was a good man. Poor Gabriella, with no one to protect her and her father from that robber. He must have been a vagrant; there has been some talk of a gypsy encampment near the river. Oh, if only you or your brother had been at the rectory..." Valerio's grey eyes well up and he wipes them with a handkerchief from his pocket.

"Indeed," Alfonso murmurs, rubbing his temples. He feels a slight throbbing, but he has not felt a jab in the last hour. He clears his throat; it feels as if it is lined with the thorns of the prickly pear. He has confided in the boy that when he and his

brother returned, they found a note from Don Simone, saying that he had come back from his visit in the neighbouring
hamlet of Riace, only to find Gabriella wild with grief over her
father. She had taken leave of her senses and was tearing at
her hair and clothes and screaming like a devil, threatening to
jump off a cliff. He felt there was no recourse but to take her
to a place where she could receive treatment for her hysteria.
Alfonso added as an afterthought that Don Simone promised
to inform the authorities about the robbery, and that he would
locate Luciano and take him with them.

"Don Simone requested that we make provisions for the
funeral." Alfonso lets out an audible sigh. "As you know, the
funeral was yesterday. The poor girl must be half-mad with
grief or she would have returned. There are arrangements
that have to be made now that she and her brother have been
orphaned, which is why we must find her."

Valerio shakes his head. "Why wouldn't Don Simone say
where he was taking Gabriella and Luciano?" His eyebrows
arch in puzzlement. "Something's not right."

Alfonso coughs, the phlegm gurgling in his throat. "That's
what worries me," he says, his voice dropping dramatically.
"They left with the mule and cart by night. What if they came
across the gypsies? Or worse, brigands?" He feigns a shudder.
"God help them." Crossing himself, he looks off to the hills.
"As new proprietor of the church and its accompanying lands,
I must do everything I can to help my staff. Which is why I
am seeking a guide to take me through the area and make
inquiries. Sooner or later, we will find them."

Valerio is biting the corner of his lip nervously. Alfonso wonders if the lad is right for the task. He is perhaps too young; he
can't be much past fourteen, if that. "I appreciate your offer
to help, lad, but I was thinking of someone perhaps a little
older, someone with a mule and cart of his own. I intend to pay
him well, of course." Alfonso watches in silent amusement as
Valerio draws himself up as tall as he can, puffing out his chest.

"I am the man in my family," he asserts. "My parents are both dead of the malaria, and I take care of my *nonna*. She would be happy for me to take this job. Not just for the pay," he adds hastily, "but because I'd be helping our friends. And we have a mule and cart."

Alfonso pretends to consider Valerio's offer. He suspects that Valerio would accompany him even without pay. He stares for a moment into those grey, lovelorn eyes and then nods. At Valerio's unabashed cry of joy, Alfonso reaches into his pocket, and hands Valerio some coins. "This is the first instalment of your payment." *We are both getting what we want*, he thinks smugly.

The boy's eyes widen; the poor bugger has probably never handled this much money in his life. When Valerio blurts out that it is far too much, Alfonso is touched by the boy's honesty. He reaches into his pocket again and takes out several more *centesimi*.

"You are doing me a favour, Valerio. And I appreciate it. Give these to your grandmother. She deserves a reward for raising such a fine young man. Meet me here at dawn tomorrow, and we will be on our way."

Valerio blinks, and Alfonso can see that he is too choked up to reply. Alfonso pats him on the back and with a respectful nod, the lad is off.

"And who says I don't treat others as I like to be treated?" Alfonso heads back to the rectory, thinking of the bottle of *nocino* in the rectory kitchen. He has had no further jabs to the head, thank God. That alone is cause for a celebratory drink.

DON SIMONE EXCUSES HIMSELF and in his absence, Gabriella limps into the adjoining room. A straw pallet is wedged into one corner, and a wicker basket crammed with herbs leans against the wall. She starts as a field mouse appears from behind the basket and skirts the edge of the room before disappearing into a crevice in the dirt floor. She shudders and despite the heat, feels a flurry of goosebumps skimming down her arms.

Her eyes are drawn to a cord that is strung from one side of the hut to the other. She notices the splatters of blood along the cord and a few errant feathers. A pigeon. Or a quail. Her gaze drops to a bulging haversack on a low bench. Her nose wrinkles at the scent of freshly killed fowl. She prods the bag with her foot and the twisted head of a pigeon pops out, its white feathers scarlet-tinged. So, the shepherd is not far off then.

The walls of the hut seem to be closing in on her. She hobbles back to the first room and out the door, where she almost collides with Don Simone. He is holding a sturdy oak limb.

He drops the limb and holds her steady by the shoulders, peering at her in concern. "Your face is as pale as the blessed host." His voice is stern. "Perhaps I should have left you with Luciano. It was madness on my part to think that you could withstand such a journey." He wipes the beads of sweat on his forehead and under his eyes. "Oh, how I wish we still had Vittorio with us."

Gabriella was present when Don Filippo advised against it, suggesting a little-known foot path through the Aspromonte mountain range that would bring them to a safe haven—a secluded Augustinian monastery run by a personal friend of his. He mapped it out for Don Simone, assuring him that the forces of law would not venture to penetrate the dense woodlands in the vicinity. Don Simone looked skeptically at the intricately drawn map with its serpentine twists, and after getting a few clarifications from Don Filippo, folded and tucked it into his cassock. "Take care of my Vittorio," he smiled ruefully at the abbot.

"It will take us roughly two more hours before we arrive at the Monastery of the Augustinians," he says now, his eyes intense, "but I cannot in good conscience allow you to travel any further until you are feeling better." His eyes drift past her to the hut. "We have no choice but to stay here for now. The afternoon heat will kill us both if we set out. Perhaps later, when the sun has gone down, you will be strong enough to go on."

"No! I don't want to stay here," Gabriella hears herself blurt out. "The shepherd has left a bag with some dead pigeons, and he'll surely come back soon. I...I don't want to be here when he comes back. He might be angry with us for trespassing. He might...." She realizes her body is trembling along with her voice, and her eyes meet Don Simone's in silent pleading.

"Oh, my dear, you have nothing to fear. The old fellow is as old as the Aspromonte mountains. And besides, I am with you. You will come to no harm."

Gabriella watches as he extracts his wooden rosary beads from his cassock with one hand. "We are not alone," he says, holding them up triumphantly. "We have the Lord with us. He will protect us."

Gabriella turns away sharply, freeing herself from Don Simone's steadying hand. *Don't talk to me about the Lord,* she wants to scream. She looks around her in agitation, feeling as trapped as a cornered rabbit. "I'm not staying," she says with the calmest voice she can muster. She draws out a long breath, fully aware that this is the first time she has defied Don Simone. Whatever demon has seized her soul to make her act this way, she has no intention of fighting. If anything, she is ready to do battle with the Lord that Don Simone holds so dear.

Crossing her arms, she watches as Don Simone blinks helplessly at her. His mouth opens and then flaps shut without a word. He cups his chin with one hand and after a moment, nods. "*Va bene,*" he concedes. "We will go." He stoops down to pick up the limb. "Use this to help you walk." He hands it to her and enters the hut to retrieve his packsack. When he reappears, Gabriella notes that he has also helped himself to the herbs. She spots two pigeon claws protruding from an outer pocket of the packsack.

"I only took one," he murmurs sheepishly. "We have little food left. May the good Lord forgive me my thievery," he says, eyes lifted to the sky.

Gabriella turns away, not wanting to show her surprise. Two commandments broken in less than an hour. Don Simone has never demonstrated such human weakness before. In one way, she finds it disturbing. She has always thought of Don Simone as a pillar of right action, a man quick to rise above the petty foibles of his parishioners. A man far removed from human indiscretions. *Perhaps nothing is as it seems*, she thinks bitterly. But then again, if a man of the cloth can justify his sins, and then seek pardon, then perhaps she can be forgiven for her crime, an act she carried out simply to protect herself.

Gabriella wipes the beads of sweat from her face with her sleeve. Her damp collar is pinching her neck, and her foot is throbbing. She looks up to the sky, but the midday sun is blinding, and she shuts her eyes. *No, you are not willing to forgive me, are you, Lord? I must suffer still. There is no justice for peasants like me.*

Stifling a sob, she begins to hobble back to the mule path. Don Simone walks closely behind her. For the first time, she feels truly alone. Not only has God betrayed her, but the man who has been her second father has let her down as well. Oh, Don Simone will say an extra rosary and pray for God's understanding and forgiveness of his actions in such dire circumstances. His conscience will be appeased. Her conscience, however, will not, for she refuses to ask God's forgiveness for sticking her knife into Alfonso Fantin's thick neck.

Damn him. He deserved to die.

PART V

ASPROMONTE:

THE BITTER MOUNTAIN

August 1862

DON SIMONE SHAKES HIS HEAD sadly at the figure hobbling ahead of him. *She has changed already.* Gabriella is no longer a tender creature suspended in a safe chrysalis, but one who is hardening in order to survive in the outside world. Her barely restrained defiance of his wishes to stay in the shepherd's hut has caused him some consternation, but he has no desire to cause her further distress. The poor child has had more than her share.

Walking at this time of day is unbearable. His black cassock is drawing the sun to him like a flame enticing a moth. His collar is drenched. Dabbing at his face with a handkerchief, he prays they both have the strength to walk the remaining two hours to get to the Augustinian monastery tucked away in a dark cleft on the northeastern slope of the Aspromonte mountain range. It is even more elusive than Don Filippo's monastery, accessible only by foot. It has been in use for three centuries, attracting the most reclusive of monks and nuns to its perpetually sheltered walls. Don Simone has never had the occasion of visiting it, but Don Filippo is on good terms with the abbot and felt it would be the ideal haven for Gabriella under the circumstances.

Gabriella is in pain but wants to go on. So be it. He has no choice but to accompany her and ensure her safety, although he's not sure what kind of protector he can be if he collapses from heat exhaustion. Unless it is a dire emergency, he never travels about the countryside at this time of day, when the sun is at its strongest. Huffing, he catches up to her. She glances at him with the barest hint of a smile, and he utters a prayer of thanks to God for this minuscule sign that perhaps Gabriella's spirit isn't completely dead. Somewhat cheered, he smiles back. "*Coraggio*," he says. "We are almost there."

"And where would 'there' be?" a voice rasps behind him.

Don Simone pulls Gabriella to him, his heart jolting. Before he can turn around to face the speaker, the man jumps out in front of him and Gabriella, one hand holding a rifle and the other clasping a bulging haversack, the same one that was in the shepherd's hut. This is not a man of the law. But neither is he a shepherd.

Don Simone feels Gabriella go rigid. Trying not to show fear in his voice, he nods congenially. "Good day, sir. We're...we're heading to...to the village. My friend, the priest, is in need of a housemaid, and I was accompanying my niece...." He has a hard time seeing the man's face under his black conical hat. The sun is throwing shadows across his features, embellishing the slant of his eyebrows, the shape of his moustache. The man is lean and muscular. His shirt sleeves are pulled up, revealing forearms that are dark and sturdy.

His pants look a size too big, held up by a rich leather strap decorated with a buckle studded with jewels. The myriad stones catch the sunlight and mesmerize Don Simone for a moment. The man chuckles and looks at Gabriella and then back at him. Don Simone catches his breath. *This man is a thief; at worst, a brigand.* His grip tightens around Gabriella, a gesture that instantly draws the thief's attention.

"It is not safe to travel in these parts without some sort of protection," the man says in a concerned tone. "There are all manner of villains lying in wait to rob you. Or worse." The man takes a step forward and tips his hat. His face is visible now, a slate of hard curves and edges, with eyes and hair as black as charcoal. His nose leans into his thick moustache; it has been broken, perhaps. If not for its awkward angle, the man might be considered almost pleasant-looking. Almost. Don Simone notices a pale ribbon around the man's neck, but the pendant is obscured. He wonders if the thief is wearing a sacred amulet of some kind; if he is, perhaps he will show respect to a representative of Christ....

"You have travelled this way before?"

Don Simone nods. "I have made pilgrimages to the Madonna of the Poppies," he lies, silently thanking Don Filippo for mapping the surrounding area for their journey.

"Then you will make your way back home. I will take your niece safely to Don Damiano."

Don Simone clears his throat, aware that Gabriella's eyes have widened. He feels his stomach muscles clenching, the blood draining from his face, but he is determined not to show his fear to this...this *vigliacco*. "With all due respect, sir, I have promised my brother that I would not leave his daughter's side. Your offer is much appreciated, but I am afraid I must decline."

"You are *afraid*?" The thief's eyes narrow into slits. "Not enough, I think." He taps the butt of his rifle sharply into the ground. "You will turn back at once."

Don Simone doesn't know if it is he who is trembling or Gabriella. He desperately thinks of something he can offer the thief. Something of worth. He wrenches the only ring he owns from his left hand and holds it out. "Please allow me to thank you for your trouble," he says as steadily as he can. He is heartbroken to relinquish the ring, not for its material worth, but for the fact that it was a parting gift from Monsignor Brunello prior to his departure for Calabria. He only hopes it will satisfy the thief.

It is a thick band of twenty-four-karat gold, with a ruby sunken within an oval silver border. The thief all but snatches it from his outstretched palm and surveys it with interest. He nods and slips it into a pocket of his trousers. "It is most kind of you, *Sacerdote*."

Don Simone feels a thread of hope....

"Now go home," the thief rasps.

Don Simone gulps. His chest tightens with the terrifying re-alization that he has nothing with which to protect Gabriella. *Nothing.* He cannot bear to look at her. And then he has a thought. He lets his arm drop from around her tense shoulders and casually slips his hand into the side of his cassock. He forces himself to take deep breaths as his hand closes around his hunting knife, trying to figure out how he can thwart the thief without getting himself or Gabriella shot.

"Hand it over."

The voice is behind him. Another thief. Don Simone makes a quarter turn and sees a figure almost identical to the first thief. The man is shorter, more robust but with the same features, all but the bent nose. This one is wearing breeches, with laced-up footwear and no stockings. The same conical hat and a gentleman's silk shirt. Around his neck, a gold chain above a thick mat of chest hair. In his hand, a polished pistol.

"You heard my brother."

Don Simone's shoulders slump. *We're finished.* He hands over his knife without meeting the thief's eyes. *Dear Lord, spare Gabriella.* He cries out as the brother wrenches him away from her. The first thief leaps to her side and grabs her by the elbow. She begins to struggle, twisting like a filmy leaf in a gust of wind, but her movements come to an abrupt end when the thief's vein-swollen hand slams against her left cheek, leaving a scarlet imprint.

Don Simone groans as the thief delivers a blow to her oth-er cheek. Gabriella collapses. Don Simone attempts to rush forward, but the thief's brother holds him back. The villain's eyes are bright with excitement; he gathers Gabriella up in his arms and disappears into a thicket. Don Simone feels the bile thrusting its way up his innards until his throat engorges. He chokes and gasps, and the acrid liquid spurts out in a gush, spraying the brother's chest with a thin, yellow film clotted with phlegm. The brother cries out in disgust and slams a fist into his stomach.

Don Simone feels himself crumpling to the ground, the brother's bile-splattered face the last thing he sees before complete darkness.

GABRIELLA SCREAMS AS THE BRIGAND THROWS her down onto the forest floor. With all the force she has left, she begins to thrash about wildly. The brigand's eyes are dilated as he looks down at her, his unshaven face glistening with perspiration. In seconds, his body has covered hers and although he is not heavy-set, his weight is enough to still her movements. He pins her arms down over her head and as his mouth comes down to the base of her neck, Gabriella hears a thundering voice ordering the brigand to release her. Light-headed, she wonders if it is God Himself. The brigand rolls off her, and as she tries to rise, her knees give out and she falls hard on the ground. She cries out as a sharp slab of rock juts into her lower leg.

She is too shaken and hurt to move. The smell of the churned-up bracken with its hint of decay is smothering, and she feels her stomach quivering with what is left of the morning's breakfast.

Without opening her eyes, she shifts painfully onto her side and almost immediately feels her stomach contract before violently expelling its contents. *I'm dying.* She sinks back to the ground. *I'm dying like a beggar, or worse still, a woman of the streets, used and tossed out.* She opens her mouth to gasp for breath and realizes the voice she mistook for God is talking to the brigand. It is controlled now, yet more frightening.

"Find your brother and get back to the hideout. *This* will bear some...discussion."

"*Sì, Capo.*"

Gabriella gasps. The brigand is deferring to his *chief*. The brigand sounds like a child capitulating to a stern parent, his voice lowered in shame. Gabriella's head begins to clamour with all the implications. She hears the footsteps of the brigand receding and then silence. Where is the brigand chief? Her stomach roils again, and she retches into the bracken. Whatever fate awaits her now can't be any better than the fate she almost experienced at the hands of that *animal*.

Yes, the brigand chief stopped one of his men from dishonouring her. But she does not want to face the man who has such power. For who could possibly stop *him*? And even if Don Simone manages to escape the clutches of the other thief and catches up to her, what could *he* protect her with? His rosary? His prayers?

Her hand instinctively feels the area that is throbbing on her left calf. There is a tear in the folds of her skirt, and at the cold, clammy sensation, she quivers, sensing that the cut is not a superficial one. At the sound of neighing, followed by footsteps crunching through the bracken, her head jerks up to see a figure standing over her, his eyes shaded under the rim of a black conical hat. His face is deeply tanned and unshaven though his moustache is trimmed. His hair is dark and longer than that of any respectable man. Something about his face unnerves her, and closing her eyes, Gabriella prays that Don Simone will appear.

A wave of vertigo overcomes her, and she realizes that the brigand chief is the cause, sweeping her off the ground as easily as if she were a wayward bough that had snapped off a tree and was in his way. He strides a few paces to his mule and promptly sets her on its back before remounting. Gabriella stiffens and as his grip on the reins tightens, she wants to scream but can't. Her powers of speech are dead; her throat is a dark, petrified tunnel with no opening.

"Hold on, unless you want to pitch forward and split your head on those stones," he rasps, barely giving her the chance to extend her arms to his waist before clicking his tongue and prodding his mule on. The mule begins its trot, and without wanting to, Gabriella's arms grab hold of the folds of the brigand chief's cloak. Her chest thrums erratically as they begin to ascend the steep mountainside, the path barely wide enough to accommodate two mules.

Oh, Don Simone, where are you? Please, dear God. Please let him be safe. She immediately stifles any further evocation, remembering that God is dead to her since taking both her beloved parents. "God!" she mutters in disgust, and feeling stronger in her fury, she surveys her surroundings. What if she were able to slide off the mule? She eyes the thick stand of trees hugging the mountainside. Could she run off into the woods and hide before the brigand chief found her? Surely she would eventually find a shepherd's hut....

She refuses to think that there could be other wayfarers that might not be sympathetic to her pleas, that might end up harming her. There had to be people who would be willing to provide her shelter and safety, especially if they knew she was evading the clutches of brigands.

She cries out as the mule veers unexpectedly and follows a rough path that skirts the mountainside. This path is much narrower, and her hold on the chief's cloak tightens as she glimpses the impossibly deep ravine. A prayer rises again to her lips. She can't help wondering how many bodies are lying on the ravine floor, broken and torn from their hellish descent.

I am in hell. With every thump of hoof on the path, Gabriella's heart pounds. When the mule sends some rocks skittering over the edge of the mountainside, she cries out while entwining her arms tighter around the brigand chief's waist, her cheek flat against his back. She clamps her eyes shut, telling herself that the mule must have taken this path countless times. Surely the brigand chief would not put his own life in danger. With eyes closed, the sounds and smells around her intensify. Perspiration rolls in droplets off her temples. Her nostrils flare at the smell of wild jasmine. If she were in a dream, she'd think she was in a heavenly garden.

A sudden rustle in the trees makes her wonder in alarm if it is a wild boar. While another scene plays itself out in her imagination, the mule swerves sharply again, and then, after another dozen paces, comes to a complete stop.

She feels the chief dismount and when she opens her eyes tentatively, he is standing in front of her, arms extended, waiting for her to jump or slide off the mule. She has no choice. He breaks her fall by clasping her by the waist, and when her feet hit the ground she sees his face clearly for the first time.

She tries not to recoil, but when he stiffens and lets his arms drop to his side, she realizes that he has seen her reaction, momentary though it was. In the stifling heat of the late morning, his sudden coldness is even more palpable, and it takes everything she has not to tear her gaze away from his strange eyes.

One green, one brown. The sunlight reflected in their canyon-like depths make her shiver inwardly. What kind of a devil has God put in her path?

The hut that he leads her to is a tangle of sturdy tree limbs, branches, and foliage.

"You will rest here," he tells her curtly, lifting the blanket hanging at the door and ushering her inside. He gestures at a thick pallet of compressed poplar leaves upon which a woven coverlet has been placed. The pillow is a rolled-up linen shirt.

Dear Mary in Heaven, don't let this happen to me. Again. Gabriella begins to shiver and realizes that the horrible clacking sounds reverberating in her ears are coming from her own teeth. She covers her face with both hands. She has never felt more alone in her life.

DON SIMONE FINGERS HIS ROSARY BEADS, Absent-mindedly watching the wisps of cloud parading in front of the moon. He stops in the middle of a "Hail Mary," struck with the way the elongated clouds resemble the filmy wings of a butterfly. He sighs, brings the rosary to his lips and then sets it down, vowing to complete the final decade once he has had a chance to...to *think*. He needs time to absorb what has happened, what is happening. To make sense out of the brigand chief, who did not hesitate to reveal his name…Stefano Galante.

Don Simone has always considered himself to be an accurate judge of character; he has been right far more than wrong when assessing the truthfulness of a confessor, ever watchful for a revealing twitching of an eye, a biting of the lip, a subtle clenching of the jaw. These telling signals have always prompted him to delve a little more into things; experience has made him realize that once over their fear of revealing their demons, his parishioners are able to arrive at the core of their inner anguish.

There is a physical forcefulness about Galante that is undeniable—his body and face could be carved from the Gallica caves themselves. There is no softness there. And his character must be stone-hard as well, to hold the position he has. This is obvious in the deference with which his band members respond to him. Don Simone harbours no doubt that the men who apprehended him and Gabriella had villainy on their mind… probably more with Gabriella than with him. His stomach muscles tighten as he recalls the events leading to the arrival of the brigand chief….

After retching all over the second brigand and fainting, he awoke confused and disoriented. And then Gabriella's screams reached him, and everything came back to him, along with the fear that the second brigand had probably joined his partner, who looked to be his brother. Wincing, he tried to get up. If it took his last breath, he would do anything he could to stop them. *Filthy degenerates.* Not knowing what he was going to do or how he was going to save Gabriella, he hurried toward the sounds, praying fervently for a miracle. The brush was thick, and the sweat trickling down his face blinded him. He tumbled over a jagged stump and lost his balance. He could see the brothers, the first shoving Gabriella onto the forest floor, and the second standing with arms crossed a few paces away, a grin of anticipation stamped on his face.

Neither of them saw or heard the horseman's approach. As Don Simone attempted to untangle the hem of his cassock from the pointed edges of the stump, a sudden stomping of hooves made him stop. Clad in black, from his conical hat to his laced-up footwear, the horseman jerked his reins and stopped in a swirl of dust.

Don Simone wanted to weep. *Another brigand.* And then he glanced at the brothers. He was astounded to see fear replacing the smirk on their faces and the steely purpose in their eyes at the horseman's command to release Gabriella. And to see their shoulders caving in submission to…their *chief.* They shuffled away like errant schoolboys after a thrashing from their schoolmaster.

And yet, despite his granite exterior, the chief's eyes seemed to soften as he took in Gabriella slumped on the forest floor. The flicker of warmth disappeared as soon as the chief's vision caught the incongruous black of his cassock draped amongst the bracken. His head riveted like an eagle, locking narrowed eyes with Don Simone for a moment before stating his name and nodding slightly, in what Don Simone wanted to believe was a sign of respect for a man of the cloth. His stomach muscles relaxed, and Don Simone instinctively knew he wouldn't be harmed.

Don Simone wonders now, though, if the brigand chief will be as honourable with a defenceless young woman as he is with a clergyman. After all, Galante could have allowed her to remain in Don Simone's care instead of ensconcing her inside his hut. Don Simone forces the inevitable soiled thoughts from his mind. Surely, the brigand chief has no intention of taking advantage of her under such circumstances. No…not if he is an honourable man.

But how can a brigand chief be honourable? After all, a brigand is a criminal, an outlaw. And one who leads a band of brigands, who orchestrates their nefarious activities, who directs them in their ungodly transgressions, who purposefully pulls them away from *the way, the truth and the life*…. Is that not the work of the devil?

With a troubled sigh, Don Simone turns his head to the darkened copse leading to the brigand chief's hut. He is utterly powerless to stop the chief from doing whatever he intends to do. He gulps, his throat constricting with a wave of guilt. Poor Gabriella. What more must she endure?

"I have failed you, my child," he whispers, bringing the tip of the crucifix to his lips. "And I have failed your father." He begins to sob quietly, his tears flowing down his cheeks and onto the collar of his cassock. "God forgive me. Oh Lord, have mercy. *Abbia misericordia.*"

GABRIELLA CAN FEEL HIS BREATH BY HER EAR. "You will be safe with me," he murmurs. Gabriella's stomach twists. Is this what she is destined for, then? To serve the whims of a brigand chief? She doubts that she will be able to thwart him as she did Signor Alfonso. And if she tries, who will come to her rescue? Don Simone is no match for any of these criminals. Yes, Stefano Galante saved her from the certain disgrace that would have befallen her at the hands of brothers, but….

"No one will dare touch you here," he says, "and you can be assured that my men will answer to me for their actions." He extends a hand at the pallet. "Lie down," he commands brusquely. "That wound needs tending."

She limps over to the pallet and when she is lying down, he lifts her skirt to survey the gash on her leg. Mortified, she looks away. Despite the afternoon heat, she is still shivering uncontrollably. She feels the chief's hand briefly on her forehead, and, with the thread of consciousness she has left, curses her inability to defend herself. He rises to get something in a basket and returns immediately. She winces as he presses a raw potato over the cut. Her teeth clench as he moves it over the gaping wound, squeezing at the same time so that the milky liquid can drip into it.

"This will prevent it from becoming infected," he murmurs. The brigand chief clamps down her leg with his hand when she instinctively tries to jerk it away. She cannot control her teeth from chattering. He reaches into his packsack and retrieves a bottle. Supporting her slumped body in a sitting position, he presses the bottle to her mouth. As the liquid squirts into her throat, she sputters and chokes; when she becomes still again, he tips the bottle into her mouth once more. When her coughing and shuddering subsides, he takes off his cloak and drapes it around her, before laying her down gently.

When she opens her eyes, she gasps at the sight of Don Simone's face above hers. Not knowing if he is part of a dream or reality, she closes them again, welcoming the embracing darkness.

STEFANO REALIZES THAT THE PRIEST has been watching his every move, his lips intoning a silent prayer. Don Simone nods gratefully when Stefano offers him the flask and takes a generous swallow. When it is obvious that Gabriella is sleeping, Stefano motions to the priest to precede him out of the hut and to the clearing. He sits on one of the stumps positioned around a fire pit and gestures at Don Simone to do the same.

"You have the manner of a doctor," the priest murmurs, gazing steadily at Stefano. "Healing hands."

Stefano laughs curtly and picks up a piece of charred wood. The innocent comment is like a burning ember in his heart. His intended reply catches in his throat, and he coughs. He pulls a knife from the folds of his cloak to whittle away at the burnt edges. He takes satisfaction at every cut, every precise incision. With every strike of the knife, he surveys the movements of his own hands in a detached manner, as if they are the hands of another. Suddenly, he stops.

Yes, he would have liked to have used these hands for healing people. He mentioned his foolish dream once to his father. Only once. Stefano pitches the wood back into the fire and turns away from Don Simone with the pretence of looking for another piece. He resumes whittling, his eyes stinging at the memories....

"Never mind such grand ideas." His father's eyes narrowed, and Stefano caught the telltale flutter that usually came before a vitriolic outburst, or at worst, a thorough beating.

He looked down at his boots, slick with manure from mucking out the stables, and then ventured another glance at his father, who had begun to pace around, his expression glazed, his mouth twisted. He stopped in front of Stefano, one hand clasping the stall gate, one hand clenching and unclenching.

"You think you're too good for your father's farm? Don't want to dirty your pretty hands?" He snorted, raking Stefano with dead, bloodshot eyes. "You think you're better than I am?"

Stefano barely saw the hand before it opened to deliver a blow to his left cheek. His knees buckled from the impact and he collapsed into a pile of dung. Stunned and unable to prevent the tears that dimmed his vision, Stefano remained sprawled on the ground. The mule's snorts and neighs rang in his ears. His father began talking again, his words muffled. He was a short man, but he stood above Stefano like a squat, grotesque giant, his eyebrows shadowing his face like heavy canopies, the folds of his chin and neck bristling with grey whiskers, his shoulders squared and menacing.

His face contorted as he spat in Stefano's face. "Just remember, *figlio mio,* you were born into dung and you'll die into dung. I didn't produce a son just for the opportunity it gave me to bed your mother, goddammit, though I'm the one who was damned, fathering two girls before you showed your face. Goddamn *piscia sangu*, all of them, including your mother." He spat on the ground.

Stefano blinked, trying to clear his vision. Every word his father had uttered was a white-hot poker searing his gut. His stomach heaved with revulsion at the stark hatred in his father's voice. He felt a sudden urge to rise up and crush the mouth that had emitted such vile obscenities about the people he dearly loved.

His father pulled out a flask and brought it to his lips. Some of the colourless liquid dribbled down his reddened cheeks and neck. He started as Stefano's dog, Argo, ventured into the barn and leapt up at him, barking.

He gave a grunt of rage and kicked Argo in the belly, sending him skidding through the dung into Stefano. With a sneer, he tramped out of the barn, slamming the door behind him.

Stefano froze. He knew that if he went after his father, he'd be responsible for making his mother a widow. He savoured the feeling of pure murderous desire, allowing it to course along his veins until he was trembling uncontrollably, as if struck with a nerve disease like old Farmer Nunzio on the other side of the village.

Argo was whimpering. Stefano buried his face in the fur of his neck, murmuring and patting him gently. "Argo, Argo," he whispered, placing a palm upon his heart, feeling his frantic heartbeats. Stefano could barely stand to look in the dog's eyes, knowing that pain would be reflected in its trusting depths. "I'm so sorry I couldn't protect you from that...that *beast*." He grimaced at the sight of the jagged cut on Argo's underbelly.

Damn the stables. Damn Papà. Much as he would like to make his father pay for what he had done, Stefano forced himself to quell his rage and tend to Argo. His fingers gently explored the area around the cut. He had learned much from his covert visits with the travelling doctor, who had allowed him to serve as an apprentice of sorts. But he was not sure if the swelling that he was feeling was the result of inflammation from a burst spleen. If it was, Argo would not have much time to live.

Stefano thought fast. If anyone could save Argo's life, it was Doctor Primo. Feeling his throat constrict, as if his father's fist was clenched within, Stefano grabbed a woven blanket hanging from a peg and wrapped it around Argo. He carried the trembling bundle outside and placed it gently into the straw-lined cart under a giant fig tree. He hitched up the mule to the cart as fast as he could, glancing several times at the farmhouse and praying that his father would not reappear and prevent him from leaving.

Stefano checked the bundle in the cart, lowering his face to nuzzle the dog. When he felt Argo shift slightly to lick the salty streak of tears on his cheeks, Stefano gulped and leapt into the driver's seat.

It was only when he had driven the mule out of his father's farm that he allowed himself to be engulfed by tears.

Stefano senses the priest's eyes on him again. His eyes shift from the carving in his hands to the eyes that hold a glimmer of invitation. An invitation to unburden his soul. His jaw clenches, and he examines the unfinished bird he has whittled. He flings it into the fire pit before gesturing at his hut. "She should not be moved. It is a pleasant night. You will be comfortable enough." He points to the edge of the clearing. "I've instructed one of my men to prepare a pallet for you behind those bushes."

At the priest's helpless nod of submission, he grunts approvingly and returns to his hut, his memories of his father extinguished.

GABRIELLA HEARS A RUSTLE AND IS STARTLED before realizing that it is the result of her slight shifting on the pallet beneath her. The smell of the brigand chief's shirt against her nostrils is familiar; it holds the same scent that assailed her when she was pressed against his back on his mule, clinging desperately to avoid being catapulted into the dark folds of any one of the countless ravines.

She attempts to lift her head, but at the accompanying rush of vertigo, she plops back onto the pallet. His scent is inescapable. He smells of the forest: the sharp tang of resin, the astringent tone of pine, and the musky body of the earth, with the summer heat trapped inside. Gabriella is both repelled and drawn to the scent. She is suddenly aware of the throbbing in her leg, and as she tries to regulate her breathing, she remembers that the brigand chief is only several arm's lengths away. She can hear his breathing, deep and even compared to the irregular thudding of her heart.

She wonders if Don Simone is awake, reciting prayers for the sorry lot they are in. There is no need for *her* to offer up any prayers. God has shown himself, if anything, to be soundly deaf as far as her family is concerned.

Another rustle. This time she knows it is not of her own making. It is coming from directly outside the hut, though it is barely perceptible. A mole, perhaps, or a hedgehog. Then she sees a telling shadow cast by the moon against the blanket suspended in the doorway. The hair rises on her arms.

The creature is, without a doubt, a woman.

The brigand chief shifts position. Gabriella shoots a nervous glance at him. He continues to sleep soundly. When she gazes back at the shadow, it is not there. A wave of nausea hits her, followed by a niggling doubt. She must be imagining things, no doubt the result of the concoction the brigand chief forced her to drink. She closes her eyes....

RUSSO HEARS GENTLE SPLASHING in the porcelain tub in the room next to his bedroom. He smiles, his quill pausing in mid-air. *Liliana.* There is nothing like the thought of a beautiful young woman to detract one from the task at hand. His letter to General Zanetti contains only the salutation. He is anxious to pen the rest of it, considering the nature of the information he is about to impart, but he allows himself pause to savour the anticipation of the evening he is to spend in the company of Liliana.

His wife Gina will be away for two weeks in the distant town of Paola. While she is fulfilling her vow to St. Francis of Paola to participate in a spiritual retreat in the monastery bearing his name, *he* will be enjoying Liliana's favours.

The country home Liliana is renting is a mere two kilometres away, but he insists that she visit him in the villa that has been provided for him in his employ. It is located a fair distance off the main road and ensconced within a thick border of century-old oaks. Her coachman drives her to a designated, secluded sideroad, where his driver, Dattilio, then takes her the rest of the way into Villa Gelsomina. It has been so named for the jasmine growing all over the property. Liliana finds the villa and its gardens charming.

Russo cannot abide the thought of the villagers knowing his private business. Dattilio is sworn to secrecy, and although his manner is off-putting at times, Russo finds him dependable in matters regarding his private life. Dattilio's daughter Elvira, responsible for housekeeping duties at the villa, has also proven herself to be trustworthy.

Elvira is paid a pretty wage for work that others, employed elsewhere, make much less, but like Dattilio, she understands that a portion of her salary pays for her silence. Russo suspects she is far more wily than her father, though. He has found her suddenly by his side on occasions when his wife was sleeping, or away, and while her father was running some errand. She has never uttered a word out of line, but a suggestive gleam in her eye on these occasions has made him aware of her silent invitation.

She is not unattractive, with a shapely body that reminds him of Gina's in the early days of their marriage, before the contentedness of domesticity added an unpleasant heaviness to her already robust frame. Elvira's hair is dark and thick, and her skin looks healthy enough. It lacks the saffron tinge of peasants afflicted with malaria or malnutrition. She has no offensive scent, and her clothes, although simple, are clean and pressed. But unlike many of his associates, he has no interest in deflowering a servant, no matter how pleasing she is in appearance. He cannot bear to think of having relations with a peasant, even one who hasn't already been contaminated with the seed of another.

Since he has brought Liliana to Villa Gelsomina, the gleam in Elvira's eyes has dulled.

She still displays her usual deference to him, but any task relating to Liliana is done with little or no enthusiasm, and in the former case, Russo is sure it is feigned. As long as she is diligent in her duties, though, he will continue to keep her, but at the first indication of insolence to himself or to Liliana, she will be dismissed.

Earlier, she shuffled out of his bathroom with the last empty cauldron of hot water, wisps of her hair damp and unfurled from her kerchief, her face ruddy from the exertion of hauling the cauldron countless times from the kitchen. She did not see him by the armoire in the shadowed hallway, but he saw *her* throwing a disdainful glance backwards at the door she had just closed before striding to the kitchen. He had stifled a chuckle, knowing full well that she wished *she* was the one about to leisurely soak in his tub. *Ah, jealousy.* Such an unpleasant vice in a woman.

Russo dips his quill again into the ornate brass inkwell, anxious to compose his letter, knowing that the hardness between his legs can only be appeased once he has fulfilled his job responsibilities for the evening. With any luck, he will be able to assist Liliana in her bathing ritual. He begins to write:

Esteemed General,

Please accept my most cordial regards to you and your wife. I pray that this latest communication finds you both in optimal health. Hopefully, your recent retreat in the Sila Mountains has restored your bronchial health. I was very pleased that you had seen fit to seek the restorative and healing atmosphere of the Sila Grande Range. I trust that further good feelings will be engendered by the news that I am about to impart to you.

My continuing investigation into the identification and whereabouts of the countless brigands in this area has resulted in a fruitful discovery. As I have mentioned in previous reports, I utilize a variety of means to procure information, such as the occasional foray into a local tavern, where, as we both know, the flow of alcohol often leads to flow of new information from the locals.

Shortly upon my entry into such a tavern—specifically, Da Matteo, in the neighbouring hamlet of Calvino, a fight broke out between two drunken peasants after a certain Luca Galante accused his neighbour Giacomo Pilone of stealing his goat. I instructed the officer accompanying me to break them up, after which he threatened them both with a severe fine if they didn't leave and go their separate ways. Fortunately, they co-operated, and once they left, the tavern occupants began to talk.

It seems that Galante is well-known for his alcohol-induced violence at anyone who is near him, mainly his family. But as seems to be the custom in these peasant communities, people do not get involved in the affairs of their neighbours. If a man deems it necessary to beat his wife or children, the villagers condone it, recognizing the unquestionable authority of the man of the house, whether drunk or not. On one particular occasion, however, the son reached his limit, and sought refuge in the outskirts of the village, hiding out in a labourer's shack on Baron Saverio Contini's estate. He knew of its whereabouts because his sister was housekeeper to the Baron.

While in hiding, the son unfortunately witnessed the rape of his sister by the Baron after his wife left to visit her family in the outskirts of Rome. The labourers had all left for the evening as well, and only the girl remained. Galante's son, blinded by rage, went after the Baron and throttled him with his bare hands, leaving him for dead, according to a goatherd passing by. The son used the Baron's mule and cart to bring his sister to the doctor in the village, and then delivered her to the safety and comfort of her maternal grandmother, rather than risking the unpredictable reaction of their father, upon learning of his sister's condition and his return.

The young man then headed for the hills and presumedly found refuge deep within the Aspromonte mountain range. The Baron survived the vicious beating and posted a ransom notice for the fugitive's capture, dead or alive. Galante's son has spent the last two years surviving—thriving, rather, first as a mere bandit, and then as a notorious brigand chief. How he has managed to elevate himself to this position in a relatively short period of time is unbeknownst to me at present; however, I imagine that he must possess some of his father's villainous attributes in order to be able to round up a willing band of outlaws that will subordinate themselves to his leadership.

You can imagine, esteemed General, my anticipation of fulfilling my mission to hunt down this reprehensible villain and bring him to justice. The loose-lipped villagers, influenced by excessive drink, soon gave me the best information of the night, which was the fact that this outlaw, this brigand, was born with a brown eye and a green eye. Just like the devil that attacked my carriage. They are one and the same. His name: Stefano Galante!

Russo sets down his quill, his hand shaking with the same excitement he felt upon first hearing the news. He hears a gentle splashing and hurries to finish the letter.

I have all I need now to pursue my attacker. A face with a name. My men will find him, hunt him down, and as instructed, bring him back to me alive.

His grip on the quill tightens. *He* will deliver Stefano Galante's final judgment. Russo laughs when he recalls the nickname Galante acquired upon achieving the lofty position of Brigand Chief: *"Il Galantuomo."* If it's the last thing Russo does, it will be to topple "The Gentleman" from the top of his mountain lair, grinding him into the dirt at his feet where he belongs.

Russo finishes his letter with the promise of a forthcoming detailed plan and signs it with a flourish. At dawn, he will have Dattilio send it on its way. He rises, feeling as charged as he did at twenty.

He steps into the room where Liliana, immersed in the claw-footed enamel tub that is still emitting steam from its rose-scented depths, awaits with a flushed face and inviting smile.

ALFONSO WAITS AS VALERIO MOUNTS his sorry-looking mule. He expressed his doubts as to the hardiness of the animal to the boy earlier, but Valerio just chuckled and told him that although Spirito might look half-dead, it was just an act so that he wouldn't be overworked. "Mules aren't as dumb as people think. They might act stubborn, but if you give them a little respect, they will do your bidding without causing you grief. Spirito will take me wherever I want; he is tireless." He offers the mule a small apple then pats him and then urges him forward with a "Bravo, Spirito!"

Alfonso nudges his mule with his heels and follows at a comfortable distance. His mule is robust, hired from the village blacksmith the evening before.

"You will want a mule that is used to heavy loads," the man advised. Alfonso was irritated at the man's eyes swept over him, openly assessing his bulk as if he were a trunk awaiting passage on a ship. "Just give me an animal that is dependable," Alfonso snapped. "You'll be well-paid. Half now, and half when I return."

"Take Borbone then," the blacksmith nodded, motioning at the animal in the largest stall. Satisfied, Alfonso paid the man and told him to have the mule ready at dawn. He returned to the rectory and found a large wedge of cheese, some cured salt pork, and a half-loaf of coarse bread for the journey.

After helping himself to a liberal amount of Don Simone's *nocino*, he decided against going to bed and instead went into Don Simone's room, hoping to find a clue to the priest's destination. Discovering nothing, he proceeded to Gabriella's room. It was stifling, with her pallet against one wall and her brother's on the other side, and a tiny shuttered window providing slivers of moonlight. It didn't take long to thumb through Gabriella's belongings in a recessed wall cupboard: a small pile of neatly folded skirts, shifts, aprons, and leggings. He tossed them back into the cupboard, pulled back the shutters to let in the moonlight, and then his gaze fell back on her pallet.

A ripple in his loins made him shiver, and he gave in to the impulse to lie down. He closed his eyes, breathing deeply, the slight scent of her still lingering on the blanket. He sprang up to remove his clothes. Sliding under the coverlet, he closed his eyes and allowed the soft fabric to smother his thoughts of revenge on Gabriella, replacing them with images of her body sprawled over his, her legs gleaming like alabaster in the moonlight. With the taste of the walnut liqueur still on his tongue, Alfonso let his wildest fantasies lull him to sleep.

Alfonso now senses that Borbone wants to overtake Valerio's mule. He tightens the reins and the mule relents. "You need a new name," he says, patting the mule's sturdy neck. "The Bourbon regime is finished. Perhaps I should call you Garibaldi. Or Victor Emmanuel, after our King." The mule snorts and Alfonso laughs. He rides behind Valerio with a smile, his thoughts returning to Gabriella and anticipating the fantasies to come....

A THUD OF HOOVES AWAKENS TONINO and the others encamped on a sparsely treed section of the mountainside. Their company commander, a ruddy-faced Sicilian of thirty-eight years, urges them to assemble immediately on the crest of the hill for the order of the day. Tonino's sleep-swollen eyes widen when another flurry of hooves approach, the scarlet-clad figure on the white stallion looming over them, scanning the regiment line with an almost leonine ferocity. Tonino averts his face to avoid the spray of dust and debris, and catches a glimpse of the General's stirrups, polished and filigreed.

They stumble to their feet and proffer a salute of respect to their General, who pauses momentarily before passing them like a sudden swirl of the *scirocco,* the capricious desert wind from Africa. Tonino and his fellow infantrymen are left breathless, the flash of Garibaldi's red shirt as blinding as the face of the sun rising over the mountains.

While the dust is settling, Tonino gathers his haversack and the rifle that he was served with and clambers up the mountainside on the heels of his comrades. The clay deposits on the barren stretch of the slope make it hard to get a good grip, and a number of them find themselves slipping, sending down showers of loose stones. Except for the occasional muffled curse, they advance in silence. Tonino breathes in the thin mountain air and trudges upward. The clumps of rock rose are glistening with morning dew, their cactus-like clusters brightening the arid slopes with yellow and reddish blooms.

The intermittent splashes of colour make him think of Gabriella: the oleander-pink of her cheeks, the gleam of her chestnut eyes, and her rose-petal mouth. Something twists in his gut, and for the first time since he joined the Redshirts, he is gripped with the fear of dying. *Of never reuniting with Gabriella.* A touch at his elbow makes him jerk around, and when he sees that it is Massimo, he smiles apologetically. Massimo gives him a reassuring pat on the shoulder while taking a deep drag of his cigarette. When he exhales, the smoke catches Tonino full in the face, making him cough and wipe his eyes, a welcome excuse to hide the real reason for his stinging eyes.

When his vision clears, Tonino continues with his company to a grassy plateau with a bird's eye view of the valley where a number of hamlets dot the landscape like clumps of mushrooms. The company commander informs them that the Royalist troops are advancing up the mountain, intent on stopping them from marching on the French garrison in Rome. General Garibaldi has spotted them through his telescope.

A murmur rustles the group and grows into agitated cries of disbelief.

"But they are our countrymen!"

"How is it possible that King Victor Emmanuel is condoning civil war?"

"It's all a ruse, just like the mission in 1860. The King has to put forth a show of protest at our forces overtaking Rome, but he secretly supports us."

"General Cialdini's troops will back off, just like the Neapolitan army did in Sicily."

Tonino hears it repeated countless times: King Victor is making it look like he's opposing Garibaldi's attack on the French garrison in order to preserve the appearance of his alliance with Napoleon III. He doesn't want to jeopardize his relationship with the Emperor....

The cries and protests come to a halt as General Garibaldi—his cheeks flushed and eyes as piercing as ever—arrives on his stallion. His full, thick moustache is trimmed neatly, as is his white-tinged beard. A black bandana is tied neatly around his neck. Despite the dust and clay, he is immaculate in his full military regalia and looks like he is about to attend a royal court function.

With a voice that is rich and brooks no argument, he booms: "I order you to resist fire. I repeat, do not initiate or respond to fire. General Cialdini's men are our countrymen. We will not open fire on our brothers. That is not why we are here. We will not be responsible for the bloodshed of our kin." He fixes those nearest him with an intense scrutiny, then shouts, "Long live Italy! Viva Victor Emmanuel!" before thrusting his way around the group to repeat his message.

Tonino feels the hair rise on his arms. He listens to the reverberations of the General's voice on the mountain, the inflections, the passion, *the fire*. He feels a warmth at the pit of his stomach that rises to fill his chest and then radiates to his neck and face. The heat snuffs out his earlier fear of dying and replaces it with a fervour that makes his every nerve tingle. "*Viva l'Italia!*" he hears himself shouting suddenly. Others repeat the cry and scurry to position themselves on the flanks of the mountain. Tonino is not sure what to expect when the Royalist troops appear. He hopes that their mighty leader will, as he did in Palermo in 1860, convince them to offer no resistance and allow him to carry out his mission to unify Rome with the rest of Italy.

A flurry of reports below them creates a sudden commotion as the Royalist soldiers advance up the slope, and Garibaldi's voice breaks through the silence between shots, urging his men not to return the fire. A bugler blows the "Cease Fire." Tonino's stomach twists. He tries to convince himself that Cialdini's soldiers are simply announcing themselves, that they are carrying out this charade as a political strategy, but when the blue-clad troops appear at the rim of the plateau, their rifles and bayonets pointed systematically at the Redshirts, the gunfire that ensues leaves him with no illusions.

With their backs to a dense stand of pine trees, his companions react in confusion. Some are frozen, incapacitated as they hear their General's voice ring out again: "Do not return the fire! Do not shoot! *Non fate fuoco!*" Some are retreating to the edge of the forest, some are flattening to the ground. The first rifle shot reaches its target, and Tonino watches as one of his comrades-in-arms flounders and drops to the ground. And then another. The royal troops begin pressing in.

To Tonino's surprise, Garibaldi is suddenly there in front of his line of troops, his arms outstretched and his hands motioning for his men to hold their fire. Tonino, trembling with indecision, swerves as a line of fire punctures the ground beside him, shooting up clay and earth. Instinctively, he shields his eyes, and when he looks up again, the fracas around him seems to intensify. General Garibaldi buckles for a moment and then again, clasping his left thigh. Tonino watches him straighten, and with blood dripping from his hand, Garibaldi continues to order his men not to shoot.

But he can no longer be heard, for some of his men on the left flank under his son Menotti, have panicked and have begun to return the fire. Some on the right under Giovanni Corrao are shooting as well. Bodies jerk and fall on both sides. In the swirl of dust and smoke, Tonino is pushed aside by a rush of retreating soldiers. Some of his comrades are stepping over each other to run for cover. In a desperate glance backward, he sees a royal officer ride up and approach Garibaldi, who is being propped against a tree by his own men.

Not knowing if Garibaldi is dead or still alive, Tonino feels himself stumble. His leg twists and when his foot makes contact with the ground, the earth crumbles beneath him. His arms and hands reach out in desperation, and his rifle slips from his grip. With every interminable jab of rock and gnarled tree trunk as he tumbles down the precipice, Tonino feels his strength depleting, and his eyes, struggling to stay open in search of something he can grab hold of, become disoriented at the whirling sensations and close of their own accord. A series of tiny frames flash beneath his lids—and then, his body smashes against a solid wall.

STEFANO TIES THE LACES OF HIS FOOTWEAR QUICKLY while watching the girl. Her breathing is regular now, and when his hand grazed her forehead the second time during the night, it felt warm but not feverish. She had stirred slightly the first time, emitting a sound like the grainy mewling of an abandoned kitten. The second time, she had remained completely still except for the erratic fluttering of her eyes under closed lids.

Stefano rises, reaches for his hat and cloak, and with a last look at Gabriella, leaves the tent. He has instructed Don Simone to remain in the campsite and not attempt to proceed with his travels, considering his ward's condition and the potential danger of falling into the path of a band with a less sympathetic chief. The priest's ready nod and nervous glance around him reassured Stefano.

He intends to find out why a priest would be travelling with a young woman through this formidable stretch of countryside. Even *he* had been apprehensive about first hiding out in a place of such reviled reputation, a dark and tangled territory that swallowed people up alive, it was said, and never allowed them to return from whence they came. The Aspromonte range was the dark heart of the South, and it beat an ominous rhythm that reverberated throughout the cavernous chambers and murky arteries of its hulking expanse. It provided darkness and refuge for those who wanted or needed it, and hopelessness and despair to those who were brought there against their will.

He was determined, though, not to let the Bitter Mountain defeat him. He spent days, then weeks and months combing different sections of it, familiarizing himself with its craggy personality, discovering its shady secrets, the mysterious and contorted folds of its verdant cape, the lichen-spotted granite cheeks of the cliffside. He gave each part of its massive body a name, for naming it seemed to tame it somewhat. *He* would become its master, he decided, after spending a restless first night in its dark embrace. A mountain could not hurt him. Not like a human. *Not like his father.*

He would conquer his fear of it.

By the end of his first week in hiding he had familiarized himself with and named several sections: *Il Boschetto di Castagni,* a grove of chestnut trees; *Via Vento,* a wind-trapped path between two cliffs; *Campo Fiordaliso,* a field of mountain cornflower; *Passo al Cimitero,* a terrifying gorge in which a dizzying drop would result in perpetual rest in its mist-shrouded cemetery; and *Caverna delle Pippistrelle,* a gaping cave that had provided temporary shelter for him during a pelting thunderstorm, only to reveal its pack of furry inhabitants upon nightfall. Fortunately, by that time, the rain had abated, and

Stefano readily left the bat-infested haven, choosing instead to walk until dawn.

On one particular day, the coral haze of dawn was breath-taking, and as he stopped to admire the strips of indigo that criss-crossed the sky like the ties of a shapely bodice, Stefano realized he had reached an unfamiliar summit. After exploring around it for a good hour, he knew he had found his haven. This mountain that would shelter him, protect him with its many hollows and copses, detract his enemies with its jagged promontories and furrowed brows, its seemingly impenetrable woodlands. "Monte Galante," he named it in wonder. *His* mountain.

Stefano looks back at his hut. This is no place for either of them, especially the girl. He recognizes her for the peasant that she is, yet he knows, without a doubt, that she has had a sheltered life in comparison to most peasants. He could see it in her face, her bearing, her eyes. She lacks skin that is the colour of tallow, and the weather-lashed face of one who spends dawn to dusk in the fields. Inky shadows do not hang under eyes that have long lost the glimmer of hope for a better life.

She has none of these features, yet there is something in her face that reminds him of a creature that has been beaten and subdued. Eyes illuminated by fear, like those of his dog Argo, or of a rabbit when it has frozen in its place, aware that it is being stalked by an unknown predator who could pounce at any moment.

Who is stalking Gabriella? He intends to find out. He himself has been stalked countless times since he went into hiding, has sniffed the predator's murky scent, has sensed its murderous intent, its desire for vengeance. And up to now, he has evaded its ruthless grip, knowing full well what would happen should he fall into the talons of his captor. For every time he has managed to outsmart the *beast*, it has become more engorged with blood lust, crazed with the humiliation of human failure and ever more determined to hunt him down.

An image of such a predator flashes in Stefano's mind. The man's chest is puffed in indignation under his medal-studded jacket. *Colonel Michele Russo.*

Russo wants his head, he knows. Stefano smiles as the light of dawn sweeps over his mountain with a gentle breeze that feels like a benevolent hand ruffling his hair. He has no fear that he will be taken by Russo. Any fear he ever had was extinguished the night his father attacked his beloved dog. That fear died along with Argo when the good doctor confirmed that the dog's spleen had shattered. And in its place, a new and much stronger feeling was born. *Revenge.*

Stefano grits his teeth as he enters his clearing. The band members have positioned themselves in their usual spots around the extinguished fire. He allows his jaw to relax as he joins them. They have much to discuss.

RUSSO NODS AT THE OFFICER WHO HAS JUST ARRIVED with his special delivery at the military station. The officer salutes him and takes his leave. Russo stares at the wooden crate on his desk. The sun streaming through the windows throws a shaft of light over his desk. Between the slats, he glimpses glass, but not the contents. He leans forward and tentatively lifts the crate, and then sets it down again. Realizing that his mouth is open, and that a drop of saliva is dribbling from one corner, he reaches for his handkerchief and wipes the edge of his lip. He clamps his lips together and swallows. He can feel his pulse quicken, and inevitably, the base of his scalp begins to itch. With a low growl of impatience, he reaches for the letter opener and relieves the itch, his eyes never leaving the crate. Taking a deep breath, he unlatches the metal clasp on the crate and lifts the lid slowly.

Russo reaches into the crate, then changes his mind and retrieves a pair of gloves from a drawer in his desk. He lifts up the jar and forces himself not to look at its contents while setting the jar down on his desk. Realizing that his hands are trembling slightly, he clasps them together and sits down.

Russo lets his eyes begin their slow ascent from his gloved hands to the jar, the contents of which are now very visible to him. He cannot help but grimace at the severed head with its thick shock of black hair undulating in the colourless liquid. The base of the severed neck is uneven in places, resembling the scalloped edge of a curtain flapping in the wind. The ears are very large, like conch shells, curved and thickly ribbed. The liquid around the head is speckled with crimson globules. Russo watches them, fascinated with their movement from the displacement of the jar.

Suddenly aware that he is clenching his jaws together, he releases the pressure, and without moving from his chair, he leans forward and twists the jar around slowly. He watches the head bob slightly and braces himself.

The face is distended in a grotesque death mask. Russo's stomach lurches uncontrollably. The eyes are bulbous and murky, full of burst blood vessels. The nose has been broken recently; it still bears splotches of purple and yellow. The mouth is gaping, its gums and teeth covered in a filmy mucous. Some of the teeth have detached from the gums, and they are resting on the bottom of the jar.

Russo starts to gag. He rushes to open a back door, and the contents of his earlier meal spew onto the ground. Coughing and heaving, he clamps his handkerchief over his mouth and returns to his office. Without looking directly at the jar, he lifts it up and places it back in the crate, closing the clasp firmly.

He didn't have to open it, but he wanted to see for himself that the bandit Agostino had met his rightful end. Adjusting his uniform and making sure his appearance does not betray his reaction to the sight of the dead brigand, Russo calls for the officer to enter and take the crate away.

After the officer leaves, Russo plucks the gloves off his fingers and hurls them into a garbage bin. He ponders the destination of the remains, a laboratory in Naples where forensic scientists will examine the head for particularities or distinguishing features that they have observed on other brigands.

Russo doesn't care what they find or don't find. His job is done. The brigand is dead.

And as distasteful as it may be, there is another brigand whose head he wants even more in a crate in front of him: "The Gentleman," Stefano Galante.

AFTER AN HOUR OF RIDING, Alfonso feels a pinch in his lower back, and although the shooting pains on the left side of his head have not returned, he feels a dull ache pulsing above his right temple. He brings Borbone to a stop, whistling to alert Valerio who has disappeared around a bend, and tethers the animal to a tree. He walks over to a bush to urinate and when he turns around, is disconcerted to find Valerio waiting on his mule, watching him.

He tightens his belt and strides over to his mule for his jug of water. At seven o'clock, the heat is already palpable. "Let me see your map," he says curtly to Valerio, who still hasn't budged.

"Map? I don't have a map." The boy shrugs, grinning. "I don't need one. I know my way around."

Alfonso looks at him doubtfully. "But you're only—what? Fourteen? Fifteen? How could you—"

"I'm sixteen," Valerio straightens on his mule, expanding his chest defensively. "And I travel these parts regularly, finding work wherever I can. My last job was in Roccella, harvesting bergamot for a foreign landowner who sells it to companies who make tea and perfume. Imagine! They can't seem to get these citrus fruits to grow anywhere else in Europe! I wish—"

Alfonso gestures curtly to stop the boy from chattering. He acknowledges silently that Valerio knows his way around, but it irks him that he is completely vulnerable and in the boy's hands. With a map at least, he could have chosen the path and gotten a sense of the territory that had to be covered. He should have thought of procuring a map before heading out. "What's the nearest town or village?" he says sharply. "And how long to get there?"

"Gioiosa Ionica. Another hour or so."

"Are there any better roads to get there?

"Roads?" Valerio gives him a blank stare.

Alfonso feels the urge to shake the boy. Perhaps he should have hired a man, not an ignorant urchin. "Roads that are not just used by mules. Roads that are wider, not full of ruts and wild grasses. Roads that don't skirt the edge of dangerous ravines."

Valerio shrugs. "Some roads will be wider when we approach the bigger towns or villages. Don't worry, Signor Alfonso. Spirito and Borbone are used to these mountain roads. Rare are the mules that end up in a ravine, and those that do were probably startled by a wild boar or wolf." Valerio jumps off his mule and saunters over to a lentisk bush to urinate.

Alfonso turns away when he realizes what the boy is doing, but not before he notices the boy's muscular legs and buttocks. He may be only sixteen, but he has the body of a man, a body sculpted by hard physical labour. Valerio may be weak in intellect—Alfonso doubts that he has received much schooling, if any—but his body, concealed under loose trousers and shirt, is anything but weak.

"Are you saying there are wild boars and wolves in this area?" Alfonso attempts to keep the alarm out of his voice as he scrutinizes the shadows of the pine and beech trees flanking the mule path.

Valerio approaches, pulling off the grey bandana around his neck to wipe his forehead and face. He chuckles, which only increases Alfonso's anxiety. "We *are* in the Aspromonte, Signor Alfonso. 'The Bitter Mountain.' With a name like that, you have to expect more than rabbits and squirrels." Grinning, he pulls out a knife from one of his trouser pockets. "But don't worry," he adds, and Alfonso wonders if the boy is secretly laughing at him, "if a wild boar crosses our path, it will make a fine supper. We'll make a nice fire and roast it." Valerio smacks his lips. "There's nothing better to eat than *cinghiale arrosto*. Unless you add it to a pot of tomato sauce with *maccheroni*."

Alfonso shudders, not at the thought of the meal, but at the vision of a hairy boar with tiny close-set eyes and menacing horns charging through the trees, sending Spirito and Borbone in a frenzy with its squeals and snorts, and streaking like a wildfire between him and Valerio, looking for some ample flesh to impale.

"Let's be on our way," he orders curtly. "If you don't mind, I would like to have my dinner in the comfort of a *trattoria* or nearby hotel, and not around a bushfire."

Valerio nods and leaps upon Spirito, unable to completely conceal his amusement. Alfonso remounts with less enthusiasm, and they proceed onward in silence, save for the occasional tune the boy whistles. The cheerful notes mingle with the twitters of sparrows and other birds perched within the shaded boughs of the arbutus and oleander shrubs flanking the mule track.

Alfonso feels a vein begin to throb near his temple, and without any hesitation, he reins in Borbone to search for a pill before the pain worsens. He washes it down with his remaining water and calls out to Valerio to watch out for a spring along the way. "*Avanti*, Borbone!" He slaps the mule's hindquarters. "Find me Gabriella!"

WHEN GABRIELLA OPENS HER EYES, she searches instinctively for Luciano. She feels a jolt of alarm as she realizes that she is alone in a crude hut, with little more than a few blankets, a packsack, and a woven basket holding a hardened half-eaten loaf of coarse bread, some shrivelled purple figs, a flask of red wine, and a wedge of cheese with a knife stuck in it. A knife like the one she dropped on the floor of the hayloft.

Gabriella shivers. Someone has cursed her family; she is sure of it. Like the families with infant boys whose doors were marked with blood in the Bible, her family has seen more than their share of blood. The blood of her mother, gushing out that awful night. The blood splattered about her father's head like the crucified Jesus. The blood squirting from Signor Alfonso's neck. Bloodshed and death. Even Nicolina, the old midwife was convinced of it when Gabriella's mother died. "*È l'invidia*," she muttered to the grieving Lorenzo. "It is pure envy that has brought death upon this family."

Gabriella lingered in the dark shadows of the kitchen, anxious to hear the words of the wise midwife whose ministrations never resulted in death. It was an accepted fact in the village that Nicolina had "feelings" or predictions that inevitably came true. No one doubted her declarations or edicts. She was well-practiced in the art of *magia* and had performed some sort of magical ritual on most of the villagers, from healing fiery rashes and unblocking intestinal obstructions, to cleansing the blood from evil spirits that were intent on poisoning it. Women covertly sought her out to obtain powerful elixirs for a number of concerns. Young women needed them to help predispose their womb to conception, older women wanted them to repel the advances of an overly arduous husband, and unmarried girls wished to draw the attention of a prospective husband.

Gabriella was around Nicolina often enough that she quickly grew aware of the midwife's ways and skills with the gifts of nature. After the death of her mother, Gabriella clung even more to her, and Nicolina began to mentor her. Gabriella listened with rapt attention to Nicolina's matter-of-fact descriptions of remedies such as herbal tonics to ensure reproductive success, healing pastes for wounds incurred in the fields, and bitter syrups and plasters for boils and hemorrhoids.

Nevertheless, Gabriella had gasped at Nicolina's assertion that envy had killed her mother. Her father had turned to look at Nicolina, his gaunt face a mask of disbelief. "Who would be envious of my sweet, kind wife?" he said quietly.

Nicolina had closed her eyes, her hands gesturing in the air. "I see someone who envies Elisabetta's smooth face and hands, who thinks she might as well be the wife of a baron with others doing her work for her. Who thinks she is favoured by the doting priest who employs her, who keeps her busy under his roof as a 'housekeeper' while her husband works the church lands like an ox. And another who wonders if perhaps the good Don Simone is giving her special blessings while she is washing his...cassock...." Nicolina's voice, which had taken a tone and cadence unlike her own, broke and she coughed to clear her throat. Her eyes opened.

"*Bastardi!*" Lorenzo gritted his teeth. "Who could have such vile thoughts? *Who?* What hypocrites in the village are spreading such filth?" He grabbed Nicolina by the shoulders. "Tell me!"

"I don't have names for you, Lorenzo. I see faces, but they are cloudy."

Lorenzo gave a barely stifled growl and began to pace the room. Gabriella saw Nicolina taking something out of her pocket—a tiny flask—and emptying some of the powder within it into a small goblet that she proceeded to fill with a walnut liqueur that was kept on the table in the rectory. It was the *nocino* that Don Simone always brought back from his monastic retreat with Don Filippo. Gabriella watched as Nicolina brought it to her father, who gulped down the alcoholic offering promptly with the midwife's assurance that the drink would stop his tortured thoughts and ease him into a restful sleep.

After Nicolina left for home, unaware that Gabriella was lurking in the shadows, Gabriella emerged from her corner and poured herself a finger of the *nocino* into the goblet as well, hoping that the sediments of powder at the bottom of the goblet would be strong enough to erase the horror of the night's events from her mind, and help her to sleep without the despairing thought of life from that moment on without her dear mother.

Gabriella blinks at the sight of a cloak tossed over a mound of blankets. She knows where she is now. Not at the rectory, nor at the Monastery of the Capuchins. Luciano isn't here of course. She lets out a breath of relief. He is safe with the Sisters at the Convent of St. Anna in Gerace. She shivers, despite the warmth inside the hut. Don Simone was right to send Luciano in the hands of the Sisters. Had he not, Luciano would be *here*, in this…*this nest of vipers*. She starts to cross herself, then groans at the ingrained habit. *No.* She is not going to depend on the Almighty to protect her. What has He protected her from so far?

The amber light filtering in through the branches of the hut walls makes her wonder how much time has gone by since the brigand chief made her drink the elderberry concoction. Perhaps *he*, like Nicolina, added some other potent ingredient to keep her subdued. She knows next to nothing about the practices of a brigand chief, but it makes sense to her that an outlaw would want to keep his captives quiet to maintain the secrecy of his hiding place.

The August sun is entering the cracks in the hut in bright shards, and Gabriella knows that before long, it will be sweltering. Being up in the mountains provides more relief than in the coastal lowlands and valleys, but even at this level, the heat is inescapable.

A murmur in the distance interrupts her thoughts. Conscious of a dull ache in her injured leg, she rises cautiously and lifts a flap of the blanket suspended in the hut opening. Her heartbeat quickens as the murmur becomes louder. Voices and footsteps approach. Gabriella casts a quick glance around, wondering at the possibility of escape. She takes a few tentative steps, wincing at the pinch in her leg. She retreats into the hut. It is futile to leave. How far could she possibly get with her injury? And for all she knows, the chief may have his men ensconced at different points, ready to spring out at her.

Given the choice, she'd rather be under the surveillance of

the brigand chief than in the company of his men, especially the brothers. Her gaze falls on the basket again. Her stomach clenches suddenly, but not from hunger....

"WHO IS IT?" HE HEARS HIS VOICE CRACK as his eyes open. The face looking down on him is a blur. He blinks several times and the filminess begins to dissipate, revealing eyes that are hazel. And lovely.

"My name is Sister Caterina."

"*Sister?*" He gazes at the white wimple framing the pale face of the girl. She can't be more than fifteen or sixteen years old. Her face is delicate, a creamy olive, with fine cheekbones and a straight nose. He watches in wonder as her cheeks assume a pink hue, and he realizes he has embarrassed her with his direct stare.

He is about to apologize, but she turns away to the ledge by the open window to retrieve a terracotta jug. Next to this *gozzarella*, a glazed brown planter is crammed with a flowering plant with white buds. She pours some water into an earthenware cup before returning to his bedside. He tries to sit up, feels his head spin, and falls back on the bed. Overcome by the chaos behind his eyelids, he does not attempt to reopen his eyes.

"Try to drink a little water." Sister Caterina's voice reaches him through the maze of lines, spirals, and colours battling between his ears. He feels her surprisingly strong arm tilt his head and shoulders up while pressing the cup against his lips. He drinks thirstily. Opening his eyes, he finishes the water. Sister Caterina refills the cup and he drinks half of the contents by himself before placing it on the nightstand. She nods and walks away briskly, her black habit billowing behind her like a dark cloud.

"Sister Caterina, please, where am I? What am I doing here?"

The nun looks frantic for a moment, and then slowly returns to the foot of his bed. He feels himself breaking into a sweat, despite the breeze that is wafting in from the open shutters of the window, and he wipes his forehead before the sweat has a chance to run down his face. He starts as he feels a stiffness around his hairline, and as he extends his fingers further, he realizes that he, too, has some sort of a covering that wraps around his entire head and one ear. Bandages. His hands descend to his face. Parts of it are bandaged also; he catches the faint smell of spirits on the cloths. The skin beyond is ridged with scratches. His hands drop limply by his sides. "What has happened? Why am I here?"

Sister Caterina's eyes shift to the doorway then back to him. "I...I don't know if I should be saying anything to you. Perhaps the Abbess Emanuela can answer your questions. I will go and find her."

"No, please. Stay." He raises his arm, and he and Sister Caterina both stare for a moment at his trembling hand. She gives a barely perceptible nod before returning to the foot of his bed. She is wringing her hands, and she, too, has a sheen on her forehead. She extricates a delicately embroidered handkerchief from a pocket within the folds of her habit and pats her face gently.

His eyes linger on the handkerchief. He cannot make out the design on its edges, and he has a sudden inexplicable urge to ask her for it. It reminds him of something—of someone, perhaps—but he can't remember why. When she places it back in her pocket, he is overcome by a sudden anxiety.

"Sister Caterina, you must help me. Please tell me where I am."

"You are at the Convent of St. Anna, in Gerace."

"Gerace?" His voice cracks.

She nods. "You were brought here on a mule cart by a goatherd. You were wounded...."

"How? Where?"

The novice's eyes widen. "You don't remember anything, do you?" Her hand grasps the iron bedpost. "Do you even know who you are?"

He blinks. Of course, he knows who he is. He is...His forehead wrinkles. He is…His hands grip the sheets. Both are now trembling. Underneath the bandages, an itch is spreading like a tenacious grass fire under the starchy fibres. He shakes his head slowly. "No." He hears the tremor in his voice. "Tell me who I am."

The novice's dismay is obvious. She wears it in her knitted brows, her face a cloak of pity.

"You were wounded in battle at Aspromonte. You were brought here to recover." She leans forward to peer at him. "*Now* do you remember?"

He closes his eyes and slumps back, shaking his head. "No, I don't remember." He places his hands over his bandaged head. "I don't remember." *Can this be happening?* He pounds the sides of the bed. "Who am I? Goddammit, *who am I?*"

When he opens his eyes, the novice is gone. He feels his tears spilling over the lacerations in his face, wetting the bandages. His vision blurred, he cannot make out who is now standing in the doorway. *Is it a child?* He blinks to clear his eyes, but the figure has gone.

He wants to call out but can't. He closes his eyes, his breath shallow, his face stinging where his tears have penetrated the bandages. His hands are no longer trembling; in fact, he can't even feel them. His stomach twists with the realization that he can't feel his legs either. Dear God, has he lost his legs in the battle? His eyes fly open in terror, but before he can check to see if he has legs or stumps, an older nun sweeps into the room holding a raised needle in her hand. Behind her is Sister Caterina, her face pale.

Before he can even attempt to protest, the old nun has advanced, her beady eyes sweeping over him with hawkish precision before jabbing a needle into his thigh.

AT LEAST HER FEVER IS GONE. Her head is clear, her thoughts coherent. Her stomach is unsettled, though, a low grumbling reminding her of its emptiness. Gabriella thinks of the bread and cheese in the basket, but she can't bring herself to go anywhere near the knife. She wrings her hands, wondering what they have done with Don Simone. The gold crucifix hanging from the thick, gold chain around the brigand chief's neck does little to reassure her that he respects a man of the cloth. She has no idea whether he wears it in devotion or for vanity, a display of a successful pillage, perhaps. If he is devoted to Jesus, then surely, he will treat Don Simone with respect and reverence.

The voices are more audible now, but Gabriella can no longer discern any movement. They must be in the clearing. One of the voices is higher-pitched; could they have abducted a woman? She rises to move aside the blanket in the doorway and sees a figure break through the trees toward her. "Don Simone!" she gasps, limping out to meet him.

"*Figlia mia*," he murmurs, embracing her. "Are you...all right?" He pulls away to scan her from head to toe. Gabriella nods, her eyes misting. Don Simone clicks his tongue sympathetically. "You have had shock after shock, dear girl. It tests your faith, I know. But we are safe for now, Gabriella. Thanks be to God."

He leads her inside the hut so she can rest her leg. He sits on the brigand's mound of blankets and shakes his head. "Falling into the hands of a brigand chief is not exactly what I was praying for, but as in all matters, we must surrender to the will of God." He sighs deeply. "What brigands do is between them and God. Who am I to judge? Perhaps some of the *disgraziati* had little or no choice about going into hiding. Look at Cosimino Rosario from Monasterace. Stealing a few figs from his boss's property. Signor Quinto Malvaso caught him red-handed. Never mind that the poor boy was desperate, trying to keep his family from starving while his no-good father drank himself into a stupor from the time the sun came up to nightfall. No, the law favoured Signor Malvaso, of course, and decided the boy needed to be imprisoned. *Over a few figs*. Why, more of Malvaso's figs fall on the ground than are picked. But does the man allow any of his day labourers to gather any? No, he is content to see them go to waste. Boys and men of lesser offences have been pursued by the law. I don't blame them for trying to get away. If I was in charge of the law...." He shakes his head again. "It's amazing how money and position can make the law blind and deaf to what's right." His eyes harden. "Don't worry, my dear, God's law will eventually prevail. The real villains will all have their day of judgment before Him."

Gabriella frowns. What comfort can she possibly get from knowing that justice might not happen until Judgment Day? She bites the edge of her lip, her stomach roiling at the thought of Alfonso Fantin. At the memory of his hands touching her so...so intimately. She wishes she were alone so she could scrub his scent and vile touch off her. She wishes she could scream her shame out, the shame of being exposed, of being used. She was pure for Tonino, pure and innocent. And now her body has been soiled by a *monster*. A beast who caused her father's death. She feels her cheeks burning. *Oh Papà, Papà. If only you hadn't shown up right at that moment. I would have endured everything and you would still be alive.* She attempts to stifle a sob and at the sudden intake of breath, begins to cough raggedly.

Don Simone rushes to pat her on the back. She takes a deep breath and forces herself to think about the present. How long can she possibly run from the law for having stabbed Fantin? She knows the law will pursue her, a lowly peasant, for a crime committed against a man of Fantin's status. The fact that he put his filthy hands on her will be of no consequence. She will not be able to defend herself. She has no money. She has no standing. And from what she has heard, it is money and standing that will always win in the courts of law.

Someone clears his voice outside the hut. Don Simone helps her up. A few seconds later, the brigand chief is standing in the opening, the blanket moved aside. He has one hand concealed within a pocket of his dark cloak, and he raises the other one to tip his hat at her, then at Don Simone. *A gentleman*. Gabriella tries not to show her surprise. From where she stands, the difference in his eye colour is not obvious. She glances away from his unblinking stare, pretending to smooth out the folds of her skirt.

"We are in the process of negotiating the terms of a...a contract, so to speak, with a visitor. My men have...*discovered* two lost travellers. Foreigners. From England. One speaks a little of our language. We are working out some details of their... safe return to their destination. Once this is done, I will see to your needs."

Gabriella looks up and meets his cold gaze. His eyes remind her of an eagle, ever vigilant, blinking only when absolutely necessary, reluctant to miss any movement its prey might make. When Don Simone nods, the brigand chief turns abruptly and leaves. Gabriella's teeth clench. Who is really the prey and the predator? For all that the brigand chief looks and acts like the latter, the fact remains that he is the wanted prey of the forces of law. He can rule over his band, over the Aspromonte territory in his own lawless way, but surely one day, the law's talons will close over *him*. *And his scruffy eaglets*.

Gabriella and everyone else in the region know quite well what lies in wait for captured outlaws. It is either life in prison, or a place outside the hamlet entrance, where their ghastly heads are propped up on pikes after their bodies are reputedly tossed into a ravine. They are the cause of a child's nightmares and turn the stomach of many an adult who leave the village in the morning for their jobs as day labourers and return at night to the sight of shadows malevolently dancing through the empty eye sockets and gaping mouths.

Savages, Gabriella has often thought, not of the brigands themselves, but of those who would defile their bodies in such a way. *Is this the work of civilized men?* she remembers crying to Don Simone, the first time after witnessing the grizzly display.

"Oh, my dear," Don Simone had wrung his hands. "If only you knew what has been done in the name of the law and civility."

"It's not right!" she had exploded in tears, afraid she would never erase the sight of the dark cloak of birds alighting on those heads, pecking and tearing, shredding and feasting. She wanted Don Simone to say something to make her feel better. She saw him open his mouth and then close it helplessly, his brow furrowing.

"No, it's not right," he said wearily, pulling his rosary beads from his cassock. "Whatever those outlaws have done, they didn't deserve to leave this world like that." He looked hard at Gabriella. "*Il mondo è cattivo*," he said. *People* are evil. There will always be good and evil in this earthly world, Gabriella. May you never fall in the hands of evil." And as was his custom since her mother died, he had murmured the familiar nightly prayer to her. "May God bless you, Gabriella, and keep you in love. Heavenly Father, grant Gabriella a good rest tonight, and send your angels to protect her. Keep her healthy, keep her strong, help her know what is right and wrong. Help her sleep the whole night through, with wonderful thoughts and dreams of you."

Gabriella went to bed, clutching her own rosary all night. In the morning, its imprint was on the left side of her cheek. Don Simone saw it at breakfast and smiled. "If God be with you, who can be against you?" he beamed, sitting down to enjoy his steaming goat's milk mixed with a splash of walnut liqueur.

Gabriella recalls, now, Don Simone's words about evil. She looks at him clasping his rosary. Even though the brigand chief has saved her, she can't shake the feeling that they have fallen into the hands of evil.

ALFONSO'S THROAT IS PARCHED from the seemingly endless trek along a path snaking through the foothills beyond Camini. The chalky white sand, reflecting the sun, has been hard on his eyes, and the occasional hot gusts of wind that churn it about, swirling the fine sand particles into his eyes, throat, nostrils, and ears, have been increasing. "It's the *scirocco,*" Valerio tells him. "The desert wind from Africa."

He pulls out his flask to splash some water in his eyes and over his face. He presses his fingers to the spot above his right temple where a faint pulsating has begun. He closes his eyes momentarily, craving respite from the light and already oppressive heat of the morning. And *quiet.* The boy Valerio has been nattering on incessantly since their journey began, any time the path widened to accommodate two riders. Upon passing a citrus orchard, he hastened to explain the entire cultivation process of the prized *bergamotto.* Assailed with the putrid scent of plants soaking in a stream, Valerio began a discourse on the production of hemp.

Coming across the ruins of a hilltop church, he went on and on about the series of earthquakes in 1783, how they had rumbled through the countryside over a period of nearly two months, destroying villages and towns, swallowing up houses, churches, people, and animals from Gioia Tauro to Catanzaro. "My great-grandmother told my mother that the houses were knocking into each other like clay pots, and the sea was churning like a sick monster, vomiting white foam over the entire beach, hissing and rising until it reached the houses, spewing them with more foam, rocks, and trees that had split like kindling." Valerio paused to wipe the spittle that had gathered at the corners of his mouth from the spirited retelling of events, and Alfonso seized the opportunity to jump down from his mule and disappear behind an arbutus shrub to urinate.

Alfonso takes another drink from his water jug before remounting Borbone. They continue along an overgrown mule track flanking a deep gorge. Valerio is silent, taking care to avoid getting tangled in the bracken. Alfonso follows him cautiously, hoping nothing causes his mule to become skittish. When the path finally splits into two, Valerio takes the west fork, where they soon find themselves between low hills cultivated with olive trees. Looking ahead, they see a hamlet chiselled into the mountainside, the stone and mortar houses all clustered together like grazing sheep.

They pass a goat herd with the scrawniest group of goats Alfonso had ever seen, and a group of washerwomen beating their laundry in the public wash house. Running about are a pack of scantily clothed children, their sun-browned arms and legs knobby and discoloured with bruises or marked with scabs. They stop and stare when Valerio says good day to the women, and Alfonso can't help shuddering inwardly at the yellow tinge in their eyes, and how they barely move when the houseflies linger on their skin. He signals to Valerio to keep going; the last thing he wants is to be in the vicinity of malaria-stricken peasants.

When they are out of sight of the villagers, they seek shade in an oleander grove, tethering the animals and handing them apples before sitting down on a knoll to have their own snack of apricots and cheese. Valerio tells him the rumours about the barefooted children; that they are most likely the *bastardi* of the Baron Saverio Contini, who, by all accounts, plans regular visits to the homes of his labourers, making sure that his officers see to their timely payment of taxes and loans, while he goes about questioning their young daughters as to their suitability for work in his *palazzo* in the town or villa by the sea. "People began to notice an increase in hurried weddings, as well as an increase in the hamlet's population," Valerio snickers. "They realized the Baron was 'questioning' the girls with his pants down, the *cornuto*. They say that at a good number of the children in the hamlet are his. He denies it, of course. He has half a dozen of his own, and if he had to support all the snotty-nosed children that he has sired, he would be as penniless as the peasants." Valerio sobers. "He's nothing but a piece of shit. *Pezz 'e merda!*" He spits, his mouth twisting in disgust. "Don't you think the Baron is despicable, taking advantage of the young women like that?"

Alfonso chokes on a piece of pear and sputters out a series of coughs. He shifts uncomfortably, his sudden thoughts of Gabriella dissipating with Valerio's pointed question. He takes his time drinking from his flask, and then, seeing Valerio's eyes still pinned on him, he nods emphatically.

"Of course," he replies, making sure his voice is inflected with just enough indignation. "The Baron's actions are unconscionable. Who does he think he is?"

Valerio starts plucking some of the pink flowers off the oleander shrubs. He gives a satisfied snort. "If he did that to my girl, I'd...I'd want to kill him. Or at least castrate him."

Alfonso looks at him sharply. "Is Signorina Gabriella your girl?"

Valerio gives him a sheepish look before averting his gaze to the leaf in his hand. "I care for her, but she doesn't have eyes for me." He looks up with a hopeful glint in his eyes. "*Yet.*"

Alfonso smiles cynically at the innocent infatuation on the boy's face.

Valerio puffs out his chest. "That's why we have to find her, Signor Alfonso. And bring her home safely."

Alfonso clears his throat again. His eyes narrow. "Don't worry, lad. We'll find her." When Valerio nods and jumps on Spirito's back, setting off eagerly, Alfonso adds under his breath, "And you can have her, little boy, once I've played my favourite game with her: The Baron and the Maid."

He calls out to Valerio that he will join him presently. Alfonso turns and disappears behind a giant clump of oleanders. With the sweet fragrance of hundreds of pink blossoms enveloping him, he relieves himself quickly, the strident buzz of the unseen cicadas around him muffling his restrained grunts of pleasure.

"GABRIELLA, I TRULY BELIEVE THIS GALANTE will keep his word. The brothers I don't trust even if they were blind. But there is a sense of honour about *him*. Yes," he says, nodding and staring at the ground, his eyebrows knit together. "That man has more decency than villainy in his bones. Or we wouldn't be standing here now, having this conversation."

Gabriella says nothing. Theirs is hardly a conversation, but Don Simone is absorbed in his rambling opinions, and she doesn't feel the need to disagree with him openly. She is reluctant to sanctify Stefano Galante simply because he hasn't done anything to them. He *is* a brigand, after all. *A brigand chief.* He has to have committed some dark deeds to garner him such a title. He certainly wouldn't have gotten it for simply being a gentleman, like his name indicates. It could have been any number of things: rape and murder at worst, or abduction and extortion at best. Either way, he is a criminal, and she can't believe that Don Simone is willing to overlook this.

"I have to sit down," she winces, limping to her pallet.

He nods. "Rest your leg. I will return in a little while."

Gabriella feels her shoulders losing some of their tenseness. She could feel a wave of fatigue sweep over her as Don Simone rambled on, and now she is almost tempted to lie down, but she has something she must do before he—or Stefano Galante—returns. She doesn't want to give herself time to change her mind. She must act now, or she might forever regret it. Taking a deep breath, she gets up and moves to Galante's pile of blankets. Approaching footsteps outside the hut startle her. She pulls the knife out of the cheese and shoves it into a deep pocket of her skirt. Plopping down on her pallet, she breathes deeply, willing the erratic pounding in her heart to subside.

"Signorina?" a voice calls just outside the blanketed entrance. Gabriella gasps softly. The last thing she expected to hear was the voice of a woman.

A new round of drumming begins against her rib cage. *The shadow wasn't a dream.*

HE MUST BE IN PURGATORY. He can barely see through the wisps of fog that float about like suspended souls. Nor can he feel anything but a throbbing in his head. He squints to try to make sense of where he is, but the fog won't clear. He shudders as a cold, clammy sensation envelops him. The oppressive fog pins down his eyelids and he wants to succumb to a persistent drowsiness, but a shuffling nearby jolts him and his eyes flutter open again. This time he is able to ascertain a shape moving over to him. It is small, it must be a child; between the ribbons of fog, he can distinguish the outline of its head, a glimpse of mouth, a body clothed in white. *An angel,* he thinks, trembling.

In the distance, a woman's voice calls out. *Is she calling for me or the child?* he wonders. He considers the possibility that the angel has been sent to lead him out of purgatory...

His heartbeat quickens. *Surely a white angel will lead me to heaven. My earthly transgressions have been few....*

He doesn't know whether to be happy or sad. Sad to leave his earthly life—although at the moment, he can remember so little of it—or happy to enter the place of eternal light.... He bows his head, a prayer springing to his lips.

He becomes aware of the exchange of voices, the woman murmuring something to the child, and the child responding. *A boy.* When the voices begin to recede, his head jerks upward. The child is gone. He recoils as if he has been slapped. Frantic, he tries to call out, but his throat has constricted. The sound it emits is nothing more than a strangled croak.

He is aware of a curtain of black approaching him, and to his horror, a pair of gnarled hands descending upon his face, prying his eyelids apart before squirting a liquid into each lower lid. The hands force his eyes shut, while other hands restrain his arms and legs. His brain swims with the terrifying thoughts of the atrocities to which he is being subjected. *Perhaps I am in hell after all....*

The rasping he hears must be the devil breathing down on him.

"Open your eyes now." A woman's voice.

The rasping stops. He realizes with a shock that *he* has been the one making those ungodly sounds.

"Open your eyes."

He obeys. He squints a few times, and a hand comes up to wipe the excess liquid spilling from his lids.

He looks past the gnarled fingers to the face staring down at him. Not the devil, nor an angel. A nun with benign brown eyes crinkling as she begins to smile.

"It's a good sign if you can see me," she says. "There should be no more fog. And if there is, we'll administer another dose of drops." She nods to the nuns holding down his arms and legs and they leave, their starched habits creating a faint breeze.

"And now, Signor Tonino, all we have to do is clear the fog from your head."

"*Tonino?*"

"Yes, your name is Tonino. And I am Abbess Emanuela."

"I thought you were the devil." His voice is still hoarse.

The abbess chuckles. "I'm sure some of the novices think the same way when they first arrive at St. Anna." She strides to the window and opens the shutters. She pours some water into the cup still sitting next to the jug and returns to offer it to Tonino. He nods gratefully and sitting up in the bed, drinks it thirstily.

"Abbess Emanuela," he ventures, "what else can you tell me about myself?"

"I will send Sister Caterina to answer some of your questions, as I must attend to another matter." She turns to leave, then stops to look at him thoughtfully. "Perhaps you can answer some questions as well."

As she turns to the right of the doorway, her steps echoing on the slate floors, he slowly gets out of bed, slips his feet into the knitted grey slippers left on the floor and sits in the wicker chair by the window. The fragrance from the creamy buds of the potted plant fills his nostrils. *Jasmine.* Star-like flowers that wait until after the sun has set to open. He breathes in the scent while looking out at the countryside that is spread below him like an endless tapestry. It seems so familiar with its crags and ravines, pastures and olive groves. The hillsides are streaked with the yellow blossoms of broom, the mountain paths edged with pink and white oleanders, giant aloe, and prickly pear cactus.

If he can remember this, then surely other memories will be restored to him. He must be patient. He feels the bandages still wrapped around his head, the scratches healing on the side of his face. He murmurs the name she has told him is his. Tonino. *Tonino*. He continues to repeat it. A patter of footsteps draws his gaze away from the countryside. He sees Sister Caterina hesitating by the door. He nods, and she enters, wiping her forehead with a white handkerchief. As she approaches, his gaze follows the movement of her hand. He can make out a delicately embroidered rose on one corner and part of an initial on the opposite corner. She tucks it beneath the cuff of her left sleeve and gives him a faint smile. "May God grant us the strength to carry on in this heat. This has to be the worst summer in years."

Tonino nods sympathetically. She must be roasting in her black habit. It falls over a crisp white shirt, the collar of which extends to just under her chin. The only exposed skin is her face below her white wimple, and her hands. "The abbess said you can tell me what you know about me," he prompts.

Sister Caterina takes out her handkerchief again and gently dabs under her eyes. Her cheeks are flushed and when she suddenly sways, dropping her handkerchief, he rises quickly to stop her from falling. He helps her into the chair, reaches for the jug to refill the cup, and hands it to her. As she drinks from it shakily, he feels a twinge of memory of another girl drinking from a cup…a girl with a handkerchief…He stoops to pick up the nun's handkerchief and notices the embroidered *P* on it. *Not the same letter.* Even so, he feels an inexplicable happiness. He holds out the handkerchief, his hand trembling. *There is a girl in my life*, he realizes. *Someone I love.*

With a sudden thrumming in his chest, Tonino takes a few

steps to sit at the edge of the bed and waits for Sister Caterina to compose herself.

"I'm sorry," she says, fanning herself with her handkerchief. "You are anxious to recover your memory. I hope I can help you."

RUSSO REMOVES HIS OVERCOAT and drapes it over an ornate walnut chair. He reaches for the bottle of Vecchia Romagna on the massive oak-and-walnut-inlaid sideboard. Pouring a generous amount of the brandy into a snifter, he watches the amber liquid swirl around for a moment. It reminds him of the golden striations of tonight's sunset.

He tips the glass, letting some of the brandy sweep across his tongue. He savours this initial indulgence before downing the rest of the brandy in one gulp. His esophagus quivers in response, and Russo feels the combined rush of pleasure and pain.

He proceeds to pour himself another brandy and then, loosening his cravat, stretches out on Liliana's settee, awaiting her entry. He shivers as he anticipates what she will be wearing. The filmy silk nightdress with the coral skirt panels resembling the reversed petals of a tulip, perhaps? Oh, how he enjoys lifting every flap, and telling her that he is in search of sweet nectar....

His wife has never been playful in their bed. She has always fulfilled her "duty" with a stiffness that has come to anger him. Unlike any woman he has ever bedded, Gina has always offered him clenched teeth and even more clenched thighs. What aroused him in their early marriage—namely, the swell of her bosom and swing of her rounded hips—eventually lost its appeal when she proved to be more of a prude than anything else, fearing that any attempt to enjoy the act would constitute mortal sin. She would whimper like a scared animal and start murmuring the *Ave Maria* every time he approached her. His varied attempts at arousing her left her mortified, and he eventually lost patience with her attempts to discourage him, so he took her out of frustration and spite, before discovering that her fear aroused him.

Eventually, though, Russo found himself yearning to mate with someone who could reciprocate pleasure and desire, and he found satisfaction in discreet encounters with the wives of other military officials whose subtle eyebrow lifts and deliberately timed glances in his direction when their husbands were engaged in conversation with others turned out to be an accurate indicator of their willingness to dally in a temporary escapade, or at the very least, a flirtatious exchange. Russo had ample confidence in his appearance, status, and intelligence, and he knew that these traits attracted women whose disenchantment in their husband or marriage was starting to show, whether in their fleeting but intent glances at him, the dismissive turn of their shoulders when their husbands addressed them, or in the more deliberate manner of finding a way to lean over to him, flaunting the curve of their bosom when in closer view.

These telltale gestures prompted Russo to come up with unique ways of meeting clandestinely with the woman, and it became a game that he looked forward to with anticipation at any social event.

In view of his new social activities, his attention to Gina languished, and she turned to religion even more, taking every opportunity to leave for a spiritual retreat in a convent. This delighted him, offering him greater opportunities for extramarital adventures.

Now, having returned from the Monastery of St. Francis of Paola, she is already involved in the preparations for the annual feast of the Madonna of the Stars at Monte Stella in Pazzano. Russo is not anxious to go home, but for the sake of propriety, he will do so. But first, he will enjoy his visit with Liliana, who is more than happy to accommodate his needs and desires in her own home.

One corner of his mouth lifts with the memory of their first encounter at the celebration marking the election win of Roccella's mayor, Pasquale Goldoni. Russo, along with anybody of standing in the community, was invited to this social event shortly after relocating in the area and assuming his new position as Colonel in charge of the repression of brigandage. Mayor Goldoni, like others in office before him, knew instinctively how to inspire and perpetuate patronage. Russo harboured no false illusions about invitation and many others by politicians and the like; the support of a Colonel in matters requiring delicate collaborations and associations is always deemed essential.

Russo usually accepted these invitations; they provided him with a pleasant diversion to his otherwise harsh profession of tracking down brigands and ordering their torture and imprisonment, and often, their hanging or shooting.

A grizzly profession, but necessary. And an official with *coglioni* is necessary if any progress is to be made in this backwards territory.

He had spotted Liliana gazing at the Ionian Sea from one corner of the spacious terrace. Oil lamps flickered along one wall, adding illumination as the sun began to set. Huge glazed pots filled with rosemary, a bay laurel, and other culinary herbs stood like sentinels at each corner of the terrace. Fancy wrought-iron planters hung over the terrace railings, and the blooms of bougainvillea, jasmine, and trailing verbena spilled over in a tangled splash of colour, like a suspended and well-used artist's palette. There were so many scents floating about that Russo felt overwhelmed. He moved around until he found a breezy spot at one end of the terrace. As he breathed in the salt-tinged air with relief, his eye wandered to the opposite side where it seemed another guest was doing the same thing.

Something in the bearing of the woman held his attention. And then, when she inadvertently turned and caught him staring, he managed a polite nod and casually looked away, pretending to search for someone among those helping themselves at the magnificent banquet table.

The long table was bedecked with bowls of fruit and platters of cheeses and spiced olives. Large ceramic trays at each end held freshly fried calamari and cuttlefish, the steam rising from the golden bundles. Alongside were glazed earthenware dishes that held stuffed eggplants and zucchini in a still simmering tomato sauce. Large ceramic bowls were filled with *arancini*, deep-fried rice balls filled with a morsel of cheese or cured pork. Baskets held wedges of coarse bread, and a series of tureens and bowls boasted a variety of vegetables, including green beans topped with slivered garlic and almonds, and salads of radicchio and arugula.

Normally, Russo would have enjoyed sampling the feast, but food was suddenly the farthest thing from his mind. He chanced another look at the unknown guest and found her looking back at the sea, which had now assumed an aura of indigo and periwinkle, with flaming streaks of red-orange above it that reminded him of the glossy skin of persimmons. And then, again, she turned and caught him looking intensely at her. This time, he saw her eyebrow lift before she looked away, and that tiny movement caused him to wonder, in tentative hope, that perhaps it was a sign.

For the next several minutes, they played their game of looking, turning away, looking longer, turning away, each initiating at one point, each feigning nonchalance. Despite his growing excitement, he sensed that something was slightly amiss. Yes, her gaze in his direction was calibrated, the slight tilt of her perfect eyebrows indicating guarded interest, but unlike other women in the past, she did not use her body in any way to arouse his senses. In fact, her stature demonstrated aloofness, and *that* aroused him even more.

Russo looked away and strode casually to a small group where Mayor Goldoni was in the middle of an animated discussion about rumours that Garibaldi was planning an attack on Venice, and that he was being paid by King Victor Emmanuel to attack the Austrians in the Balkans.

Russo waited until the mayor paused, then diverted his attention with a diplomatic but meaningful wink and tilt of his head. Goldoni, wiping his perspiring brow, stepped aside, blinking at Russo, as if expecting to hear some previously unrevealed political secret involving the recently established liberal government. He started when Russo inquired as to the identity of the woman at the terrace railing, and then his features smoothed out and he returned a conspiratorial wink.

"Heavens, Colonel," he murmured, cupping Russo's elbow as if they were intimate friends. "That is Signora Liliana." He explained that she had been widowed for over a year, at which time she had left her villa in the Bay of Naples and moved to a villa in the sunny coastal town of Roccella. She had an ample estate and a number of holdings and had only recently begun appearing in public.

Goldoni must have seen the gleam of interest in his eyes, as he gushed, "Would you like an introduction?"

Russo smiles at the memory of her gaze when the mayor led him across the terrace to make the introduction. Her ebony eyes locked with his, and up close, he could marvel at the impossible perfection of her widow's peak, and her flawless skin.

The hand Russo extended was accepted with not the usual limpness from women whose eyes hinted at lust but whose sweating hands indicated insecurity; rather, Signora Liliana's clasp was cool, firm, and lingering. He caught her fleeting gaze on the ring finger of his left hand. He didn't know if he imagined that she gave his hand a slight squeeze before releasing it, despite her observation of his marital status, but even the remote possibility sent his pulse into delirium, and for the first time since he had strayed from his wife, he felt flustered and almost inept, knowing that he could not employ his usual tactics of the hunt with this woman. This knowledge compelled him to leave the event early after a brief and polite exchange between them and the mayor. As he left Goldoni's villa and returned to his carriage, where his driver Dattilio awaited, he could barely restrain his body from trembling with the almost desperate desire to find a way—*any way*—to have this woman.

Russo smiles indulgently as Liliana's soft footsteps tread across the terracotta floor. She has been especially attentive since the attack on his carriage by the brigand chief, murmuring during the most intimate of moments how devastated she would have been if the *cornuto* Stefano Galante had maimed him, or worse.

Russo feels himself hardening now as he has done every time Liliana hastened to stroke him reassuringly after her husky declarations. She would render him almost delirious, squeezing and releasing, her supple body pressing into him like a contented kitten. The mere mention of the brigand chief made his insides roil, and combined with the deliberate pressure of Liliana's fingers, Russo would have to restrain himself from screaming. He began to indulge himself in the fantasy of Galante being bound and gagged in a corner of the room while forced to watch him and Liliana in their passion.

He wanted to relish each lingering thought of Galante squirming at the sight of Russo exploring Liliana's ripe body. He wanted the brigand chief to see what was *his* as he proceeded to peel off each item of her clothing with painstaking slowness, until Liliana's body was quivering with expectation at Russo's imminent conquest. He imagined Galante's eyes smouldering, his body writhing within the restraints as Liliana was completely exposed and shuddering from the release of her pent-up frenzy. And his complete satisfaction as he finally quenched his own passion, with Galante's eyes at his backside.

"*Vieni*," she is beckoning now, one hand outstretched. She is wearing something he has never seen before, a black, slightly transparent gown that clings to her body, its lacy designs emphasizing her most forbidden places. The breeze from the far window in her room wafts past her, causing ripples of movement all across the silk. He groans, and as he sets down his tumbler and strides to her, she laughs in that way that makes him want to rip the silk to shreds.

"Come, my lover," she laughs again. "Come and tell me about your day. I want to hear about every brigand bastard you captured."

GABRIELLA'S BREATH CATCHES IN HER THROAT. She's not sure what to say, what to do. *Should I go outside?* she wonders. *Or should I tell the woman to enter?*

"Signorina?" The voice is low for a woman, raspy, reminding Gabriella of old Nicolina.

"*Un momento*," she calls out, deciding it would be better to step outside the hut. She rises, and despite the day's heat, feels a shiver run down her arms. When she steps outside, she is surprised to see the figure of a man about ten paces away, and then realizes it *is* a woman, a woman in a man's clothes. She is slight, her pant legs baggy below a grey linen shirt, the seams of which hang midway between her shoulders and elbows. The shirt is tucked in, the sleeves rolled up, and the belt that encircles her willowy waist is buckled at the first hole, leaving a long leather strip that the woman has wrapped several times around yet still manages to hang down. Her footwear is the only part of her clothing that seems to fit correctly, laced snugly up her calves to enclose the bottoms of the trousers.

Gabriella's gaze moves upwards, and she is startled to note that the woman's features are ashen and made even more so in proximity to the grey shirt. Her face is angular, with unusual eyes of a colour Gabriella can only liken to the silver-grey underside of olive leaves. Her hair is concealed under a blue bandana, although a few light brown wisps have strayed. Gabriella gulps. Of all the perils she had imagined befalling her while journeying with Don Simone, encountering brigands, male and female, was not one of them.

This *brigantessa* is now smiling at her, a thin-lipped curve that makes her cheekbones jut out even more. She has stopped and is an arm's-length away from Gabriella. Gabriella shifts uncomfortably from one foot to the other.

"The chief has asked me to come and talk to you," the woman says in a voice that has little inflection. "He wants you to understand that it is safer to remain with the band than to continue on your own with the priest." Her eyes flash, and her mouth collapses into a sliver. "The chief has punished the brothers; you can be sure that they will not be stepping foot anywhere near you or the priest." She motions to the thicket leading to the clearing. "The chief wants me to stay close to you, while he is settling matters with some…misguided travellers. I am to see to your protection, in case other dangers should arise."

Gabriella blinks. *Other dangers?*

The *brigantessa's* eyes narrow. "I do not want to alarm you, Signorina, but we *are* in the Aspromonte mountains. There are natural dangers here, like wolves and wild boars, but even wilder are the rival bands of brigands. Consider yourself lucky to be with us. Palma's band would have eaten you alive, and you would have fared no better with Crocco and his criminals."

Gabriella's stomach twists. The woman before her is an outlaw herself, a criminal of God knows what crime. She shivers. How can she trust her or her chief?

"My name is Dorotea," the woman rasps. "The chief told me your name." Her gaze drops to Gabriella's shifting feet. "He said you were injured. Go rest now. He will most likely want to move on at dusk, and you won't be able to make much ground unless your wound has a chance to heal."

Gabriella nods and retreats into the hut, realizing she hasn't said a word to the *brigantessa*. She lies back on the pallet and despite the oppressive August heat, draws a blanket up around her. She listens to the receding shuffle of Dorotea's feet and then closes her eyes, wishing that she would soon awake from this horrible dream of brigands and their women, of wild men and beasts, and find herself once again safe in Camini, waiting for her father to come back from the fields, and Tonino to embrace her with promises of a lifetime together.

Smothering a sob in her palm, she squeezes her eyes shut

to block the dream she knows is a reality, but in spite of her efforts, Dorotea's silver-grey eyes won't disappear.

RUSSO DIPS HIS QUILL INTO THE INKWELL, anxious to share his latest news with General Zanetti....

Esteemed General,

It is my sincere hope that this letter finds you in optimum health and spirits, and that you are continuing to recover from your recent illness. It is not without a little envy that I think of your extended stay in the Sila mountains under its verdant canopies. From my singular visit to that area in 1852, I have fond recollections of treks to the heights of Sila Grande, from where the heavens seemed an arm's-length away, and whose wooded flanks plunged into a valley quilted with a patchwork of green, yellow, and brown. I can still picture the ripple of the smaller crags with their clay façades baking in the haze originating from the African scirocco. From where I stood with my colleagues, three seas were visible: the Ionian to the east, the Tyrrhenian to the west, and the Mediterranean to the south. It made one feel like an eagle, so majestic were the earth and seas spread out before us.

I am hoping you have found this poetic preface to your liking, dear General, aware that I am of your fondness for the romantic works of Alessandro Manzoni and the like, but I will proceed forthwith to inform you of the matters upon which I have been commissioned to report. By the time this correspondence reaches you, the remains—or more specifically, the head of the brigand chief Agostino Pizzelli—will be transported to the military station in Naples, from where it will then be turned over to the appropriate forensic specialists for examination.

Allow me to expound on some details. The brigand Agostino was smoked out of his mountain cave, captured, and, as justice dictates, has been summarily executed for his exceedingly long list of crimes. After his hanging, he was decapitated and exposed at the town entrance in the usual way—on a pike. However, due to our order to send the head to Naples for forensic study, the head did not remain long in exposition before being crated and duly forwarded to the Neapolitan officials.

Two of the chief's band members were with Pizzelli and met with the same demise, thus joining their chief in this most symbolic exhibition, one on either side. I am certain that this display has resulted in the temporary paralysis of the rest of Pizzelli's band. It is my hope that this will deter the brigands permanently; however, being under no illusions, I will continue to direct my forces to maintain a high level of vigilance, ensuring their readiness to respond to bands that are determined to persist.

As for the members of Pizzelli's band, six out of the twelve brigands were captured soon afterwards, and as a consequence, the band has collapsed. The four who remain at large have been spotted by our informers in an area that we have reinforced with additional surveillance, and I am quite confident that by the time you receive my subsequent correspondence, they will have been apprehended. For the present, I have ordered the six captives to be imprisoned and questioned under duress of potential hanging or shooting. I have no doubt that some, if not all, will capitulate and enlighten us in tracking down both remaining brigands and the band's supporters and informers, most likely relatives of the same.

Every battle won in this war on brigandage is significant, and in the wake of this successful mission, it is my fervent desire to forthwith deliver similar information to you about the brigand chief Stefano Galante, whose capture and arrest will continue to be on my list of priorities, along with those in his company. Although he leads one of the smallest bands in the territory, he has been most successful in his nefarious undertakings, eluding the forces of law for much too long. This can only be credited to a chain of informers that are masterful in covering their tracks and their connections to Galante.

Although the latter may not have the same dark history as Pizzelli, who, by all accounts, fully merited the nickname "Assassi-

no," Galante has been credited with at least a dozen kidnappings and subsequent extortions in the past year alone. My sources tell me that he and his band members are concentrated within the Aspromonte mountain range near Gerace. The Aspromonte is notorious for brigand activity, its dense woodlands and ubiquitous caves and hollows providing perfect hiding places for such villains. Hamlets are scattered about this territory, with homes clustered atop many a vertiginous summit like a multi-layered nest. The peasants who venture along the mule tracks and narrow roads have little to fear; the brigands prey mainly on visitors, especially those travelling by horse and carriage, many of whom are foreigners or gentry.

As you well know, dear General, my own carriage was apprehended by the brigand chief Galante, who was far from a "gentleman" in his treatment of myself and my companion. "*Galantuomo*" indeed! Had his band members not alerted him with their gunshots, forcing him to flee, I harbour no illusions as to what might have happened next. As it were, his mission was partially successful, having robbed my companion of articles of the finest gold, some of which were treasured heirlooms.

But now I have some treasures of my own...the discovery of Galante's identity and his village. My men are on tight patrol in Gerace and the surrounding area, ready to pounce on anyone who offers the slightest clue as to Galante's hiding place in the Aspromonte. If the villagers cannot or are not willing to provide any information with reasonable means on the part of my forces, then I will give the order for my officers to proceed in ways that are more...effective. If these peasants do not have the mental capacity to understand reason, I must employ any measures I have at my disposal to make them capitulate. Brigands like Galante cannot survive on their own without the occasional support of their friends or relatives who find ways to sustain them with food, supplies, and even weapons. In fact, these *manutengoli* are just as guilty as the brigands themselves.

It is my hope that the next several days will be fruitful in this regard, as I send my forces into Galante's village of Calvino to interrogate every last villager as to their knowledge of Galante's whereabouts, or their possible collaboration with him. We will employ all means available to us in order to gain the villagers' co-operation. Our first stop will be the home of Galante, and his immediate family.

As has occurred in previous undertakings of this kind, I anticipate success, as my team has become quite skilled in extracting information from peasants with their convincing methods of interrogation. I cannot resist wondering, dear General, if Galante, upon his capture, will show himself to be the *"galantuomo"* that he is reputed to be.

I will, nevertheless, demonstrate some restraint in my enthusiasm for now; I look forward to sharing my celebratory news with you in the very near future. Rest assured, esteemed General, that my intent is to destroy this scourge that has afflicted this territory. As always, I wish to express my gratitude for your faith in my leadership in the repression of brigandage, and I vow to persist in my mission until the scores of brigands poisoning this region with their abject lawlessness are brought to justice. Long live King Victor Emmanuel II! Long live united Italy!

As I complete this present communication, I send my regards to your dear wife, along with my best wishes for her health as well. And, I remain, as always, ready at your command, with the highest regard and respect, on this, the 17th day of August in the year 1862.

Your devoted comrade in the battle against brigandage,
Lieutenant Colonel Michele Russo

GABRIELLA EMERGES FROM A THICK ARC OF BUSHES. The edge of her skirt catches on some brambles, and as she tries to pull it away, it tears. She bends to extricate the material with her fingers and pulls back in pain as a thorn pricks her thumb. Almost immediately, she feels a throbbing sensation, like tiny needles shooting paralyzing stingers throughout her flesh. She stifles the urge to cry out, lest the brigand chief or one of his band members appear, and hobbles back to the hut. Don Simone is pacing with his head down, his lips moving noiselessly. He looks up, alerted by her shadow on the ground, and holds up his beads. His smile freezes and his eyebrows thatch together in a furrow. "What's the matter, my child? What has happened?"

As Gabriella shows him the ripped hem of her skirt, she realizes that her thumb has started to bleed. At Don Simone's worried look, she feels her eyes welling. She lets them spill over unchecked, until Don Simone's face is a blur in front of her.

"*Figlia mia*, don't despair. Come, sit down on this stump. Let me take a close look at your thumb."

Gabriella wipes her eyes with the backs of both hands. "I'm not crying about my skirt or my thumb. I'm upset about… about…."

"I know, child," Don Simone murmurs. "You've been dealt a hard blow, first losing your mother, and now your father." He bends down on one knee, retrieves a handkerchief from within his cassock, and wipes the blood from her thumb. "And now this business of going into hiding…." He shakes his head. "Thank God we have come this far in safety."

"God?" she rasps. "Am I to thank God for taking both my parents from me, for leaving me and Luciano orphans? God has damned me and my family."

"Gabriella, don't—"

"Don't what? Don't blame God for sending Signor Alfonso to ruin me and kill my father? For leading me to this nest of vipers?" Her voice breaks, and she feels the hot tracks of fresh tears run down her cheeks. She meets Don Simone's shocked eyes defiantly as she rises from the stump. "God be damned."

Don Simone gasps, his body going rigid as a stalk of canna drying in the sun. Then his shoulders sag. He says nothing for a few moments, and Gabriella hastily wipes away her tears, thinking he has left. But he is still there before her, motionless except for the twitching of his fingers around his wooden rosary.

He seems to be struggling for words; she watches his mouth open and close several times. His face, usually pale, is flushed, and glistening with perspiration. The mid-morning sun is already oppressive, elbowing its way through the gaps in the woodland to make its presence felt in the clearing. Gabriella shifts uncomfortably, her armpits and neckline already drenched. She watches the flurry of emotions on Don Simone's face: shock, disbelief, confusion, and sadness. And then his eyebrows are knitting together and the sadness disappears. He draws himself up, his blue eyes darkening, his eyelashes fluttering wildly. "Gabriella! 'Thou shalt not utter the name of the Lord in vain.'"

The angry flash in Don Simone's eyes stuns Gabriella. He has never looked at her this way before. Not even years ago, after her mother died, when he caught her pouring some of his *nocino* into a cup when she thought he had retired to his room. Not when she had left one of his treasured volumes out on the terrace, after promising him that she would take good care of it. *The Lives of the Saints.*...

She had finished her morning chores and Luciano was still napping. She flew to her room to retrieve the book, anxious for a few moments of time alone in her favourite spot. She climbed up the two sets of stone steps flanked on the outer railing by a canopy of vines and settled into the wide wicker chair in one corner of the terrace in the shade of the *giuggiola* tree. It was a glorious fall day, and the oblong berries hung in thick clusters above her, their reddish-brown skins gleaming in the early afternoon sun. She grabbed a handful and began to flip through the illustrated plates in the book, while munching contentedly.

A soft breeze ruffled her hair, and suddenly she realized that she was happy. The patter of the pigeons strolling about the terrace, warbling; the haze in the distant stretch of mountains, their tips poking the occasional cloud; the endless strip of Ionian beyond, azure with streaks of purple; the trill of a sparrow or the piercing cry of a goshawk; the bracing smell of rosemary in their glazed pots: All gave her such a sense of contentedness that she put the book down for a moment, and continued to look about her in wonder.

For the first time since her mother had died, she acknowledged that she was still able to be happy. She felt herself smiling then and proceeded to immerse herself in Don Simone's book. She couldn't read all the words—Don Simone had only recently begun to teach her to read, declaring that as long as she was living at the rectory, he would "elevate" her learning—but she didn't mind. The illustrations were mesmerizing; the saints with their robes of magenta and royal blue; their faces luminous below golden haloes; and others, wearing hardly anything, like poor *Santo* Rocco, his ribs protruding in sharp angles, his bare limbs covered in open sores and scored with bloody gashes. At the sight of him and other saints like him, Gabriella would cross herself and utter a prayer: "*Santo Rocco*, protect me and my family from all diseases. *Santa Lucia*, keep my eyes healthy. *Sant'Antonio*, help us to keep bread upon our table. *San Nicola*, keep us safe from natural disasters...."

That day, in the middle of one of those prayers, Luciano woke up screaming, and Gabriella, in alarm, jumped out of the wicker chair and tossed the book down on it, rushing to see what had befallen her brother, who usually woke up as placid as a lamb. She rushed to their room and found him crouched in horror on his pallet. His eyes were fixed on a black snake that was weaving its way through the vines outside the window, its body slithering purposefully over the window ledge. "Don't move," she told him, and scurried to fetch the straw broom she kept in the room. She edged the tip of the handle slowly to the writhing body, and once the snake had begun to curl around it, she flung it over the edge of the windowsill. She looked down into the rectory court-yard, catching a last glimpse of its tail before it disappeared behind a shrub.

She shivered at such an evil omen, and realizing it was starting to rain, closed the shutters and proceeded to comfort two-year-old Luciano, who was still shaking in fear. She wrapped a blanket over him and carried him down to the rectory kitchen, promising him his favourite treat, a beaten egg yolk sweetened with sugar and wine must. They sat in front of the fire as she spoonfed him his *uovo sbattuto* while listening to the crackling wood chips and the rain clicking an erratic beat on the clay roof tiles.

And then she remembered the book. She flew around the kitchen to the door that led outside, raced up the two flights of stairs to get to the terrace, where she pounced on the book, its maroon leather cover dripping. She tucked it under her vest and scurried inside, almost tripping on the slick steps.

Inside, she came face to face with Don Simone, who had just returned from a home visit on the outskirts of Camini. His overcoat was still on, and rainwater was sliding off his shoulders and dripping on the tiled floor. His gaze went from her to Luciano, then back to her and the book she was holding. Haltingly, she began to explain what had happened with the snake, and when she started to apologize about the book, Don Simone held up his hand to stop her. Expecting Don Simone to scold her, as he sometimes did to the congregation during his sermons, she stood biting her lip remorsefully, waiting for him to tell her that she would no longer be entrusted with any of his books. He hung up his overcoat and looked at her gravely.

"You did the right thing, child. You protected your little brother." He reached out for the book and Gabriella handed it to him in embarrassment. "I'm sorry," she blurted.

Don Simone propped it up near the heat of the fire and then turned to face Gabriella again. "You are forgiven," he smiled. "It won't be so bad once it dries." He peeked into the small earthenware bowl streaked with the remnants of Luciano's treat. Patting Luciano, Don Simone's face broke into a grin. "I don't suppose I could have an *uovo sbattuto* as well?"

Gabriella wishes Don Simone were grinning now, instead of fixing her with a scowl. "Now is not the time to abandon your faith, to distance yourself from God," he admonishes, his eyes boring into her. "Yes, I know you feel that God has abandoned *you,* has left you without parents. Taken Tonino away from you. It's hard to have faith under such terrible circumstances. But believe me, Gabriella, you must have faith now more than ever. *Coraggio!* Listen to these words from Proverbs: 'Wait on the Lord, be of good courage, and he shall strengthen thine heart; wait, I say, on the Lord.'" Don Simone gazes at the sky and then back at Gabriella. "As sure as the sun rises every morning, God is with you, Gabriella. Don't cast Him away. Instead, 'cast thy burden upon the Lord, and he shall sustain thee.'" Don Simone's voice is gentle, yet full of conviction. "The Lord will not fail you."

Deflated, exhausted by her spurt of anger, the heat, and the throbbing in her thumb, Gabriella cannot find any words with which to reply. She looks at her thumb and is alarmed at how swollen it has become. She hears Don Simone gasp before taking her hand again to look closely at the puncture. The tip of the thorn is still embedded in the flesh. Don Simone quickly extracts it with his fingertips, then reaches into his cassock for a flask. Gabriella winces as the alcohol sears the puncture wound. She feels battered, her leg and foot still aching, and now her thumb. And worse still, the constant pain in her heart, a pain that she cannot imagine ever subsiding. She thinks of everything and everybody she has lost.

Oh Tonino, how I wish you were here with me now. She turns away sharply from Don Simone, deliberately suppressing any words of gratitude, and biting her lip hard, she re-enters her hut.

ALFONSO CRINGES AT THE SUDDEN JOLT above his left ear. At that moment, Borbone veers to one side, neighing, and it is all Alfonso can do to remain in the saddle. When Borbone calms down, Alfonso catches up to Valerio, who is shirtless, his body as bronzed as a gleaming hazelnut. Alfonso has removed his outer jacket but cannot bring himself to take off his vest, let alone his shirt. He has no intention of breaching decorum, even in this godforsaken territory, where the only people they have encountered are peasants like Valerio, or worse.

Within a half-hour, they arrive in Locri. Valerio's inquiries about Don Simone and Gabriella are met with unconcealed interest. Why would Signorina Gabriella be travelling with her brother and Don Simone? Did something happen? Some kind of *disgrazia*? Where is her father? Why is the red-faced stranger looking for them?

Valerio, open-mouthed, turns to Alfonso. Without dismounting, Alfonso explains that robbers or brigands broke into the priest's home, stole what they could, killed poor Lorenzo Falcone, and fled. The poor girl, who could not bear returning to the place she and her father and brother called home for fear of the brigands returning, left Camini with her brother, under the protection of Don Simone. And *he,* Alfonso Fantin, as the new proprietor of the church estate, needs to settle affairs with the priest and his employees before returning to Turin.

The look of interest on the villagers' faces changes instantly to disdain. "Go back to Piedmont where you came from," yells an old goatherd, pounding the ground emphatically with his stick before waving it at Alfonso. "Leave the church to the people who believe in it. Damned Piedmontese," he spits before sauntering off. "It's not enough that they're taxing us into our graves. They have to take our religion away from us too."

Alfonso watches as the faces below him began to contort in anger. His heart jolts at the possibility of a peasant altercation. A snot-nosed boy picks up a stone and hurls it at him, catching him on the thigh. Alfonso nods to a white-faced Valerio and they make haste to leave amidst the raucous shouts of the peasants.

"And you, Valerio, what are you doing in the company of a *diavolo*? He'll take you straight to hell, boy."

They continue for a stretch without talking. Alfonso's heart has calmed down, but there is still a throbbing in his temples. Nearing the hamlet of Calvino, they come upon a watermelon vendor by the side of the road. Valerio haggles with the peasant until he nods with satisfaction and stoops to pick the biggest melon. Moments later, they stop to refresh themselves under the shade of a huge holm oak. Valerio splits open the melon with his knife, cutting thick wedges for them and for Spirito and Borbone. Alfonso swipes the flies away from the sweet red fruit, cursing in-between bites.

Once they have refreshed themselves, they proceed onward, passing long stretches of olive groves and the occasional farmhouse and vineyard. As they enter the hamlet, stopping at a public fountain, Alfonso inquires as to a tavern, where they can rest and have some decent food before questioning the villagers. Valerio dashes his hopes by telling him that they will have to travel another narrow stretch before arriving at a tavern on the outskirts of Gerace.

Reluctant to face another group of disgruntled peasants, Alfonso sends Valerio to the *piazza* to make inquiries about Don Simone and Gabriella, advising the boy not to mention the other facts, lest the villagers harbour the same resentments. Valerio unties his shirt around his waist and puts it back on before sauntering jauntily up the main road, whistling a cheerful tune and nodding a greeting to a few old men sitting on dilapidated wicker chairs outside their doorsteps while engaged in an animated game of *briscola*. Alfonso sees them glance curiously in his direction, but he turns away, unwilling to give them any indication that he intends to approach, and instead, proceeds to tether the horses and wait for Valerio's return.

It has been a good twenty minutes since Valerio set off for the *piazza*. Alfonso winces at the sudden pangs in his head. He waits anxiously by the public grotto that houses a tapped spring, and beside which stands a stone-built shrine dedicated to the Madonna of the Poppies. He lets Borbone and Spirito satisfy their thirst and while they busy themselves nosing the red berries on the nearby arbutus shrubs, Alfonso wanders over to the shrine to gaze at the statue of the Madonna with its fading and peeling paint. Around the periphery of the statue, the flower bed is a tangled mess of knapweed, ivy, jasmine, and heather. His eyes travel up to the face of the statue. Unlike the body, it is flawless, its peachy skin slightly more flushed at the cheeks, and lips the same tint as the red poppies painted at the base of the statue. Alfonso finds himself mesmerized by the black eyes that seem so lifelike, like polished river stones. So very much like...Gabriella's.

He starts at the shuffle of footsteps behind him and turns to find a panting Valerio.

"I spoke to the priest, Don Damiano; he said he hasn't heard from Don Simone, but that he might be making his way to Gerace, where he usually goes for his retreats."

"Well done, Valerio. Let's go, then."

"But Signor Alfonso, the Monastery of the Capuchins does not allow women. He couldn't possibly be taking Gabriella there."

Alfonso hesitates, his controlled excitement at Valerio's news diminishing. He shakes his head. "Nevertheless, it's a start." He gestures at the animals. "All right then. Let's be on our way, and once we reach the tavern, we'll eat properly and get a well-deserved rest. We can continue our search in the morning." His hand flies to the side of his head, and he curses under his breath. "Is there a pharmacy of some sort there? I will need to procure more medicine for this blasted head pain; I don't want to run out in the middle of this godforsaken countryside."

Valerio nods again, and they remount, the sun at their backs as they head off. To Alfonso's relief, the boy is quiet, and all they hear are the fading cries of the old men at their card game, and the trill of the ever-present cicadas.

As the village disappears around a bend, and they begin to ascend a side road that is flanked by brambles and ferns,

Valerio begins to sing a spirited folk song, much to Alfonso's dismay. He allows Borbone to fall back, annoyed with the boy's endless cheerfulness, and resigns himself to the sound of Valerio's ardent voice, with its crackles and pitch leaps. He wonders if the boy is thinking about Gabriella as he sings:

When I saw you at the river doing your washing,
holding the handkerchief I had given to you,
My eyes locked with your piercing dark eyes,
My heart beat fast; I couldn't help but sigh.
My Calabrese girl, for you I would die.
Tirulaleru laleru la la, 'sta calabrisella morire mi fa,
Tirulaleru, laleru la la, my Calabrese girl, for you I would die.

"Sentimental fool," Alfonso murmurs, and dismisses the sudden goosebumps on his arms as the result of a northerly breeze. The image of Gabriella's eyes and those of the Madonna of the Poppies intertwine in his mind at regular intervals as they ascend the steep mountain path to Gerace, distracting him from the vertiginous edges of the mule track and the darkening shadows. Valerio eventually stops singing, but just when Alfonso begins to silently rejoice, the boy begins yet another folk song, resonating with the joys and sorrows of love. As they reach the outskirts of Gerace, the sound of the cicadas have diminished along with the daylight. Valerio finally stops singing and coaxes his exhausted mule on to the final stretch before they reach the tavern. Alfonso, sighing with relief, follows with a smile. Decent food and a clean bed are all he wants.

And oleander-scented dreams of Signorina Gabriella.

PART VI
LA BRIGANTESSA
August-September 1862

G ABRIELLA RETREATS INTO THE HUT, breathing hard. Her leg is throbbing, though not as intensely as the previous day and night. Her thumb is still painful and the sweat that is already trickling down her face and neck and under her petticoat is causing an unbearable itchiness. She extracts her handkerchief from her skirt pocket and wipes her face and under her collar. She wishes she were by the river in Camini, washing clothes and cooling herself off. She fingers the embroidered "E" on the now soiled handkerchief and wonders what horrible fate awaits her and Don Simone. Her instinct urges her to pray, but she represses it, and instead makes a silent appeal to her dead mother. *Help us, Mamma. Wherever you may be, send us an angel of mercy to protect us, to lead us away from this place. And please, please send one to Tonino.*

Gabriella brings a hand to her mouth, thinking of the last moments she spent with Tonino. *Where is he now? Is he safe? Will he return to Camini alive? How will he ever find me? Will Galante release me and Don Simone?*

She starts at the approach of footsteps. The blanket at the doorway is pulled aside without warning and the brigand chief enters brusquely, the panels of his black cloak resembling the dark wings of a vulture. Gabriella gulps, clenching her handkerchief.

"Sit down," he orders. "There are instructions I need to give you."

Gabriella slips the handkerchief back in her pocket and walks to her pallet. There is no other place to sit, other than on *his* pile of blankets. She slips her hand into the pocket of her skirt, touching the knife she placed there earlier, and she pauses, wondering how successful she might be at plunging it into him, before he can....

And then she feels the brigand chief directly behind her, and her head jerks slightly in alarm. His breath is even, fanning the side of her neck and face. Her fingers tremble. She clenches the knife handle and then releases it. Whatever she might be able to do to him, she would ultimately have his band to deal with. The brothers. The *brigantessa* Dorotea. Her heart pumping, she turns without looking at him, and lowers herself onto the pallet, wincing slightly.

He crouches down and she opens her mouth to scream when he lifts the hem of her skirt, only to realize that he merely wants to examine the wound on her calf.

"No infection." He readjusts her skirt but does not rise. "You'll be able to travel if we need to leave, but for now, you and Don Simone will remain here with the band." He stands, and when she tentatively looks up, his eyes are narrowed. "It will be necessary for you to wear the appropriate clothing," he says, pausing to make a sweeping gesture with one hand, "for this kind of life."

Gabriella blinks. At the sound of footsteps, she turns to the doorway, where a slight movement of the blanket makes her release her pent-up breath. *Don Simone.*

"*Permesso?*"

A female voice. Gruff, barely audible. Gabriella bites her lip, disappointed.

"Come in." Galante waits for the *brigantessa* to shuffle forward and then he turns to the woman, who is holding a roughly folded pile of clothes and a pair of scuffed footwear. "Leave them with me," he orders. "And get started for your uncle's place. Take Gaetano's mule. Fill one of the saddlebags with some of the remaining wild fennel, in case you're stopped." He pauses and Gabriella watches as Dorotea hands him the pile. He tosses the footwear on the ground near Gabriella's feet. Dorotea's arms drop and she continues to stand there, her lips parting as if she has something she wants to say.

"Well, what is it?" Galante says, his jaw flicking impatiently.

"You told me you wanted me to watch over the girl." Her voice is so low Gabriella can barely make out what she is saying.

Galante's jaw clenches. "You will do that when you return with the supplies. We're running low. We'll need whatever your uncle can spare."

Dorotea continues to stand sullenly, her angular face appearing even more stark. Gabriella watches the rise and fall of her chest under the coarse linen shirt. In her oversized trousers, Dorotea could easily pass for a man.

"What is it?" Galante says pointedly.

"What will I offer my uncle?"

Galante nods and fishes inside one of his pockets. He hands the *brigantessa* a clump of assorted bracelets and gold rings decorated with precious stones. Gabriella gasps softly.

"I will expect you back tomorrow morning, once you meet with…" he glances sideways at Gabriella, "with our other associate." He waits as Dorotea plunges the jewellery deep into a trouser pocket and then he turns back to hand Gabriella the pile of clothing, which, she can now plainly see, consists of a man's trousers and shirt. She rises and takes them, standing awkwardly while Dorotea, her mouth twitching, glances from her to Galante with a gleam in her hooded eyes. Without responding, the *brigantessa* adjusts her bandana, turns sharply, and leaves the hut.

Gabriella's eyes drop to the clothes in her hands. She feels her stomach clenching. *How can I wear these?* She looks frantically at the doorway, willing Don Simone to appear and somehow convince Galante to leave her be, but she knows her hope is futile.

The brigand chief lifts a hand to touch Gabriella's hair and she stiffens, holding her breath. *Where is Don Simone? I will use the knife if I have to, the consequences be damned.*

She hears Galante's deep intake of breath, and despite her earlier vows, begins to silently recite a *Pater Noster*. To her relief, Galante turns and leaves the hut.

Gabriella crosses herself, and with a heavy heart, begins to take off her clothes.

DON SIMONE IS SEATED ON A STUMP in the shade of a giant chestnut tree, where the brigand chief told him to sit. He has no intention of disobeying the chief's orders. Although the spot offers him some respite from the burning sun, his cassock is soaked through in places; it feels like he has collected pools of sunlight in every fold. He wipes his brow and looks at the hut, biting on his lower lip. His wooden rosary is wrapped around one hand, but he is not reciting any *Ave Marias* or *Pater Nosters*. His mind is occupied with thoughts of Gabriella, and what the brigand chief is saying. Or doing. And now the *brigantessa* Dorotea has entered the hut with a pile of clothes.

A flash of green diverts his attention and he spends the next few moments watching a lizard skitter past his foot. It stops suddenly, frozen in position, and then darts away, its tapered tail the last thing Don Simone sees before it blends into the forest bracken.

He looks back at the hut. Dorotea is walking out, her mouth a thin line, her reed-thin body as stiff as the canna stalks Gabriella uses to entwine garlands of drying figs. She strides past him without a glance, disappearing through a thicket, and while Don Simone shakes his head, bemoaning her lack of respect for a man of the cloth, the brigand chief emerges as well. His face, darkened by its stubble, is marred by a deep frown. Don Simone shifts uncomfortably on the stump, and the movement catches Galante's eye.

He advances and is soon standing next to Don Simone, his conical hat casting his face in shadows as he looks down. Despite the fact that he is wearing a substantial black cloak, no doubt weighted down by any number of weapons concealed within its folds, his face gives no indication of discomfort. Wiping a rivulet of perspiration trickling from one side of his own face, Don Simone hopes that the thick gold chain and crucifix around Galante's neck is a genuine sign of the man's sympathy and respect for their shared religion. He wonders if he dare question the chief.

He reciprocates Galante's nod and attempts to rise, but he steps on the hem of his cassock and throws himself off balance. The brigand chief's arm shoots out to steady him, and after regaining his composure, he decides he must make an appeal to Galante. "Signor Galante, may I broach some matters to you—some matters that concern Signorina Gabriella and myself, and our unfortunate predicament?"

The brigand chief raises an eyebrow.

"Oh, oh, not *this* predicament," Don Simone hurries to explain. "I meant the—the situation that compelled us to leave our hamlet, and why we must continue along our way."

Galante glances at the hut and then back at Don Simone. "Come, we can have this discussion in the hut with Signorina Gabriella."

"No! I mean, I'm sorry, Signor Galante, but I fear this may be too much for my ward, in light of her injuries and disposition. Could we not discuss this privately, at least for the moment?" He watches the flicker of emotions on Galante's face while moving his fingers up and down his rosary beads.

"Very well," the brigand chief rasps, gesturing to a circle of stumps several yards away.

When they are both seated, Don Simone feels Galante's expectant gaze on him. "The Signorina was forced to leave Camini. She stabbed a landowner who was staying at the rectory." He fingers his rosary nervously. He pauses for a moment, wondering how much he should divulge. The news about the sale of the church lands? The arrival of Alfonso Fantin and his brother?

Don Simone proceeds with this, his tone measured and his voice steady. When he gets to the part about his discovery of Gabriella in the barn, he can hear his voice quaver, and as he attempts to regain his composure, he sees Galante glance sharply at the hut several times. Don Simone swallows and continues with his account of the sight of Gabriella's father at the foot of the stairs with his head smashed and bleeding, Gabriella sobbing hysterically, and the prone body of Alfonso in the hayloft, his neck slit and slimy with blood after Gabriella attacked him to defend herself.

At Galante's intake of breath, Don Simone pauses, takes a deep breath himself, then continues telling him about Gabriella collapsing in the rectory, the return of Luciano, the preparations to leave Camini to find a sanctuary for Gabriella and prevent her certain arrest, their flight out of Camini and stay at Don Filippo's monastery, their decision to relinquish Luciano into the hands of the Sisters, their discovery that Fantin survived and that the forces of law were searching for them, and their entry into the Aspromonte mountain range.

At this point, Don Simone hesitates; Galante knows everything that has transpired since then. He feels the brigand chief's eyes fixed upon him unblinkingly. Perhaps he just imagined Galante's reaction at the news of Alfonso's attack upon Gabriella. In his chosen way of life, an assault upon someone, whether man or woman, would be considered an ordinary circumstance, he thinks.

However, he *did* rescue Gabriella from being assaulted by one of his own band members, he tended her wound, and he administered some medicine to bring down her fever. But *why?*

Don Simone shakes his head, wanting to rid himself of any supposition as to why a brigand chief would curry favour on Gabriella. He must convince Galante to let them go on their way to the Augustinian monastery suggested by Don Filippo.

The sooner they are out of the Aspromonte, the better. "So you see, Signor Galante, how essential it is for me to find refuge for Signorina Gabriella. She is truly an orphan, and she will need to be taken care of in a safe place, where she might, God willing, eventually regain her strength."

"And her brother?" Galante's eyes narrow. "Where is he?"

Don Simone shakes his head. "My dear associate Don Filippo felt he would be safe in the care of the Sisters at the Convent of St. Anna in Gerace. Once the situation was resolved, we would return to the monastery for Luciano. And then we would all return to Camini," he ends wistfully.

"And how do you suppose the situation will be resolved?" There is a bitter twist to Galante's lips. "A peasant girl stabs a landowner who is attempting to rape her and flees, leaving him for dead. He survives and engages the forces of law to find her and bring her to justice." His eyes bore into Don Simone. "As far as I can see, the resolution you seek would require a miracle."

Don Simone searches the brigand chief's face for signs of mockery but sees none. His eyes drop to the heavy crucifix hanging at the apex of Galante's throat and he sighs. "Yes, my son, I suppose we do need a miracle. And I will have to leave that in God's hands. The only thing I can do is to get Gabriella to a safe place."

"She's safe *here*."

Don Simone swallows. "But...but we're in the wilderness. There are dangers...."

"Danger will not befall her while she's with me," the brigand chief drawls. "You have nothing to fear."

"But she—*we*—can't live like *brigands*," Don Simone gasps.

Galante gives Don Simone a measured look. "Letting you go would not only put you in more danger, it would put me and my band in danger. You could be intercepted and questioned by the carabineers, who have their ways to make you talk, or you might fall into the path of other bands of brigands. Bands whose chief would be the first to pitch you into a ravine before feasting on Signorina Gabriella and then tossing her to his men for the crumbs."

Don Simone winces. Is Galante truly concerned, or is he attempting to conceal his real motives toward Gabriella by making the other bands in the area seem like savages?

"I don't imagine you and the girl will be here forever," Galante says wryly. He glances again at the hut. "But we don't think of more than one day at one time. We survive on the hare we catch today, not on the wild boar we hope we will catch in one week's time. For now, you and the Signorina will remain under my protection." He stands up, the set to his jaw brooking no argument, and Don Simone's stomach churns with the realization that he and Gabriella are as helpless as newborn chicks nesting in the shadow of an eagle.

"Before I forget," Galante says, fishing into a pocket, "I believe this belongs to *you.*"

Don Simone gasps softly as the brigand chief holds out his ring. He nods, speechless and puts it back on his finger. As Galante strides away, his dark cloak flapping at his sides, Don Simone hears a shuffle from the hut. The brigand chief stops to look as well.

The blanket is drawn aside, and as Gabriella emerges, Don Simone inhales sharply. This is not the child in his care, the girl he knows. His gaze travels from the brown linen shirt to the well-worn trousers tapering to below her knees. And to her calves, emphasized by light stockings and laced–up leather footwear. No, this is not Gabriella; this is a *brigantessa*. Their eyes lock, and his heart constricts. *Oh, my poor child, what in God's name is to become of us now?*

THE FIRST CROWING FROM THE COURTYARD below his window makes him stir, but it isn't until the rooster's raucous cries have incited the warbling of the hens and pigeons that Tonino awakes. He tentatively brings his fingers up to his face and remembers that his bandages have been taken away by Sister Emilia, with assistance from Sister Caterina. Tonino sits up cautiously, not wanting to send his head in a spin with a quick movement, and then notes with pleasure that his shirt and trousers have been washed, ironed, and placed on his chair. He dresses and shuffles over to the window overlooking the courtyard.

The convent is awakening. Sister Anna is rustling about the glazed terracotta herb pots squatting on the low walls of the courtyard, collecting basil, rosemary, parsley, and sage for the day's meals. Sister Nora is whisking the bird droppings from the earthen floor with her enormous straw broom before scattering grain to the clustering hens. Tonino turns away at the sound of the soft shuffle of the sisters' feet on their way to the chapel; the officious clearing of the throat belongs to the abbess, whose confident, staccato-like tread on the slate floors of the convent is also easily identifiable.

When he looks out the window again, Sister Nora has gone, leaving the bolder hens to squawk at each other, trying to get to the last morsels of grain. Sister Anna, her basket spilling over with herbs, has caught his movement in the window, and has shyly looked down and scurried out of the courtyard.

Heavier footsteps approaching his room draw his attention to the doorway, where Sister Caterina is entering with a tray of steaming goat's milk and freshly baked sage and lemon *biscotti*, a dusting of ash still visible on their lightly charred edges. She sets the tray down on the table by the window, and leaves him to enjoy his breakfast alone, reassuring him that she will be back shortly. He nods and sits down, biting into his milk-dipped biscuit while allowing the events of the previous evening to flood his memory.

The abbess had received some extraordinary news from Don Filippo, abbot at the Monastery of the Capuchins, and she in turn relayed the news immediately to Tonino, while Sister Emilia removed the rest of the bandages from his head. The room suddenly tilted around him, the bodies of Abbess

Emanuela, Sister Emilia and Sister Caterina closing in on him like a murder of crows, their habits a black blur. He remembers being made to drink some kind of spirits, the liquid burning his throat but helping to clear his vision, and he listened to the abbess's news while Sister Emilia wiped the beads of sweat from his temples.

Garibaldi. Wounded at Aspromonte. His son Menotti injured as well. Defeated by General Emilio Pallavicini and the Royal troops. Transported by stretcher from the mountains to the coastal town of Scilla, where he rested overnight in a shepherd's tent, and was placed the next morning on a man-of-war, the *Duca di Genova,* along with Menotti, ten officials, and the three doctors. Seven *garibaldini* dead, five from the Royal army. Dozens wounded. Some of the regular riflemen, who in the ten-minute skirmish had left their positions to join up with Garibaldi's volunteers, were rounded up, arrested, and shot as traitors. When Garibaldi's men realized that their General had fallen, some retreated into the forest.

Tonino suddenly envisions the wave of volunteers rushing back from the Royal Army's attack, a wall of bodies and arms swinging into him, pushing him to the forest's edge. There, his foot caught on a tangled root, precipitating him over a ridge and miraculously, onto a ledge padded with overgrown shrubbery instead of into the endless depths of the ravine....

Tonino sets down his cup of milk, his stomach lurching with the renewed acknowledgement that their mission has failed. *Rome is not ours.* The realization sits hard in his stomach like a granite boulder.

But Garibaldi is alive. And *he* is alive. His head slumps forward into his hands as a new memory surfaces, those precious seconds before slipping over the edge: Massimo, reaching forward to grab him but failing as his own back suddenly stiffens and his body crumples, his face ashen with the realization that he has been shot. Tonino feels his throat constrict. Massimo's face will haunt him forever. *Why did Massimo have to be one of the seven?* His poor family. Tonino's stomach lurches. Massimo will never have a family of his own. He will never meet a girl, experience love….

Gabriella! My girl. Tonino lets the memories swarm him. Her embrace by the river. Her treasured handkerchief, her skin the scent of oleander blossoms. Camini….

Tonino looks down at the lemon sage biscuit crushed between his fingers. He brushes the crumbs away and breathes deeply in the attempt to calm the pounding of his heart. *I must get back to Gabriella.* He feels his eyes misting, and when he hears someone re-entering, he blinks rapidly.

"My name is Sister Renata," the nun is saying. She is holding a young child by the hand. Tonino wipes his eyes. *A boy.* He is not a vision. *He* is the one Tonino mistook for an angel.

"Luciano," Tonino hears himself croak. *"Luciano!"*

ALFONSO NODS DISMISSIVELY AT THE MOON-FACED innkeeper and promptly shuts the door. He glances about the room. It is furnished with two single beds and nightstands, each on opposite whitewashed walls. The room itself is small, but the higher-than-usual ceiling makes it feel bigger, although the cobwebs suspended in each corner are somewhat disconcerting, swaying gently with the slightest flow of air. Otherwise, the room is fairly clean, the wide floor planks obviously swept and oiled. As in the room in Naples, chamber pots have been supplied, tucked under each bed, but there is also a more private water closet at the end of the hall outside their room, pointed out to them with an air of pride by the innkeeper himself moments earlier, as if, Alfonso thinks scornfully, he were displaying a room of distinction. Yes, it is certainly a step up from that hovel in Naples, but only a step.

He deposits his packsack on the bed nearest the window and opening the shutters, looks out onto a tangled garden. A stretch of prickly pear bushes thrives among the wild *macchia* vegetation beyond. The setting sun is leaning into the wooded flanks of the distant Aspromonte range, casting its bronze glow along and down its granite ridges. Alfonso turns from the window, leaving the shutters open to let in a breeze. As the door opens and Valerio enters, having tended to Spirito and Borbone before leading them to the *locanda's* stable, the noises emanating from the tavern cut into the silence, and his senses are suddenly aroused by smells of meat frying.

He motions to Valerio to set down his packsack on the bed closest to the door and to accompany him to the tavern. He is surprised when the boy's eyes widen and his cheeks flush deeply. His mouth opens and he sputters for a moment, until he is finally able to voice the words. "I'm s-sorry, Signor Alfonso. I don't have…I mean, I have brought some cheese and bread…."

Alfonso holds up a hand. "Now, now, young man, surely you must be tired of cheese and bread. Come, it's on me. You've done quite an adequate job leading us through this wretched countryside. A hearty meal is the least I can offer you to show my gratitude that I'm still alive and not in a heap at the bottom of a ravine, or worst still, impaled by a wild boar." He chuckles at the disbelief stamped on Valerio's face. "Not used to this kind of treatment, are you? *Andiamo!* If the food tastes as good as it smells, I'll buy us both a second serving!" He slaps Valerio on the back and ushers him out the door and down the hall until they come to a narrow stairway leading down to the tavern on the main floor.

The smells have intensified, and the satisfied looks of the patrons eating from steaming plates heaped with dark meat and a chunky sauce pleases Alfonso, who chooses a corner table. He pushes a still hesitant Valerio over to a chair and then sits down and loosens his vest. A woman with tired eyes and a gaunt face approaches their table, and he immediately orders a bottle of wine and two plates of the stew the others are having. She nods, and turns quickly away, but not before he notices how her eyes sweep over the fine cloth of his tailored jacket and trousers, and the gleaming details of his boots.

He watches her as she leaves, her long-sleeved grey tunic tied at the waist by a twisted cord of some sort and draped over a linen skirt that reaches to her boots. A few moments later, she re-enters with a covered tureen and two plates, and is followed by a boy of roughly fourteen, who is holding a jug and two terracotta goblets. The boy murmurs something to Alfonso, his eyes lowered deferentially, but Alfonso fails to understand the dialect. He sees Valerio nodding, though, and shrugs, his eyes now shifting to the woman. He watches as she sets down the tureen without a word, lifts the lid, and ladles a generous portion of the stew onto a plate, sets it before Alfonso, then puts a smaller portion on Valerio's plate.

"Fill it," Alfonso snaps, unable to conceal his irritation. "He's a young man, not a child. And bring us some bread." She casts a sideways glance at him as she is leaving, starting when he adds, "Now!" He turns to Valerio, who is perspiring, although Alfonso suspects it is more from embarrassment than from the steam rising from his plate. As the boy fills their goblets with a murky red wine that looks as dark as the meat sauce, he says, "Ask the boy what kind of meat this is."

"Oh, I can tell you, Signor Alfonso. It is *cinghiale*, fried with onions and garlic, and with a sauce of tomatoes and eggplant."

"Wild boar?" Alfonso chuckles. "Well, I suppose it's better that I'm eating *it* instead of it eating *me*." He puts a forkful of the meat into his mouth and nods appreciatively. He notices that Valerio hasn't begun to eat; he is waiting for Alfonso to give him a signal, no doubt. He laughs. "Are you waiting for me to feed you?" He takes a drink from the goblet, grimaces, and spears another piece of meat, watching Valerio with amusement. "*Mangia*. This will put hair on your manhood."

Valerio chokes on his first mouthful, and blushes deeply as the woman, who has returned with a bread basket and has heard Alfonso's remark, lowers her gaze and purses her thin lips. Alfonso takes a hunk of bread, slides the bottle of wine over to the woman, and growls, "Take back this bloody piss and bring me the best wine you have. The best, you hear?"

He brings a piece of meat to his mouth, sucking the sauce from the bone. He calls out to the retreating grey skirt, "And bring us more meat!"

BY THE TIME STEFANO RETURNS TO THE HIDEOUT after hearing Tomaso's reciprocated bird call, it is almost midnight. He has no intention of retiring to his hut, though, until Tomaso fills him in on the events of the day. Once the brothers have tended to Stefano's mule and have retreated to their lean-to, Stefano saunters to the gathering place. Tomaso is standing, waiting for him.

Stefano sprawls out on a mossy bank while Tomaso sits on one of the stumps. Stefano listens avidly as Tomaso begins his account.

Shortly after Stefano left with the brothers, Don Simone and the girl ate some bread, onions, and olives provided by Gaetano. The priest then opened his breviary and read a few passages. The girl stayed for the first passage, then excused herself and still limping slightly, made for the hut, where she spent the better part of the afternoon. The priest seemed saddened by her departure but cheered up when Tomaso stayed on to listen. Gaetano returned late in the morning, with a plump string of fowl and two rabbits. He arranged himself at the far limits of the clearing, so he could also listen to Don Simone and proceed to pluck and skin his catch without offending the priest's sensibilities. The priest appeared delighted at the brigands' display of faith, and even more so when the men recited a decade of the rosary with him. All three retreated to their respective resting spots while the sun was at its highest, the only movement coming from the girl, who left Stefano's hut momentarily in the mid-afternoon for the privacy of the woods. The priest, hands still clasping his wooden rosary, retreated to his pallet and fell into a slumber that lasted into the evening.

At dusk, Gaetano set about preparing the animals on a spit over a bed of hot coals, careful not to send plumes of smoke into the sky. When the food was ready, he signalled to Tomaso to have the priest and the girl gather around the fire for the rationing, saving a portion for Stefano and the brothers.

After the meal, which the girl barely touched, she returned immediately to the hut, and the priest took out his beads and his breviary once again. He voiced his praise to God for the bounty he had just enjoyed, thanks to the generosity of the band members, and for the opportunity to share His word with an audience, albeit a small one. The priest engaged Tomaso and Gaetano in another decade of the rosary, and then got up and walked about as contentedly as a small child stooping to gather acorns under the forest canopy, before returning to his shelter for the night.

Stefano nods without a word and Tomaso leaves to assume his watch further down the mountain. Stefano pulls out a cheroot and gazes alternately at the sky and his hut. He breathes in the night air and smiles with satisfaction at the outcome of today's mission. He and the brothers accompanied their "visitor"—an engineer by the name of Rosario Talese—to the edge of the village of Canolò, where he was to spend a fortnight with the mayor. During their trek, Stefano listened to his incessant nattering with amusement, attentive to how his information might better serve him, although, from the expression on the faces of the brothers, it was clear that they would have liked to employ one of their many ways to stifle the man's nervous chatter.

Talese and the mayor were to discuss some engineering modifications to the main road. It posed an ever-present danger as it snaked through a perilous stretch of jagged clay hills that occasionally shifted, sending loose wedges of white stone hurtling down the sides.

The villagers were still dealing with the after-effects of the earthquake of 1783, which had altered the landscape by swallowing half the village, and slamming mountain against mountain, building against building. Even all these years later, the *Passo dei Mercanti* leading from Canolò through the mountains into the western part of Calabria was still hazardous, having recently sent a chunk of clay hurtling into the path of a team of horses transporting the carriage of a visiting landowner from Reggio. The resulting death of one horse and the driver, and the near death of the landowner, precipitated the latter, after recovering from his multiple bruises, to recruit the best engineer from Naples to examine the stretch and prepare a plan to restore it in order to ensure the safety of The Merchant's Pass to travellers and villagers alike.

Stefano exhales a long wisp of smoke, sending it upward. He cocks an ear at a slight rustling, and realizes it is caused by Don Simone, shifting on his pallet at the edge of the clearing beyond the arc of pines. He breathes in the night air, enjoying the peacefulness and the sounds that always soothe him after a long day: the faint gurgle of a distant stream, the rustling of the dormouse through the bracken, and the haunting call of a distant wolf.

He drops the cheroot stub and stamps it out with the tip of his boot before extracting a purple bag from the inside of his cape. This had to be one of his most efficient and successful missions, thanks to a most co-operative captive and an even more efficient mayor.

Stefano had ordered Raffaele to hide Talese in one of the caves skirting the base of Canolò, while Roberto passed Stefano's carefully written ransom request to a terrified goatherd who happened to be getting some refreshment for himself and his herd at a mountain spring, and who promised to deliver it to the mayor personally. The goatherd, abandoning his goats to nibble on a patch of hillside overgrown with broom, scurried into the village. He alerted the mayor as to the brigands' request, and waited while the mayor, who was on the verge of appealing to the police force to investigate the cause of the engineer's tardiness—Talese had been expected to arrive the day before—sprang into action and amassed the funds in three hours, without even attempting to barter for a lower ransom. He needed the engineer, and nothing was going to prevent him from carrying out his election promise of repairing the mountain pass. He handed the goatherd a bag holding the requested ducats, and sent him on his way, even promising him a generous stipend if he ensured the engineer's safe arrival in Canolò.

Stefano watched and waited atop Mastro on a bluff high above the village, able to see both the cave where Talese and Raffaele awaited, and the transaction between the goatherd and Roberto. After the goatherd disappeared, Roberto put his time to good use, distancing one of the animals from the rest of the herd, before cornering and slaughtering it. He sliced up the meat into large pieces before tossing them into a sturdy packsack, and then flung the carcass into a nearby ravine. After splashing the blood off his hands and arms at the well, he assumed his post behind a large boulder and awaited the return of the goatherd.

By late afternoon, the goatherd reappeared, handed the bag to Roberto, who made him promise to sit by the rock while he went to retrieve the engineer. Roberto undoubtedly would have left the man trembling with fear, leaving him with no uncertainty as to his fate if he disobeyed and strayed from the spot to alert anyone who might be passing by. In fact, Roberto later revealed that he had pulled out a goat leg from his bag and waved it at the ashen-faced goatherd to emphasize his point, before dashing away. A half-hour later, Stefano watched as Talese was thrust at the goatherd, who embraced the engineer as if he were his own long-lost son, and escorted him back to Canolò, unharmed as promised by the brigand chief.

When the men had disappeared around a bend, Roberto gave his warning bird call and set out with Raffaele to meet up with Stefano at their pre-arranged spot. Stefano immediately delved into the bag and gave the brothers their share for their work in the mission. They pulled out their wine flasks to celebrate in the glen where their mules were tethered, and after a snack of hardened cheese and prickly pears that grew in profusion along the periphery of the glen, Stefano headed back to Monte Galante, with the brothers close behind.

Stefano slips a hand underneath his cloak to grasp the scapular of the Madonna. Ordinarily, he would have descended the mountain to leave an offering at the Shrine of the Madonna of the Poppies in Calvino, but he is anxious to get back to his hideout. He rises and after taking a glance around, he strides to his hut, pausing at the doorway to see if his entry has caused the girl to awaken.

She does not stir from her position on the pallet. His blanket lies partially over her fully-clothed body. Dorotea's clothes. Or rather, her dead husband's. They are too large for Gabriella, but they do what they are now meant to do: hide her gender and help her in her role as *brigantessa*. It is simply not practical to roam the countryside in a dress, not only because of the endless walking and climbing up and down mountains and hillsides, especially during the night, but also because of the nature of some of the brigands they might encounter.

Better to look like a man in these wild Aspromonte mountains. Although, he has to admit, the law tends to demonstrate more clemency with female brigands than with males. Females are more likely to end up in prison or sent to labour camps instead of being shot instantly, hung, or decapitated like many brigands. The most fortunate of the brigands are served with a sentence of life imprisonment.

Stefano rubs the stubble on his face as he looks down upon Gabriella. It is hard to believe that at best, life imprisonment awaits her for the crime she committed. The crime of self-defence for trying to protect her honour. He walks over to his blanket and removes his boots and cloak. She is so beautiful. *Innocent.* His stomach twists at the thought of the man who

attempted to defile her. *Bastardo!* He would like nothing better than to meet him face-to-face. To slam his knee into his
groin, watch him crumple, watch his swine face contort with
pain. Stefano looks at Gabriella's face, peaceful in sleep, and
breathes deeply. Her hair is spread out on his blanket in rip-
pling waves. He can't help himself from reaching out to touch
it. He is only inches away when her eyes fly open, and before
his hand moves any further, she has sprung one arm out from
under her blanket and is pointing something at him, her hand
clenching it tightly,

Stefano arches his eyebrows at the glint of his own knife
and slowly withdraws his extended hand. "I was wondering
when you were going to try to use that," he murmurs, his eyes
meeting hers unwaveringly.

ALFONSO TAKES A TENTATIVE SIP OF THE WINE, ready to give the
server—the same boy who brought the first bottle—a stinging
reproach, but decides that it is tolerable, and although it hardly
compares to the wines he deems tolerable back home and usually avoids, Alfonso accepts that he cannot expect any better,
given his whereabouts. He flings several coins onto the table,
and nods to the boy, whose furrowed eyebrows have ironed out
in relief. When the boy has retreated into the kitchen, Alfonso
sits back, satiated from the second serving of *cinghiale* stew,
and swirls the dusky red wine over his palate.

He catches Valerio's eye and winks. "Are you sure I can't
tempt you with this..." he inclines his goblet, chuckling, "nectar
of the Calabrian gods?"

Valerio shakes his head, and then flushing, nods. "No, Signor
Alfonso. I mean, yes, I'm sure. *Grazie,* you've been generous
enough."

Alfonso shrugs. "Suit yourself." He reaches into his jacket
and pulls out his pocket watch. "I'll be finishing my wine and
retiring shortly. We should be heading out before dawn if we
don't want to roast in the heat of the day. With any luck, we

might be able to garnish a clue about Signorina Gabriella." He grimaces at a dull ache that has begun to tap along one temple. "Perhaps we should start enquiring at the Monastery of the Capuchins. The abbot may have received some news from Don Simone. As you mentioned, the good priest embarks on regular retreats in these parts, and therefore, the monastery seems to be the logical place to begin." His eyes narrow. "I understand there's also a convent here, but as it is located centrally, I doubt Signorina Gabriella would be refuged there."

He sees the boy's eyes light up. "Oh, Signor Alfonso, perhaps they are safe within the monastery walls, and we won't have to travel further." A shadow of wistfulness darkens his expression. "I hope we are the first to find them. Although, if they are not there, then I shall be glad that Colonel Russo and his men will be searching for them as well; I would not like to think of the trouble that could befall them in these parts, finding themselves in the company of gypsies or brigands." Staring past Alfonso, he shudders before crossing himself.

Alfonso senses a figure hovering nearby, and when he diverts his gaze from Valerio, he sees the woman holding a plate with wedges of cheeses and several plump black figs. His eyebrows tilt questioningly, and she haltingly explains that the dish is complimentary, from the proprietor of the tavern, in appreciation of the Signor's patronage. Alfonso smirks; he has been informed about the prevalent system of patronage in the south, both by his brother and some of his gambling companions. Rarely is a kind gesture made without some sort of expectation in return, if not in monetary remuneration, then in some other manner. Again, he catches the woman's eyes flitting slyly from the gleaming buttons on his jacket to his ring as she sets down the plate. He has obviously made some sort of impression with the owner, with his fine clothing and demands for the best wine. And with *her.*

Alfonso nods and the woman turns away to tend to another patron, who has taken a seat near the bar. He takes a fig, peeling back the black outer layer, and breaking it open to reveal the seedy flesh inside. He brings it to his mouth, enjoying its succulence and texture, while passing the plate to Valerio. Alternating between the cheeses and the figs, they finish off the plate. Alfonso leans back with a groan. "I'm finished. No more for me."

Valerio nods and sighs contentedly. "Again, thank you, Signor Alfonso. I am going to head back to the room now."

"Go ahead, lad. I'll be up once I've paid my dues."

Alfonso looks around the tavern. Most of the men have left, save for a couple of elderly gentlemen and the man at the bar. The latter's hand clasped around a flask is gnarled and pale, reminding Alfonso of the hairless claw of a chicken. When the man turns slightly, peering past the swinging kitchen doors, Alfonso catches sight of a face that is as colourless as the skin on his hand except for the prominent network of veins pulsing at his temple and down his gaunt cheek. Alfonso looks away, slightly repulsed, and starts when he realizes that the woman is at his side, holding a piece of paper in her hand.

Annoyed at her stealthy return, he takes the bill and surveys the amount scrawled on it. As he withdraws a pouch from his vest pocket, extracts the required amount, and sets it down on the table, she nods and slips it into her apron pocket. To his surprise, she does not leave. He looks up at her, wondering at her audacity, knowing he has paid more than enough for the meal, and frowns.

"I beg your pardon, sir," she curtsies again, her eyes lowered. "I could not help but overhear you mention the name of someone you are searching for...."

Alfonso straightens immediately, his eyes blazing. He watches as her eyes slowly travel from the floor, to his trousers, then up his chest to his face. For the first time, his gaze meets hers directly, and he is struck by the pallor of her eyes. Again, she shifts her gaze, *as she should,* he thinks, seeing as how she is speaking to someone in a class above hers.

"Gabriella Falcone," he prompts sharply. "What do you know of her? Has she been here? Is she with the priest, Don Simone? Or her brother?" A flicker in the depths of her eyes makes him blurt out, "I will gladly reward you for any information you can give me."

Hesitating, she looks over to the bar where the grizzled man is making his departure, turns slightly as if she needs to approach him, but then redirects her gaze at Alfonso.

"I...I have heard some things in the village...." Her eyes sweep downward and settle for a fraction of a second on the pouch still in Alfonso's hands. Concealing his contempt, he stands and pulls out the chair Valerio had used. He watches a flush suffuse her gaunt face as she sits down primly, her shoulders rigid and not touching the wicker spindles. She keeps her hands in her lap, and is motionless, save for the nervous tapping of one foot against a chair leg, which, Alfonso suspects, she doesn't even realize she's doing.

He opens up the money bag a little wider so her shifting eyes can catch sight of the coins within. He sees her thin lips part slightly, and to his disgust, a tiny drop of spittle bubbles at the edge of her mouth before dribbling down. Yet, despite the revulsion he feels for a peasant who is obviously adept at procuring what she can for herself, he feels a strange stirring. She may not be a *whore* in the usual sense of the word, but a whore nonetheless, ready to sell her knowledge for money, instead of disclosing it readily, as a good citizen would do. He feels himself grinding his teeth, and he takes a deep breath, knowing he has to control himself if he is to gain the information he wants.

"You have been most hospitable," he says in his most genuine, appreciative tone. "Please allow me to offer you a heartfelt sign of my gratitude." He extracts a fistful of *ten centesimi* coins that he knows will make an impression and watches with satisfaction as her face brightens. "*Prego.* Please accept my gesture of thanks."

He places the coins on the table, and after a momentary hesitation, she takes the money and shoves it into a deep pocket inside her apron. Alfonso catches a glint of gold encircling a red stone on one finger.

"Now, Signora, please tell me what you have heard about the Signorina Gabriella, my dear niece. As you may have surmised, she has been missing from her village—Camini—and you can imagine that our family is most preoccupied as to her safety. I have been scouring the countryside with a guide, and as of yet, have discovered nothing." Alfonso pauses, letting his head droop in one hand. He sniffs, wipes an imaginary tear, and looks at her piercingly. "You must help; I must bring Gabriella back, God willing, safe and unmolested. I don't even want to imagine what may have already befallen her...."

"I have heard," the woman speaks in a low voice, making Alfonso lean forward, "that this Gabriella and a priest are in the company of some outlaws. *Briganti.*"

Alfonso draws back, his gasp genuine. "What about her brother? He is missing as well; he is no more than seven years of age."

"There has been no mention of a boy." The woman purses her thin lips.

"Where did you get this information? Where were they last seen? Did *you* see them?"

The woman's eyes flutter wildly and she recoils; Alfonso realizes he has plunged forward, his face only inches away from hers.

"I heard some talk at the public fountain." She looks away. "They were seen by some shepherds in the mountains beyond Calvino, an hour or so away. I did not see them."

Alfonso stares at her profile; something in her manner and in her denial does not sit well with him. From the set of her jaw, he doubts that she is willing to disclose any further information. He pulls out a few more coins and slides them over. He is willing to eke out whatever details she is withholding, no matter how many lira it takes. He raises his fingers to his temples, both pulsating now.

"How can I get a message to the brigands?" he wonders aloud, rubbing his temples. "To let them know that I would pay for the release of the girl?" He looks up, and she is staring straight at him, her eyebrows raised.

"I know a goatherd from that area," she says. "He is a cousin. Perhaps I could pass the message to him; he may come across Galante or his men."

"Galante?" Alfonso says sharply.

She fidgets in her seat. "He is the chief of the band roaming the area. It is common knowledge. He is wanted for a crime he committed near Calvino."

Alfonso jerks from the nerve pain above his ear that feels like a jab from a forger's iron. He restrains himself from grabbing the wench's arm and twisting it until she spits out whatever else she is keeping back. He is willing to wager that she knows much more than she is revealing to him. He feels it in his gut, and as she reaches for the money, he scrambles to come up with a plan. "Perhaps you could tell this goatherd cousin of yours that I will pay twice the amount if he can find the girl and bring her to me here."

He opens up the money bag and lets the woman see its full contents. "Now, of course, if *you* were to find Gabriella and bring her to me safely, the money would go to *you*." He watches her expression as she considers his offer.

"Actually," she murmurs, "I do help my cousin Ilario from time to time with his herd. And Stefano Galante—the brigand chief—used to be a friend of Ilario's, before he went into hiding. He's from Calvino."

"Stefano Galante." Alfonso swallows. *Gabriella, in the hands of a brigand chief.* He hoped to discover her in the safety of a monastery, not in the wilds with a wanted criminal. He rams his fist on the table, making the woman tremble. Right now, he does not even want to imagine what Galante might have done with her. "What does he look like?" Alfonso demands.

"He is about your height, Signor, with dark hair. He is easily recognizable; he has one brown eye and one green."

"Will you inform your cousin of my request?"

The woman nods, and for the first time, attempts a half-smile. "I will leave tomorrow before dawn; he or I will return the day after tomorrow."

"Whoever returns with Gabriella will get the rest of the money." His eyes burn into hers. "And if she is rescued from the brigands before they can compromise her in any way...the reward will be even greater."

"If it is of any reassurance to you, Signor, the brigand chief Galante is known as '*Il Galantuomo*.'"

Alfonso wants to reach out and slap her. *The Gentleman* indeed. With trembling fingers, he extracts another handful of coins, and instead of placing them on the table, holds them out to her. When her hand closes over the money, briefly brushing against his fingers, he clasps her hand tightly. "I expect, Signora, that should you or your cousin not return with Gabriella, the money I am entrusting you with will be returned to me. *In full*." He gives her a piercing look. At this proximity, he can see that her eyes are of a grey-green colour that reminds him of the lagoons in Venice, murky and impenetrable most of the time, but flashing with silver glints when pierced by the sun. He waits until she nods, then releases her hand, stroking her ring as he lets go.

He rises from his chair, and she does the same, lifting her skirts slightly before turning on her heels. As she swirls away, Alfonso catches a glimpse of a dagger strapped to her leg above one boot. She strides through the kitchen doors, and above the clanging of pots, Alfonso hears the angry voice of the owner: "Dorotea! What took you so long? There are dirty pots stacked as high as heaven. Get to work, goddammit. I don't pay you to stand around like a whore waiting for a lick and a promise!"

GABRIELLA'S EYES WIDEN. "YOU...YOU *KNEW*?"

Stefano nods, his gaze never leaving her eyes. "I make it a point to know where all my weapons are." He slowly sits back on his pallet. "Keep it; you need it more than I do." He shrugs off his cloak, revealing the array of knives and pistols within its inner folds.

"How do you know I won't try to use it during the night?"

Stefano's eyes narrow. "Because I don't plan to touch you, Signorina, and if I don't come near you, you won't have cause to stab me, will you?"

He sees Gabriella's face twist in confusion. "How do I know you won't come near me? You were just about to—"

"Touch your hair," he says gruffly. "Nothing more." He tilts his head at the knife still pointed at him. "You can put that down, Signorina. I will not touch you. Or are you afraid to trust a brigand?" As soon as he says it, he regrets the words. *Of course she is afraid to trust him*. He is an outlaw, a wanted criminal, a man no decent woman would go near.... And especially after her experience with that bastard Alfonso Fantin, how could she possibly trust any man? He knows that if he wanted to, he could lunge at her and in seconds the dagger would be in his possession. But he is reluctant to do so; her eyes are already brimming with barely concealed fear.

"Why should I trust a *brigante?*" Her voice trembles. "And how do I know you won't touch me?"

Stefano shifts on the pallet so that that he is resting on his side on one elbow, his chin in his hand. He breathes in deeply, stares at her eyes, then her hair. Her dark, silky hair. "I wanted to touch your hair," his eyes meeting hers, "because it is just like...my sister's." He watches as her eyelashes flutter wildly. "You see, Signorina Gabriella, my sister, like *you*, was attacked by a wealthy landowner. He brutally raped her and left her to almost bleed to death in the cornfields behind his estate."

He pauses at Gabriella's gasp. Her fingers slacken, and the knife falls to the floor. Neither of them reaches for it.

"Patrizia was his housekeeper," he continues, changing his position to lie flat on his back. He stares up at the crude ceiling of intertwining branches. "She was going to be married in a few months' time. I was working at a neighbouring village and left early to meet her so we could walk home together." He turns his head to Gabriella. "I arrived too late."

He sees that tears are welling in her eyes. "I killed him with my bare hands," he rasps. "At least I thought I did. Then I hitched up the mule and cart and brought Patrizia to the village doctor and then to our *nonna's* house. She was too ashamed to return home." He feels his jaws tighten. "She miscarried after two months. That was two years ago. She still lives with *nonna,* but she doesn't speak. The doctor said the shock has left her mute. And who will have her now?" he growls, his fists clenching. "He ruined her life. So now you understand, Signorina Gabriella, why I have no intention of touching you. You are safe with me." He reaches for his cloak and extracts a pistol. "Take this," he says, setting it down near her pile of blankets. "You might need it one day."

RUSSO IS IN FULL UNIFORM, RIDING AHEAD of his rifle regiment and behind a half-dozen cavalrymen. He finds the heat unbearable. He curses under his breath and runs an ungloved hand over his scalp. He cannot wait until nightfall; the mission will be over, and he will be recounting the events to Liliana, including, hopefully, the news that he has captured Galante.

He slows his horse down to a trot as the road forks off into two narrower paths. He notices a few wide-eyed youths pausing as the regiment marches past them. Their skin is sallow, their clothes tattered. A goatherd heading outside the village starts cursing when the incoming troops cause the goats to scurry off in every direction. One skitters beside one of the more volatile horses, and the rider tries unsuccessfully to steer his horse away. It startles, and Russo watches as it rears up, its hooves smashing against the goat's head. The goat crumbles to the ground in a lifeless heap, the gash spurting blood like a fountain.

The officers continue onward, ignoring the wailing of the goatherd at the side of his dead animal. Russo dismounts and hands the reins to one of the foot soldiers. He conceals his irritation as he walks over to the goatherd who is sobbing as if he has just lost a child, and extracts some coins from an inner pocket. "Please accept my apologies for this unfortunate mishap," he says, wondering if the old man is mourning the loss of what the goat might have fetched him at market. "I trust this will compensate you for your loss."

The goatherd wipes his bloodshot eyes with the sleeve of his shirt and takes the coins. He murmurs a garbled reply of thanks and shuffles away, shouting to one of the boys to run off and fetch him a cart to transport the goat back home. Russo remounts and continues on his way, impatient to begin the mission in Calvino.

When one of the officers on horseback doubles back and informs him that they are approaching the Galante farm, Russo feels a twinge of anticipation. He bids them continue to their pre-assigned posts; *he* will be the one to make the official call. He will be accompanied by two carabineers who are to wait for him outside while he interrogates the family members. While he is engaged in this task, the riflemen have been instructed to disperse throughout the hamlet, with each horseman stationed at any possible road or path leading out of Calvino.

When the last of his men disappears around a bend, Russo dismounts. One of his men, Rodolfo Farina, proceeds to tether his horse and the other, Silvio Bertoli, follows several paces behind Russo, his hand over the pistol in his pocket.

Russo strides up the main path to the farmhouse. He pounds on the doorway and waits, taking in the ramshackle appearance of the house with its small, curtainless windows and lichen-spotted stone walls, one of which is draped with a tumble of ivy. The main door, splintered and charred, looks as if it has been struck by a bolt of lightning.

Russo knocks again, waits a few seconds, then with a nod instructs Silvio to enter the house and search the rooms. He continues along a straw-scattered path to the barn, which is bigger than the house but just as dilapidated. As he approaches its double doors, one creaks open and a ruddy-faced man appears, his brows knit together under a woven, wide-brimmed hat. He is a head shorter than Russo, with sagging jowls and vein-splattered cheeks. His arms jut out like sturdy tree limbs, with exposed forearms that are brown and pink in places where the sun has scorched the skin. His legs seem shorter than his arms, and twice as stocky. The dank odours of the barn have emerged with the farmer, and Russo also catches the scent of alcohol—something stronger than just wine, though. He looks beyond the man and catches sight of a flask containing a colourless liquid. *Grappa.*

"Signor Galante?"

Russo tilts his head questioningly, realizing that the man has been scrutinizing him.

"*Sì, Signoria Vostra.*" Galante removes his hat and tips it. "In what manner can I assist you, Sir?"

A shuffle behind Russo alerts him to Silvio's return. He lifts an eyebrow.

"There is nobody in the house," the officer tells him. "There are signs of women's clothing, and some beds that haven't been slept in."

Russo is aware of Galante's startled gaze from him to his officer.

"What has happened?" Galante cries. "Why are you here?" His face reddens even more, and his mouth gapes open, showing tobacco-stained gums and several missing teeth. Russo tries not to grimace.

"We are here to obtain some information, which I am confident you will readily provide," he says smoothly. He turns and instructs Silvio to wait for him with Rodolfo. "I am certain Signor Galante will be most co-operative." He makes his voice silky, almost a caress. When they are alone, he asks, "Where is your family? Your wife?"

"My wife is in Gioiosa Ionica with one of my daughters, sir."

"And your son?" Russo keeps his voice pleasant.

Galante's face hardens. Russo can see his jaw clenching several times before he spits out, "My son? I used to have a son before he abandoned me. I can barely keep up with the work on this farm without him."

Russo takes a step closer. "Where is he now?"

Galante looks at him sharply. "I don't know. He hasn't shown his face in two years." His mouth twists bitterly.

"And no one in these parts has come across him?" Russo's nostrils flare at the smell of mingled sweat and manure that he realizes is smeared on Galante's trousers and boots.

"Not that I'm aware of. Whether they have seen him or not, my neighbours and friends know better than to mention his name to my face."

Russo gazes intently at Galante for a moment. "You must have an *idea* as to his whereabouts." He takes a step back, his stomach contracting at the stench of cow dung.

Galante's mouth twists. "He can be in hell for all I care. *Vigliacco! Disonorato!* He has dishonoured me and put a stain upon our family." He turns his head and spits, leaving a yellow glob on the ground.

"I understood he acted to avenge the assault of his sister." Russo is genuinely puzzled. How could the old man be upset at his son for going after the man who raped his daughter?

Galante's eyes cloud over. He wipes the beads of sweat on his upper lip with his shirt sleeve and rasps, "With *that,* I have no cause to be angry. I...I am enraged over the fact that he went into hiding like a coward, instead of attempting to defend himself. I could have had the parish priest speak on his behalf, ask for clemency.... But no, Stefano didn't give me the chance; he chose instead to break his mother's heart and my balls, leaving me to do all the work on the farm." He laughs without humour, a harsh croak that stabs the air like a vulture's cry.

"And these past two years, he's managed to maintain himself quite well, from what I hear, living the life of a brigand." Galante sneers. "Apparently, he enjoys collecting travellers these days. The fellow his band released after they got their ransom money said he has a young lady and a priest with him...."

Russo stiffens. "Well, well," he murmurs. *How very fitting that the girl I seek for attempting to kill Fantin is in the company of the very brigand I intend to destroy.* He smiles, savouring the thought of a double victory.

Galante clears the phlegm in his throat again, and as Russo takes in the man's hunched shoulders and grizzled head bobbing as another mucous-filled splatter is ejected, he is hard-pressed to see any similarity between the pathetic sight before him and the man's brigand son.

"Colonel Russo!"

Russo swivels at the sharp tone of urgency. Silvio is striding over to him with his hand clasping a purple bundle. Russo's eyes narrow as his officer hands him a half-dozen small bags of purple cloth, at the centre of which is embroidered the initial "G" in yellow thread. With a self-satisfied smile, Silvio extracts another such bag from his pocket and hands it to Russo, informing him that all were concealed under the hemp-filled pallet in the bedroom occupied by Galante and his wife. It is the only bag that is not empty.

Russo loosens the drawstrings and peers at the contents, his mouth pursing as he withdraws a thick gold necklace and two gold rings, and a silver brooch studded with an assortment of precious stones. The sunlight catches on the facets of emerald, ruby, and amethyst, and as Russo smiles at the significance of this discovery, Galante rasps, "What is this all about?"

Russo looks at him coldly. "You tell us, Signor Galante. You claim to know nothing of your son, to have had no contact with him, yet items that obviously bear his mark and the fruit of his chosen *labour* are found under your pallet."

Galante's face blanches. "Under *my*...?" His eyes dart wildly from Russo to Silvio. Russo watches as his lips clamp shut, then open to stammer, "My...my wife! This is *her* doing! I know nothing about this." His cheeks begin to redden in uneven splotches, and although his surprise seems genuine enough, Russo is not completely convinced that he is as innocent as he implies of having any connection with Stefano. Or of benefitting from any of Stefano's successes. Perhaps his outward disdain for his son is a deliberate act to protect himself. But why would he be so quick to heave the blame on his wife?

Russo looks down at him. Whether he is lying or not, it is obvious that Stefano has at least maintained contact with his mother, who has provided him with hand-stitched loot bags embroidered with his initial, and who has, in turn, been provided for with some of the spoils of his pillages. There are other things that are not so obvious, though. Many questions have yet to be answered....

Russo exchanges a glance with Silvio. He gives him a slight nod then moves aside. Silvio plants himself in front of Galante, forcing him to back up. Silvio thrusts out a beefy hand and with one solid push, he sends Galante hurtling backwards into the barn with a grunt. Russo's mouth curves into a smile. Silvio has a knack of *preparing* people for questioning. Once he is done with the old man, Galante should be quite ready to provide Russo with the truth, and hopefully, the whereabouts of his son.

Ignoring the thuds and cries from the barn, Russo strolls a short distance away, admiring how the stones on the brooch glitter in the sun.

TONINO STARES FROM THE NOVICE TO LUCIANO, who is still

holding Sister Renata's hand tightly. He sees confusion flit across both their faces for a moment, and then he realizes that the boy hasn't placed him yet. Luciano would recognize him in regular clothes, but here, in this bed, someone from Camini would probably be the last person he would expect to find. And even if Luciano did recognize him, he wouldn't associate him with his sister. He doubted Gabriella would have divulged their exchange to him, their mutual promise of love. *But why in heaven's name is Luciano here?*

"Do you know each other?" Sister Renata says, her eyebrows peaking.

"Now I know!" Luciano tugs at her hand excitedly. "Tonino, the butcher's son! I couldn't tell at first with that bandage covering his face."

Tonino lifts his hand to feel the linen cloth Sister Emilia reapplied the night before, after his wound had started to bleed again. She applied a thin salve of rosemary and honey and then a fresh cloth to cover it. "To stop the flies from landing on your face," she said with a smile.

"You are both from Camini?" The nun's voice is incredulous. "How strange."

"What is Luciano doing here?" Tonino cannot keep the urgency out of his voice. "*What has happened?*"

Sister Renata looks flustered. She opens her mouth and then clamps it shut, her brows furrowing. "I...I am not at liberty to say, Signor Tonino."

"Indeed you are not, Sister Renata," Sister Emanuela says, appearing in the doorway. "Thank you for your discretion in this matter. You may bring the boy to the refectory for a bowl of pigeon soup. I wish to speak with Signor Tonino."

"*Sì, Badessa.*" Sister Renata looks relieved as she curtsies and shuffles out, leading Luciano by the hand.

"Abbess, what has happened?" Tonino leans forward. "I need to know."

He watches the abbess studying him for a moment, her hands

clasped in front of her heart as if in prayer. "I'm sorry, Signor Tonino, but I cannot in good conscience divulge any matter relating to the boy to anyone but his immediate family. I hope you understand. I am the only one here at the Convent of St. Anna who is aware of the entire circumstances of Luciano's arrival, and I cannot break confidence." She nods and begins to walk away.

"Abbess, please. Gabriella and I...." he says, pausing to wait until she has turned around to face him, "are promised to each other. I was intending to marry her once I returned from the mission with General Garibaldi." Tonino searches her face for a sign that she will relent, but when it remains impassive, he adds, "Her father Lorenzo and mine are best friends. The first thing I plan to do when I get back to Camini is to ask him for his consent."

The abbess's head lowers and Tonino notices her mouth has settled into a grim line. *Something terrible has happened to either Gabriella or her father.* He grips the edge of the sheet. "Abbess Emanuela, *please*, what in God's name has happened?" He feels a sudden heaviness, as if a giant hand is on his chest, trying to prevent him from taking a breath.

The abbess draws in a deep breath and then exhales slowly, while reaching into her habit pocket for her rosary. She sits down in a wicker chair near the side of the bed. "In view of the circumstances, it is perhaps best that I inform you of what has transpired." She looks at him steadily. "Signorina Gabriella is safe. She is with Don Simone. I'm sorry to have to tell you, Signor Tonino, that her father is dead."

Tonino's heart plummets. Signor Lorenzo, *dead*. He shakes his head. *"How? What happened?"*

The abbess reaches over to place a comforting hand on his arm. "Signor Tonino, what I have to tell you is not pleasant, but please remember, Signorina Gabriella is safe at present...."

"At present? What danger was she in before?" Tonino feels the room closing in on him, the scent of jasmine wafting in

from the window ledge suddenly nauseating, his happiness at seeing Luciano shattered.

"The new owner of the church lands attempted to…to take advantage of Gabriella when she was alone. Her father returned from the fields and tried to stop him but he fell down the stairs of the barn loft and struck his head, dying instantly. Gabriella stabbed Signor Fantin." She pauses momentarily as Tonino tries to take it all in, his eyes blinking rapidly.

He sits up, cringing at the pain that has begun to throb on one side of his head.

"Don Simone found her and they left Camini with Luciano, seeking refuge at Don Filippo's monastery here in Gerace. A few days later, Don Filippo heard that Signor Fantin had survived and was seeking the support of the military forces under Colonel Russo to pursue and arrest Gabriella for her crime. Don Filippo thought it best that Luciano be brought here to our orphanage for safety, and that Don Simone find a place of hiding for Gabriella that nobody knows he is associated with." She pauses, squeezing Tonino's arm sympathetically. "I'm sorry. This is too much for anyone to digest…."

Too much. Tonino shakes his head, stunned. The pain he felt slamming into the side of the mountain is nothing compared to what he feels now. He is disjointed, and his limbs are numb. He closes his eyes, his breathing shallow. He wants to scream, to pound the walls, to *kill*. Yes, he could easily kill the bastard Fantin for attempting to lay a hand on his sweet innocent Gabriella. He squeezes his eyes, trying to keep out the sordid thoughts of Gabriella being—

He hears the abbess telling him she will return with some chamomile and fennel tea to ease the shock he feels, and as her footsteps recede, his ears reverberate with silent screams. He collapses against his pillow, his bandage soaked with fresh blood from the gash that has reopened.

BY THE TIME DOROTEA APPEARS THROUGH THE THICKET, walking alongside Gaetano's mule, Stefano and the rest of the band are sitting on the stumps around the fire pit. Stefano lights a cheroot and watches the *brigantessa's* approach. The brothers, as usual, have taken their places next to each other. Although there is a two-year age difference between them, they are as close as fraternal twins, choosing to spend most of their time together. Roberto, the younger of the two, is surprisingly the more aggressive, though, and Stefano has witnessed on several occasions how Raffaele has tried to diffuse his brother's fiery temper during a mission. As chief, Stefano has had to show his teeth a few times to keep Roberto subdued. Just like in a wolf pack.

Roberto's face bears the signs of Stefano's handiwork for accosting Gabriella. It is swollen and mottled with bruises. One eye is almost shut, and the other seems aflame, it is so bloodshot. His right ear has an open gash.

Gaetano, equipped with his assortment of knives and knap-sacks for his daily trek to fetch game, is whittling away at a branch. His weathered face is impassive, almost bored, as he awaits the report from Dorotea. He rearranges his cap over his grey-flecked hair, his eyes regularly scanning the fringe of woods beyond the landing for any hint of animal presence.

And finally, at his side, the ever alert Tomaso Salino, his boyish enthusiasm tempered by his efforts to emulate the measured words and actions of his chief. Stefano smiles. Tomaso is what he imagines a younger brother would be like. And unlike most brigands, there is an air of innocence to him, a healthy lust for life, without the core of cynicism that hardens with every experience of social injustice that has led one to become a brigand in the first place.

The priest, Don Simone, has also joined them at their cir-cle, sharing a chunk of coarse bread from a loaf that is being passed around along with a pan of fried onions and wild fennel gathered by Gaetano the day before. Don Simone murmurs his request to say grace, and he seems to glow with pleasure as he proceeds to recite the blessing, with the addition of an impassioned entreaty to God to keep everyone within the circle in His care.

Stefano is not surprised at Signorina Gabriella's absence. This is all too much for her, as it would be for any young, innocent girl. He gazes at the advancing figure of Dorotea. Even *she* must have been innocent once. Long before he knew her....

As Dorotea enters the clearing, the brothers jump up to take the saddlebags off the mule and plop them inside the circle. She lifts the strap of her own bag off her shoulder and sets it on the ground beside her stump. She sits down with a sigh, and then looks up at Stefano expectantly. He holds up a hand for her to wait, and then nods at Roberto and Raffaele to empty the contents of the bags.

Stefano nods in satisfaction. Dorotea has done well. Her uncle and other supporters have demonstrated their generosity once again. The contents are jammed in the first bag: three coarse woollen blankets, two black cloaks, two pairs of faded trousers, six pairs of woollen socks, and six bandanas. Stuffed beneath the clothes are assorted cloths, various ropes, a jumble of tools, two pistols, a fistful of knives and daggers, a flask of alcohol, a large tobacco pouch, and several pipes made from the woody roots of erica shrubs on these Aspromonte slopes.

Stefano gestures to the members of his band and they advance, helping themselves to various items except the weapons; they know that *he* will distribute those among them personally.

The second bag consists of food offerings that will keep the band comfortable for at least a week, even without Gaetano's success: a burlap bag filled with onions, garlic, and potatoes; another brimming with kale, wild fennel, dandelion, sprigs of rosemary and sage, chamomile, and bay laurel; two small wheels of sheep's cheese, a string of peppered sausages, a bag of cracked, oven-baked olives, and a string of tiny red peppers, each run through with a needle and thread, and joined in the form of a necklace. And in a separate bag, within giant fig leaves bound tightly with twine, are freshly butchered segments of goat.

Stefano nods with pleasure at Dorotea. "Well done. With your gifts and the goat Roberto also brought back, we'll be feasting for a week." He gestures to the brothers to refill the food sack and what's left from the first bag, and once this is done, they all turn to Dorotea expectantly. The supplies are necessary, but her report even more so, the information vital for their next move. "You may begin, Dorotea," he says, crossing his arms.

She looks at him steadily. "Colonel Russo has been in the outskirts of Gerace, not only in search of brigands, but for a girl who has gone missing." She darts a glance at the priest, whose eyes have widened at the news. "The talk at the tavern is that she was travelling with her brother and parish priest."

"Where exactly was Russo seen?" Stefano's eyes narrow.

"He has been seen in Locri and Roccella; now he is in Gerace. His men have been riding about, combing those areas as well."

"Where are they heading? What have you found out?"

Dorotea's eyes shift to Don Simone and then back at him. "He and his men plan to remain in the Gerace area for a day or two before heading deeper into the Aspromonte mountains. Russo has given the order to his men to employ any necessary means to locate *Il Galantuomo* and his band." She slips a hand into her trouser pocket and extracts a folded piece of paper. Stefano takes it, his brows furrowing as he reads the notice.

"I'm worth that little," he jokes wryly at the bounty Russo has set for his capture. His eyes harden and swoop over to Dorotea. "What else did you learn from our informer? Are we in any immediate danger?"

Dorotea shakes her head. "He says Russo is planning a surprise 'visit' to Calvino. He wants to squeeze any information he can out of the villagers. Get some of them to bend under pressure and reveal what they know about you or where you may be. He plans to start with your family."

"Did *you* make contact with my family?"

"I inquired at the tavern. Your mother left for Gioiosa Ionica with your younger sister; your cousin Rita has gone into labour. They left this morning, an hour before sunrise." She coughs to clear her throat. "Your mother left this for you with my uncle." She reaches into her left apron pocket and pulls out a half-dozen purple pouches with the letter G embroidered in the centre with yellow thread. "She sends her love and prays for your safety," Dorotea tells him gruffly, avoiding his eyes while holding them out to him.

Stefano feels a tightness around his heart. His mother has always been with him in spirit. Since leaving home, he has found ways and people to get messages to her, knowing that above all, she needs to know he is safe, and she, in turn, has supplied him not only with unfaltering messages of love and support but also with an occasional coin or two that she has managed to conceal from her husband, and the cloth pouches for Stefano to use to deliver his gifts to the Madonna of the Poppies or to those in dire need.

He nods his appreciation and turns brusquely to the others, making sure to look at everyone individually. "Be vigilant. There may be more activity in these parts since Russo's postings have been distributed. Trust no one outside our usual supporters. In these times, anybody might feel compelled to pass information to the *carabinieri* if it means feeding their family. Gaetano, you may go. Take something with you." He gestures to the bag and Gaetano approaches to cut himself a wedge of cheese and a sausage link before turning and sprinting into the forest. "Roberto and Raffaele, you can venture down the mountain. Watch for any sign of Russo's men, with or without their horses. Dorotea, you can tend to the food storage, and then check up on Signorina Gabriella." He pins her with an intense gaze. "See if her leg wound has healed. And bring her something to eat." Dorotea nods stiffly before heaving the food bag over her back and disappearing through the thicket.

Stefano nods in satisfaction and turns to the youngest brigand. "Tomaso, take the weapons." He sees Tomaso's eyebrows rise. "Yes, I'm leaving this responsibility up to you. You are ready." He waits until Tomaso has gathered up the items and then murmurs so that only he can hear, "There is no one I trust more than you." He gives the brigand a pat on the shoulder and then turns to the priest.

"Don Simone," he says, gesturing at the sack with a pair of trousers and a cloak still unclaimed, "perhaps you might wish to take those. If we are suddenly forced to leave the mountain to seek refuge elsewhere, you might find clambering up and down the mountain ledges rather unpractical in a cassock."

The priest looks startled as he considers this possibility and then reluctantly nods, crossing himself with his rosary before stooping to pick up the items. He tucks them under one arm and heads to his shelter, the fluttering hem of his cassock edged with a fine dusting of clay from the dry ground.

Alone, Stefano walks to the edge of the clearing. He stands, one hand against the rough trunk of a giant ilex, and stares beyond the valley to the mist-covered hamlets in the distance. *So, Russo is planning a visit to Calvino*. His stomach clenches, and he inhales and exhales deeply, thanking Providence that his mother and sister will not be subject to Russo's interrogation. His father, he has no concerns for; he knows nothing about Stefano, as his wife has kept their communications a secret. Stefano has no illusions as to what would happen to his mother if his father ever discovered her deception. It pains him deeply to know what his father is capable of—even as a child, he would notice the yellow and purple bruises on his mother's face and arms when her sleeves were rolled up to wash the laundry at the river. It would make his insides tighten with revulsion and fear, fear that one day his father's rage would get the better of him and he would kill her.

After Argo died, it took everything Stefano had not to run away. He despised his father and could hardly bear to look at him. He daydreamed of ways he could make his father pay for what he had done to Argo, and for the way he treated his family. He hadn't yet sunk to beating his daughters Patrizia and Marina, but if he didn't take a belt to them, his tongue lashed them just as hard. He yelled at them for being too slow with the chores, for not preparing food properly, for not having his clothes mended.

When his eldest daughter Patrizia told him she had sought work as a maid at the estate of Baron Saverio Contini, he flew into a rage, accusing her of flaunting herself, acting like a *puttana* for having offered her services to Contini. He grabbed her by the hair and tore open her bodice, demanding if she had let the Baron touch her there. And for what price? Patrizia managed to tear herself away from him, sobbing, and ran to the room she shared with her sister Marina. His father stormed about the kitchen, calming down only when his wife reassured him that Patrizia would turn over three quarters of her salary to him, and keep the rest for her dowry. Placated, he left to go work in the stables.

The sight of him filled Stefano with revulsion daily, and it was all he could do to not show it. He dreamed of the day he could leave. Every time his father's words invaded his thoughts—"You were born into dung and you'll die into dung"— it hardened Stefano's resolve to prove him wrong. To get himself away from the yoke of poverty and the even more painful yoke of his father's domination. *I deserve better,* he told himself. He conjured up thoughts of how he could be free from his father, how they could *all* be free from his tyranny, but never did he imagine that the opportunity would arise from the tragic circumstances of Patrizia's rape.

Stefano grits his teeth at the memory of his father in the stable. The life he has adopted, the life of a *capo brigante,* is, in some ways, better than the life he had. And it was the price he gladly paid to avenge his sister's ruin. He is free of his father, for one thing. Stefano turns away from the edge of the mountain and heads in the direction of his hut.

He has every intention of keeping Signorina Gabriella from falling into the hands of either Russo or Fantin. It was destiny that brought her into his life, and although he cannot imagine as yet how either of their destinies will play out, he will, as brigand chief, do whatever he must to keep her safe. *Even if it means killing.*

RUSSO LOOKS BACK AT THE HAMLET OF CALVINO. He has ordered his men to retreat and to return to their regular posts. Some of them left reluctantly, so consumed were they by their own inner fire. Russo watched, body arched forward as he straddled his mule, while some tossed their torches carelessly into the ditches flanking the main road as they left the hamlet, making the dry grass and shrubbery sizzle.

Some came stumbling out of the houses with their uniforms in disarray, their eyes glazed with violent passion. He saw one of his men enter a house and pull his patrol partner off a girl of no more than fifteen or sixteen. From the street, Russo could see her cowering in a corner of the room, her skirts hiked above her trembling knees, her eyes two dark plums in a face the colour of ashes.

Four of his men had bound the wrists of a dozen men, young and old, and were prodding them on with the butt of their rifles through the *piazza* and on to the main road. In the glen just outside the limits of the hamlet, the officers would reclaim their horses and accompany the men, two leading in front, two in back, to the station, where they would be locked up for further questioning the following day.

Russo took a deep breath and pressed the mule onward, trying to ignore the jarring sounds of the screaming children and the high-pitched wailing of the women, some of whom tried, in desperation, to approach Russo with hands linked as if in prayer, begging for the release of their husbands or sons. When one of the women came close enough to grab his trouser leg, hurling profanities at him, he flicked his crop at her hand and she fell back, screaming.

Now, as Russo begins to ride past the Galante farm, he glances at the receding barn with contempt, grimacing with the recollection of the man's rust-brown face, splattered with blood and dung, his body a misshapen heap in the fetid, urine-soaked straw. He wonders how Stefano will feel when he hears the news about his father's death....

When Silvio rushed out of the barn to let Russo know that the elder Galante had suddenly clasped at his chest and collapsed, Russo went back to check on the old man. There was nothing to be done; Galante's face had already turned chalky, his mouth open and twisted in an agonized death mask. Russo had shaken his head and motioned for Silvio to leave him be; he would send the appropriate villagers to tend to him. After Silvio left to join Rodolfo, Russo grabbed the bottle of *grappa* on a bench, opened it, and lay it next to Galante's body. He left the barn as the alcohol poured out....

Stefano will surely want to attend the funeral. But then again, he must know that Russo will have his *carabinieri* posted in and around the hamlet in the next two days of official mourning and for the funeral and subsequent procession to the cemetery. Russo doesn't imagine Galante would attempt such a move; he is experienced enough in matters involving the law. Perhaps he will send one of his band members in his place. Or come disguised. Russo knows Galante is not stupid, or he would have been apprehended a long time ago. No, the brigand chief will likely not risk showing his face anywhere near Calvino.

But, Russo reasons to himself, Galante will surely try to make contact with his informers. Consequently, he will instruct his men to be watchful for any signs that might lead to a connection with Galante such as a farmer who strays a little too far from the field, or a youth who carries a sack out of the hamlet limits, or even a washerwoman who takes up at a different spot by the river.... Anybody could be a brigand informer, providing him with information about the forces of law, their position and presence in the area. Or they could simply be supporters, supplying an intermediary with foodstuff, blankets, supplies, and even weapons to deliver to brigands who are relatives or friends.

If Russo could identify some of Galante's supporters in Calvino, he could easily find out if they were hiding any of the brigands in their own home. As far as Russo is concerned, and he knows that General Zanetti shares this sentiment, anybody harbouring a brigand is just as culpable as the brigand and deserves to be treated as such.

Russo jerks back the reins and his horse comes to a stop, panting heavily. He pats the horse's glistening neck. They must stop soon to refresh all the horses before they collapse in the heat. Russo feels his jaw tensing at the thought of the brigand chief. There is no resemblance between the old man and his son, at least not outwardly. The latter must have inherited his features from his mother's side.

Despite Galante's different-coloured eyes, Russo has to admit that the brigand's looks are striking. Even Liliana hinted as much, jesting during one of their lighter conversations that it was a pity that brigands as handsome as Galante were wanted by the law, when there were plenty of women who would want them even more. Russo stiffened, recalling the slow ascent of the brigand chief's hands up Liliana's legs. She must have seen the cold look in Russo's eyes after her comment, because she immediately added, "Peasant women, that is. Women who are contented with rough men and their rough habits." And then she had begun to stroke him. "Men who hardly ever wash," she continued, her voice as silky as her touch. "Or change their clothes. *Dirty* men." She led Russo into the room where her bath awaited and proceeded to help him remove his clothes before inviting him into the steamy tub. "I like my man clean."

Russo thoughts are interrupted by a raspy throat-clearing, and glancing behind him, he realizes that Dattilio is trailing him, followed by Russo's two armed horsemen, Silvio and Rodolfo. Dattilio confirms that they will shortly be arriving at the public fountain between Calvino and Gerace, where they will be able to stop to refresh themselves and the horses. Russo nods, relieved, and moves on.

Russo is anxious to get to the station in Caulonia and plan his strategy for the next three days. Now that he knows Galante has his clutches on Gabriella, he is all the more hungry to see the brigand chief captured and punished. And there is also the question of the boy and the priest....

He sighs in relief when he spots the fountain set a short distance from the side of the road. Some of his men are already there, refreshing themselves and their horses. He dismounts, waits for them to move off, then leads his horse to the trough below the running stream of water. While he is filling his flask, he notices a youth atop a grizzled mule approaching the fountain. The lad, riding shirtless, is no more than sixteen, with a shock of hair that almost covers his eyes. Russo watches in amusement as the mule comes to an abrupt stop, refusing to budge, to the consternation of the boy. No amount of prodding incites the animal to move, and the youth finally jumps off his back with a string of curses and pulls an apple out of the saddlebag. He begins to cajole the animal in a gentler tone, and the beast, unmoved, snorts and looks away, ignoring the apple.

"*Dai*, Spirito, *muoviti*! Move, you stubborn son of a bitch!"

Russo laughs outright, and the boy, aware of being watched, lets out another mouthful of curses that precipitate guffaws from the rest of the men. The boy slaps the mule's rear in resignation and walks to the fountain sheepishly, nodding respectfully to the men in uniform. "What else can you expect from an ass?" he says to nobody in particular, before bending to drink noisily at the fountain. "He'll come around eventually. Spirito knows who's really the boss." He splashes water over his sweat-beaded face and chest, before plopping down in the shade of a giant chestnut tree.

"Where are you from?" one of Russo's men asks him.

"Camini, sir."

"That's a fair distance from here. What brings you to these parts?"

The youth hesitates. "I...I'm helping someone who is searching for a young lady in Gerace."

"And are there no young ladies in Camini? Or do the young ladies in Gerace have some special quality that we are not aware of?" The group around him burst into fresh laughter and Russo watches with amusement as the youth's cheeks redden.

Another carabineer pipes up, "And what are *you* doing to help this 'someone' find a lady? Are you hoping to carry her back to him on your ass?"

The youth jumps up, his face reddening. "Signor Alfonso is not looking for a lady. I mean, he is, but not for..." he stops, floundering at the amused faces, then spits out, "...for *that!*"

Russo's eyes narrow. "Enough with the teasing, officers." He motions for his men to move on. They remount, and still chuckling, set off. Dattilio stays behind, along with the two armed horsemen.

"Signor who?" Russo walks over to the boy.

"Signor Alfonso Fantin, sir." He bows his head respectfully at the sight of Russo's medals.

"And *your* name?"

"Valerio, sir. Signor Alfonso hired me as a guide to search for a girl who has run away from Camini. She is travelling with our *parocco*, Don Simone. And her brother Luciano."

Russo purses his lips. "And this would be the Signorina Gabriella Falcone."

Valerio's eyes widen. "How do you know? Has the news spread this far already?"

Russo gives a wry smile. "Signor Alfonso appealed to me to join in the search for the young lady. I have been somewhat occupied with matters of a most urgent nature, but I have informed my men to be watchful as they conduct their usual rounds in the area."

Valerio gazes at him in wonder. "Ohh…would you be…?"

"Colonel Michele Russo, yes." Russo looks down at the boy who is nodding, his eyes wide with something akin to awe or disbelief.

"Well," Valerio says, "I will have to tell Signor Alfonso that I met up with you. I'm sure he will be very pleased."

"Indeed," Russo cannot help smirking, wondering at Alfonso's obsession in finding the girl. He obviously had no wish to leave the matter entirely in Russo's hands. There must be something more to the story that he hasn't revealed to Valerio. Or to *him*. Why else would he go so far as to hire a guide to search the area? Does he hope to find the girl first? And if so, why?

"Where would Signor Alfonso be at present?" He looks at Valerio intently.

"We're staying at Giacomo's Tavern on the outskirts of Gerace, but Signor Alfonso is not there at the moment. He went in search of a pharmacist to get some medicine for his headaches. He asked me to ride about, inquiring as to the appearance of Signorina Gabriella, Luciano, and Don Simone." He shakes his head ruefully. "Nobody has seen any sign of them."

"Mmm." Russo casts a glance at the darkening sky. He would like to confront Alfonso as to why he isn't leaving the matter in the hands of the *carabinieri*, but his first priority is meeting with his men to discuss the strategic plan for Calvino. "How long will you be staying at the tavern?"

"At least two days. Signor Alfonso wanted to make inquiries at the monastery. He thinks perhaps the abbot there may know something…."

Russo smiles. He has no intention of revealing that Gabriella and the priest are in the hands of brigands. The less information Fantin knows, the better. Valerio has provided Russo with everything he needs for now. As soon as he gets back to the military station in Caulonia, he will assign an officer to track Alfonso's movements. He looks back to where Dattilio is standing, waiting for his order to move on.

"I think Spirito has regained his spirit to travel," he says, nodding at the mule, who is slowly approaching. "I bid you farewell. And please tell Signor Alfonso that I will make it a point to seek him out before he leaves Gerace." He responds to Valerio's nod of respect and remounts. Turning the horse in the direction of Caulonia, he sets off, sending the dry earth of the road scattering behind him.

GABRIELLA STRETCHES HER LEGS TENTATIVELY on the pallet. The discomfort has subsided from her calf wound. Her thumb is still tender, but she decides to remove the linen cloth binding it to let it breathe. The worst ache, though, is one she can never imagine subsiding: the ache of sadness and longing. *Papà. Luciano. Tonino. At least Luciano is in a safe place, cared for by the nuns. Papà is gone forever. Did I even embrace him before he left for the fields that morning? Show him, at least, how much he meant to me?*

He was not a man to be free with his words of affection, and even less so when his Elisabetta died, but Gabriella and Luciano had always sensed his devotion. He was like the craggy limestone hills around Camini—hard, weather-beaten, marked with the shadows of a hard life—but with a face and eyes that reflected his love, just as the white rock-faces reflected the rays of the sun. Gabriella tries to console herself that he has joined his wife in heaven, but then finds herself wishing selfishly that he were alive for her and Luciano instead.

Thinking about Tonino only causes her despair. She can hardly bear to think about the feel of his lips on hers, the way his strong arms embraced her by the oleanders, the heady perfume of the pink blossoms gently wafting over them by the river. Gabriella does not even attempt to console herself. *With what? The hope that Tonino will still be alive when—if—I ever return to Camini? Why would God grant me this favour, this act of mercy? There is little mercy in this world*, she thinks bitterly, rising from the pallet. *At least for the Falcone family.*

Gabriella feels her stomach contract with hunger. She declined the portion of goat offered to her last night around the fire. Gaetano had cooked it over kindling gathered from juniper shrubs; she had heard him explain to Don Simone that it made the meat sweet and spicy. But she could not bring herself to taste anything that had been killed at the hands of Roberto, and when he appeared with the others after Gaetano had finished roasting it, she murmured to Don Simone that her stomach was unsettled, and that she just wanted to rest. He insisted she take a wedge of the coarse dark bread with her, and she complied before retreating, aware of Galante's dark eyes following her up to the hut. She lay down on her pallet without touching the bread. It is still where she left it, on top of her skirts at the foot of the pallet, a fly working industriously on one corner.

She stiffens at the tread of footsteps outside the tent.

"Signorina?"

Dorotea. Gabriella pushes aside the curtain and steps out. She squints at the brightness of the day. She must have slept much longer than usual. The *brigantessa* is holding out a bundle containing a wedge of cheese, coarse bread, and several black figs. "The chief said you needed to eat. You must maintain your strength. I brought back a good supply."

Gabriella's insides contract again and she relents, nodding. She sees Dorotea's face relax approvingly. Gabriella walks over and sits on one of the stumps, and when the *brigantessa* follows her, she tilts her head questioningly. "The chief wants me to reassure you that you are in no present danger," Dorotea says, one corner of her mouth twitching as if undecided whether to stretch itself into a smile. Gabriella notices something flash as Dorotea gestures, and when her hands become still, Gabriella sees that it is a gold ring with a red stone. As the *brigantessa* sits down on a stump opposite her, Gabriella's gaze is drawn to a glint above her boot. *A polished dagger.*

"A *brigantessa* is especially vulnerable," Dorotea says huskily, meeting her gaze. "She has to learn to protect herself without depending on the help of her fellow brigands or brigand chief."

Gabriella doesn't know what to say. She tentatively bites into the bread and chews it slowly, looking at the ground.

"You'll come to no harm here." Dorotea's voice has softened, and Gabriella looks up, wondering what severe circumstances induced her to go into hiding. To become a *brigantessa*. Dorotea's eyes are strangely compelling—pools of silver-green with a speck of black for a pupil. Shadowed arcs hang below them like half-moons. With a grey bandana drawing back most of her hair, she is all sharp angles. No tender jawline, no shapely lips, nothing at all that hints at tenderness.

Dorotea's eyes narrow. "The chief has made it clear to us that you and Don Simone are to be protected at all costs. He has asked me to be your guardian."

"Guardian?" Gabriella murmurs. "Don Simone—"

"You need more than the protection of a priest here." Dorotea's mouth twists into a grim line. "Prayers aren't quite enough to keep the lawmen away. Or brigands from other bands." She slides her hand down one trousered leg until it clasps the alabaster handle of the dagger. "And you can't always know whom to trust." She releases the handle and leans closer to Gabriella. "You can trust *me*, Signorina." Her eyes flicker. "You will be safe with me."

A bird call makes her turn sharply to the entry into the clearing. "That is Tomaso's signal," she says, rising. "He has seen something from his lookout or heard some news from one of the goatherds in the area. I must go." She begins to walk away, then turns to Gabriella.

"Forget who you were or where you came from," she advises

gruffly. "You're a *brigantessa* now. You're going to have to learn to live like one. *If* you want to survive."

ALFONSO DRINKS THE NERVE TONIC the pharmacist recommended and grimaces. He takes a swig of the wine to rid himself of its foul taste and starts sputtering. The wine is no better. He chides himself inwardly for not demanding the same wine he had the night before. Looking up from a corner table in the dining room of the tavern, he sees Valerio walking over to him. The boy has an excited air about him and Alfonso wonders if he has gleaned some valuable information about Gabriella.

He motions for him to sit down. "What is it, Valerio? You look like you have something of importance to share with me." He raises his eyebrows expectantly.

Valerio nods. "You will be happy to hear who I encountered at the roadside fountain, Signor Alfonso. It was no other than Colonel Russo. He was there with some of his officers. I heard them talking amongst themselves about their mission in Calvino, searching out a brigand chief by the name of Stefano Galante. Imagine, a *capo brigante*!"

Alfonso straightens in his chair, his eyes narrowing. "Did they capture him?"

"No, but they arrested a dozen men. They're bringing them to the military station in Caulonia."

Alfonso has a troubling thought. He looks at Valerio squarely. "What did you tell Russo?" He deliberately keeps his voice calm, reluctant to show Valerio that he is upset over the news of Russo's presence even if Russo *is* doing what he is supposed to be doing, as leader of the forces of repression against the brigands. "Did you tell him we were searching for Gabriella?"

"Yes, of course," Valerio nods emphatically. "And Colonel Russo said he and his men are also engaged in the search for her and her brother. And the priest. He told me to tell you that he'll be stopping in to see you in the next day or two."

Alfonso nods slowly. *Damn.* He wanted his search to be a private affair. At least, private from Russo. Yes, he asked Russo to intervene and help find Gabriella. He wanted the law on his side; besides, Russo's men could comb the area more efficiently than *he* could.

But somehow, he couldn't help holding on to the dream that *he* would be the one to find Gabriella first. He *had* to find her first. He was so close. The *trattoria* owner's niece, Dorotea, seemed so certain that she could find Gabriella and bring her back to the tavern. The last person Alfonso wants around when that happens is Russo.

Alfonso struggles to keep his annoyance from Valerio. *Stupid peasant! Doesn't have the sense to keep his mouth shut.* He should have ordered him to wait here at the tavern instead of traipsing all over the place, chattering like an old washerwoman by the river. He turns to the boy with a forced smile. "Let's hope he will come to tell me he has found Gabriella."

Valerio nods vigorously.

Alfonso makes up his mind quickly. He must send Valerio back to Camini. If luck is on his side and Dorotea comes back with Gabriella before Russo shows up, then he can't have Valerio in the way. He puts a hand on the boy's shoulder. "I am confident Gabriella and her brother will be back in Camini in no time. With Colonel Russo and his men in the vicinity, there is no need for me to go any further. I will stay here and wait for him, but there is no need for you to do so."

"But—"

"Your grandmother needs you more than I do at present, Valerio. You have taken me this far, and I am most grateful for your diligence in ensuring a safe journey." He pulls out his money pouch from a slit inside his vest. He withdraws several coins and hands them to the boy, a sum that is double the amount he had promised. "I am obligated to you." He puts up a hand when Valerio starts to sputter an objection.

"You must take this, Valerio. It will help ease your *nonna's* financial burdens."

Valerio looks at him misty-eyed. "*Grazie,* Signor Alfonso. You are very generous."

"You're welcome, my boy. Now get going. I have every reason to believe I will be back in Camini with Gabriella very soon."

Valerio nods and leaves. Through the open shutters, Alfonso watches as Valerio makes his way over to Spirito, untethers him, and plods off with a happy whistle.

"Good riddance," Alfonso murmurs. "Go back to the hole you came from." He bangs his fist on the table and a robust server comes scuttling out of the kitchen, wiping her greasy fingers on her apron.

"Bring me your best *Greco,*" he orders. "This wine is shit."

GABRIELLA CAN SMELL THE SCORCHED LANDSCAPE long before the brigand chief tells her they have reached the outskirts of Calvino. They dismount in silence, and after Mastro is tethered, Gabriella quickens her pace to try to keep up with Galante's long strides. From various heights on Mount Galante, they could see fires smouldering across fields like crimson veins, igniting dry bundles of hay or flax, devouring huts and barns. Now, as they approach the houses on the outer edge of the hamlet, the undistinguishable clamour they heard on the slopes becomes clear. Women are shrieking, their faces distended and streaked with soot. Their children are wild-eyed and crying, their noses dripping with black-tinged mucous. They are clinging to their mothers' skirts while their mothers circle about, pulling at their hair, pummelling their own chests in frantic despair. When they see Stefano, they rush to him, tugging at his cloak, their voices a chorus of agony.

Gabriella stands a few paces behind him, horrified. She hears them telling him how the forces of law descended upon Calvino like a plague of locusts, smashing their way into homes, hurtling the women aside to search for their husbands and when they found them, either in the fields or returning to their homes, beating whatever information they could out of them. Some of the women weren't so lucky as to get tossed aside; they were dragged into back rooms and interrogated, before being stripped and ravaged, sometimes by a half-dozen soldiers.

Gabriella gasps and chokes on her own saliva. Her eyes fill with tears. She wants to cover her ears to any further atrocities, but she can't seem to feel her fingers or limbs. Someone shoves past her to get to Stefano. "They destroyed my family," the woman sobs, her hand clawing his arm. "They tried to make my husband admit he was providing you with supplies and weapons, and when he tried to deny it, they smashed his head against the fireplace." She covers her face with her hands and when she opens her bloodshot eyes, they are directed at Gabriella. "One of them took my daughter on the floor. *On the floor.*" She gives an uncontrollable shudder. "*Bettina is only fourteen.*"

Stefano steps forward and embraces the woman. He murmurs something in her ear, but Gabriella cannot hear what he is saying. He turns to the group and urges them to gather at the Church of the Madonna of the Poppies, where he will return after checking on his family, once he determines that it is safe to do so. He tells them that their dead husbands have become martyrs and will suffer no more in this earthly hell. He orders the boys and the few men who are in the crowd to gather blankets, food, water, and whatever weapons they can find, and to bring them to the church, for there will be many more villagers needing comfort and support tonight.

Stefano takes Gabriella by the arm and leads her away from the group. He takes a darkened path around the periphery of the village and then cuts through a field and past an animal enclosure. The goats and the sheep seem unsettled, emitting strident bleats. *Even they know something terrible has happened,* Gabriella muses sadly.

"My mother's house," Stefano says suddenly, and his voice

wavers for a moment. He rushes inside, his cloak flapping behind him and while Gabriella waits, she prays that his mother and sister have not been brutalized.

She stiffens when she hears footsteps approaching and is relieved to see a boy, not an officer, hiding in wait for Stefano. "The Signora and her daughter are not home," he tells her, out of breath. "My mother saw Stefano heading in this direction and wanted me to give him this message. They went to Gioiosa Ionica; the Signora's niece is expecting her baby."

"Thank you, Alberto." Stefano emerges from the house, relief in his voice. "Take this to your *mamma*." He reaches inside his cloak pocket and a moment later hands the boy several coins. Alberto runs off and Stefano gazes at Gabriella. "He didn't mention my father. I'll just go and have a look around."

Gabriella is thankful for illumination provided by the half-moon while she waits for Stefano. Her thoughts are dark enough, with the horrors she has just seen and heard.

She startles at Stefano's return and then searches his face. It is expressionless.

"My father is dead," he says. "The animals have been released. Men were there; you can see boot prints on the ground leading to the stable."

"How?" Gabriella whispers.

Stefano takes a deep breath. "It was obvious he was beaten. I found him lying in cow dung."

TONINO WAKES UP IN A SWEAT. Plagued by an onslaught of nightmares, he has barely slept after hearing the news about Gabriella. In the first dream, Gabriella appears at the crest of the mountain, holding Luciano's hand, when a line of infantrymen charge and run at them, bayonets gleaming in the sun. In the second, Gabriella is lying on top of a mound of bracken, tied up under a chestnut tree with a cord around her ankle. A big hulking man whose face is obscured advances toward Gabriella. Tonino runs to stop him, aware of his dishonourable intentions, but his legs cannot make any headway. When the man sinks to the ground in front of Gabriella, blocking her from Tonino's view, Tonino wakes up screaming, "Let her go or I'll shoot you!"

Moments later, Tonino is sitting up in his bed; the novice Caterina is wiping his face with a cool, wet cloth and telling him to calm down and take deep breaths. Sister Emilia enters, opens the shutters, and proceeds to inspect the bandage on Tonino's cheek. "No fresh blood," she says, nodding approvingly. With deft fingers, she removes the bandage. "The cut has closed nicely, but it won't hurt to apply a little more salve to it."

While she is applying a balm of aloe, rosemary, and honey, the abbess enters. Tonino raises his hand to block Sister Emilia from continuing her ministrations. "Abbess, I must leave! I must let my family know I am alive. By now they must have heard something of the events at Aspromonte. And I must find Gabriella and bring her and Luciano home." He hears his voice break. "I'll find some way of clearing her name."

The abbess's eyes flutter and she hesitates. "Signor Tonino, outwardly it seems that your injuries have shown healing. However, we are not just concerned about your physical well-being. You have suffered a great trauma—"

"I appreciate your concern, Abbess. But knowing Gabriella is somewhere out there in God knows what kind of trouble is far greater suffering for me. I can't just wait here and do nothing." He turns to get out of bed but falls back, gasping at the sharp pain in his ribs.

"Signor Tonino," the abbess says softly but firmly. "Your ribs need time to heal. We cannot see the exact damage you have suffered inside."

Grimacing, Tonino forces himself to sit up again. "Please, Abbess Emanuela. I will be fine."

"And how do you intend to help Gabriella if you can barely move? Allow yourself one more day at least, Signor Tonino. Have faith that Don Simone has found a place of refuge for

Gabriella and that she is in no danger. In the meantime, we will fortify you with a hearty bean and lentil soup." She smiles. "It is full of iron. Surely your ribs will be stronger after a bowl or two."

Tonino sighs and nods. The abbess is right. He can't imagine riding a mule or even sitting in a cart in his condition. He must rest. He leans back and watches the sisters leave the room and then a thought occurs to him. Perhaps it would help if Sister Emilia were to bind his chest.... A whirring noise catches his attention and he gazes at the window. A hummingbird is suspended in flight by the jasmine flowers, its red throat and green body glimmering like jewels, its wings fluttering too quickly to be perceived by the human eye. For some strange reason, the sight of such minuscule perfection brings Tonino some comfort, and for a few moments, he allows himself to believe what another part of him wants to doubt—that God is keeping Gabriella safe.

GABRIELLA STARES AT STEFANO. *His father is dead.* Yet Stefano's face is not showing any shock or sorrow. His mouth is drawn into a thin line, and his eyes are narrowed, causing his brow to furrow, but his expression is otherwise impassive.

When the boy is out of sight, Stefano says, "It's out of my hands for now. I moved him to a corner, on a bed of clean straw." He turns away and Gabriella stares at his rigid back, wondering what emotions must be churning deep inside him. Is he feeling guilty for his part in his father's death, no matter how indirect it was? And what about the havoc wreaked upon Calvino in order to track *him* or the people that have a connection to him?

"We must return," he rasps, and without waiting for her to reply, he turns back in the direction in which they first came. She has no choice but to follow him, ever conscious that in her male disguise she is also a target for any carabineers who may have lingered in Calvino to see if Stefano would appear.

She stumbles over brambles and is glad that she is not impeded by her skirts. Picking herself up, she hurries to try to catch up with Stefano. He seems barely aware of her presence, and she wonders why he wanted her to come with him in the first place. She recalls the look of dismay on Don Simone's face when he found out that Stefano was taking her to Calvino.

He tried to dissuade the brigand chief, but Stefano merely lifted his eyebrows at Don Simone's nervous supplication and assured the priest that Gabriella was as safe with him as with Don Simone.

Gabriella watched the anxiety and uncertainty settle on Don Simone's face, and she instantly felt a rush of affection for him for caring about her. No, it was *more* than affection; it was *love*. Her eyelids prickled at the acknowledgement that Don Simone had been in her life for as long as she could remember, and he had watched over her and nurtured her alongside her parents, who had devotedly served him. He had always been *family*.

After Stefano left her to get ready for the journey, she rushed over to Don Simone, telling him about the chief's sister and reaffirming that Stefano had no bad intentions when it came to her.

"Take this," Don Simone urged, handing her his wooden rosary. "I will have a small measure of peace knowing the good Lord is accompanying you. May you be blessed as are these beads, and may you return safely and speedily to me."

Gabriella hesitated. Surely Don Simone hadn't forgotten how she felt about God's place, or rather, absence in her life. She took a deep breath and with a resigned nod, placed the rosary in the pocket of her trousers. As Don Simone's face brightened, Gabriella conceded to herself that considering his feelings ahead of her own wasn't as painful as she thought; in fact, she had to grudgingly admit that her small gesture of acceptance brought her a measure of peace as well.

Now, heading to the Church of the Madonna of the Poppies, Gabriella fingers the beads in her pocket against her mother's handkerchief. Although it must be well past midnight, some of the villagers they pass are huddled on doorsteps, their faces dappled from the glow of candlelight, their voices rising and falling. Some are heading to the *piazza* and the church, carrying blankets and baskets of food. Small children are still up, some disgruntled and crying, some running about in a frenzy. A smell of burning still lingers in the air.

Suddenly, Stefano turns down a narrow lane. He stops at an arched wooden doorway, knocks, and enters without waiting for anyone to open the door. Gabriella steps inside and follows Stefano through several dark rooms and up a few cement stairs to a second level before he stops abruptly. A shaft of moonlight enters an open balcony door and Gabriella sees the person Stefano must have been looking for. The girl is huddled on her pallet, her eyes fluttering open as Stefano approaches. She recoils when his shadow looms over her, but then relaxes when the moonlight reveals his features. "Bettina," he murmurs, drawing the blanket by her side over her. "I'm so sorry this happened."

Gabriella swallows. *Bettina. The fourteen-year-old girl.*

One of her eyes is swollen, and the skin around it has already darkened like the skin of an eggplant. Gabriella watches as she erupts into tears. "Papà refused to tell them anything," she sits up, gulping. "They had received a tip that Papà was providing supplies for you and your band. I thought they would try to find the money you gave Papà to pay for his medicine, but they weren't interested in money." She covers her face with her hands. Stefano cradles her in his arms and between sobs, she says, "They killed him and then laughed about it as they were leaving. One of them returned to search up here, and when he saw me, he grabbed me and dragged me downstairs and...and..."

"*Sh, sh,*" Stefano murmurs. "Don't talk about it anymore, Bettina. I will make them pay for what they've done, do you understand? Anyone who hurts my family or friends will pay if it's the last thing I do." With one arm he motions to Gabriella to approach. "Bettina, I have a....a friend with me. She will help you while I go to the church and see what has to be done. Your mother and neighbours are waiting for me there. I won't be long." Bettina lays back down on the pallet and closes her eyes. She says, her eyes still closed, "Another officer came and dragged him off me, saying that Colonel Russo had given the order for all his men to leave Calvino at once. He had left the door open....The Colonel was on his horse, watching from the road. When he saw me on the floor, he *smiled*."

Stefano curses under his breath, and Gabriella notices that his hands are both clenched. He glances at her without a word and leaves, the door slamming violently behind him.

Gabriella's heart twists when she looks down at Bettina. The girl's lower lip is quivering, her teeth occasionally clattering together. Gabriella stoops to caress her forehead and squeeze her hand. "I will bring you a cup of *camomilla*," she murmurs. By the time the tea has steeped, Stefano has returned with Bettina's mother, who embraces Gabriella tearily and takes the cup of tea from her.

Stefano leads Gabriella back to the church of the Madonna of the Poppies to help the families whose huts or houses were burnt down to settle for the night. Pews have been moved and the villagers are setting down whatever they have been able to salvage or recover, their voices echoing in a cacophony. Gabriella helps distribute blankets and food that have been collected by the boys and men of Calvino. She seeks out mothers who seem to have their hands full, trying to comfort screaming babies or restrain children who are overly rambunctious, and is gratified to see the appreciation in their tired faces.

She glimpses Stefano slipping coins into the palms of the villagers, reassuring them he would be providing them with more in the days and weeks to come. He vows to find ways of getting money to them even if Colonel Russo steps up his forces in the vicinity. Gabriella watches the men of Calvino embracing him, shaking his hand vigorously, patting him on the back. Some women are drying their tears, kissing his hands, blessing him aloud. Others are weeping noisily, wringing their hands, lamenting the arrest of their sons or husbands.

Stefano speaks to all of them, and to Gabriella's surprise, none of them are hurling accusations of blame at him; no one is maligning him for being the cause of the attack upon Calvino. Some are yelling out curses to Colonel Russo and his *diavoli,* for who other than devils would set fire to huts with people and animals still in them? Destroy their homes and their means of subsistence? Ruin the lands on which they labour for the meagre pay that keeps them alive?

It is a miracle that nobody was killed as the flames devoured what they could. An old farmer named Rocco Taverniti emerged screaming from his hut, awakened from a nap by the crackling of flames on one corner of his straw pallet that swiftly reached his legs. He ran out of the hut and threw himself into a pile of fresh dung to snuff out the flames. His adult sons carried him to the river to clean him off, and after applying a cooling balm of aloe over his inflamed skin, his wife tore strips off her skirts to wrap around his burns. Feverish with shock, he was brought to the church, and his sons set him down on a pile of blankets in an alcove below the statue of his namesake, *Santo* Rocco, venerated for healing diseases and plagues of the body.

His wife is still hovering over him in the alcove, one hand clasping his and the other fingering the beads of her rosary.

Gabriella's attention is drawn to a couple weeping over the loss of their animals, entrapped in a barn that was torched by some of Russo's cavalrymen. The couple had cowered behind a thick arbutus hedge, helpless to save their animals. "*Povere bestie,*" she sobs against her husband's chest. "Those poor beasts. Their cries are ringing in my ears. May God damn the men who could do such a thing. May He send them straight to hell, so they can roast in the flames, like my poor animals! May they know nothing but suffering to the end of their days!"

Gabriella turns away, sickened by the thought of any animal suffering in such a way. She notices Stefano murmuring something to the parish priest, Don Damiano, before handing him a purple bag that the priest immediately slips within the folds of his cassock. Moments later, while she is crouching to tend to the scraped knee of a youth no older than Luciano, she senses someone behind her, and turns to find the old priest watching her with a benevolent smile. "*Che Dio ti benedica*," he blesses her, making the sign of the cross above her head. Gabriella, flustered, rises to nod respectfully, but someone has called out to him and he has already turned away.

By midnight, the din has subsided. The children are asleep on the makeshift beds, along with most of the parents, and the few that are still awake are either kneeling in front of a statue in the nave, whispering prayers, or saying a rosary at their pew. The heavy oak doors of the church are open, letting in a warm breeze, and some of the men have shuffled outside to sit either on the steps of the church, or on stone benches in the *piazza*, their low voices mingling with the rustling leaves of nearby eucalyptus trees.

Satisfied that the villagers are taken care of, at least for the present, Stefano informs Gabriella that they need to return to Calvino. Gabriella sighs with relief when they reach Mastro. For the entire journey back to Calvino, Gabriella closes her eyes and allows herself to press against Stefano, her arms and hands entwined around his waist, mustering just enough concentration to keep herself from falling.

RUSSO POURS HIMSELF A GENEROUS SHOT of brandy and savours it slowly before getting to the task of updating General Zanetti about his recent mission....

Illustrious General,
The region is buzzing with the news of General Garibaldi's defeat at Aspromonte. The peasants seem to be quite sympathetic

to his plight, despite the fact that he represents the newly unified Republic, the notion of which is confusing to them in their limited understanding of political affairs. Again, dear General, these simple folk are a contradiction unto themselves, which is, perhaps, the very reason there is so much turbulence in their lives. A violent, passionate people indeed!

As you recommended in your previous letter, I undertook a mission yesterday in Calvino for the main purpose of tracking down the brigand chief Stefano Galante and his band, as well as his supporters. As the villagers had no reason to expect such a manoeuvre, they were caught unawares, and as a consequence, my forces were able to apprehend a dozen men suspected of being either supporters or informers of Galante.

As family is usually the first to be implicated, I undertook to question Galante's immediate family members myself. The senior Galante was the only member present; his wife and daughter were in the neighbouring town of Gioiosa Ionica, assisting a relative in childbirth. Although Luca Galante made his disdain for his son's lawless pursuits quite clear, I could not ascertain with certainty whether his proclamations were genuine or feigned, and therefore, I instructed my assistant to utilize more rigorous procedures to encourage his truthfulness. Unfortunately, the brigand chief's father became belligerent, having previously consumed a good measure of grappa, and forthwith attempted to strike my assistant with a sickle.

My officer had no recourse but to try to protect himself, and rightly so, being a lawful servant of His Excellency King Victor Emmanuel, and an ardent combatant of lawlessness and corruption. The elder Galante collapsed and we were not able to revive him. Earlier, we discovered items that would indicate that Galante's wife has been in contact with her son, and he has been rewarding her with some spoils from his robberies. I have every intention of pursuing my investigation upon her return to Calvino.

As I mentioned earlier, esteemed General, a dozen villagers

have been arrested. They have been brought to the station and will be detained behind bars until I am satisfied with their testimonials. None have as yet provided any sufficient information as to Galante's hiding place, but as with Galante's father, they will receive forceful incentives to co-operate.

Would that we could carry out our mission without the use of extreme measures, but as has been proven innumerable times, the scourge of brigandage in this territory has only been deterred or extinguished by the same means with which the brigands conduct their affairs. An eye for an eye! This biblical law of retribution seems to be the only law these brigands understand.

And so, dear General, we will continue to use any means at our disposal to ensure a successful mission. For this occasion, it meant setting fires, smoking some of the suspected informers out of their hovels, and imposing pressure on those we questioned. We left the villagers with no doubt as to our position and scope of our military operation. We gave them the succinct message that they would have a reprieve during the night and for an additional day, providing them with ample time to figure out how they would deliver Galante to us, or else direct us to his hideout. Those who co-operated would receive a monetary reward and immunity from hanging or imprisonment. I truly believe, General, that this tactic will prove to be fruitful.

I anticipate the success of our mission in the next few days, not only in capturing the brigand chief Galante, but also in finding a young woman who is presently under his protection—a peasant by the name of Gabriella Falcone, who, after stabbing a landowner, fled her hamlet of Camini with her brother and the parish priest. The landowner, Alfonso Fantin, approached me to pursue the girl in order to make her pay for her crime. So, dear General, my intention is to capture and arrest both a brigand chief and a *brigantessa*, the former for the crime of murder, and the latter for attempted murder.

As always, I send my warmest thanks for your continued support in this and all my missions, and I avow my utmost respect and compliance for your every command. Signed on this, the 7th day of September in the the year 1862.

    With faithful obedience, I remain, your servant,

    Lieutenant Colonel Michele Russo

THE RIDE BACK SEEMS ENDLESS. Gabriella can feel every rut in the road, every vertiginous curve. She clings to Stefano frantically, her stomach heaving. By the time they reach the foothills of Monte Galante, Gabriella is cringing from stomach cramps. She does not realize she has cried out, and when Stefano reins in Mastro and dismounts, helping her step down, he searches her face with narrowed eyes. "Sit down for a few minutes," he orders, and pulling out a flask from his saddlebag, instructs her to take a drink. "More," he says after her tentative swallow. "You look like the Holy Ghost."

Gabriella complies, shuddering as the alcohol burns a path down her throat. They sit without talking for a few moments, looking out at the valley below.

"How are you feeling now?"

Gabriella clenches her jaw. Her stomach is still agitated, but the sadness and helplessness she felt when she arrived in Calvino has been replaced by something much stronger. *Fury.* Fury for the plight of Stefano's neighbours, and at the senseless barbarity and lust of the carabineers. Disgust at their abject disregard for justice. *Justice!* How disillusioned she was to think that the enforcers of the law would be upholding it. Whether or not the villagers had leant Stefano any support, they were condemned. Made to pay for Stefano's lawlessness. Gabriella realizes with horror that if this is what they would do to an entire village, her fate or that of Stefano's, as wanted outlaws, would be far worse.

Stefano repeats his question. Gabriella turns to meet his gaze. His look of genuine concern makes her eyes well up. "I feel sick for what has been done to those poor people. To Bettina and your father. To those who have had nothing to do with you. And even to those who *have* supported you. Brought you some bread or fruit. They didn't deserve to suffer. To *die!* To have their homes destroyed, set on fire. To have their wives and daughters violated. What kind of *law* is this?"

"I am a wanted man, Gabriella. Wanted for attempted murder." Stefano's voice is calm. "The law will use any means to find me."

Gabriella shudders. *She* is also wanted. She may have escaped being violated by Alfonso Fantin, but how can she escape the law forever? And what will they do to *her* when they find her? How will she ever find a way to convince them of her innocence so she can reunite with Luciano and return to Camini? And to Tonino, if he is still alive....

"*Andiamo.* Let's go, Gabriella. We'll be safe on Monte Galante. Have faith." He helps her remount, and as they ascend the mountain slope, with the scent of resin in the sultry breeze and wisps of fog suspended over the black depths of ravines, Gabriella acknowledges that perhaps faith is, after all, the only thing that she shouldn't run away from.

STEFANO PEERS BETWEEN THE FOLIAGE of a lentisk bush. He is almost certain that the whistle he heard several moments earlier originates from one of his informers, but he will not act precipitously and advance into the glen without first verifying the identity of the person.

Dorotea informed him in private that the informer would be waiting at their usual meeting spot early in the morning, when the man's boss would most likely still be sleeping. Stefano left his hideout on Monte Galante and descended the mountain with Mastro, tethering him under a beech tree and then continuing down the slope on foot, pausing every few moments to listen for the signal.

It could very well be a trap. Stefano is not so naïve as to believe that one of his informers could never be pressured to reveal what he knows about *him*. Anything could make a man blurt out a confession. The promise of money. The threat of torture to himself or his loved ones. Not only is a suspected informer vulnerable to the will and force of the law, but even more so are the brigands in the chief's band.

Stefano does not allow himself to trust anyone implicitly. Even if one's intentions are honourable, one can be made to bend easily under the right conditions. He is well aware of a number of brigands who succumbed and betrayed their chief. Used the excuse that they needed the bounty money to take care of their children, who were dying of starvation or sick with malaria. Or simply decided that being hanged was too high a price to pay for their loyalty to their leader. The incentive of receiving immunity from any of their previous crimes as brigands and reacceptance into the village or town from which they fled to go into hiding, has always attracted a band member who was tired of life on the run, tired of never knowing how many days he would have to go hungry before the next meal. No, *he* would not be such a fool as to jeopardize his own life by trusting anyone completely.

Stefano's ears suddenly pick up the soft tread of footsteps on the mossy ground, and his eyes narrow, anticipating the appearance of his long-time friend and informer since he has been in hiding. If Stefano had to trust anyone, it would be *him*. He has known the old farmer since he was a youth, travelling about the villages and hamlets seeking work as a day labourer. He would often stop at the farmer's hut, located in the valley between Gerace and Calvino, and rest for a few minutes while his old friend gathered some chicory or wild fennel for him to take home to his mother.

Despite his grizzled appearance, the old man has an intelligence and intuitiveness that have served Stefano well. The latest information he gave Dorotea has been invaluable. Russo's intention to move his forces into Calvino was not a surprise to Stefano. His friend has been fastidious in his observations of Colonel Russo, since being hired as his driver, handyman, and manservant. Now Stefano is anxious to find out the details of Russo's next move.

Stefano smiles as the old man emerges from the thicket. As he advances into the sun-dappled glade, Stefano gives a soft whistle to announce his presence before stepping out from behind the lentisk bush.

"*Salve*, Dattilio," he smiles. "Come and share a flask of wine with me. I'm anxious to hear your news." He extends a welcoming hand. "Let's sit down."

Dattilio nods. He takes the flask from Stefano and gulps thirstily. He wipes his lips with the back of his hand and frowns at Stefano. "Russo wants your head in a jar," he rasps grimly, "just like the brigand Agostino. He's had it in for you since you attacked his carriage." He spits to one side. "The bastard has been more demanding than usual since he took up with that *puttana*. She treats me like a leper. If I knew I could get away with it, I'd show Signora Liliana what an old leper is still capable of." He makes a crude motion toward his genitals. "She and Russo both need a good lesson," he grunts. "And if *I* can't teach it to them, then I hope *you* can."

THE STRIDENT CRY OF A GOSHAWK cuts into Gabriella's dreams. When she realizes it is real, she opens her eyes. The sun is beaming through the slits of the hut's ceiling. Gabriella shifts to look over at Stefano's pallet and is not surprised to find it empty, although she has to admit that she is disappointed. Stefano's presence brought her some measure of comfort when they returned from Calvino. He followed her into the hut, retrieved some bread from the basket near his pallet and handed it to her, insisting she eat it to settle her stomach and to preserve her strength. He procured another flask, this one filled with just water, and left it by her pallet. He would be back shortly, he told her, after meeting with his band to discuss their plans should Russo succeed in tracking them.

"Have faith, Gabriella," he reassured her again, his deep

voice softening. "You will be safe with me even if we must evacuate."

She saw the sincerity in his eyes and felt ashamed that she had ever been taken aback by their strangeness. She had been so quick to attach a superstitious belief to his eyes, the belief that something that wasn't *normal* was a bad omen, or worse, connected to the devil. She nodded, overwhelmed with humility, and caught his nod and a flash of a smile as he left.

Chewing small bites of the coarse rye bread, she prayed for his safety and the people of Calvino until her eyelids felt heavy....

And now, even after a few hours of deep sleep, she still feels the same, the memory of her time in Calvino no less distressing. She sits up, rubbing her eyes. Her hair has tumbled out of her bandana, and while she is rearranging it into a bun and adjusting the bandana, she hears footsteps approaching.

"Signorina Gabriella?"

Dorotea. Gabriella hurriedly steps out of the hut. "Yes?"

Dorotea squints at her, the sun in her eyes. "The chief gave me instructions for you," she says. "He had to leave early this morning with Tomaso to take care of some business. He is concerned for your safety and has asked me to take you to my uncle's tavern on the outskirts of Gerace." Gabriella's face must have displayed surprise and uncertainty, for Dorotea quickly adds, "He said not to worry. He will meet up with us at the tavern after dusk, and then we will continue on to Calvino. Our informer has told him that Colonel Russo and his men have received word of the abduction of the son of a baron in the town of Siderno, and are occupied in pursuing the suspected brigand, which will allow the chief to return to Calvino unhindered."

Gabriella wonders aloud, "Stefano told me I would be safe *here.*"

She sees Dorotea's eyebrows rise at her use of Stefano's given name. "You will be safe with *me,*" Dorotea says stiffly. "These are the chief's orders."

"But what about Don Simone?" Gabriella says. "He *is* coming with us?"

Dorotea falters. "Well…ah…no. He is staying here with the brothers and Gaetano. No danger will come to either of you," she says more gently. "The chief wants you to have a proper roof over your head. And proper food." She steps closer to Gabriella and places a hand around her shoulder. "You have seen the chief. He is not the villain the law makes him out to be. He told the band what happened in Calvino, and new plans have been made. One of those plans is to get you to my uncle's tavern for now."

Dorotea's voice takes on a note of urgency as her grey-green eyes gaze directly into Gabriella's. "*Please*, Signorina. *We must leave at once*."

Gabriella stares at her for a moment. The *brigantessa's* eyes don't waver. Gabriella sighs. She is not looking forward to the ride down Monte Galante and through the countryside, but she trusts Dorotea more than she does the brothers, especially when Stefano is not present. "*D'accordo*," she concedes. "I'll be ready in a few minutes."

CHEWING ON THE TIP OF A REED, Stefano sits under the shade of a beech tree for a momentary rest, watching the figure of Dattilio get smaller and smaller until the mule path twists and he disappears from view. Although Dattilio's tone was urgent, appealing to Stefano to return to the hideout until he sent word or came back himself to verify that Russo or his men were not lurking in the area, Stefano is not unduly alarmed. Nevertheless, he will call a meeting to plan an alternative escape from Monte Galante should their hideout be compromised.

He rises, stretches, and pats Mastro affectionately before mounting. As the mule continues plodding its way up the narrow winding path to the summit of Monte Galante, Stefano envisions all the possible escape routes he and his band members could take. He has not even made this information known to *them*.

No, there are some secrets better kept to himself. Divulging them could jeopardize his freedom....

His mouth twists bitterly. He has a freedom of sorts, living the life of an outlaw. The freedom to roam over Mount Galante and a stretch of the Aspromonte range, ruling over his band like the Apennine wolf with his pack, keeping them in line as any competent pack leader would. And those who stray from his leadership end up like Dorotea's husband Paolo, cornered and shot by the carabineers.

She was lucky she hadn't ended up riddled with bullets like him. She had strayed behind him to refresh herself at a mountain stream and he had ventured ahead, ignoring Stefano's earlier orders to stay at the hideout after receiving a tip that some carabineers were combing the foothills for signs of brigand activity. From his vantage point, camouflaged behind a stand of pines, Stefano had seen at least a dozen carabineers advancing up the flanks of the hills like ants.

Paolo ignored Stefano's warning, driven by the desire to lay in wait for one particular carabineer who had harassed and threatened Paolo's family and friends. Pressing ahead, he fell into a trap, and was instantly surrounded by four carabineers who opened fire simultaneously. Hearing the shots, Dorotea retreated as stealthily as she could. She arrived back at the hideout after a long trek, her face mottled from exertion and fury. "I swear I'll find out who Paolo's killers were," she hissed, her gaunt face streaked with tears and dirt. "I'll make them pay...."

Stefano presses Mastro over to the thicket opening. He gives his bird call signal to Tomaso, who answers it and then repeats it, alerting the others to Stefano's return. As Stefano enters the clearing, his band members come rushing out to meet him except for Dorotea. *She must be with Gabriella.* He dismounts, tethers Mastro to a sturdy branch of an arbutus tree, and swirls around to find Don Simone shuffling over to him as fast as he can.

"Signor Galante!" The priest's cheeks are fever-red and glistening, and he is gesturing wildly toward Stefano's hut. "Signorina Gabriella is gone!" He gasps, swallows, and crosses himself. "I went to check on her after I awoke and there was no answer. Thinking she was asleep, I went back to my own hut." He starts wringing his hands. "I returned after a short while, and when nobody answered, I went in. Gabriella was gone." He blinks rapidly, and Stefano can see that his hands are trembling. "And Dorotea as well."

Stefano feels an intense heat building within his chest. *What has Dorotea done?* He has noticed her watching Gabriella a number of times when she thought nobody was looking. At first, Stefano thought they were simply looks of jealousy, but now he realizes it was more than that. Dorotea assumes that intense scrutiny when she is planning an act of banditry that she will carry out herself. *What scheme is she involved in that has led her to disobey my orders and take Gabriella away?* he wonders uneasily.

He is sickened to think that Dorotea found a way to convince Gabriella to leave Monte Galante with her. *But why? And where could they have gone? Where is Dorotea taking her?*

He turns quickly to the brothers. "Do you know where Dorotea went?"

Roberto looks at Raffaele and then back at Stefano. "She said she was going on a lucrative mission...and it had to be just her, and that the girl would be helping...."

Stefano's nostrils flare. "Where?" he barks.

"I'm not certain, but I think she said she would be stopping in at her uncle's tavern outside of Gerace."

Stefano's eyes flash dangerously. "Roberto and Raffaele, stay here and guard the hideout. I am placing Don Simone in your care." He shoots them a piercing glare. "Do *not* move from here unless you get word only from me or Dattilio. Gaetano, stay close to the hideout. You may continue to hunt but not with firearms of any kind. Tomaso, scour the foothills, and

I will venture out to Gerace. I intend to find Gabriella and Dorotea and bring them back with me."

He shoots a glance at Don Simone. "Keep praying," he advises the priest grimly. "Gabriella needs prayers now more than ever." He strides quickly to Mastro and with a nod at Tomaso before remounting, he heads down the mountain, one hand on the reins and one over the scapular of the Madonna at his chest.

PART VII
ENCOUNTERS
September 1862

ALFONSO CLOSES HIS SHUTTERS and stretches out on the bed. The medicinal treatment the pharmacist in Gerace gave him seems to be effective; he hasn't experienced any jabbing pain since he took the tincture of valerian root and willow earlier this morning.

He enjoyed his solitary breakfast in the dining room without Valerio's incessant chatter. The coffee was surprisingly good; the variety of breads, cheeses, and cured meats extensive. He particularly enjoyed the generous slices of *soppressata*, a delightfully oversized pork sausage seasoned with dried chili peppers and fennel seed.

Now, hands crossed over his sated stomach, Alfonso considers whether he should wait at the tavern for the rest of the day or venture to the monastery and churches clustered on the foothills. It has been a day and a half since he spoke with the owner's niece. *Dora,* he believes her name is. *No, Dorotea.* As for Colonel Russo, he has not made an appearance at the tavern as yet. Could he have already left the area?

Absorbed in his thoughts, he barely hears the knock at his door. As the tapping continues, he jumps up, then strides over to the door. The youth who served him the wine the night before last is standing before him, his hands entwined.

"Signor Fantin, I have a message from Signora Dorotea."

Alfonso's eyebrows lift. "*Prego,*" he nods, his stomach lurching with excitement.

"She is wondering where you would like to meet. She says she has some news to give you."

Alfonso studies the youth's face for a moment. From his impassive expression, Alfonso concludes that he knows nothing about Dorotea's news. "Tell her to come here," he says, and seeing the instant look of shock on the boy's face, realizes that it would not do for the owner's niece to be in his room unescorted. "Is there a private salon where we might meet?"

The youth's forehead wrinkles as he ponders the possibilities a few seconds before shaking his head. "The only salon we have is being used at the moment."

Impatient, Alfonso fishes a couple of coins out of the pouch inside his vest and hands them to the boy. "Well, how about you tell her to come here. Then, when she returns to the kitchen—our meeting shouldn't take more than a few minutes—you may come up and I'll give you the other half for your trouble."

Money solves so many of life's problems, Alfonso thinks with a smile as the youth bolts away. He paces the room, opens the shutters. He wonders if he dares hope Gabriella will be with Dorotea. At the tentative knock a few moments later, his heart drums even faster.

It is only Dorotea. He motions for her to enter and then closes the door. With her back to him, he quickly turns the key in the lock position. He pivots to face her. "Did you find her?"

She looks at him for a moment and then nods, biting her lip.

"Well?" Alfonso tries to keep the annoyance out of his tone. Her grey-green eyes look glazed, almost frozen, reminding him of the icy etching on windows on a winter day. Her face is even more bony and pale in the light of the day.

"She is waiting in one of the rooms." Dorotea begins to say something else, then hesitates. *She wants the money promised her,* Alfonso realizes. He slides his hand into his vest pocket. Without counting the money that he extracts, he gives her a handful of coins and she nods, slipping them into an outer pocket of her skirt.

"What room is she in?" he asks evenly.

"She's in room six on the main floor, the room down the hall from the kitchen."

Alfonso nods. "Where did you find her? Was the priest with her? How did you get her here?"

Dorotea looks like she is not sure what information to divulge. He takes a step closer and she blurts, "She was in the Aspromonte mountains with the brigand chief Stefano Galante, as my cousin mentioned. The chief left to do some business, and I told Gabriella that he had asked me to bring her to my uncle's tavern for safety, since Colonel Russo and his forces were in the area, scouring the mountains and valleys for any sign of either of them. He would come back for her later."

Alfonso stares at her intently. "It sounds like this Galante has gained Gabriella's trust."

Dorotea's eyes narrow. Her jaw tenses, and Alfonso purses his lips. *Dorotea is jealous.* A dozen thoughts jumble together all at once, and then, suddenly, everything becomes clear to him. The boots. The dagger. *Dorotea is a brigantessa.* She is part of Galante's band and has known exactly where to find Gabriella the whole time. And now she has pulled one over on her chief, bringing Gabriella to the tavern while he is away. Her motives? Jealousy and greed. She wants Galante for herself as well as the money. Alfonso would be willing to bet the church lands that he is right on every count.

He will not let her get away with her deceptions, though. She might think she has the upper hand in her little game, but he intends to play his own game with the wench. He grabs her by the forearm. "Did the bastard touch my niece?" he rasps. "He's had her for days. Am I to believe that the brigand chief nicknamed '*Galantuomo*' was truly a gentleman with a beautiful young woman like Gabriella? What kind of a fool would believe that?" He grabs her by both shoulders. "Tell me what he did to her. Tell me!"

Dorotea winces. "Don Simone was with her much of the time."

Alfonso feels his anger mounting. "Even at night? Where did she sleep?" He shakes her, and her head lops against his chest and then back. Her eyes widen. Alfonso pushes Dorotea back onto the bed, his excitement mounting. She stumbles and in a moment, he has pinned her to the bed. "Did he touch her here?" He covers her breast with one hand and squeezes roughly. "What about here?" He yanks up her skirt and slides his hand up her leg. "Did he take her virginity? Tell me, you brigand bitch."

Dorotea begins to writhe and manages to move her head forward enough to sink her teeth into his left arm. He cries out and retracts his free arm to whip her across the face. He catches her hard on the cheek and ear, sending her skidding off the bed. Her dagger falls out of her boot and clatters onto the floor. Alfonso swipes it and advances. She is breathing hard, one side of her face already swelling and mottled red and purple. Her bandana has fallen off, and her hair is a tangled swirl.

"Give me the key to the room," he growls.

She reaches into a pocket of her skirt and hands it to him. She begins to back away, her eyes blinking rapidly. Alfonso follows her. As she reaches for the handle, still facing him warily, he lunges at her and with a heavy swipe of his arm, knocks her over. She tumbles sideways, her head hitting the wooden post of the bed with a loud crack before she crumples to the floor, moaning.

Alfonso leans forward, extracts the money from her pocket, and puts it back inside his vest. Her whimpering both disgusts and excites him. He drops down, lifts her skirts, and tears her leggings off. She groans as he flattens her and begins writhing. His release comes quickly, and after several moments of intense breathing, he rolls off her clumsily. Her face is turned away, her jaw slack.

He reaches for her bandana on the floor. Standing above her, he pats the sweat off his face. With a sneer he flings the cloth at her. *The brigantessa is getting everything that she deserves.*

"Thank you for your trouble, *puttana di brigante*." Taking a deep breath, he heads for the door, the key to room six tight in his hand.

DON SIMONE TAPS HIS FOOT NERVOUSLY as Tomaso follows Stefano out of the clearing. If ever he has felt powerless over anything, it is right now. *How did this happen? How could Gabriella be convinced to leave the hideout without me?* He shakes his head dolefully, walking in circles around the stumps in the gathering place. He searches his mind for words of comfort and wisdom from the Bible, with the hope that they will help ease the terrible guilt he feels for not protecting Gabriella better.

The sound of someone clearing his throat reminds Don Simone that he is not alone. He stops and realizes that the brothers are each sitting on a stump, watching him. Roberto has refilled his pipe and is tapping the tobacco down while gazing at him stonily, the bruising exacted by the chief still visible on his face. Raffaele, with whom Don Simone has not had any contact since he splattered him with vomit, is tapping his foot against the edge of the stone, his eyes as murky as his expression. Don Simone notices him glancing at the ring that is back on his finger and now wishes he had deposited it within his cassock, out of sight.

Who is to say that Raffaele won't attempt to retrieve it, or do something worse, now that the brigand chief has left? Don Simone is hard-pressed to imagine what moral tenets the brothers adhere to, if any, since they joined Stefano's band. But perhaps he is being too harsh. Yes, they had every intention of abducting Gabriella and using her to satisfy their animal passions—or at least Roberto did—but perhaps, like their chief, their initiation into brigandage was a result of a situation that forced them into committing a crime. It could have been poverty, or desperation, or injustice that had propelled them to resort to such measures....

Don Simone stifles the fear that is threatening to overcome him. He is in the company of two criminals, yes, but he must believe that the good Lord has better plans for him than allowing him to perish in the wild Aspromonte. He must think about Gabriella now, not himself. And yes, of course, he must pray for Gabriella's safety. He will not stop praying until she is standing before him, untouched and unharmed. Looking past the brothers to beyond the clearing, he wishes he could just find a way to go in search of Gabriella.

Another clearing of the throat. He looks first at Roberto, then at Raffaele. *Coraggio,* he tells himself. He must draw upon all the reserves of courage he has. Of faith in God as well. He mustn't waver in the face of adversity; isn't that what he has been telling Gabriella throughout their journey? To trust that God will protect her?

A sound in the bushes near the entry of the clearing makes them all startle. Roberto throws down his pipe and reaches for his pistol before leaping over to Don Simone. Raffaele sprints in the opposite direction to the edge of the forest, his hand extracting a pistol before disappearing through the trees.

The carabineer who appears is pointing his rifle at them. Don Simone feels Roberto's breath on his neck. Two armed men, and *him* between them. His thoughts of faith and trust in God dissipate as he feels his blood congeal. He trembles as Roberto presses closer against him, grabbing his left shoulder while extending his right hand to aim his pistol straight for the carabineer.

"Put down your rifle unless you want the good Father to go straight to heaven," Roberto yells out.

Don Simone watches the merest flicker of uncertainty in the carabineer's expression. *Someone's going to die.* He gulps and shuts his eyes. Is he a hypocrite then, for thinking that perhaps God *has* forsaken them?

Roberto's fingers are digging into his shoulder like talons. He winces, and as a shot is fired, his stomach contracts. A scream in his ear forces him to open his eyes. Don Simone feels his knees buckle. As he falls to the ground, he waits for the sensation of unbearable pain searing through his heart and lungs, but it never comes. He sees Roberto writhing on the ground, three fingers of his hand blown off, and the rest a scarlet pulp. His pistol has skittered several yards away.

Don Simone's breathing is shallow, and he makes no attempt to get up. He watches the carabineer approaching quickly, his rifle aimed at Roberto. The brigand is emitting moans that make the hair on Don Simone's arms rise, The carabineer proceeds to plant a boot firmly on Roberto's good hand, and then points his rifle and blows a hole through the brigand's head.

Don Simone begins retching as his eyes take in the bloody mush splattered on the ground. When he finally lifts his head, his eyes too blurry to identify the man who is now standing next to the carabineer, he hears the voice of the carabineer.

"Colonel Russo, I am indebted to you for your timely intervention. Had you not shot him first, I might have ended up where he is now...."

AFTER RIDING ON RUT-FILLED MULE PATHS for almost three quarters of an hour, Gabriella was relieved to finally stop. There was no sign of any activity at the tavern. Dismounting, Dorotea quickly tethered her mule to a post and ushered Gabriella inside through a side door and down a dark corridor to a far room on the main floor, a room she also opened with her own key. The walls were a pale yellow-lime, and one shuttered window kept out the light but not the heat.

An iron washstand in one corner held a white enamel bowl filled with water. After dipping a face cloth into the bowl, Dorotea squeezed it out and wiped her face. She dipped it into the water again, twisted it and handed it to Gabriella. Although the water looked clean enough, Gabriella saw a dead fly floating in the bowl. Masking her distaste, she took the cloth, and while Dorotea bent down to tighten the laces on her boots, Gabriella set it back on the stand and proceeded to open the shutters on the far wall. She leaned out onto the windowsill and felt a rush of gratitude that they arrived in safety. No carabineers, no brigands, just a bevy of quail rustling through the woods.

The sky was just beginning to show hints of the approaching dawn with its pale coral streaks, the sun arching above the horizon. Other than the faint crowing of a rooster in the distance, the air was still. Gabriella felt a twinge of uneasiness. *Did I do the right thing in leaving the hideout with Dorotea?* she wondered. *Should I have talked to Don Simone myself?*

Gabriella closed the shutters, leaving open just a crack. Dorotea instructed her to stay in the room until she returned. The chief would likely be back in an hour or two, Dorotea reassured her. Gabriella nodded and sat down in a wicker chair in one corner of the room, feeling the tension compressed within her muscles and joints. She eyed the single bed, and after walking over to examine it for any sign of infestation, she pulled off her boots and lay down on top of the faded green coverlet. The bed was comfortable and felt luxurious after sleeping in Stefano's hut. Gabriella wanted to close her eyes and rest, but her thoughts kept her awake. Thoughts about Dorotea's plea and what was to come....

She let out a long drawn-out breath, wondered if she could allow herself a nap. She couldn't remember feeling as tired as she did. Drained. Even the toil of harvesting olives from the church lands or of pounding bundles of flax to soften and prepare the fibres for weaving didn't compare with her present fatigue. The throbbing in her thumb and leg wounds had subsided, but the pain of her father's death and the uncertainty of Tonino's safety were always there. Her only consolation was that Luciano was being cared for by the Sisters at the Convent of St. Anna, and would be there until she returned for him.

Gabriella opens her eyes and blinks at the sunlight streaming into the room from the slit between the shutters. She *has* napped. Surely more than an hour has passed. *Where is Dorotea? Stefano?* She stands and tries to stretch the stiffness out of her body from sleeping in trousers. She bends down to put on her boots. While she is lacing them up, she hears a key turning in the lock. She rises, her pulse quickening. *Stefano.* The door opens. Her heart begins to clatter against her ribs. *Alfonso Fantin.*

Gabriella takes a step back, bumps into the bed, and stops herself from falling back. The room feels stifling. Alfonso's face is flushed, dotted with beads of sweat. He watches her but doesn't move, like a cat who plans to amuse itself with a cornered mouse by flipping it about and watching it squirm and flounder before clamping its jaws into its neck. Alfonso moves one arm forward and she stiffens. The scent of his perspiration hits her and her stomach roils.

She doesn't have to glance about to know that there is no escape. Even if she were to dash for the window, by the time she threw open the shutters, he'd be upon her. Her neck prickles. She takes in the wide bands of dampness at his armpits, his chest and stomach rising and falling. Her gaze drops to the white alabaster handle of the dagger sticking out of his right pocket. Her eyes fly up to his face that is openly smirking now. Gabriella gasps. *So this is Dorotea's doing.* She has no time to wonder how or why; her instinct tells her she has to somehow try to stall Alfonso. He wants his revenge. It is clearly stamped on his face. And she has no illusions as to what form it will take.

The same anger that she felt after seeing the destruction in Calvino begins to suffuse her now. As Alfonso takes a step forward, she draws herself up and takes a sharp breath. "The brigand chief is on his way. He will be here at any moment."

Alfonso smiles and stops. "The '*Galantuomo*'? You're not counting on *him* to rescue you, are you, Signorina Gabriella? Surely, you must realize by now that Dorotea had to fabricate a story to get you here."

"How did you know where to find me?" Gabriella keeps her voice calm.

Alfonso smiles. "I hired a guide to help me search for you. Your friend, Valerio." His smile widens as she gasps. "We needed lodging for several nights; he suggested this place. Dorotea served us and overheard our conversation." He licks a droplet of sweat from the corner of his mouth. "She had 'heard' that a girl and a priest were in the company of a brigand chief. I made a deal with her to find you and bring you here." He takes off his jacket and flings it in one corner. "I don't have time to give you the details. I have something to give you in return for the present you left me...." He twists his head to show Gabriella his neck scar. "I owe you a debt of gratitude for not taking my life."

When he turns to face her again, the amusement is gone from his eyes. They are narrowed, ugly. Gabriella feels her anger mounting even more than her fear. *He* was responsible for her father's death; *she* is the one who should be filled with revenge. And she *is*. She wants to pummel him, slap him, claw his eyes out. *Kill him*. Her thoughts fly to the knife she has strapped to her leg as Stefano instructed her to do the night they left for Calvino. *She has no time to reach down for it and unstrap it.* Her stomach muscles tighten. *God help me*. She takes a tentative step back along the side of the bed. Alfonso could pounce and be on top of her in seconds, but he simply takes another step forward, his eyes gleaming lustfully. With every step she moves back, he moves forward, until he is only an arm's-length away. A shadow by the window distracts her for a second. He notices her glance and looking over his shoulder, laughs. "I have waited long enough for this moment, Signorina Gabriella." He advances purposefully.

Gabriella stiffens. Nobody can save her. Not Stefano, not Don Simone, nor God himself. Alfonso stops to fling off his vest and unbutton his shirt, revealing the golden-brown thatch on his chest. The bile rises in her throat. It reminds her of the straw in the hayloft. When Alfonso looks down to unclasp his trousers and remove his belt, Gabriella has a flash of memory: "You might need it one day." Her heart drumming, she plunges her hand in her trouser pocket and extracts the gift Stefano gave her.

Pointing the pistol at Alfonso, she waits until he looks up and as the smirk on his face freezes along with his body, her hand trembles. She will surely hang for this. Or at best, wither away in a prison workhouse. She will never see Luciano again. Or Tonino, if he's alive. And if she doesn't shoot, Alfonso will take what he has wanted from the beginning...her body, her dignity, her purity. Everything she wanted to give to Tonino as his wife.

All her life she has thought about others. *Done for others.* Tended to her father, a shadow of a man since his wife died. Cooked for him, cleaned, tried to bring him some comfort in his grief. Put on a brave face while grieving herself. And Luciano? He might as well have been her son; she has been more of a mother to him than a sister. Other than suckling him, she has raised him almost from the beginning. Without complaint or remorse, she has spent her youth and young adulthood sustaining both of them. And she has also done her part for Don Simone. Kept house, tended his animals and garden, cooked, washed. Yes, he, too, is family. She has done it all for her family. And she has never looked at taking care of the ones she loves as a hardship

But now she can't think about them anymore. She must think about herself. *Yet why is this so difficult to do?* She wavers as Alfonso puts his hand up tentatively. His forehead is peppered with sweat.

"I beg you to put that down, Signorina. I....I promise your safe return to Camini." His nostrils flare. "I will tell the authorities that it was an accident. You will not suffer any consequences."

Gabriella hesitates. *Could he be telling the truth?* She hears the fear edging his voice. Does she have it in her to kill him?

She senses a shadow falling across the window behind him. In the second that she looks at it, he lunges for her. Her gaze flies to his face. The fury in his eyes. The cruel twist of his lips. *His true intent.*

Without hesitation, she pulls the trigger and fires.

AS HIS OFFICER ACCOMPANIES THE PRIEST out of the clearing, Russo makes his way around the hideout, pistol in hand. His eyes take in the circle of stumps, the path to the night shelters, and the upper bench of the mountain where a hut has been constructed with branches and blankets. *Galante's den.* Smiling, he dashes over to it.

It was by sheer luck that he had come across this wildly overgrown trail that to a regular eye seemed impenetrable. He had, at the last moment, changed his mind about accompanying his men in pursuit of a brigand for a recent abduction in the town of Siderno. Upon their departure, Russo and two of his officers—Rodolfo and Silvio, the ones who accompanied him to the Galante farm—nosed about the foothills in the area, hoping to uncover a clue or a villager that might be tempted to talk. A piece of brightly coloured cloth tangled on a bramble bush caught his eye as he was scanning the wooded slopes for any sign of movement. His men went off to investigate, returning with the exciting news of a hidden path much farther up the mountain and directions for it.

Russo congratulated them before ordering Silvio to investigate other entry points to that particular path, and Rodolfo to trail behind *him.* He then proceeded up the mountain to venture onto the hidden path. If they were fortunate enough to have finally found Galante's lair, *he* wanted to be the one to drag the brigand chief away from it. After a dizzying ascent on a serpentine path that skirted cavernous ravines, Russo was glad to reach a glade that led inward. He tethered his horse at this point, and advanced quietly, careful not to snap a branch and reveal his presence.

The woodland resins hung heavy in the early afternoon air. Russo almost cried out when a squirrel's scolding call shattered the silence. Pushing away protruding boughs, he had the odd sensation that the forest was closing in on him, sucking the oxygen out of his lungs. He stopped, took a swig from a thin flask within his vest, and wiped his brow. His scalp was beginning to tingle uncomfortably and as he scratched at it, a movement through the trees caught his eye. His officer, Silvio Bertoli, aiming his rifle at a brigand standing next to a priest.

"Put down your rifle unless you want the good Father to go straight to heaven," the brigand barked.

Russo advanced quickly and immediately aimed for the brigand's hand, wanting to keep him alive for questioning. Unfortunately, his carabineer proceeded to approach the wounded brigand and blow out his brains, In any other situation, that would have been acceptable as far as Russo was concerned. There were too many brigands and simply not enough time or resources to proceed with such frivolous things as trials.

Russo questioned the priest instead, pleased that he had found him. Don Simone, his face ashen, was barely coherent, mumbling only that Galante was gone, and that Gabriella was with a *brigantessa* named "Dorotea." Impatient, Russo ordered his officer to take the priest back to the military station in Caulonia to recover from the shock. The girl couldn't be far off, and neither could Galante. *How wonderful it would be*, he thought, *if I came upon the two of them together….*

Russo now pulls aside the blanket and enters the hut. His gaze falls on two pallets that still have indentations and he is taken aback when he spots the neatly folded clothes that must belong to the girl. There is no sign of violence, of rape.

Even if Galante has been a "gentleman," he will still hang, Russo thinks grimly. *I will see to it.* The brigand chief may not have been a degenerate with Gabriella, but he has caused enough havoc during his rule to warrant a punishment more severe than life imprisonment.

Shoving his pistol in his holster, Russo grabs a dark cloak that is hanging over a protruding branch on one side of the hut. He rifles through the hidden pockets and discovers two daggers and a purple pouch with Galante's initial embroidered on it. Loosening the drawstring, he discovers a gold bracelet, a pocket watch, and several rings. He looks closely. No, not Liliana's. He feels his jaw clenching. Stuffing the bag in his trouser pocket, Russo spins around and strides out. He clambers up the ledge behind the hut and scans the valley below. He can make out the figures of the priest and his officer descending the mountainside. *Quite the eagle's view.* No wonder Galante has not been apprehended. Even if somebody *had* discovered the mountain trails, Galante would have spotted them and left long before they had reached the summit.

Russo jumps down from the ledge and returns to the meeting area. Skirting the mangled body of the dead brigand, he glances around before moving over to the path his carabineer took. A rustle in the bracken makes Russo stiffen. He lets out a breath when he sees that it is a squirrel. Nevertheless, he reaches for his pistol.

"I wouldn't do that," a deep voice advises.

Russo freezes. His gaze moves upward in the direction of the voice. The man he desperately wants is watching him steadily from the ledge that Russo has just vacated. Despite the heat of the day, Galante is wearing a dark grey cloak. It takes Russo a second to realize the brigand chief has a pistol in his hand, and the barrel is pointed at *him*. He must stall him. *Damn it, where is Rodolfo?* Russo meets Galante's gaze. Those strange eyes stare at him without blinking, and Russo's jaw clenches as he tries to conceal how unnerved he feels, as vulnerable as he did when Galante attacked his carriage and bound him up.

"I will see to it that your sentence is reduced if you turn yourself in," he says evenly. "Life imprisonment instead of hanging."

"That's generous of you, Colonel Russo, but I'm not *at the end of my rope* yet," Galante drawls, his lips curling into a sneer.

Russo's scalp is on fire, but he knows better than to make any sudden move.

"My men are on the mountain. It will only be a matter of time before they surround you. You may wish to reconsider, Signor Galante, before they appear and swarm you. They will have even less mercy on you if I am....hurt."

"Your men, *Colonello,* are otherwise occupied. And I have no intention of hurting you, unless it is to defend myself," Galante says. "I simply want you off the mountain. *After* you drop your pistol on the ground." His eyes narrow menacingly. "And trust me, if you even attempt to use it, I'll shoot off every finger on both your hands and you can join the brigand Roberto in heaven if there's anything left of your soul after I've riddled it with bullets."

Russo's stomach twists. His forehead is prickling with drops of sweat. Galante has him by the balls. *Again.* He considers his limited options. Drop his pistol and walk away unharmed, if he is to believe Galante—which he doesn't—or take a shot at the bastard.

"I'll leave the mountain," he calls out in a conciliatory voice. He watches as Galante nods and lowers his hand slightly. *Now,* an inner voice urges. Russo drops to the ground, and in mere seconds, grabs his pistol and aims at Galante. By this time, Galante has already fired, sending up a spray of dust by Russo's face as the bullet hits the ground by Russo's ear. Russo shoots again, and is stunned to see Galante's body jerk back, his shoulder a splotch of crimson.

I have done it! He watches as Galante staggers backwards before tumbling over the edge of the mountain.

Russo picks himself up, dusts himself off, places his pistol back in its holster, and lets out a deep breath. His heart still pounding, he strides to peer over the edge, and sees a series of sharp ledges and woodland skirting the impenetrable depths of a dark ravine. His stomach churns with mixed feelings. *He wanted Galante alive.*

He can't help feeling cheated. Cursing, he heads down the mountain.

THE GUNSHOT IS LIKE THUNDER IN THE SMALL ROOM. Gabriella watches Alfonso begin to collapse. He falls backward, his head hitting the slate floor with a sickening thump. Blood oozes out of his chest like a blooming poppy. Dazed, Gabriella looks up to see the slit between the shutter doors widening to reveal Dorotea.

Dorotea leaps into the room, her silver-green eyes surveying Alfonso's body with a satisfied gleam. One side of her face is bruised and swollen. She is no longer wearing her bandana. Her hair is a rat's nest.

"Let's get out of here," Dorotea rasps, grabbing her arm. "Out the window."

Gabriella follows her, not because she wants to, but because she can't stay with Alfonso.

To her surprise, there is nobody about, nobody scurrying to question them. Dorotea helps her mount the mule and then jumps up herself before heading in the direction of the main road.

Dorotea spurs the mule on, and Gabriella hangs on desperately, wondering at her chances of survival should she tumble off. After an interminable stretch, Dorotea slows the animal down until they arrive at a tapped spring off the road.

The sun is high above them. Gabriella feels drenched and is glad to jump down and refresh herself. She pulls off her bandana, wets it, and after twisting it, wipes her face and neck. Dorotea splashes water over her face and drinks, and after letting the mule drink, she leads him away from the road and through a thicket. Gabriella follows her and when they come to a mule path, Dorotea turns to speak to her. "This trail will lead us back to Monte Galante and the hideout," she says expressionlessly. "After a short rest." She sits down on a grassy knoll, snipping off the nearby grasses absent-mindedly.

Gabriella stares at her, her stomach churning. She hates Dorotea for having deceived her, for having sold herself to Alfonso, but how can she completely hate someone who has been a victim of Alfonso herself? Gabriella cringes at the sight of Dorotea's face and torn clothes.

Dorotea turns as if she can feel Gabriella's gaze on her. Her mouth is drawn in a thin line and the expression in her silver-green eyes has hardened. "He took the money he owed me," she says. "And my dagger." Her jaw clenches. "And he put his filthy hands on me. I would have killed him if I could."

"He tried to...to take advantage of me, too," Gabriella chokes on her words. "My father tried to stop him, but Alfonso pushed him down the stairs and he died." She cannot prevent the tears from streaming down her face. "Alfonso came after me again and I stabbed him. It was the only way to stop him."

"But he didn't die," Dorotea says slowly. "Is that why he came after you?"

Gabriella nods. "Don Simone wanted to bring me to a safe place." Her words catch in her throat. "He knew the law would be on the side of a wealthy landowner, not a peasant, no matter what the reason."

To her surprise, Dorotea nods.

"We had to place my brother in a convent." Gabriella chokes up. "Don Simone thought that it would be the best thing for now. And he was going to bring me to another place, but we were stopped—"

"By Roberto." Dorotea's eyes pierce hers. "And rescued by the chief."

Gabriella wipes her tears with her mother's handkerchief. "Stefano told me about his sister, how she was brutally raped by the man she worked for. Stefano said I reminded him of Patrizia...."

The expression on Dorotea's face makes Gabriella falter.

Dorotea thought Stefano was interested in me. She watches as Dorotea turns away, pretending to brush off a fly. *So that was why she had no problem making a deal with Alfonso....*

Gabriella looks at Dorotea's angular face, her willow-thin body. The dark purple splatters on her cheek. *Poor creature.* Like any animal in the woods, she had to do what she could to ensure her survival. And survival for a brigand or *brigantessa* has its own rules.

"We should go." Dorotea jumps up and turns to the mule.

The bushes behind her open and a carabineer emerges, clasping Dorotea's arms before she can reach for her pistol. He jerks them behind her back and handcuffs her before pushing her down to the ground. She grunts as she lands hard on her knees. Two other men appear, one in a colonel's uniform. Gabriella, immobilized, meets the colonel's eyes. He looks down at her, not unkindly, and calls her by name.

"Signorina Falcone, I am Colonel Russo. My men and I heard your account of the circumstances that led you to go into hiding. You are no longer wanted as a fugitive. Please know that I will officially have your name cleared upon returning to the station in Caulonia. We will proceed there shortly." He pauses, waiting for her nod of understanding. "Don Simone is there presently. I will see that arrangements are made for your accommodations for the night. At dawn, you can head to the Convent of St. Anna to fetch your brother."

Gabriella stares at him in disbelief. Colonel Russo's expression hardens as he turns to Dorotea. "Bring her back to the station," he orders his men. "Once she is behind bars, you can go in search of Galante's other brigands." He looks at the *brigantessa* disdainfully. She tries to struggle as one of the officers drags her off the ground, but he stuns her with a backhand to her unbruised cheek, and she lets out a tortured groan. Gabriella covers her face in distress as they walk away.

"Come, Signorina. You are safe now. The *brigantessa* will be imprisoned for the rest of her sorry life, and the countryside has been purged of two of her cohorts as well." He gives her a satisfied grin. "Yes, two members of the infamous Galante band are dead: Roberto Pellegrini and the brigand chief himself, '*Il Galantuomo*.'"

DON SIMONE IS NOT ABLE TO HOLD BACK HIS TEARS when he hears the news that Colonel Russo has arrived and that Gabriella is with him. He makes the sign of the cross and murmurs a prayer of gratitude to the Blessed Virgin for granting his request that Gabriella be found and safely returned to him. *These last few hours since Colonel Russo departed to search for Stefano and Gabriella have surely aged me,* he thinks with a heavy sigh.

In the small waiting room at the station, he has spent the time thinking of all the possible situations Gabriella might find herself in. He didn't want to believe that Gabriella was dead, or injured, or suffering in any way. At one point, he yelled out, desperate to stop the thoughts swirling around in his head. Tormenting him. A carabineer on duty came over to reassure him that the Colonel or his forces would find Gabriella. Don Simone began reciting the rosary without his beads. Yes, he hoped Russo would find her, but that would certainly mean her arrest.

He lost track of how many decades he went through. How many Sorrowful and Glorious Mysteries. Occasionally, he would drift off, his eyelids drooping in exhaustion. When he finally opened his eyes after a particularly long stretch, he realized that dusk was approaching, and the bad thoughts reignited. Scenes flashed through his mind incessantly: the sight of Roberto, his hand a bloody pulp and his brain shattered; the body of Lorenzo, broken and bleeding; the mask of horror and shock on Gabriella's face in the barn; Gabriella huddled next to Luciano on the mule cart, her body barely bigger than his; the frightening encounter with the two brigands in the mountains of Aspromonte; and the rescue by their chief.

Stefano Galante. For all that he is a wanted outlaw, Don Simone prays that he won't end up like Roberto. Yes, he has sinned, but he has more good in him than evil. Don Simone has always sensed it, from the time he rescued Gabriella from Roberto, from the way he tended to her injury and fever. He has caught the brigand chief gazing at the valley from his mountain ledge, his hand clasping his scapular, his lips sometimes moving in silent prayer. How could anyone with such devotion for the Madonna be unworthy of forgiveness and redemption?

Absorbed in his thoughts, Don Simone does not hear the carriage wheels come to a stop in front of the station. But when the carabineer suddenly leaves and then returns moments later with the news of the arrival of Colonel Russo and Gabriella, Don Simone jumps up, overcome with emotion. Wiping away his tears, he opens his arms to her when she precedes the Colonel into the room. She says nothing, but she clings to him, hiding her face against his cassock. Colonel Russo nods to Don Simone before ushering the carabineer into an adjoining room. Leading Gabriella over to the bench, he murmurs, "Don't worry, my child. I'll find a way to prove your innocence."

Gabriella's head jerks up. "Oh Don Simone, of course you don't know…Colonel Russo overheard me talking to Dorotea about Signor Alfonso. He knows everything." Her eyes fill up. "I don't have to run away anymore."

Don Simone intertwines his hands and shakes them toward the ceiling. "*Grazie, Dio mio*." He clasps Gabriella's hands, beaming. "You see, my dear, I told you to have faith that God would take care of you." He smiles reassuringly. "And now that the Colonel knows what happened, I'm sure he will pursue and arrest Signor Alfonso."

Gabriella takes a deep breath. "Signor Alfonso is dead. And Dorotea has been arrested. They've brought her here." She looks at him pleadingly. "So much has happened, but I can't bring myself to talk about it now. I just want to get Luciano and go home."

Russo re-enters, with the carabineer behind him. "It's too late to head back to Camini now," he says. "Once Dorotea is given a cell, you and Don Simone will be accompanied to the Monastery of the Capuchins in Gerace. And tomorrow you can retrieve your brother at the Convent of St. Anna. From there, you will be provided a mule and cart to bring you back to Camini." He smiles benevolently. "And the story will end happily for us all." He nods and leaves, motioning for the carabineer to join him.

Don Simone puts a protective arm around Gabriella. "This nightmare will be over soon," he murmurs. "Thank God. We will sleep well tonight. I will say extra prayers for Tonino and Stefano Galante. I don't think the chief will fare well when Russo finds him." He shakes his head, his mouth pursed.

Gabriella's body stiffens; her face is a grey veil. "Stefano is dead, too," she chokes out the words.

Don Simone gasps; he slumps down on the bench, wringing his hands. He thinks of Roberto and wonders if Stefano met a similar fate. "Dear God, I thought I knew what justice was, but now…now I'm not so sure anymore."

"*Justice*?" Gabriella's eyes are smouldering. "You know what justice is, Don Simone? It's an excuse for the law to commit the horrible crimes they profess to fight against." Her body is trembling. "And that kind of 'justice' is the work of Satan himself."

WHEN GABRIELLA WAKES UP, she stares at the unfamiliar ceiling and it takes her a few moments to realize where she is. Her gaze settles on a simple crucifix on one wall and she slowly makes the sign of the cross. She pushes away the twinges of guilt for her lapse of faith and reminds herself what Don Simone has told her on many occasions—that everyone has times when their spirit falters, especially after the unexpected or tragic death of a loved one.

Thank you, God, for keeping Don Simone and I from harm.

And Luciano. I am sorry if I have offended you. Suddenly, her eyes prickle and she squeezes them shut, overcome with humility. She reaches under the covers and plunges a hand in her pocket to retrieve her mother's handkerchief. She dabs her eyes and then traces the embroidered initial with a sigh. *Please let Tonino be alive.*

Her stomach clenches and she realizes how terrified she is to go back to Camini and discover that Tonino is dead. If only she *knew* that he was alive. She would be filled with joy, knowing everyone she loved would be reunited in Camini with her. Yes, she would still be in mourning for her father, but having Luciano, Tonino, and dear Don Simone would give her a reason to be happy. She rises and walks to the cell window. A rooster crows from a nearby courtyard. It makes her think of the morning the hen crowed for her mother and the time it happened to her. Her mother died, but *she* is still alive. Her misfortunes have not killed her.

Gabriella takes a deep breath. The window opens under a canopy of chestnuts; their scent is particularly fragrant at this time of year. She looks down at her *brigantessa* clothing. *Alfonso Fantin was my Goliath,* she muses. And she mustered the courage to battle him with the tools she had. With no one to help her. *Except Stefano.* Her fists ball up. She will have to do the same in Camini. She will have to muster the courage to resume some sort of life for herself and Luciano, especially if Tonino is—

She brushes the thought away. She will find out soon enough if he is alive, and until then, she will think only of Luciano and her responsibility in raising him. And the sacrifices she is going to have to make....

An exchange in the courtyard below breaks through her thoughts. She sees two Franciscan monks gathering herbs from glazed pots, murmuring in excited tones.

"Can you believe it, Brother Sebastiano? A brigand's pouch left in front of the monastery steps. Brother Salvatore says it was filled with coins and that the abbot was overjoyed, for now he will be able to arrange for repairs to the chapel that have not been undertaken since the earthquake of 1783."

"It is a blessing indeed, Brother Rocco."

"And the abbot says that there is enough money in that little purple bag to provide more charity meals to the hungry. God knows the peasants haven't fared any better since Unification."

As the monks walk off, basket of herbs in hand, shivers run down Gabriella's arms. She looks across the valley to the dark mountains in the distance. There is a halo of mist encircling them and the dawning sun is just starting to illuminate their heavily wooded slopes. One of those mountains is Monte Galante. She gulps. *Could Stefano have survived? Could one of his supporters have informed him as to the situation with Alfonso and my whereabouts? Is this his way of sending me a message?*

She shivers again. Mere days ago, she thought of the brigand chief as nothing less than a monster, yet now she feels a surge of hope that he is alive and has thwarted Colonel Russo and the forces of law. For it is the law that failed Stefano, his sister, and countless others who have been trod on by the wealthy and entitled, and who have suffered injustice and humiliation with no recourse but to take to the hills and skulk like wild animals with the constant threat of pursuit, capture, torture, and death. Or life imprisonment, if luck is on their side.

Yes, she prays fervently that Stefano is alive, for he deserves better than to be hunted down like a wild boar and ripped apart by the dogs that disguise themselves as lawmen. He deserves to be cleared of his crime, an act that anyone might be pushed to commit when a family member's honour is compromised.

Gabriella draws in a quick breath as something flickers in the distance. She squints but sees nothing. A bird, perhaps. She knows that she is being foolish, that nobody on those slopes could possibly see her, but she waves anyway. With lifted spirits, she leaves the cell and goes in search of Don Simone, ready to head to the Convent of St. Anna. She can't wait to hold Luciano in her arms again.

"I'm sorry, Signorina Gabriella," Don Filippo says kindly, then adds moments later, "Don Simone is battling a high fever. He can't possibly accompany you further. When he recovers, he will return to Camini."

Gabriella swallows. "But how will I—?"

"Brother Rocco will take you to the Convent of St. Anna. And then he will see you and your brother safely home in Camini. *Coraggio, Signorina*. All will be well...."

TONINO PUTS ON HIS BOOTS. Even they have been cleaned and polished. His clothes, washed and pressed. His wounds, tended and healing. The Sisters of the Convent of St. Anna have looked after him like family, feeding him soups full of "substance," as Abbess Emanuela liked to say. Soups that not only satisfied the body's needs, she assured him, but the spirit as well. The nuns grew or raised everything they cooked, taking pride in their every effort to honour the Creator for the gifts He provided.

Tonino owes them so much. He wishes he had something to offer them to show his appreciation of their benevolence, not only to him, but also to Luciano.

The boy has thrived under their care. Tonino has watched how they have tended to him like doting aunts, encouraging him to finish the last spoonful of the wild fennel or pigeon soup, or instructing him in some way, such as how to snip off leaves of basil properly from the pots in the courtyard, or how to soften the fibres of linen or broom by pounding them with a *manganeddhu*, a wooden pallet, before the Sisters can begin to weave them into blankets, rugs, or *fisculi*, the small wicker baskets used to hold ricotta cheese.

Tonino feels an ache in his chest thinking about how Gabriella must be suffering, being separated from Luciano. And not knowing where she is or if she's safe. He has convinced the Sisters that he is well enough to return home. He must inform his family that he has survived the battle at Aspromonte, and then set out to find Gabriella himself.

Moments later, he is explaining this to Luciano, kneeling in front of the boy, who has been snipping herbs for the cook in the courtyard.

"I will find Gabriella and return with her to fetch you," he murmurs, clasping the boy's small hand. "Then we will return to Camini. I promise."

"And Don Simone?" Luciano says brightly, his eyes wide.

Tonino smiles. "And Don Simone. We can't forget the good priest."

He squeezes Luciano's hand and rises. Abbess Emanuela and Sister Caterina are standing behind the boy, their faces gleaming under their wimples despite the fact that the sun hasn't even reached its mid-morning strength.

He nods to each of them respectfully. "When I return, Abbess Emanuela, I will have the gifts that Luciano wants, and also something I want to give to you, to express my gratitude for your kindness and care, and to all the Sisters as well. I will never forget it."

The abbess shakes her head. "Your gratitude is gift enough, Signor Tonino. Now be on your way, young man. And may God be with you. Don't forget to take this sack from Sister Caterina; she has packed some figs and cheese and other surprises for your journey."

Tonino thanks them warmly and walks away without looking back. He doesn't want Luciano or the Sisters to see the fear in his eyes, the fear that he won't be able to keep his promise to the boy and return with Gabriella and Don Simone....

Squeezing his eyes to curb the tears that are prickling the corners, Tonino leaves the convent and strides to the mule cart that awaits him a few paces away. The abbess has insisted that he be driven to Camini, instead of riding a mule himself. He nods at the driver, a labourer called Cristoforo, who transports the Sisters' woven blankets, rugs, and baskets to sell at markets in the neighbouring hamlets. Tonino makes himself comfortable against one side amidst the neatly stacked baskets and he signals to the driver to start off.

Tonino listens to the clip-clop of the mule's hooves on the cobblestone path as it approaches the turnoff that will lead them through the countryside to Camini. The cart suddenly jolting to a stop unseats him. He hears Cristoforo mutter a curse as he rights himself and readjusts a few tumbled baskets. The mule neighs and Tonino watches Cristoforo jump down and direct the mule to back up. Looking past him, Tonino watches the approach of another mule transporting a cart. The path is too narrow for both carts.

When Cristoforo has backed up the mule to allow sufficient room for the other driver to begin to pass, he jumps back into his seat and waits, calling out a greeting to the driver when he is close enough to recognize him.

Tonino leans to one side to wipe his forehead with his shirt sleeve. He should have thought to ask for a straw hat from the Sisters.

As the cart rumbles past, he sees that there is a passenger in the back as well. He glimpses the man's back and his bandana. The mule comes to a stop in front of the arched convent doors and Tonino watches the driver jump down before extending a hand to the man in the back. Tonino watches, puzzled. *Is the man sick or injured, needing to recover at the convent?* "I'm going back for a hat," he calls out to Cristoforo. "I'll be back in a moment."

Tonino jumps down and begins to walk over to the cart. The passenger has descended and is brushing some straw off his trousers. He is thin, his shirt hanging loosely from his shoulders, his trouser legs ballooning with unfilled space. His hair is surprisingly long.

Tonino watches as the driver lifts some sacks out of the cart and begins to haul them to the front entrance. The passenger lifts his hands to adjust his bandana and turns to swat at an insect flying past his face. Tonino stops in his tracks and blinks, his heart drumming erratically. It is not the hair that has tumbled out in waves that makes Tonino want to sink to his knees, but the eyes that have always reminded him of the Ionian Sea during a winter storm.

And the cheeks, flushed like oleander blossoms....

GABRIELLA MUMBLES UNDER HER BREATH and makes a tight knot behind her head. She is grateful for the bandana and the brigand clothing. Wearing her regular clothes would have caused her no end of discomfort in the full sun. She does feel conspicuous though and imagines that the good Sisters will be taken aback by her appearance.

She inspects herself again for any errant wisps of straw and dust, then turns to Brother Rocco, who has deposited the last of the baskets near the entryway. She motions at the convent door. To her surprise, she cannot voice her request to be taken to Luciano. She knows she will lose her composure if she does. And she wants to present a stoic front, not just to the Sisters, but to Luciano. There is no time for weakness now. She bites her lip.

Brother Rocco nods and pounds the massive oak door several times with the iron knocker. Gabriella's heart begins to pound in response. She realizes she is holding her breath. She looks at the doorway, willing it to open. She expels her breath slowly. *Where is everybody, anybody?* She is tempted to pull the door open herself and run from cell to cell until she finds Luciano. She wants to hold him, *needs* to hold him. Take him back to Camini and start a new life. She frowns at Brother Rocco. He holds up a hand. *Pazienza.*

Yes, she knows she has to be patient. She bites her lip so hard, she tastes blood. She wipes her face with her sleeve. The heat is monstrous today. She can feel the beads of sweat trickling over her forehead, their saltiness licking at her lips. Every second is too long. Too much time to think. She doesn't want to think right now. She wants to scream. Her nostrils flare at the perfumed scent of the jasmine flowers and potted oleanders lining the last stretch of the path to the convent.

Brother Rocco, seemingly unperturbed by the heat or the delay, taps on the door again. Gabriella stares unblinkingly at the motion, counting each tap silently.

When the door finally opens, Brother Rocco greets the abbess and Gabriella bows respectfully, her eyes misting. When she looks up, the abbess is looking at something over Gabriella's shoulder and smiling.

Gabriella turns and blinks at the approaching figure. When her eyes clear, the first thing she sees are the oleander flowers in his hand.

AUTHOR'S NOTES

La Brigantessa is a work of fiction based on true events that took place in the aftermath of Italy's Unification in 1861. I have at times taken liberties with some dates and locations. Any details in the novel that deviate from historical facts with regards to time, places, and events have been included to enhance my fictional story. Although my novel is set in Calabria, brigandage and its repression occurred in other regions as well. I have used the names of real places and towns as well as fictional locations.

Years ago, my mother had mentioned an ancestor who had passed on stories of Giuseppe Garibaldi. My imagination went wild. It is very likely that any one of my ancestors had witnessed or come into contact with this charismatic leader in his quest to unify the south of Italy and Sicily with the rest of Italy. He had passed through many towns in Calabria, inspiring young men to join his army of "*Camice Rosse*" or "Redshirts" as they were known. On his march toward Rome, which had yet to be united, there was a skirmish in the dense Calabrian mountain range of Aspromonte, and Garibaldi was wounded.

I was so fascinated with the history of Calabria that I decided to write a novel based on true events. I had purchased a suitcase full of books during a trip to Italy, books that dealt with every aspect of life in Calabria, especially in the post-Unification years, that is, 1861 on. I read about Garibaldi and Cavour, the politics of Unification, the cultural traditions, the role of women, the food, the superstitions, the role of the Church in this period, the hardships suffered by the agrarian population in the south, and the subsequent rise and repression of brigandage. My goal was to bring this fascinating period of southern Italian history to life, because it is a part of my history.

During a subsequent trip to Italy in 2010, I explored the area in and around the Aspromonte mountain range of Calabria, where brigandage flourished and also where an historic battle took place. General Garibaldi was injured in the Battle of Aspromonte (1862) while attempting to march north to liberate Rome from French protection and unite it with the rest of Italy. I stood by the tree against which Garibaldi was placed after being shot. It stands within an iron enclosure, a plaque marking its historical significance. I could hardly believe that I was standing in a place where 148 years earlier, part of Italian history was being enacted!

Except for Garibaldi and a few other historical figures, all the characters in my novel have been invented, along with their names. Any similarity to real people is purely coincidental. They are representative of figures in this particular time period and setting: a peasant girl and the young man who has asked for her hand, the parish priest who employed her and her father, the wealthy landowner from the North, the brigand chief, and the colonel in charge of the forces of repression of brigandage, a phenomenon that flourished from 1860-1870, a turbulent decade known as "*Il Decennio di Fuoco*," The Decade of Fire.

From my extensive research, I was able to glean insights into the people and circumstances of the agrarian south in the years following Unification. This was a troubled time, where peasants were rebelling against the harsh policies of the newly formed Piedmontese government. These Southerners were struggling with increasing poverty as a result, and many turned to the dangerous life of brigandage. They were forced to go into hiding in wild territory such as the Aspromonte mountain range in Calabria, where the dense woodlands and caves provided refuge and safety.

The law sought to pursue, capture, and destroy the brigands and anyone who harboured them. The brigands were organized in bands, and each band had a chief whose authority was unquestioned. Sometimes the band included the wife or lover of the chief or of one of the brigands, and these women—the *brigantesse*—participated in the nomadic and dangerous missions undertaken to survive.

In my novel, the order of Colonel Michele Russo to attack brigand chief Stefano Galante's hamlet of Calvino and the punitive actions of Russo's soldiers are representative of the harsh measures the Piedmont government took toward those with anti-Unification/pro-Bourbon sentiments. I researched the devastating massacre at Pontelandolfo and Casalduni in Campania on August 14th, 1861, which inspired me to include a chapter in *La Brigantessa* with similar tragic events.

Naming Gabriella and Tonino's hamlet "Camini" was an indulgence I permitted myself, since Camini, Reggio Calabria, is where I was born. Although I was only three when my family immigrated to Canada, I have always felt a strong connection to my motherland and to my relatives in the south. In writing this novel, I wanted to honour the lives and sacrifices of my parents and ancestors, and the people of Camini and Calabria in particular.

REFERENCES

ITALIAN SOURCES

Alvaro, Corrado. *Gente in Aspromonte*. Milano: Garzanti Libri, 2001.

Alvaro, Corrado. *Itinerario italiano*. Milano: Gruppo Editoriale Fabbri, Bompiani, Sonzogno, Etas, 1995.

Alvaro, Corrado. *La Calabria. Libro sussidiario di cultura regionale*. Reggio Calabria: Iiriti Editore, 2003.

Angilletta, Domenico. *Camini: Tra paesaggio arte e storia.* Soveria Mannelli: Rubbettino Industrie Grafiche ed Editoriali, 2009.

Berto, Giuseppe. *Il Brigante.* Milano: Arnoldo Mondadori Scuola, 1989.

Bourelly, Giuseppe. *Il brigantaggio dal 1860 al 1865.* Potenza: Edizioni Osanna Venosa, 1987.

Brandon-Albini, Maria. *Calabria.* Soveria Mannelli: Rubbettino Editore, 2007.

Calabria Sconosciuta: Rivista Trimestrale di Cultura e Turismo. Reggio Calabria: Falzea Editore, Aprile Giugno 2004.

Caligiuri, Mario. *Breve storia della Calabria dalle origini ai giorni nostri.* Milano:Tascabili Economici Newton, 1997.

Casaburi, Mario. *Donne di Calabria. Nobili e borghesi tra Unificazione e avvento del Fascismo.* Catanzaro Lido: C.B.C. Edizioni, 1998.

Cava, Tommaso. *Analisi politica del Brigantaggio Attuale Nell'Italia Meridionale.* Ristampa dell'edizione di Napoli, 1865. Napoli: Arnaldo Forni Editore, 1983.

Cavallaro, Alessandro. *Il barone di Montebello e la strage degli Alberti di Pentidattilo.* Reggio Calabria: Laruffa Editore, 2002.

Comi, Silvana. *In Calabria con Swinburne. Letture da "Travels in the Two Sicilies."* Calabria: Edizioni Parallelo, 1976.

Crupi, Pasquino. *Il paesaggio storico Calabrese nei testi letterari tra ottocento e novecento.* Reggio Calabria: Città del Sole Edizioni, 2007.

De Leo,Antonio. *Briganti sbirri cafoni e manutengoli in Calabria: Note sul brigantaggio calabrese negli anni 1799-1870.* Cosenza: Pellegrini Editore, 1981.

De Simone, Eugenio. *Atterrite queste popolazioni. La repressione del brigantaggio in Calabria nel carteggio privato Sacchi-Milon. 1868-1870.* Cosenza: editoriale progetto 2000, 1994.

Di Lampedusa, Tomasi. *Il Gattopardo.* Milano: Feltrinelli Editore, 1999.

Dorsa, Vincenzo. *L'origine greco-latina delle tradizioni calabresi*. Catanzaro Lido: C.B.C. Edizioni, 1998.

Douglas, Norman. *Vecchia Calabria*. Firenze: Giunti Gruppo Editoriale, 1992.

Dumas, Alexandre. *Viaggio in Calabria*. Messina: Rubbettino Editore, 1996.

Fenaroli, Luigi. *Flora mediterranea*. Firenze: Giunti Gruppo Editoriale, 1998.

Furfaro, Lina. *Il monastero di Sant'Anna. 91344-1891*.. Gioiosa Jonica: Corab Edizioni, 1998.

Garibaldi, Giuseppe. *Memorie (a cura di Alberto Burgos)*. Udine: Gaspari Editore, 2004.

Gaudioso, Francesco. *Calabria ribelle. Brigantaggio e sistemi repressivi nel Cosentino (1860-1870)*. Milano: FrancoAngeli, 1996.

Grignola, Antonella e Ceccoli, Paolo. *Garibaldi: Una vita per la libertà*. Firenze-Milano: Giunti Editore, 2004.

Irving, Washington. *Storie di briganti italiani*. Milano: Einaudi scuola, 1994.

Lear, Edward. *Diario di un viaggio a piedi. Reggio Calabria e la sua provincia. 25 luglio-5 settembre 1847*. Reggio Calabria: Laruffa Editore, 2003.

Mack Smith, Denis. *Cavour e Garibaldi nel 1860*. Torino: Giulio Einaudi Editore, Reprints Einaudi, 1977.

Mack Smith, Denis. *Storia d'Italia 1861/1969*. Roma-Bari: Editori Laterza, 1982.

Meridiani Calabria. Rivista Mensile, Luglio Agosto 19960

Montanelli, Indro e Nozza, Marco. *Garibaldi. Ritratto dell'eroe dei due mondi*. Milano: SB Saggi, 2002.

Nisticò, Ulderico. *Storia delle Calabria*. Cosenza: Edizioni Brenner, 1984.

Romeo, Domenica Gabriella. *Artigianato tradizionale e arte popolare in Calabria*. Reggio Calabria: Laruffa Editore, 2004.

Romeo, Pietro A. *Ippolita, sorella del brigante Musolino*. Reggio Calabria: Laruffa Editore, 2007.

ENGLISH SOURCES

Abba, Giuseppe Cesare. *The Diary of one of Garibaldi's Thousand.* Westport: Greenwood Press, 1981.

Alvaro, Corrado. *Revolt in Aspromonte.* Norfolk: New Directions, 1962.

Barish, Eileen. *The Guide to Lodging in Italy's Monasteries.* Scottsdale: Anacapa Press, 2003.

Coccioli, Carlo. *The Little Valley of God.* New York: Simon and Schuster, 1957.

Douglas, Norman. *Old Calabria.* London: Picador Travel, 1994.

Duggan, Christopher. *The Force of Destiny: A History of Italy since 1796.* London: Penguin Books, 2007.

Gissing, George. *By the Ionian Sea: Notes of a Ramble in Southern Italy.* Evanston: Northwestern University Press, 1996.

Guernsey, Alfred H. "Three Months With Italian Brigands." *Harper's Magazine,* August 1866 issue.

Hibbert, Christopher. *Garibaldi and His Enemies.* London: Penguin Books, 1987.

Hobsbawm, E. J. *Primitive Rebels: Studies in Archaic Forms of Social Movement in the 19th and 20th Centuries.* New York: W. W. Norton & Company, Inc., 1965.

Jepson, Tim. *Wild Italy.* San Francisco: Sierra Club Books, 1994.

Lawrence, D. H. *D. H. Lawrence and Italy.* London: Penguin Classics, 2007.

Lear, Edward. *Journals of a Landscape Painter in Southern Calabria,* [etc.]. Charleston: BiblioLife, 2016.

Lintner, Valerio. *A Traveller's History of Italy: Fifth Edition.* Brooklyn: Interlink Books, 1998.

Mack Smith, Denis. *Cavour and Garibaldi 1860.* Cambridge: Cambridge University Press, 1985.

Moens, William John Charles. *English Travellers and Italian Brigands: A Narrative of Capture and Captivity.* London: Hurst and Blackett, 1866. Digitized: University of Pittsburgh Library System.

Montgomery, Michael. *Lear's Italy: In the Footsteps of Edward Lear*. London: Cadogan, 2005.

Pirandello, Luigi. *The Oil Jar and Other Stories*. New York: Dover Publications, Inc., 1995.

Rotella, Mark. *Stolen Figs and Other Adventures in Calabria*. New York: North Point Press, 2003.

Seton-Watson, Christopher. *Italy from Liberalism to Fascism 1870-1925*. London: Methuen & Co. Ltd., 1967.

Talese, Gay. *Unto The Sons*. New York: Alfred A. Knopf, 1992.

Trevelyan, George Macaulay. *Garibaldi and the Making of Italy, June-November, 1860*. London: Phoenix Press, 2001.

Viviano, Frank. *Blood Washes Blood: A True Story of Love, Murder, and Redemption Under the Sicilian Sun*. New York: Pocket Books, 2001.

ACKNOWLEDGEMENTS

There are so many people to thank for their part in my writing journey to complete *La Brigantessa*.

When I first conceived of the idea for this story, incredibly twenty years ago, my father was the first person I interviewed. I asked him to tell me about the tradition of the hog slaughter, which eventually became the focus of the first chapter. I only wish I had recorded him. His kindness, intelligence, and compassion have inspired me in so many ways throughout my life. He, along with my devoted and hard-working mother, taught me many life lessons, and I honour their sacrifices and hardships as immigrants by writing about the land of their birth, the land they loved but had to leave in the economic crisis of the sixties.

Throughout the long and winding road to publication, I have been blessed with the constant support of my husband Nic, who encouraged me to believe in myself as a writer and to invest in my growth. He read every draft, provided insights, and contributed in countless ways while I immersed myself in my fictional world. Nic has always supported my big dreams through thick and thin. Our children Sarah, Jordan, and Nathan continue to cheer me on.

Many family members and dear friends—including my "Craft & Chat" and "Lively" groups—have demonstrated ongoing enthusiasm for my project. Special thanks to my brothers Cosimo and Pat Micelotta & families, and to my (late) Zio Pietro, Zia Elsa, and cousin Mary Adavastro.

Friends provided me with helpful research material. Helen and J.P. Mayer gifted me with—among other sources—an article from an actual 1866 issue of *Harper's* magazine: "Three Months With Italian Brigands" by Alfred H. Guernsey which prompted me to further research the ordeal of William Moens in his book *English Travellers and Italian Brigands: A Narrative of Capture and Captivity*. Victoria Salvas contributed research involving Calabrian country life, traditions, and folklore.

I am grateful for the support of my friends and colleagues in the Association of Italian-Canadian Writers, the Canadian Authors Association, and in the Sudbury Writers' Guild, who have inspired me with their stories, books, and writing journeys. As an executive member of the Calabria Social Club of Sudbury and member of the Società Caruso Club, I have enjoyed the friendship and support of my fellow members in our goal to promote the Calabrese and Italian culture.

I am thankful to Dr. Joseph Pivato, who accepted my very first short story for *The Anthology of Italian-Canadian Writing* (Toronto: Guernica Editions, Inc., 1998).

I acknowledge the John D. Calandra Italian-American Institute at CUNY (City University of New York) for accepting my proposals in 2008 and 2010 to present a paper at their annual conference. It was there that I met Rossana Del Zio in 2008 and Paola Melone in 2010, both of whom shared useful research information for my novel.

Over the years, I have had the valued support of esteemed Professors of Italian at Laurentian University in Sudbury Diana

Iuele-Colilli and the late Paul Colilli, whose encouragement of my writing and invitations to read in their classes and conferences were much appreciated. At one such conference, author Maria Coletta McLean invited me to submit my stories for a collection which was shortly thereafter published as *Mamma Mia: Good Italian Girls Talk Back* (Toronto: ECW Press, 2004). Maria and editor Joy Gugeler were very supportive and I appreciated their validation. Maria's memoirs about her little village of Supino are heartwarming and they resonate with readers who wish they, too, could experience life in Italy.

Prolific historical fiction author Mirella Sichirollo Patzer's beautiful books have inspired me with their captivating characters, settings, and rich story details.

Multi-talented and award-winning actor, writer, and playwright Michaela Di Cesare—whose latest play, *Successions,* was staged at Montreal's Centaur Theatre—continues to shine and inspire in her varied and outstanding ventures.

I gratefully acknowledge the support of the Ontario Arts Council for granting me a Writers' Works in Progress Grant in 2006 for *La Brigantessa*. This validation from the four-person jury helped boost my resolve to keep researching and writing. The OAC is a vital organization in supporting creators in all artistic fields.

In the same year, multi-award-winning author Nino Ricci's critique and encouragement of my first chapter during a workshop for the Sudbury Writers' Guild were especially valued and motivating, helping me to persevere until I completed the novel in 2012. From the time I read Nino's first book, the internationally acclaimed *Lives Of The Saints* in 1990, I was captivated by his stellar writing.

Hugely successful author of historical fiction and thrillers, and of *Page-Turner: Your Path to Writing a Novel that Publishers Want and Readers Buy,* Barbara Kyle evaluated my manuscript in its third draft in 2012. Her insightful suggestions and guidance were invaluable.

Internationally acclaimed and best-selling author Gail Anderson-Dargatz has been an inspiration with her superlative writing and teaching. I participated in her week-long "Writers' Camp" in Providence Bay, Manitoulin Island, in 2015.

Much gratitude to Joseph Kertes, founder of Humber College's distinguished creative writing program and multi-award-winning author, whose workshop I attended in Parry Sound in 2014, inspired me to polish my final draft, which I then submitted to Inanna Publications.

And finally, infinite thanks to the amazing and tireless team at Inanna Publications: to outstanding publisher and editor-in-chief Luciana Ricciutelli, publicist extraordinaire Renée Knapp, exceptional copy-editor Adrienne Weiss, and designer Val Fullard for the stunning cover. I have been enjoying Inanna books for years and am very proud to be one of their authors.

Heartfelt thanks to all!

Rosanna Micelotta Battigelli was born in Calabria, Italy, and immigrated to Canada with her family at three years of age. She is an alumna of The Humber School for Writers and her fiction has been published in fifteen anthologies, including *A Second Coming: Canadian Migration Fiction* (2016), the "Folktales" issue of *VIA* (*Voices in Italian Americana*) (2017), *150 Years Up North And More* (2018), and *People, Places, Passages: An Anthology of Canadian Writing* (2018). A collection of short fiction entitled *Pigeon Soup and Other Stories* is forthcoming from Inanna Publications in 2020. Since retiring from teaching in June 2015, Rosanna is pursuing her literary goals full-time. She lives in Sudbury, Ontario.